A Calling to Love

Anita Wolfe

To Mary,
With Love,
Anita
Wolfe

PublishAmerica
Baltimore

ISBN: 1-60813-155-6 (softcover)
ISBN: 978-1-4489-9457-1 (hardcover)
PUBLISHED BY PUBLISHAMERICA, LLLP
www.publishamerica.com
Baltimore

Printed in the United States of America

For my dad and minister, Barry, and my sister, Brenda

And in the memory of my mom, Theresa, who read my book and encouraged me.

Chapter I

Michael Donnelly sits on a bench by Lake Erie watching gentle waves roll over the rocks. Michael, at twenty-six, stands at six foot, two inches with a slim athletic build. He has thick, black hair and intense brown eyes. Michael inherited his father's chiseled features. His parents had raised him in a mansion. His mother, Sophia, who is the picture of sophistication, always has a tailored appearance and never has a hair out of place. She loves spending time at her country club and had often brought her children with her. Michael spent much time there swimming and golfing, but his favorite sport had been tennis for which he won many trophies.

His father, James Donnelly, owns and runs his own company. An older version of his son with a mustache and a distinguished appearance which commands attention and respect, he raised Michael with high hopes that his son would go to Harvard Law School to become a successful attorney. His father, devastated, became angry when his son chose to go to seminary instead of Harvard.

Michael came to Erieton to spend the week at his denomination's annual conference. Ministers bring their families to this small vacation community where they stay in old, quaint cottages. Michael's conference consists of all of the churches in the eastern half of Ohio which is divided into districts headed by a District Superintendent.

Ministers with their church delegates attend conference sessions in a large auditorium during the day and spend time with their family and friends during the evenings. Michael came alone staying in one room he rented in a large boarding house close to the auditorium.

Tomorrow, Monday morning, conference will begin and Tuesday evening, Michael will be ordained a minister having completed his student pastorate. The last time he saw his parents, they had a large argument. Now, he doesn't know whether they will come Tuesday or not. They made it perfectly clear that they do not approve of their son becoming a poor minister.

His ex-fiancé, Barbara Stark, broke up with him because she refused to live as a minister's wife. Barbara, one of his best friend's little sister, had a crush on Michael most of her life. Michael made it all the way to college before she finally captured his attention. They dated for three years and became engaged. However, she did not believe in his calling. When he left home for seminary, she returned his engagement ring.

In seminary, he met and dated a pretty young woman named Monica Popavich. Monica, having been at the seminary herself, would have lived happily as a minister's wife. She was willing to do everything that Barbara had run away from, but on a personal level, outside of the church, he did not find a strong enough personal connection. He felt no chemistry. He liked her, but he was not in love with her.

Now Michael sits on a bench in Erieton watching ministers arrive with their families and greeting old friends, all alone as he prepares to begin his ministry.

Monday morning, Michael walks to a small restaurant, Regina's, for breakfast. Regina's has indoor and outdoor seating. He purchases a cup of coffee and a bagel at the window and takes a seat at an outdoor table. Before he orders, Rev. Martin Stevens, his conference appointed mentor, joins him. Martin is in his late forties with a kind face. He has jet black hair which is graying at the temples. Martin has a presence that demands attention when he enters a room. A strong, yet tender loving man, he exudes a spiritual air about him.

"I've been looking for you," Martin tells Michael as he sits. "Did you get an appointment yet?"

"Yes, last week. I should have called you," Michael replies.

"Wow that is last minute. So tell me."

"Well, I have my own church. I didn't really want an associate position. It is a nice little church, Trinity in Ambrose."

Martin seems surprised, "Really? My daughter belongs to that church."

"Really?"

"She is here this week. I'll have to introduce you. She always came here with us, but for the first time she is here as a delegate for her church, or should I say, for your new church," Martin informs him.

Martin and Michael discuss his new appointment and ordination tomorrow. Michael recounts his argument with his parents and explains that he doesn't know if anyone is coming. However, in case someone does come, he plans to drive around tonight to find a restaurant for afterwards.

Martin hadn't realized that no one had planned a party for him. Most of the others had halls or a cottage for large parties. Martin intends to call his wife before session to see what she can come up with for him. Martin assures Michael that he and his wife will be there and finds out that if everyone invited comes there would only be ten people.

"Sadie!" Martin spots his daughter.

Sadie heads straight to the table. Martin introduces her, "Michael, this is my daughter, Sadie."

Michael stands, struck by her beauty. Sadie has thick, long, brunette hair, dark, lively eyes and a radiant smile. She is petite with a sculpted body from her daily exercise. Sadie looks up at Michael who must be a foot taller than her. The phrase tall, dark, and handsome crosses her mind.

"This is Rev. Michael Donnelly," Martin continues, "He's the young man I have been mentoring. Ready for this? He has just been appointed to your church."

Sadie is surprised because Michael looks so young, "Wow, nice to meet you."

She reaches across the table and they shake hands. His broad, warm hand seems to swallow up hers. He smiles warmly down at her.

"Join us," Martin invites. "I'll go to the window and order you something to eat."

Michael and Sadie sit down as Martin leaves them. As he waits in line at the window, he watches the two.

"So, you are our new minister. We will be working closely together. I'm not only the conference delegate; I am the Sunday School Superintendent, Bible School Director, and Children's Choir Director. I'm also in the chancel choir and the substitute organist." Sadie lists.

"Is that all?" he teases with a smirk.

"So you better be real nice to me. I can make your life easy or a living hell," she flirts.

Michael chuckles, "Good to know. Does your husband mind you volunteering so much of your time?"

Sadie squints at him, "Subtle, no I'm not married."

Michael laughs.

Martin watches his daughter flirt who he has not seen his daughter flirt in years. The three eat breakfast and then part ways to attend the opening session. The Conference begins with a worship service that many families attend which includes a memorial service for all of the ministers and ministers' wives who had died the previous year.

Joy attends the service with her husband. Before she leaves, Martin asks her if she can pull a party for Michael out of her ear. Making no promises, Joy agrees to try. Joy is loving and energetic. She is thin and petite with shoulder length blond hair and sparkling eyes.

During the lunch break, Joy and Sadie walk down to the Erieton Hotel. While it had once been beautiful, it is now ancient, but still contains a fancy restaurant. Joy speaks to the manager about reservations for twelve sectioned off for an ordination party, but he turns them down. They already scheduled one of the ordination parties in their party room. The rest of the restaurant is for small groups.

Sadie steps up to talk the manager into changing his mind. As she discusses it, she uses a flirtatious tone, tipping her head, and flipping her hair. The manager finally agrees to save seating in the corner for the party. Joy teases her daughter all the way back to the auditorium for flirting to get her way.

Following the afternoon session, Sadie finds Michael in the back of the auditorium. The noise level in the building is high, so Sadie touches his arm to gain his attention and nods to step outside to speak.

She explains that her father asked her mother to find a place for him to go after ordination and that they were able to obtain reservations at the Erieton Hotel three blocks away. He is grateful. She volunteers to show him where it is to see if he is satisfied. As they walk through downtown, Sadie answers questions about Erieton. Sadie came for a week every year for her father's conference since she was a baby with her mother, older brother and two younger sisters. It had been their main vacation every year and while her father had long meetings, the family enjoyed it as a resort. The restaurant appears nice to him and he likes that it is close by.

Tuesday evening, Michael waits nervously on a corner in front of the auditorium with his robe over his arm to see who comes. Martin and Joy meet him first with Sadie who also has a robe over her arm. She explains to Michael that she is in the conference choir and they all bring their robes from their home churches. Michael thinks Sadie looks pretty in her light weight sundress and her hair pulled back with a matching headband.

Michael visibly relaxes as he sees his parents, sister, brother, and one of his friends coming down the road. He greets them introducing them to the Stevens. Sadie notices the tension between Michael and his parents. His sister is the only one who hugs him warmly.

Shortly, Rev. Rob Foreman and his wife, Bonnie, walk up embracing Michael.

Michael's parents do not like the Foremans. Rev. Foreman had been the minister of the church Michael attended in college where they became friends and where Michael had discovered his interest in the church. It had been Rev. Foreman who first talked Michael into being a lector doing readings and leading other various parts of the church services. It had been there where Michael received his calling, and his parents blame Rev. Foreman for Michael becoming a minister.

Soon Sadie reminds Michael they should go. The pair head around to the back of the auditorium while Joy shows the rest inside. Sophia is unimpressed with the old auditorium and hard auditorium seats. Joy is careful to be sure that Sophia has an aisle seat. As they walk to their place, Carol overhears people excitedly discussing parties for others and feels terrible that her family had not thought to plan a party for her brother. Her parents are not celebrating Michael's becoming a minister.

As Sadie and Michael enter in the back, people seem to be worked up into a frenzy. They learn that the organist tripped on the way up the stairs hurting his wrist, and now there is no one to play for the service.

Sadie grabs Michael's arm, "Quick, stop me. I'm about to do something stupid."

He doesn't know what she means as she approaches her choir director, "I play the piano. I have subbed for our church organist many times."

When asked if she is any good, she responds, "I'm better than dead silence. I'll be sight reading, so there will be mistakes."

Michael laughs at her response. Taking her up on her offer, everyone prepares for the service. Her parents are shocked when Sadie sits at the organ. The organist sits next to her so that he can pull out the correct music and give her the cues. He also knows how he has his stops set. Sadie's hands tremble as she begins. Each tiny mistake sends waves of heat up the back of her neck, but she plays very well and no one notices any errors except for the organist sitting next to her.

As Sadie plays the Prelude, the seven men and two women making their ordination process down the center aisle in their black robes. While many mothers and wives cry with pride, Sophia cries with disappointment. This is not the future she and her husband had pictured for their beloved son having wanted him to be a powerful attorney. They wanted him to have money and live in the lap of luxury and do not understand why Michael would choose to live on a minister's salary and work for a denomination which mostly has small poor churches.

The Bishop of this East Ohio Conference presides over the ceremony. Martin robes up and sits up front as Michael's sponsor. Michael appears dignified and reverent as they process in. The new ministers sit in folding chairs on the stage.

They open the service with a hymn, prayers and a greeting. They reaffirm their baptism. The chairperson of the Board of Ordained Ministry presents the candidates to become ordained elders. As he reads their names, each stand.

The service continues with prayers, scriptures, and a sermon. As the choir sings the anthem, Michael watches and listens as Sadie sight reads. He notices no mistakes and marvels at her skills and at her bravery to volunteer to do this in front of so many.

The Bishop leads a very long litany which describes the ministry and the duties Michael will be facing. "Do you believe that God has called you to the life and work of ordained ministry?"

Michael, with the others, responds, "I do so believe."

The long litany continues. The Bishop then takes each candidate up one at a time. Michael is first as he kneels down on the kneeler. His family and friends are invited to stand. The Bishop, the Chairperson, a guest bishop, his new district superintendent, and Martin, as his sponsor, all lay hands on his head as they pray.

The Bishop prays, "Almighty God, pour upon Michael James Donnelly the Holy Spirit for the office and work of an ordained elder in Christ's holy church."

All respond, "Amen."

The bishop continues, "Michael James Donnelly, take authority as an elder to preach the Word of God, and to administer the Holy Sacraments, in the name of the Father, and of the Son, and of the Holy Spirit."

All respond, "Amen."

The choir sings a choral response as the Bishop hangs a red stole around Michael's neck which represents the yolk of the Lord and the red represents the Holy Spirit and then it is the next candidates turn. Michael returns to his seat and his family and friends sit.

His parents are almost overwhelmed and unsure of how to feel about any of this. It all seems foreign to them and all so serious and sacred. It feels odd to see their son like this.

After the service, they gather outside. Martin suggests that they take pictures before Michael takes his robe off. Michael declines because he is uncomfortable. Martin insists that later in his career, he will wish he had pictures from this day. When no one has a camera, Sadie pulls one out of her purse which her dad had suggested that she bring.

Despite his protests, his sister, Carol, agrees. She arranges the groups while Sadie snaps pictures. Carol feels embarrassed that no one thought to bring a camera. She feels terrible that they didn't do anything nice for her brother as she notices other large groups excitedly celebrating around them.

Once finished taking pictures, Sadie conveys that it was nice meeting them and begins to leave. Michael's family and friends wait and watch as he catches up to her, blocking her way. He invites her to go with them, but she declines not wishing to intrude. She had only come because she belongs to the conference choir.

"Come on, you made the reservations, you played for the service, and we are going to work closely together. You represent my future congregations," he persuades.

Smiling, she agrees to join them. As they walk, people fuss over what a wonderful job she did playing the organ for the service. Michael shares the story of her volunteering.

Her mother then embarrasses her, "When Martin told me that Michael didn't have anywhere to go afterwards still yesterday, I went down to the Erieton Hotel to make reservations, but the manager turned me down flat. Luckily, Sadie came with me. She flirted with the guy until he figured something out for us."

Michael, walking with his brother, Sean, and best friend, Graham, looks over at Sadie.

She turns to the three, "I did no such thing. Besides, it's not my fault that men are dumb enough to fall for that." The men laugh as she walks ahead with her head held high.

Sophia and James are unimpressed with the old hotel, but Carol whispers to them that they didn't provide anything nicer for him. During the dinner, Sophia begins to ask negative questions about ministry to Michael's frustration. She asks Pastor Rob and Martin what the hardest part of ministry is to them. Michael rolls his eyes. The ministers agree that having no set hours makes it easy to work too many hours, but it is nice that their hours are flexible.

Sophia then asks their wives, Bonnie and Joy, the hardest part for them. They agree it is making each parsonage work.

Bonnie shares a story: "When we had a teenage son and two middle school daughters, we moved to a small parsonage. Downstairs the living room, dining room, and kitchen were lined up and upstairs there was a master bedroom and one regular room. We gave our daughters the master bedroom and our son the other room. We put our bedroom in the dining room. Our bedroom was the center of the house with no doors."

Sadie's mother then relates a similar story with her four children in a small ranch house where she had done her best to make a bedroom for her middle school aged son in an unfinished basement.

Sadie interrupts, "Uh, Mom, you two are scaring the hell out of Mrs. Donnelly. Michael, what do you think of your parsonage?"

He responds, "It's nice. I'm by myself and I get four bedrooms."

"What do you think of the front bedroom?" she smirks.

"You mean the nursery?" He tells his family, "The one room has a mural of a cartoon forest with little animals. They said that the person who painted it without permission promised to remove it if I request it."

"So, do you want it removed?" Sadie inquires.

"No. I just won't use that room." Michael thinks for a moment, "Wait. Did you paint it?"

"Yes."

"It's good. So you're an artist?" he asks.

"No. I cheated. I copied coloring book pictures on a transparency and used an overhead projector to trace, then paint." she explains.

"Clever. Did you do the Noah's Ark in the church nursery?"

"I did it with the youth group," she replies.

Carol points out, "Well if you are there two to eight years, you could get married, have children and use the room."

"I guess that's true," Carol watches as Michael glances down the table at Sadie.

Sophia continues to ask negative questions but the ministers and their wives give every answer a positive spin. Sophia asks if all ministers are so positive about their hardships.

Sadie answers, "Ministers spend much of their time studying the Bible for sermons and Bible studies and everywhere they go, they pray for people. With that much time spent in prayer and Bible study, they develop a close relationship with God that brings them peace and a positive attitude."

Michael smiles at her.

"Very well stated," Rev. Foreman compliments.

"I get that crap from my dad," she remarks.

"Sadie!" Joy reprimands.

Taken by surprise, Michael and most of the others laugh. Her wit and attitudes amuse him.

After dinner, Martin and Joy hand Michael a gift. He opens it to find a beautiful purple embossed stole to wear over his black robe for worship. Rob and Bonnie also give him a present which he unwraps to find *The Book of Worship*. His brother Sean gives him a statue of Jesus with his hands lifted as if giving a blessing. Michael teases him that it looks like Jesus is signaling a touchdown. Carol presents him with a desk set for his office that includes a name plate which reads "Rev. Michael Donnelly" with a cross on each side of his name. Michael really likes it. His parents only give him a card with money. Michael tells them he will use it to pay for the furniture he just purchased for his new home. His friend, Graham, hadn't thought about giving a present for the occasion and Sadie didn't know that she would be attending his party.

At the end of the evening, his father, James, insists on paying for everyone's dinner. Michael thanks the Stevens for all they did for him and says goodbye to Rob and Bonnie who gush about how proud they are of him.

As Michael walks his family back to their car, Carol asks him how long he has known Sadie and is surprised to learn that he had only met her yesterday. She teases him about the obvious attraction he has for her especially when he chased after her to convince her to join them for dinner. Pushing each other around as they had done since childhood, Michael puts her in a headlock.

James shakes his head, "For heaven's sake son, you are an ordained minister now. Let your sister go."

Chapter II

Michael spends Wednesday bored in meetings. He notices Martin and Sadie on the other side of the room. He daydreams about Sadie who is pretty and funny. She understands ministry and has lived in parsonages her whole life. She sounds as if she is the volunteer youth minister and could be the church organist. Sadie would make a wonderful minister's wife.

Session finally ends. As Michael walks down the road, a bicycle cuts close in front of him. Sadie, on the bike, circles back around coming to a stop in front of him. She looks cute in a simple t-shirt, shorts, and a ponytail.

"Hey Michael," Sadie greets him, "Have big plans tonight?"

Michael smiles, "Hello there. I have no plans for tonight. There's not much to do here when you're alone."

"Well, I'm the delegate for your new church, so protocol dictates that we need to go out to lunch or dinner sometime this week," she informs him.

"Oh really? You want to go out tonight?" he invites.

"Don't look at me like that. It's not a date. It's business," she stresses.

"Sure it is," he flirts.

"If you are going to be that way, forget it," she begins to ride off, but he catches a metal rack on the back of her bike lifting it just enough for the back wheel to be off the ground.

"Now wait a minute. I get it. Dinner is just business. I would like to hear about the church and town."

Sadie agrees. The restaurants in Erieton are busy, so Sadie suggests they drive to the next town to a unique restaurant with good sea food. She provides Michael with the cottage address and rides off.

Her mother cooked spaghetti for supper. Sadie tells them that as delegate, she plans to eat with her new minister. Her two younger sisters don't think anything of it, but Joy and Martin glance at each other. Sadie hurries to the bathroom to freshen up.

Her sisters' jaws drop open when Michael arrives to pick-up Sadie. They did not expect a young, tall, handsome man. Their surprise increases when Sadie returns. She has changed into a cute one piece short outfit, lightly applied make-up, and brushed her hair out. Her parents and sisters watch out the window as Michael opens the car door for her.

The restaurant, Harbor Light, looks different from any restaurant Michael had ever seen. Long rows of picnic tables set on a plain cement floor. The food is served on Styrofoam plates to be eaten with plastic utensils, but the food tastes delicious.

When the waitress comes for their order, Sadie requests separate checks. Michael contradicts that one check will do. They go back and forth until Michael remarks that she won't win this one. Once they order, Sadie reminds him that this is not a date.

"Why is that so important to you? Do you have a boyfriend at home?"

"No. I just don't date."

"You don't? Why don't you date?" he leans forward.

"Because I believe most men are scum and can't be trusted," she answers matter-of-factly.

"What do you base this hypothesis on?" he wants to know.

"Life. Moving on, I want to talk to you about Bible School," she changes the subject.

Last year Dorothy Martin ran a Bible School for kindergarten through sixth grade in the late afternoon. They only enrolled eleven students. They wanted to cancel it for this year, but Sadie pushed to take over. Now people are fighting her on her plans, so she lobbies for Michael's support.

She plans to hold it at seven in the evening because of working parents. She wants to provide a nursery and add a youth group project. She thinks Michael should run an adult Bible study.

Her plans include more advertising including the local newspaper and fliers passed out at the Fourth of July parade. Michael agrees with her plans. Sadie suggests the two of them go to the Christian bookstore in Erieton during break tomorrow to select materials to which he agrees.

From here, the conversation turns to more personal topics. He discovers that in the fall, Sadie will begin her third year as a first grade teacher at Ambrose Elementary and that she is the high school flag corps advisor. She believes her teaching is a calling just like ministry.

Sadie elaborates, "My senior year of high school, I wanted to be a professional pianist. I planned to go to a conservatory. However, things changed when I began failing biology. I never failed a class in my life. My father studied all evening for a test with me, but I still failed. My father went to school and asked if he could see the test, but the teacher said since he used the same tests every year, he never allowed the students to keep them. So dad asked to see a blank one, but the teacher refused.

"My father became so angry, that he demanded that I be allowed to drop the class even though that was against policy. The principal allowed me to drop the course. Now I had a study hall, lunch, and another study hall, so the guidance councilor sent me across the street to aid for a kindergarten teacher.

"I fell in love with it and knew for a fact that I was to be an elementary teacher. I went straight through college in four years. I'm now working on my Masters in Curriculum and Instruction with a Reading Endorsement, but I think I'm taking this year off. I need a break from classes."

Not sure why, Michael tells her the beginning of his interest in the church. "My parents took me to a large fancy Episcopal church occasionally growing up and my grandmother took me to a Bible school in some small church every summer.

"The first weekend of my sophomore year in college, my friends and I went for a long walk. We passed a small brick church with a sign out front with the times of the services. The next morning, Sunday, when I woke up, I pictured the sign in my head. So out of curiosity, I attended the service. I slid in the back pew. I know it sounds crazy." His friends and Barbara made fun of this story.

"It doesn't sound crazy. It sounds like God called you to church and you heard Him." To his surprise, Sadie understands.

He continues, "For six weeks I slid in the back pew. On my way out, I always bypassed the minister, but on the sixth week, he excused himself from his greeting line to catch me. He said he wanted to talk to me and asked me to wait in his office. So I did.

"He came up to find out who I was and if I needed anything. At first I gave monosyllabic answers, but I eventually relaxed and we talked. I asked him questions about prayer. He asked if I read the Bible. I said no. It didn't make sense to me.

"The next week, I went through his line. He told me he wanted to give me something, so I waited in his office again. He gave me a red Bible called *The Book*. It was easy to understand. He showed me that at the beginning of each book was a summary plus other information like about who wrote it. He told me to start with the Gospels and then read Acts and Romans.

"I attended church every Sunday my sophomore year and none of my friends noticed. That minister was Rev. Foreman who you met yesterday. Rev. Foreman and I became friends. After a year, he began to convince me to take part in the service as a lector. I noticed that he gave me more parts of the service than other lectors. He somehow knew that I was heading this way before I did.

"I was in college earning a business degree with plans to attend Harvard to become a great lawyer with my friends. Man, were they shocked when I opted for a seminary instead of Harvard."

They realize they have been talking for two hours, so he drives her back to Erieton. She tells him to park where he is staying and she will walk.

Since it is still early, Sadie invites him for walk to the pier. They talk all of the way and sit on a bench on the pier. Sadie asks why he didn't know if anyone would come yesterday.

He leans back with a sigh, "My parents are wealthy. I have had a privileged childhood. They are not happy that I plan to live on a minister's salary. Then last week, I went home for dinner. I had a substantial trust fund. I told them I planned to turn it over to them because there is no such thing as a rich minister. They didn't want me to give my money away. We had a large, rather loud argument. That was the last I had seen them, so I wasn't sure what they would do last night."

Martin and Joy take a walk on the pier and spot Michael and Sadie deep in conversation. Martin enjoyed mentoring Michael. He thought Michael was one of the best candidates for ministry that he had worked with. Sadie's apparent attraction surprises Martin because she hadn't been attracted to anyone since she left her fiancé three years ago.

Michael leans toward her, "So, what happened in life to cause you to not trust men?"

Becoming uneasy, she stands, "We should head back."

He cocks his eyebrow, and then follows her. Her sudden withdrawal takes him by surprise, because they had been talking so easily. A little girl runs toward them calling Sadie. They follow the girl to a sobbing mother sitting by a baby in a stroller.

Sadie sits by her, "Peggy, what's wrong?"

"Oh, I don't know. I don't think I'll be ready by next week. I hate moving. I'll miss you," she hugs Sadie.

"School's out. I'll come and help you pack. I am amazing at packing. Nothing I pack will break. My mom taught me well." Sadie promises.

"Sadie, will you stay with the girls while I go find Bill? We'll be right back," Peggy begs.

"Sure. We'll take them over to that playground," Sadie agrees.

At the "we", Peggy looks up at Michael, "Who is this?"

"Oh, he's just a friend. Go find Bill."

As they walk to the playground, Sadie explains to him that Peggy is the minister's wife who currently lives in Ambrose and these are the little girls for whom she had painted the cartoon forest.

Michael inquires, "Why did you make it a point not to tell Peggy who I am?"

"She was crying about missing me. I didn't think it was the right time to tell her I'm spending the evening with her husband's replacement."

Michael nods.

The two play with the girls who are three and one. The tiny tots are adorable. Michael enjoys watching Sadie play with them. She cuddles and coos over the baby. She tickles and chases the toddler. He likes the feel of the chubby little arms around his neck when he picks the three year old up. Sadie changes the baby's diaper and then places both girls in baby swings leaving Michael with them while she disposes of the dirty diaper and washes her hands.

As he gently pushes the swings, a man walks up to him, "Do I know you?"

Michael looks at him, "I don't think so."

"Then why are you pushing my daughters?"

Michael glances at the girls and then back at him, "I'm with Sadie."

Just then Sadie returns. She introduces Rev. Bill Harper to Rev. Michael Donnelly. She tells Bill they just had their delegate dinner.

Bill whines, "Oh man. I had mine at lunch. My new delegate is almost seventy and obese and you get Sadie. That's not fair."

Michael laughs. Sadie teases, "See, I didn't make up the delegate dinner." Michael laughs again.

The two ministers talk about the church as Sadie plays with the girls. As they part ways, Bill wishes Michael good luck and warns him not to turn his back on Mac Macintyre.

Michael walks Sadie to her cottage as the evening grows dark. He points out that she is good with kids and that if she wants kids of her own, she'll have to learn to trust a man. Sadie rolls her eyes, "Whatever."

Thursday morning, Martin and Sadie take their seats in the auditorium. Before session begins, Michael plops down next to Sadie. As the morning drags on, Sadie keeps cracking jokes and making sarcastic remarks to Michael. Martin leaves to talk to a friend. Sadie bends down taking Michael's small notebook and pen from under his seat. He watches her from the corner of his eye as she writes something. She lays the pad of paper and pen on his lap having drawn out a hangman game. Michael attempts to keep a straight face. He hasn't seen this game in years. He plays it with her until he finds the answer, "I'm so bored."

Her dad returns confiscating the notepad, "What are you two, in high school?" The pair attempt not to laugh.

During the morning break, Martin tags along to the bookstore. He runs into an old friend to visit, but keeps an eye on his daughter. She and Michael become engrossed with their Bible School project. They impress Martin with their give-and-take as they discuss their selections. Sadie planned a 'Miracles of the Old Testament' theme, but willingly changes the theme when Michael comes up with 'The Power of Prayer'. They find children's picture books about Bible Stories involving prayer like *Elijah and the Burning Altar, Jonah and the Big*

Fish, Daniel in the Lion's Den, plus two from the New Testament. They also find a children's prayer book. Plus they discover an adult book concerning prayer, *To Pray Like Jesus.*

They place a rather large order in the name of the church. Sadie leaves her name as the Bible School Director, but promises that Rev. Bill Harper would come in as the current minister to sign off on the order. The couple is a half hour late returning to the meetings.

For lunch break, Martin walks to the cottage for a sandwich with Joy, but Sadie accompanies Michael to Regina's. They take a seat inside for the air-conditioning. When the waitress comes to the table, Sadie requests separate checks. Michael rolls his head and states one check will do. Sadie opens her mouth to protest, but Michael holds up his finger and gives her a look that causes her to quickly give in.

During the afternoon session, Sadie inquires about his evening plans, of which has none. Her mom is preparing tacos for supper and Sadie invites him. He doesn't want to intrude, but Martin calls Joy on his cell phone and arranges it. When they arrive at the cottage, her sisters, Mary and Lucy, who are three and five years younger than Sadie are dancing around the living room to a pop song. They grab Sadie who joins them. Michael watches for a moment enjoying their energy.

Martin turns to Michael, "Daughters."

He leads Michael out on the porch to visit while they wait for supper. Sitting on the padded white wicker furniture, Michael checks over his shoulder for Sadie, then leans forward to inquire, "I want to ask you something. What happened to cause Sadie's attitude towards men?"

"Oh you noticed," Martin leans back. "She had some rough times in college. She had a very ugly breakup with her fiancé, but she feels very private about it. It's up to her to tell you. If I wasn't a minister, I might have beaten the crap out of him.

"Here's a story I probably shouldn't tell you. Sadie and two of her friends went to a party at a fraternity house. One of their friends disappeared so the two searched for her. They went to the basement where they found a guy guarding a room. Sadie flirted with him while her friend got down on all fours behind him. Sadie pushed him over her friend. They ran into the room to find their missing friend being gang-raped by three frat brothers. Two had already raped her and the third was pulling down his pants. The boy in the hall followed them into the room closing the door. The two girls pulled out pepper spray and quickly sprayed all four of them. Then they grabbed them by the shoulders kneeing them each in the groin. They rushed to dress their friend, but the buttons were missing from her blouse. Sadie was wearing a sports bra, the kind that many people choose to jog in, so she took off her shirt and gave it to her friend. The boys still tried grabbing them. They kicked and shoved their way out."

Michael shakes his head, "No wonder she looked at me odd when I mentioned that I lived in a frat house."

"Dad, what are you two talking about?" Sadie, standing in the door, demands.

Martin and Michael jump. Martin answers, "I told him about the fraternity party."

"Why?"

"I don't know," Martin shrugs.

Sadie appears angry. She shakes her head, "Come eat." She disappears back into the cottage.

Martin whispers to Michael, "I wouldn't ask her about her ex-fiancé tonight if I were you."

Over supper, her youngest sister, Lucy who just graduated from high school, complains to Sadie, "I don't like that you're a delegate. This is our last evening here and we have hardly spent any time with you. We didn't play miniature golf or shuffleboard."

Michael knows that he is the real reason Sadie hadn't been around.

"You're right. After supper, let's go down and play," Sadie offers.

Mary thinks that Sadie should stay with Michael. She has not seen her sister so lively around a man in years.

"You know, since our brother Luke couldn't make it this year, we have an odd number for shuffleboard. Michael, do you want to be our fourth?" Mary suggests.

"No, I don't want to intrude," he declines.

"Who's going to be Lucy's partner?" Mary asks.

Mary and Sadie yell in unison, "Not it."

Lucy crosses her arms acting offended. The sisters begin sticking their tongues out at each other. Michael cocks an eyebrow at the group. Mary informs him, "Now you have to go. You're Lucy's partner."

The group plays shuffleboard first. Lucy and Mary sit at one end while Sadie and Michael head to the other end. Sadie pushes her disk in the center of the ten point triangle. It's Michael's turn. She keeps bumping him and grabbing the end of his cue pole to keep him from knocking her disk out. He makes her sit on the bench, but she uses her cue pole to try to trip him up. He still manages to knock her disk out.

Next, they walk down to the miniature golf. Michael claims he never played, but on the three warm up holes, he sinks each with one shot. He explains that he golfs; he just never did it with windmills and bridges. They bet loser buys ice cream. Three of them can sink most in two or three taps, but Lucy plays poorly. On the sixth hole, she whacks her ball off the green into a nearby bush stomping her feet with frustration. Michael retrieves her ball. He shows her the line on the putter that she is supposed to line up with the ball and hole. He takes the next three holes to improve her game. As he leans over Lucy, Mary teases Sadie that she should ask for lessons.

In the end, Lucy still loses. When they reach the ice cream stand Sadie instructs Lucy to save her money for college, but before Sadie can pay, Michael bumps her out of the way so he can pay.

"Your need to pay makes you a chauvinist, you know," Sadie accuses.

Michael shrugs, "Probably, but I don't care."

Mary and Lucy decide to look through shops leaving Michael and Sadie alone. Michael and Sadie take a long walk around Erieton. Sadie reminisces about her childhood vacations here. They also discuss his new appointment. She warns him that his new church's finances are a mess. That is why Rev. Harper is moving. They can no longer afford his salary, so they rolled the salary back to a first year minister.

He reminds her that when he went to college his plans were to be a lawyer, so his bachelor degree is in business and finance. He suggests that maybe God is sending him there on purpose to help. Sadie agrees that that must be it.

As they walk up in front of her parents' cottage, Michael points out, "Do you realize we spent every evening this week together? I'm glad I met you here. I had a good time."

"Well, I felt sorry for you since you were whining about being alone," she teases.

Sadie knows from the warm look in his eyes and small smile on his lips that he is about to kiss her. He moves closer brushing her hair off her shoulder. Sadie's heart pounds. Just as he is about to lean down, Sadie drops down to one knee to untie and retie her shoe. When she stands back up, she shakes his hand and talks fast.

"I'm glad I met you too. It's good to be friends since we will be working together. Once you move in we will get to work on Vacation Bible School. I'll probably see you tomorrow. Good night." She runs into the cottage leaving him standing there shaking his head.

From the open front window, he overhears her sisters chastise her, "What's the matter with you? He was about to kiss you."

"No he wasn't," he hears Sadie.

He walks away thinking, "Oh yes I was."

Friday morning, Martin and Sadie arrive for the last session. Sadie doesn't see Michael. She feels nervous about seeing him after her whacky behavior last night. The Bishop calls the meeting to order, but no sign of Michael. She wonders if he will avoid her today. About ten minutes into the meeting, he appears plopping into the seat next to her acting the same as any other day.

The session ends with official closing of conference and a thunderous round of applause. Outside Martin shakes Michael's hand wishing him good luck serving his first church and reminds him that he is only a phone call away if Michael has a question or needs help with anything.

Michael invites Sadie to walk down by the lake one more time before they leave. Sadie declines because she should help clean the cottage, but Martin assures her not to worry about the cottage. Michael and Sadie walk along the lake. He points out a flat boulder in the water, so they climb down over large rocks to sit on the boulder. Sadie leans back on her elbows lifting her face toward the warm sun. Michael sits with his arms wrapped around his knees looking down at her.

"When I was in college," he begins, "I had a fiancé. She loved me when I was going to be a lawyer, but when I went to seminary, she gave the ring back. How about you? Before you decided that all men are scum, did you have a serious boyfriend or fiancé?"

"I never said all men are scum. My dad and brother are good men and I have a couple friends who are good guys. I just think more than fifty-percent of men are scum." Sadie explains, avoiding the question he was actually asking.

"I see. What happened with your fiancé?" he persists.

"How do you know I had a fiancé? What exactly did my father tell you?" she demands.

He admits, "Just that you had a fiancé and it ended badly."

"Well, that's true," Sadie stares off over the lake, "We probably should be going."

Sadie climbs back up the rocks. Striking out again, Michael follows. Michael reaches the grass first taking her arm to help her down. Instead of letting go of her arm he pulls her to him, "Come here."

He slides his other hand under her hair cupping the back of her head. He leans in, kissing her gently on the lips. At first she freezes, but soon she returns the kiss. Releasing her arm, he reaches for the small of her back pulling her closer and kissing her more firmly. She lays her hands on his chest her heart pounding.

The kiss ends, Sadie opens her eyes staring into his intense gaze. Her chest tightens as panic sets in. She pulls away babbling.

"I'm sorry. I think I gave you the wrong idea. I just want to be friends. We will be working together. I'm one of your parishioners. I better go. I'll see you next week. Good luck with the move. I'm sorry."

She hurries away. Although he is disappointed that she pulled away, he feels hopeful because she returned the kiss first. He thinks there is something cute about the way she babbles when nervous. He is curious about what had happened with her fiance and why she runs away from the topic, literally.

Chapter III

Most churches bringing in a new minister pay for a large moving van and movers. Ambrose's Trinity is spared the expense. Michael moved from his parents' home to a fraternity house, to a furnished apartment by the seminary. All he requested is a small u-haul and some church members to help him unload.

The men mostly help him unload boxes. He has a computer desk he places in the small den off the dining room and a set of weights with a workout bench he hauls down to the basement. He also owns a small entertainment unit he sets in the living room by the picture window.

The kitchen has a breakfast nook with a built-in table. He informs the men that he ordered a living room suit and bedroom set to be delivered later that day. The men decide to bring one of the old, beat-up, long, rectangle tables which seats eight and several gray metal folding chairs from the fellowship hall in the church for him to use in the dining room for now.

The men leave and Michael settles in to wait for his furniture delivery. The kitchen door faces the driveway that leads to the church parking lot instead of a road. He walks through the kitchen turning into the dining room. One end leads into a small den and the other end boasts a large archway into the living room. The fireplace at one end of the living room can be seen from the dining room and the other end has the staircase leading to the four bedrooms. Across from the stairs is the front door which leads to a porch where Peggy left the porch swing since her new parsonage had nowhere to hang it. He sits in the living room on the floor with his back against the wall.

He hears the kitchen doorbell. Assuming his furniture has arrived, he opens the door to find Sadie and invites her in. She first checks to see if he is okay with her and with being just friends. He assures her he is fine. She opens the door to retrieve a large flat present she brought him.

"What's this for?" he asks.

"It's a combination of ordination and first appointment gift. I was unprepared at your party," she explains.

"You didn't have to."

"I know. So, open it."

Michael lifts the present onto the kitchen table to open. It is a painting of a carpenter's workshop during Biblical times. A toddler plays in the light from a doorway. A man raises a hammer which casts a shadow that looks like a cross over the toddler. Apparently, the painting depicts Joseph working with a young Jesus playing in the shadow of a cross.

Michael likes the painting and plans to hang it above the living room couch. Sadie sees the church table and gives Michael a strange look. Michael shrugs telling her it was the idea of the men from church since he does not have any dining room furniture. Sadie notices the lack of furniture and boxes. She discovers that he does not have much. He doesn't have items like a vacuum, cleaning supplies, or a decent set of dishes.

Sadie offers to help and instructs Michael to pick up a notebook and pen. They walk from room to room writing a list of basic needs. In the bathroom, he doesn't have a shower curtain, soap dispenser, waste basket etc. His furnished apartment had a full size bed and he chose a queen size bed at the store, so he does not even have bedding.

The furniture arrives. He selected a beautiful cherry wood bedroom set. For the living room, he picked out black leather couch, love seat, and recliner. He bought glass end tables and a coffee table with black legs and edging. He also purchased black lamps with white shades trimmed in black.

Sadie starts to leave when Michael asks where he should go to start buying things on the long list. When she inquires if he wants help, he admits he does. He has money saved to set up housekeeping, but is not sure where to start.

On their way shopping, they stop at a restaurant for a late lunch. When the waitress comes to the table, Sadie requests separate checks. Michael runs his hand over his face. He orders her to stop that, and then informs the waitress that one check will be fine.

Sadie takes him to Wal-Mart. They are playful as they select their purchases. She teases him with pretty flowery selections and will not permit him to buy ugly or plain items.

Sadie and Michael turn down the aisle with the bathroom sets. Sadie stops in front of a selection of matching items, "Hey, look at this set. It is perfect."

Michael turns to see her in front of a set covered in little yellow duckies, "Ha, ha, very funny."

He continues to look, but Sadie picks up a plastic duck shaped waste basket and a shower curtain covered with yellow smiling duckies swimming in a pond with cattails. Michael notices her placing them in the cart.

"No, no, no," he returns to the cart removing the two items. As he replaces them on the shelf, she is setting a matching toothbrush holder and soap dispenser in the cart. He takes those back out as well returning them to the shelf while she grabs a bath mat and toilet brush holder. Before Sadie can reach the cart, he catches her around the waist pulling her away from the cart and up against him.

"Hey, you stop that. Now put that stuff back," smiling, he pulls her back to the shelf. Giggling, she puts the items back.

He chooses a shower curtain with a black and white pattern with squares and circles. Sadie teases him about his taste for black. He even selects white dishes trimmed with black. She selects cleaning supplies and a vacuum for him. They eventually agree, buying most of his basic needs. She suggests that he waits on the bedding to buy better quality elsewhere.

Once they unload the car back at the parsonage, Sadie invites Michael to go for a walk. His church is located on the main street in town across from the public library. His is the only house on the block. They walk two blocks passing the post office and many little shops. She stops at a hardware store.

Instead of going to the main entrance, she goes to a door on the corner and pulls out a set of keys to unlock it. Inside, a set of stairs climbs straight up to the next floor. Michael has no idea where they are going. Curious, he follows her up. At the top of the stairs, Sadie unlocks the only door which is on the left leading over the hardware store. Inside the door, to the right is a hall with several doors, to the left is a bathroom, and straight across from the door is a dining room. At one end of the dining room is the door to the kitchen. The other end opens into a large living room.

"This is your apartment?" he asks looking around.

"Yes. It's old, but it is big for the money and close to everything. My school is only six blocks from here. Weather permitting, I walk or ride my bike. My church is close." Pointing out her living room window, she says, "See that bar across the street down on the corner? One of my best friends owns that. So I hang out there a lot. I'm not a lush; I just love spending time with my friends. Have a seat. I'll be right back."

Michael looks around. Her apartment is clean and neat. She likes knick-knacks and silk flowers. She has an electric piano with a magazine rack stuffed with music.

There are photographs and prints hanging on the walls. He notices a portrait of Sadie's family when Martin and Joy were younger. Sadie must have been about twelve, her older brother Luke was thirteen, her sister Mary was nine, and Lucy was seven. He smiles at the attractive minister's family and the sweet little Sadie.

Sadie returns with a set of pastel plaid sheets and a soft purple blanket. Michael cocks his eyebrow.

"I know they are girly colors, but you are borrowing them from a girl."

Sitting beside him, she hands him a catalogue to look at bedding. She points out ones that look like a quilt. He shakes his head. He points out some plain solids. Sadie says no even though they are for him. She also will not allow him to look at anything black. She finds one that is micro suede with browns and brown paisley forming a pattern. He likes them.

Sadie leads him to the hall. The first bedroom contains bookshelves and her computer desk. They order the bedding on line. He takes the sheets and blanket saying goodnight. He feels the urge to kiss her goodnight, but thinks better of it. She offers to help him unpack tomorrow and he accepts.

The next day, Sadie impresses Michael with how quickly she can unpack and set up house. He had been raised with servants. She had been raised doing chores and helping her parents with their moves. He did his best to keep up with her and stay useful.

She even brought leftovers for lunch and they order a pizza for supper. Sadie tries to reach the door first to pay for the pizza, but Michael comes up behind her wrapping his arms around her waist, he picks her up, and moves her so he can pay.

As they finish up, Sadie informs Michael that she won't come around the rest of the week. She figures he needs the next four days to work at church, unpack his office, and prepare for his first service. He agrees.

They both lean back on the kitchen counter tired from a day of hard work. Michael leans down around and kisses her on the mouth. Sadie returns the kiss and then pulls away.

"I'm not dating you," she reminds him.

"I know. You've said," he kisses her again placing a hand on each side of her leaning on the counter.

"Then why are you kissing me?"

"Well, for one thing, I want to," he gives her a quick kiss then adds, "And you are letting me." He continues to kiss her.

Sadie pushes him away, "Stop it. We are just friends. I mean it." She leaves.

The next day, Michael walks around the church trying to picture his new life as a minister. He sits in the back pew in the sanctuary which while much smaller than his parents' home church; he sees it as warm and inviting. Simple wooden pews with a center aisle fill the room. The side windows have colored small diamond shaped design. The front wall boasts a large cross hanging in front of burgundy drapes. A burgundy rug covers the altar area and runs down the center aisle. The choir loft is split in two on both sides. The altar sets in the center with a gold cross and candle sticks on both sides. An organ sets on the left side beside a lectern and the pulpit with the minister's chair sets on the right.

Michael walks to his office to meet his new secretary, Sue Anderson. She is a middle-aged woman who is a little frumpy with glasses and has short tightly curled hair. While friendly, his age seems to bother her. However, after two mornings working with Michael to set up his office and prepare for the Sunday service, he quickly wins her over.

The night before his first service, Michael can't sleep. His thoughts drift back to college and his life at the fraternity house.

Colby Stark and Graham Worthington had been his best friends since kindergarten. They lived together at college. They planned to eventually open their own law practice: Worthington, Donnelly, and Stark. Graham and Michael cruised through school, but Colby struggled. Graham and Michael tutored him, especially Michael.

Michael's sophomore year, Graham and Colby never noticed that he attended church every week. They assumed he was jogging or swimming. However, his junior year, Michael's girlfriend, Barbara, began her freshman year. She noticed after Saturday night dates or parties, that Michael disappeared every Sunday morning.

One evening, Michael sat alone in his room reading the Bible Rev. Foreman gave him. He found some of the Old Testament stories crazy and amusing. Graham, Colby, and Barbara decided they wanted to go out and stormed his room to take him with them. Michael slid the Bible under his pillow, but while he was getting his jacket, Barbara pulled it back out to see what he had hidden.

His friends were surprised that Michael had been sitting around reading a Bible and teased him. Barbara put it together with Sunday mornings asking him if he went to church. Michael admitted it.

That Sunday was the first time Michael was going to lector. Rev. Foreman talked him into doing the readings. He felt nervous.

Graham, Colby, and Barbara showed up at the church out of curiosity. They didn't see him in the sanctuary. They returned to the entry way thinking they must be at the wrong church. An elderly woman greeted them. Barbara asked if she knew Michael Donnelly. The lady told them of course she knew him and that he was here somewhere.

Almost time for the service to start, Michael walked down the hall with Rev. Foreman. When he saw his friends, he ducked into a room. Rev. Foreman followed him.

"I change my mind. I can't do the readings today," Michael panicked.

"Who are those kids you saw before you dove in here?" Rev. Foreman asked.

Michael rolled his eyes, "They are my friends and girlfriend. They think it's weird I'm going to church. I don't want them to see me up front."

Rev. Foreman reprimanded him, "You are not supposed to hide your faith."

Michael shrugged, "Yeah, I don't care."

"You committed to do this, so do it. We are late. Let's go," he ordered.

Michael followed him out. He didn't see his friends and hoped that they left. The organ played as Michael walked down the aisle beside his minister. He passed his friends who were sitting in a pew visibly surprised to see him walking up the aisle. He sat up front during the announcements. Then he went to the pulpit where he read the Call to Worship, led the litany, and then read from the Old Testament. His voice's deep tone sounded rich and full.

When he finished, he went and sat with his friends for the rest of the service. On the walk home, they wanted Michael to explain why he was involved in a church, but he didn't know how to explain it. It was just a feeling, an interest.

The next Saturday, the fraternity house planned a blow-out party. Michael always had two or three beers over the course of the evening, but didn't get drunk. That night, his friends pushed him, pushed him hard to get drunk. They handed him about six jell-o shots. They pushed other drinks. Michael became drunk and walked wobbly.

The three friends watched a frat brother drink from a beer bong, a long tube with a funnel on top. When he finished, others yelled for who's next. Graham volunteered Michael.

"No, no, no, no, no, no," Michael stuttered.

Graham taunted, "Come on Bible boy."

Graham pulled on his arms and Colby pushed. Once in front of the beer bong, Colby pushed the back of Michael's knees with his foot. On his knees with people chanting, Michael took the tube in his mouth while Graham poured beer into the funnel. When he drank all he could stand, Michael couldn't find his balance to stand, falling over. His friends laughed.

A girl named Brittany helped him up. She led him to the other side of the room where she began kissing him. He told her he had a girlfriend, but she replied, "So do I." Another girl, Allie, began to rub his back. He stumbled away.

"Don't go now. The party is just starting," cooed Brittany who pushed him. Losing his balance, he fell on the couch. Brittany and Allie each kneeled on either side of him. While one kissed him on the mouth, the other kissed his ear and neck, taking turns. Michael began to return their kisses.

Barbara showed up looking for her boyfriend. Graham and Colby tried to stop her, but they were drunk too. She walked past him with the girls and murmured, "Oh get a room."

She stopped. Going back to the couch, she takes a closer look realizing it was him.

Grabbing the girls by the back of their hair one at a time, she pulled them off, "Get off my boyfriend you skanks."

With the girls gone, Barbara turned back to Michael who slurred, "Hey Barbie, what's up?"

His friends laughed hysterically as Barbara screamed, "Augh!" and stormed off. Michael jumped up to follow her, but was overcome with nausea.

Colby yelled, "He's gonna blow!"

Graham handed him one of the buckets setting around just for this purpose. Michael dropped to his knees vomiting. When he had purged himself, he crawled up on the couch passing out for the night.

The next day, Barbara came to confront Michael ready for a fight, but couldn't find him. She located her brother and Graham, but no one could find him.

Since it was Sunday morning, Barbara suggested the church. They drove over, but church had ended and the building was locked up. After looking everywhere they could think of, at one o'clock, Barbara called the police.

The detective's in charge main concern was that the last time seen, Michael had been wasted. The possibility of alcohol poisoning or an accident was high. Police and campus security searched. His parents were notified and two hours later they arrived on campus.

The detective discovered that two of the frat brothers had made a video that night. He showed it to Graham, Colby, Barbara, and his parents. The tape showed Michael watching someone on the beer bong. Then his friends pushed him into a turn despite protests. They also captured him making out with two girls at the same time as well as Barbara catching them. The boys taping the event can be heard laughing.

James was angry that his son could be pushed around like that by his friends. He wished his son was stronger than that. He also didn't understand the Bible boy comment.

Sophia was furious that his friends would hurt her son. While the detective left them for a minute, she smacked both Colby and Graham across the face. Terror filled her with the fear that he was dead or seriously hurt.

The president of the university was on the scene threatening to close the fraternity house and place everyone caught drunk on tape on probation.

At seven o'clock that evening, Michael walked up on the lawn asking an officer what was going on. The officer radioed the lead detective, "Hey Bruce, guess who just came home?"

Michael walked into the house not expecting to see his parents. His mother threw her arms around him and cried.

Michael stuttered confused, "I don't understand why I was reported missing. I always go off on my own on Sundays."

Barbara, crying, explained that she called because he had been so drunk. The detective sent the search party home. He then sat Michael, his parents, and friends down at the table wanting to know where he had been.

Embarrassed, Michael explained, "I woke up at ten o'clock on that couch. I had vomit on my shirt and I felt sick. I went up to my room, changed clothes, and brushed my teeth."

The detective interrupted, "Wait a minute. You were on the couch in the main room until ten and no one saw you?"

"Everyone I saw was sleeping," he shrugged. "I put on my sunglasses and left. I still felt half drunk and hung over. Bobby, who didn't go to the party was leaving for work and gave me a ride to church."

Colby and Graham shook their heads and rolled their eyes…

Rev. Foreman had been worried about Michael not coming for the first time especially since he had been upset about his friends the week before. Twenty minutes into the service Michael staggered in wearing sunglasses with his hair a mess. He slouched down in the back pew holding his head.

After the service, Michael attempted to bypass Rev. Foreman, but the minister excused himself from the greeting line and went after him. Grabbing his arm, he demanded Michael wait for him in his office.

When Rev. Foreman entered his office, Michael was lying on the short couch with his knees draped over the arm. Rob slammed the door startling Michael and hurting his head. He ordered him to a chair and took the sunglasses off him. His bloodshot eyes appeared incapable of focusing. Rob asked several questions, but Michael couldn't seem to think clearly enough to answer.

Once Bonnie, Rob's wife, saw Michael, she insisted on taking him to the parsonage. At the parsonage, Rob again questioned him but gave up. Michael fell asleep on the couch for hours.

When Michael woke, Bonnie gave him a full, healthy dinner. Michael told them about being pushed around by his friends trying as hard as they could to get him as drunk as they could. Rob lectured him about standing up to his friends, about not drinking and about going to church. Then Rob drove him back to campus.

After Michael finished his story, the detective asked about the night before. All he remembered was the beer bong, vomiting, and that he passed out. He insisted he didn't remember anything in between. To his embarrassment, the detective showed him the tape. He had forgotten about the girls on the couch.

After the detective left, Michael apologized over and over to Barbara. She forgave him, because the video showed exactly how it happened. She made him promise never to get so out of control drunk again to which he gladly agreed.

Then his parents lectured and interrogated him. They asked him question after question about the church and the minister. His dad asked him about the extra classes he has been taking. The second half of his sophomore year, he began taking religion courses as electives. His father informed him that those are not needed to be a lawyer. Michael defended himself by pointing out that he was earning a major in business with a minor in political science. As long as he made the Dean's List each semester, who cared if he took an extra class?

However, his father did not understand Michael's curiosity in this area and continued to interrogate him with questions about Rev. Foreman and why this man had taken such an interest in his son.

Michael became frustrated, "Why do you seem more upset about my attending church than me getting wasted and having a threesome?"

Chapter IV

The alarm goes off. The time has come for his first service in his first church as an ordained minister. He prays hard that God will guide him this day.

The morning at church consists of people being surprised, amazed, and some even horrified by his age. Girls in the youth group giggle and point, developing immediate crushes. Sadie introduces him to Mac Macintyre who looks at Michael as if he were an idiot who couldn't possibly do this job.

During the service, Sadie as conference delegate introduces Rev. Donnelly to the congregation. She also gives a thorough conference report. She had paid attention after all. The service runs smoothly. Sadie loves his deep rich voice. He gives a sermon he had prepared for a seminary class about ministry, dealing with Jesus' Sermon on the Mount.

Since the choir disbanded for the summer, Sadie sings for the special music. She performs a contemporary song. Michael loves the sound of her voice. To him, she sounds like a professional singer.

After the service, the women's group set up a reception for their new minister. They serve sandwiches, veggies and dip, cookies, coffee, and punch. Sadie introduces Michael to Colleen and Aidan. Colleen, who has been her best friend since high school, sometimes attends church with Sadie, but Aidan never goes with them. They are here today because they are curious about the new minister who so obviously has Sadie's attention. Michael's good looks surprise Colleen.

"Rev. Donnelly, this is Colleen Quillen and Aidan Phillips. They are my closest friends. You are performing their wedding in November."

"I am?"

Colleen explains, "Rev. Harper said that the new minister would do our wedding. So how many weddings have you performed?"

Michael smiles at her.

"Have you done any?" she asks worriedly.

"Not exactly," he hedges. Although he completed his student pastorate having performed a few funerals and baptisms, a wedding had somehow never come up.

Colleen is not sure how she feels about this.

"Well, someone needs to be your first," Aidan states with confidence.

Over the next four weeks, Michael works closely with Sadie on Bible School. He decides not to make any further advances. He still wants to date her, but thinks it would be best to give her time to become comfortable and trust him.

Kirk Donaldson provides them with a large six foot by four foot, flat piece of wood for a sign to advertise their Bible School out in front of the church. Sadie brings Michael a piece of paper with her design for it. He approves it. She places it in the copy machine and sends a transparency through the bypass. Michael and the custodian, Don, carry the wood down to a tarp in the fellowship hall. Using an overhead,

Sadie paints. When his office hours end, Michael runs home to change. He returns to the fellowship hall where Sadie is only half way done to spend several hours helping.

Michael finds Sadie a breath of fresh air. She is lively, witty, and easy to talk to. She tells him that her father always says, "Sadie's report cards often read, talks too much in class and now a school pays her to talk all day in class, an irony of life."

Michael laughs. Sadie always makes him smile, laugh. The urge to kiss her returns, but he does not act on it.

As they finish, Sadie quickly turns around knocking into Michael. Her one inch paint brush hits his arm leaving a large green patch on his bicep.

"Oh, I'm so sorry," she apologizes.

"That's okay. Don't worry about it," he assures her.

With a sparkle in her eye, she steps closer, "Wait, I'll fix this."

She quickly slaps the paint brush on both of his cheeks.

He jumps back, "Hey, how did that help?"

"Now it matches."

He holds up his paint brush which is covered with blue, "Oh yeah, come here."

Laughing, she runs from him but he is quit. Catching her arm and pulling her close, he dots her forehead, cheeks, and then her nose while she screams, laughs, and attempts to pull free. Out of breath and still laughing, they set down their brushes to admire their handy work. The large sign advertises the Vacation Bible School for all ages with the dates for the first week in August and the seven o'clock times. There is a picture of happy children playing in the grass under a blue sky with a cross up in the clouds next to the theme, 'The Power of Prayer.'

They look at each others' paint covered faces and begin to giggle and chuckle once more, when they here the door upstairs. Someone is in the church. Not wanting to be seen with their faces covered with paint and having obviously been playing around, Michael grabs Sadie's hand and quickly pulls her into the kitchen beside the large refrigerator where they can't be seen. Holding onto Sadie's shoulders, he pulls her up against him while they wait.

The custodian, Don, enters the fellowship hall calling, "Reverend? Sadie?" He stops in front of the sign to admire their work. Shaking his head, he picks up the brushes they had left unclean and heads over to the utility closet to wash them out.

While the water is running, the two quietly slip out of the kitchen, through the hall, and up the stairs. Keeping their heads down, they hurry to the parsonage to wash up.

"Would you like to go out to eat?" Michael invites.

Sadie, noticing the warm look on his face as he gazes at her, becomes nervous. She keeps telling him that she won't date him, but she can't seem to stop flirting with him. She makes excuses and leaves.

The year before the church enrolled eleven children in Bible School. After the last day of registration, Michael's count comes to seventy-two people from nursery to the adult class. Many people are not members which brings a good opportunity to attract new membership. Bible School also provides the church members the opportunity to get to know their new minister.

On the first day, Michael calls Sadie, "I want to sit down with you to go over the opening for this evening. I know you will run it and teach the songs, but I need to know what you want me to do and when."

"I'll be home until I leave for church. Stop by anytime." Her door buzzer sounds, "Where are you?"

"Downstairs," Michael admits. Hanging up, Sadie hits the door release and Michael climbs up the stairs where Sadie is waiting for him.

"Give me a few minutes to get dinner in the oven. We can talk while it bakes. Do you want to eat with me? I'm making breaded chicken breast, roasted potatoes, and salad," she offers and he accepts.

He leans in the doorway to talk while she prepares the meal. While it bakes, they sit together with a notebook. Some parishioners give Michael a hard time about his age and do not have much confidence in him as of yet. Rev. Harper had little to do with Bible School; she wants Michael to be seen. She already told many of the teachers and people working on it that Michael came up with the theme.

Originally, she would do the entire opening and the minister would only say a quick prayer. She decides Michael should be more active. Most of the time will be used up with the singing. She suggests that he be in charge of the memory work. They divided the Twenty-Third Psalm into four parts. Each day the students will memorize one part and any child who can recite the whole thing on Friday can choose a prize from the treasure chest. The teachers will listen to the recitations, but Michael can explain it, encourage participation, and go over each part. At the program on Sunday, children can go to him for the prizes.

Feeling prepared, they relax and enjoy dinner. As they leave Sadie's apartment for church, they run into Mac Macintyre coming out of the hardware store. Mac acts cold and suspicious about their new, young minister coming out of Sadie's apartment.

The pair opens Bible School together. Their plans work like clockwork. Sadie welcomes everyone and introduces the first songs with a high energy level. Within minutes she has most of the kids excited and singing. Once she has them wound up, Michael takes over introducing the Memory Challenge and the theme, "Power of Prayer." He leads a prayer, and then Sadie takes over organizing an orderly dismissal to classes while introducing the teachers. Michael and the adults adjourn to the lounge. Sadie is free to help where needed.

The first night is a success. Kids leave wound up and jumping around. The adults are in good moods and chatting. Sadie's goal in the opening had been to help put Michael in a good light, but many, mostly women, notice the chemistry between the two as Michael and Sadie led together as a team.

Tuesday evening, before Bible School, Michael walks around the breezeway greeting people as they arrive. A five year old girl with long blond hair and big blue eyes pulls on his arm.

"Excuse me mister," she calls, "Are you the preacher?"

"Yes I am," he answers. He towers over the tiny girl. She curls her finger in a come here motion, so he squats down.

"If you're the preacher, than you are friends with God, right?"

Michael smiles, "Yes I am."

"Yesterday, the teacher said that God will hear my prayers. She also said it is good to ask people to pray for you." Her r's sound like w's. She sounds like she is calling him a pweacher and asking him to pway for her. "I thought since you are friends with God, He would hear you for sure if you pray for me."

"I'd be happy to pray for you," he stands up looking around. "Come here."

He leads her to a chair by a small end table. Lifting her onto the table, he sits down next to her, "Now, what exactly are you praying for?"

"I don't want to have to leave my apartment. I heard Mommy say if we lose it, she doesn't know where we would go," she looks at him with pleading eyes.

Michael is surprised that the prayer is so serious, "Where is your Daddy?"

"I don't know. He doesn't live with us. He might be dead, I think. I heard Mommy call him a deadbeat," she answers in the sweetest voice.

"I don't think he's dead Sweetheart. I will pray for you and we will talk again, okay?" Michael assures her.

"Okay," she jumps down skipping off not waiting for the prayer.

Michael heads to the sanctuary. Before Sadie begins the opening, he pulls her aside pointing out the little girl. He requests that after the classes begin, for her to find the girl's registration form and bring it to him even though he will be with his group. He wants to see it before the girl is picked up.

Once classes begin, Sadie slides into the lounge, hands him the sheet and quietly leaves. While his class works on a quick writing exercise, he reads the sheet over: Kelly Mitchell, five years old, Westbrook Apartments, Mother Alice Mitchell, works at Wal-Mart, not a member of his church, no father listed.

After classes, many of the children tear around the fenced-in playground. Michael stays near the gate. A small woman with stringy blond hair arrives. She should be pretty, but looks as if life has beaten her down. She calls for Kelly. Michael introduces himself and asks if he can talk to her in private. She nervously agrees sending Kelly off to play. He leads her to his office.

"She isn't in trouble already, is she?" Alice nervously sits.

He assures her that is not the case relaying the conversation he shared with Kelly. Alice appears embarrassed. Michael offers to help her. It takes several minutes to persuade her to open up to him about her situation.

Alice divorced her husband almost a year ago for domestic violence. Although the court ordered child support, she has not received any money for the past four months and does not have the money for a lawyer and court fees to go back and fight for it. Now she is short two hundred fifty dollars for the rent and the building manager offered to make up the difference for her in return for sexual favors. Alice breaks down in tears.

Michael hands her a tissue and goes into the secretary's office. Unlocking a filing cabinet, he takes out a cash box with discretionary funds and removes two hundred fifty dollars recording the withdrawal in a small notepad inside.

Alice refuses the money at first, but accepts it with a little persuasion. He convinces her to meet him again tomorrow at one o'clock. By the time they return to the playground, only Sadie and Kelly remain. Although curious, Sadie knows not to ask because being a minister, much of his interactions are confidential.

Alice returns to the church the following afternoon with Kelly in tow. She can barely afford a sitter for her work hours. Michael, having called Martin Stevens for advice about how to help, plans to take her to the welfare office. Alice refuses the thought of welfare, but Michael convinces her to look into it for Kelly's sake.

Michael takes Alice to the welfare office where she is given food stamps, health care coverage, and lists of community resources. She is also offered up to five thousand dollars which will be returned when her ex-husband pays up his back child support. She is then sent to the department for child support where her ex-husband's driver's license is immediately revoked until arrangements are made to garnish his paycheck. They are then sent to the office of community housing to apply for section eight to help with her rent until the child support is straightened out.

Once back in the church parking lot, Michael lifts a sleeping Kelly out of his car, buckling her into her mother's car. A grateful Alice thanks Michael for all his help inviting him to dinner at her apartment to thank him properly. He declines. Moving closer, she asks him to reconsider as she brushes her breast across his arm. Stepping back, Michael tells her not to worry about it, helping is what a minister does and he makes a hasty retreat.

The next morning, Michael, wearing his clerical shirt and black suite, visits the Westbrook manager's office. He explains to the manager that if he bothers Alice or Kelly in any way again, Michael will personally see to it that criminal and civil sexual harassment charges are filed against him. If he tries to remove her from the building, he will bring charges against him. The manager attempts to deny the allegations, but under Michael's intense stare he promises to leave Alice alone.

Friday night, Bible School ends a success. The people who attended Michael's study found him well-prepared, insightful, and knowledge-able. Many members begin to accept him as their minister. The children love him. While Michael doesn't know it yet, Alice and one other family became interested in the church during the week and will join.

After Michael locks up the church, Sadie says she'll see him

Sunday. Being a hot August evening, Michael offers to buy her an ice cream cone to celebrate the week. They walk a couple blocks to a nearby ice cream stand close to the high school.

As they eat their ice cream and slowly stroll toward Sadie's apartment, Michael declares that they made a great team and he enjoyed working on Bible School with her. He suggests maybe she can relax next week before she starts back to school.

Sadie laughs, "I'll be gone all next week. I'm going to a college campus in Pennsylvania for band camp. I'm the flag corps advisor."

"You do keep busy," he comments. "How about tomorrow, you and I go see a movie. I'll take you to dinner first."

"Dinner and a movie? I don't know. That sounds an awful lot like a date," she points out.

"So what? We have a good time together. Would it kill you to go out on a date?" he argues.

"You never know?" Sadie teases.

They finish their ice cream as they near her apartment. Michael asks, "Do you think I am one of the more than fifty percent of men you consider scum?"

"Heavens no, you are definitely one of the good ones."

"Then let me take you out tomorrow," he pushes.

"Sorry, no. I'll see you Sunday," she unlocks the door, "Goodnight. Thanks for the ice cream."

Michael catches the door before it shuts following her into the stairwell, "I have one more argument for why you should date me. Come here."

He grabs her kissing her hungrily having held himself back for over a month. She returns the kiss as he wraps his arms around her. She does not pull away, but waits for him to stop. He leans his forehead on hers.

She whispers, "Michael, I am not going to date you."

Frustrated, Michael steps away leaning his back against the wall, "I want to know why."

Sadie leans against the opposite wall staring at the floor, "I don't want to risk falling in love with you."

His eyes widen, "What? Why?"

Her eyes remain fixed on the floor, "I don't want to end up with a minister."

He never expected that to be the reason. He had assumed it had something to do with the ex-fiancé. Barbara left him for that reason, but Sadie would make a wonderful minister's wife. She is so active in the church. She knows how to run things, she understands church politics and she possesses a strong faith.

Her gaze slowly moves up to his face, "You have to understand, I did my time in a parsonage. Every two to eight years you are going to move. I would lose my job. I could never earn tenure. I would always be trying to start over. With years of experience making me expensive, schools tend to hire the newly graduated.

"Also, I'd have to leave my friends. There are three women and two men in this town who I love dearly and I have been with since college, one since high school.

"Another heartache is you have to go wherever the Bishop sends you. You can't choose your house or the town and you are expected to act like you're happy about it. Do you know how much of Ohio is country? I am not a country girl and the inner city scares me.

"You are the first man I have even been tempted to date in the past three years, but I can't. The cost of being with you is too high."

Michael just stares at her not knowing what to say. A tear rolls down Sadie's cheek. He crosses to her pulling her into his arms and laying his cheek on top of her head holding her for a minute. Kissing her forehead, he quietly leaves. Sadie sits on the stairs and cries.

Chapter V

Friday evening, Michael sits in front of the T.V. bored and restless. He walks out on the porch to sit on the swing Peggy left behind. Other than church, he has not seen Sadie for two weeks. When he is not working, he is alone.

He hears the marching band in the distance. Checking his watch he thinks it is too early for halftime. It must be the pre-game show. Although he never cared much for football, he takes a four block walk to the stadium.

Several people and children from church greet him as he leans on the waist high fence by the field.

"Rev. Donnelly, right?" a pleasant man asks.

"Yes," Michael turns toward him. He looks familiar.

Extending his hand, he reminds Michael, "Aidan Phillips. You are doing my wedding in November."

"Oh yes, I remember you," Michael shakes hands. He is a friend of Sadie's. Aidan hasn't been to church since Michael's first Sunday about two months ago.

"Who are you here with?" Aidan asks.

"Oh, I'm on my own." Michael replies.

"I guess you've only lived here two months. It must be hard to be new in town. I'll tell you what, come sit with us," he invites.

Michael accepts his offer following him up into the stands. Three beautiful young women sit on one bench and Aidan joins a man sitting behind them.

"Reverend, this is Colleen, Brenda, Stephanie and Steve. This is Reverend Donnelly," Aidan introduces.

"Michael."

"Oh," Stephanie claps her hands together, "You must be Sadie's hot minister."

Michael cocks his eyebrow. Aidan warns, "I must warn you, these are Sadie's best friends. Anything you say, she will know."

It occurs to Michael that he is sitting with the three women and two men that Sadie spoke of. The girls are thin and stylish. Stephanie has long full blond hair, blue eyes and seems flirtatious. Brenda has short red hair, green eyes, and appears a little cynical. Colleen has long kinky sandy hair, green eyes, and is bubbly. Aidan and Steve appear to be in good shape. Steve is average height, curly hair and wears glasses. Aidan is tall and wears a buzz cut. Aidan is engaged to Colleen and Steve and Brenda are married.

Michael enjoys sitting with this lively group. As halftime approaches, Aidan warns Michael to stay seated because halftime is important to the girls.

Colleen turns around propping her elbows on Michael's knees. "Sadie was in the flag corps her first two years of high school, but then her family moved the summer before her junior year. She had missed the spring tryouts for our flag corps which I was in. Sadie and I became good friends over the summer. I talked our advisor into putting her on the squad as an alternate. She marched all but two games. The following year, she was the squad captain. I helped her make up two of the routines they are doing tonight.

"Sadie hated moving to our town. It is too country for her. That same summer, my mom and step-dad were going through a divorce. We were both miserable, but we hooked up. We have been inseparable ever since."

They watch the halftime show. The marching band is impressive. For the one song, the flag corps lays down their flags and picks up colorful derby style hats that Sadie sets out for them. The girls perform a Broadway style dance with their hats.

After halftime, the group visits and watches the rest of the game. As the game ends, Aidan invites Michael to walk with them to Duffy's, a bar that Steve and Brenda Duffy own. Michael remembers the bar Sadie pointed out across the street from her apartment.

Michael hedges, "I'm not sure Sadie would be comfortable with that."

Colleen pats his knee, "I bet she'll be fine with it. Trust me, I know her."

Steve interjects, "We know that you wanted to date her. I'll tell you, you are probably lucky she said no. Sadie is a bit of a whack job."

The girls turn to give Steve a dirty look. Michael laughs. He had wondered how much they knew. He didn't know whether he should go to the bar or not. Sadie might not like it and he is a minister now. The girls run to meet Sadie in the band room, while the guys stand around waiting. They soon return with Sadie. Michael feels a bit nervous and out of place.

"Hey Sadie," Aidan calls, "Is it okay with you if the Reverend here goes to the bar with us?"

"Of course it is," Sadie walks up to Michael, "I've always said I want to be good friends. Besides, apparently it is a good thing I wouldn't date you, being I'm a whack job and all."

Steve grabs an imaginary knife and plunges it into his chest falling backwards. Michael catches him.

As they walk up the hill Aidan repeats his warning to Michael, "I told you, they tell each other everything. For example, we know that you have kissed her three different times."

Michael feels embarrassed as Colleen adds, "We also know that you are an awesome kisser."

Sadie covers her face with her hands. Stephanie grabs hold of Michael's arm leaning on him.

She purrs in a sensual voice, "If Sadie won't date him, maybe I should."

She gives him a little pinch.

"Hey," Michael jumps and moves away from her.

Colleen cries, "Oh my god, tell me she didn't just goose my minister."

Steve shakes his head, "You are going straight to hell."

Aidan leans on Michael, "Reverend, that girl needs saved."

"Yeah, but I'll try from over here," he replies.

At the bar, they push two tables together and order drinks and Buffalo wings. The three guys sit on one side, Colleen and Brenda sit across from them and Sadie and Stephanie sit on the ends.

Stephanie, with an evil gleam in her eye, apologizes, "I'm sorry if I embarrassed you Reverend. To make things even, I know how I can embarrass Sadie. She called the day she met you. Do you remember how you described him?"

"Big deal," Sadie looks at Michael, "I said you are tall, dark and handsome."

Stephanie continues, "You also said that if he weren't a minister, he could always be an..."

A piece of celery hits Stephanie in the forehead. Everyone looks down the table at Sadie.

"Oops, it slipped," Sadie threatens, "There are knives on the table too, you know."

Colleen speaks up, "Stop embarrassing these two. Poor Michael isn't going to want to come back."

"No," Steve begs, "Finish the sentence. If he weren't a minister, he could always be an..."

"No way, let it go." Colleen declares. "Now, no more talk about underwear models."

Michael's eyes widen as Steve and Aidan loudly laugh. Sadie slides out of her seat onto the floor under the table.

The girls leave to dance. Later, Sadie sits at the bar on a swivel stool with Brenda and Colleen standing across from her. The guys and Stephanie sit at a table close by.

"You know Reverend, you've kissed Sadie before. What do you think she would do if you just walk over there and kiss her now?" Steve harasses

Michael just cocks his eyebrow, so Steve repeats the question to Sadie.

She answers in an uppity tone, "I would smack him across the face."

"Good to know," Michael takes a drink of beer.

"Oh, she hits like a girl," Steve persists. "I dare you to kiss her."

"Steve!" the girls yell.

Michael realizes that as the new guy, he is basically being hazed tonight by her friends. He wants to win her friends over and he likes the idea of kissing her again. Aidan can tell that Michael is considering it.

Aidan joins in, "I double dare you."

"You two stop it," Brenda chastises. "You are acting like you're in high school."

"We spent the evening at the high school," Aidan points out. "I triple dog dare you to walk over there and kiss her."

Michael takes a swig of beer and then agrees, "Okay."

He stands and moves around the table. Sadie freezes asking her friends if he is actually coming over. They look over her shoulder at him. Michael takes her by the shoulders and turns her toward him. She places her hand on his chest.

"You are not seriously going to kiss me on a dare are you?" she demands.

"I probably shouldn't," Michael agrees, "But, what the hell."

Still holding her shoulders, he quickly leans down and kisses her on the lips. The kiss lasts longer than her friends expected. He finishes and walks back to his seat to hoots and applause.

"You're an idiot," Sadie snaps.

Michael looks up at her, "I'm an idiot? For one thing, you forgot to slap me. For another, you kissed me back."

"I did not," she denies.

Her friends respond, "You did too."

The next Friday, Michael sits in the kitchen trying to decide if he should go to the game or not. He changes his mind every few minutes. Someone knocks on his door. Aidan and Steve are on their way to the game and stop by to see if he wants to walk down with them. Decision made, Michael walks with them.

The Ambrose Comets win again. The group waits for Sadie outside the band room. Teenagers are running around excited about a dance that night. As Sadie joins her friends, a cute young girl, with three friends in tow, run to Sadie.

"Miss Stevens, Miss Stevens," the girl cries, "I don't think I can do it. I'll just die."

"Jessica, calm down dear. I promise you won't die," Sadie comforts, "You have your friends with you. Don't cry in front of him, just look annoyed. Save all tears for the girls' room."

"What if he says something that I don't know how to answer?" Jessica quivers.

"When in doubt, hold up your hand and say, whatever." Sadie advises. "You can do it. We practiced yesterday. Stand up to him. He's nothing but a jerk."

"Okay Miss Stevens. I'll try. Will you be home if I need you?" she whines.

"No, I'm going to Duffy's, but I have my cell phone if you need me," Sadie promises.

With a deep breath, Jessica and her friends head for the dance. Sadie's friends ask about it, but she thinks they should wait until they are away from the school.

As they walk up the hill, away from the school, Michael asks, "What are you doing Sadie? Teaching the next generation to be bitter and distrustful of men?"

Anger shoots through her. Swiftly, she turns shoving him with the palms of her hands. "Me?! You think this is my fault? She's fifteen!

You think I want her hurt and bitter?"

"Sorry," Michael backs off throwing his hands up.

Poking him in the chest with her pointer finger several times, she growls, "That sweet little girl had a crush on a big, strong football player. He found out and asked her on a date. She was thrilled. On that date, he talked her into giving him a blow job. It was the first time she did anything like that. The next day, he dumped her and he told his friends what she did. Now several guys are asking her out in disgusting ways. How is any of that my fault?"

She gives him a final shove and storms up the hill.

Steve whispers, "Smooth move."

Michael whispers back, "Oh shut up."

Once at the bar, they ask Sadie how she told Jessica to handle it. Sadie lays out her basic plan for them. Jessica and her friends will walk up to him when he is with at least two friends. She'll say, "I can't believe what you are saying about me. Stop it."

Then one of her friends will talk to one of his friends, "What makes sense to you? She did what he said so he dumped her or she refused to do what he said and he dumped her?" Most boys won't understand why he would dump her.

"I told them, don't deny anything, don't admit anything, and stick to the truth. I also said not to stand around and argue, just walk away," Sadie finishes.

Michael leans forward, "So basically your client is guilty of the charges and you created reasonable doubt without perjury. You should have been a lawyer."

"I could never be a lawyer," Sadie leans forward too, "I cannot defend the actions of men."

She jumps up leaving the table to dance. Her girlfriends join her. As they go crazy to an up tempo song, Michael leans back shaking his head. He thinks it is hard to defend men when you have Alice's ex-husband, her building manager, the three frat guys who raped Sadie's friend, this football player, and whatever Sadie's ex-fiancé did.

Michael lowers his voice and quietly asks Aidan and Steve, "Sadie's father told me a story about Sadie and a friend rescuing another friend at a fraternity house. Do you know who he was talking about?"

Aidan and Steve, shocked, do not answer right away. Finally, Steve whispers, "My wife, Brenda, was the one raped. Sadie and Colleen saved her."

Michael shakes his head watching the group of beautiful, energetic girls dance. They are survivors.

A slow song begins. Steve goes to his wife and Aidan goes to his fiancé. Stephanie dances with someone she just met. Michael catches Sadie as she leaves the dance floor.

"Come here," he pulls her back to the dance floor swaying her to the music. He whispers apologies for his thoughtless comments earlier. She accepts and lays her cheek on his chest.

Later, Sadie's flag girls show up at the bar excited. Sadie's plan worked. No one knew for sure what happened anymore and in the confusion they think the issue will be dropped. Logan, the date, was furious. The girls hug Sadie and leave. Michael comes up behind her and squeezes her shoulder.

Tuesday morning, during office hours, Michael receives a phone call to inform him that one of his parishioners, Ed Hart, will be taken off life support at three o'clock this afternoon. Michael promises to be there.

When he arrives at the hospital, a tiny, skinny, elderly woman, Betty is holding her husband's hand. Although his eyes are open, he doesn't move. Michael greets Betty and then prays for Ed and reads scripture. The doctor comes in and removes Ed from the machines. Betty trembles, so Michael places his arm around her.

After the doctor finishes, he informs them he doesn't know how long it will take for him to die. It could be a few minutes or a few hours. Betty sits at his side talking to him and stroking him. Betty is all alone, so Michael stays. The heart monitor still displays a heartbeat. Betty tells Ed it is okay to go now, not to worry about her. She tells him she loves him over and over assuring him that she loved her life with him and to go on ahead, she'd catch up later.

Over two hours later, the heart monitor displays a flat line. He is gone. A nurse turns off the machine and a doctor is called to pronounce him dead. Betty crawls up into the bed with him and sobs.

A nurse tells Betty she needs to leave now, but Betty doesn't move. The nurse looks at Michael who walks over and gently pulls her off the bed. Her legs refuse to support her. Michael tries to hold her up, but she collapses. Not sure what to do, he lifts her up in his arms and carries her from the room. She weighs very little. He sits her on a couch in a waiting room and sits beside her. She buries her face in his chest crying.

She looks up with pleading eyes, "What am I supposed to do now? We were married for fifty-six years. What am I supposed to do now?"

Michael prays for an answer. All he can think to say is, "You'll just have to take it one day at a time for now."

He sits holding her allowing her to cry out her sorrow. After about twenty minutes, her children, who are in their fifties, arrive. One look at Michael and their mother and they know. The son promises his mother that he will take care of her and that she is not alone.

Finally, Michael is able to leave. When he climbs out of his car, he stares at his house not feeling like spending another long evening alone. He had never seen someone die before and he feels a little shook up.

Michael walks down the street to Sadie's and pushes the buzzer. When she answers, he says it's Michael. She pushes the door release, so he can climb up.

He leans on the doorway, "I'm sorry to bother you, but I had a hard day. I need someone to talk to."

Sadie invites him in. They sit at the dining room table, while Michael shares his burden of the day while Sadie quietly listens. When he finishes, she tells him to stay put and she'll be right back. She goes in the kitchen to heat up leftovers for him and serves him salad, chicken rice casserole and cuts up an orange. He hadn't realized he was hungry until he ate.

After he finishes, she asks if he wants to head home or stay to watch some T.V. He chooses to stay. They sit on the couch, but after a few minutes, she looks over at him discovering him asleep. She gently pulls his feet up and slides him down a little placing a throw over him and sliding a pillow under his head.

She sits on the floor by the coffee table grading papers. Her eyes keep wandering over to Michael with his thick mop of black hair. He has a strong jaw line with a clef chin. His cheekbones are prominent and his eyebrows are thick and dark. His lips are inviting. His kisses have ranged from gentle and tender to forceful and demanding. If she closes her eyes, she can almost feel his kiss.

He sleeps soundly for almost two hours. Sadie kneels beside the couch leaning her elbows on the edge. Overcome by temptation, she gently kisses his lips. He opens his eyes.

"Did I fall asleep?" he asks.

Sadie laughs, "Only for two hours."

"I'm sorry," he sits up.

"It's okay," she assures him and walks him to the door.

"Thanks for being a friend tonight. I needed it," he begins to leave, but stops, "Uh, Sadie, did you wake me with a kiss?"

"What do you think?"

He shakes his head, "Don't admit anything. Don't deny anything."

He leans over kissing the top of her head and leaves.

Chapter VI

Wednesday morning, Michael jogs before he needs to be in the office. He rounds a corner running into Aidan and Steve coming the other way and stops to talk. Aidan tells him they work out regularly with a variety of exercises. Michael comments that he does too so they invite Michael to join them; he accepts. Enjoying having friends to workout with, Michael begins meeting his new friends to workout on a regular basis.

Thursday evening, Steve and Aidan go to the church with Michael. Michael had told them that the kitchen sink in the church is acting up and Steve had offered to look at it. As they walk through the fellowship hall, they pass an aerobics class consisting of about twelve women of varying ages including Colleen, Brenda, Stephanie, and Sadie.

Michael notices Sadie working out in small shorts and a tank top with her hair pulled up in a ponytail. He tries not to watch, but his eyes keep wandering over in her direction. The women seem to be half kick boxing and half dancing to music with a driving beat.

The large window over the counter between the kitchen and the fellowship hall is open. As Steve and Aidan work on the sink, they notice that Michael keeps looking over at the group of women.

"They get quite a workout, don't they," Aidan comments.

Michael turns back to Aidan, embarrassed to be caught watching.

Aidan sits on the floor looking up at Michael, "You really like her, don't you?"

Shocked, Michael denies his feelings, "What? No, not really."

"Huh," Steve scoots out from under the sink, "I didn't know ministers could lie."

Michael stares at the floor with an embarrassed grin.

Steve is able to unclog the sink saving the church a plumber's bill. Michael thanks him. As they leave, the women are about finished with their workout and are lying on mats on the floor stretching and cooling down. The sight is too much for Michael who looks away and hurries out of the hall followed closely by his friends.

Friday evening, Michael does not plan to go to the football game because it is an away game and it looks like rain. Aidan comes to the door to invite him to ride with them. Michael declines, but Aidan orders him to grab a jacket and an umbrella.

"What do you have that is better to do?"

Michael shrugs and gets his jacket. They have Steve's minivan. Steve and Brenda sit in the front, Aidan and Colleen sit in the middle and Stephanie sits in the back.

"I'm not sitting back there with her," he protests.

"Oh, she's harmless," Aidan insists and then orders, "Hey Stephanie, no touching the minister."

On the drive out, Colleen worries about Sadie, "It is damp and chilly out tonight. I wonder how Sadie is holding up."

Michael inquires to what she means. She explains that Sadie has a bad hip that acts up especially in damp, cold weather.

When Sadie steps off the school bus, she walks to the bag with the flags and the box of props. Her heavy, long raincoat is missing from the box. Jessica admits she moved it to look for something and must have forgotten to put it back. Sadie knows this will be bad for her hip.

As Sadie's friends take a seat in the stands the band marches by their bleachers. Sadie limps beside the band as a drizzle falls. Colleen notices immediately the missing raincoat.

By the second quarter, a steady rain begins to fall. Michael watches Colleen fret and wring her hands. He climbs down next to her.

She worries, "Where the hell is her raincoat? She has a heavy, long raincoat that helps. Cold, wet jeans plastered to her are the worst. Damn it. She tries so hard. She exercises everyday to try to be healthy and keep her hip working. After this she will probably limp for days."

"What exactly is wrong with her hip?" he asks.

"She broke it once ending up in a wheelchair. She was determined to get back-up on her feet despite all the pain," her eyes tear up.

"How did she break her hip?"

Colleen sighs, "I'm sorry, but Sadie feels real private about that. Only she can tell you."

Michael's eyes widen, "Colleen, does this have to do with her ugly break up with her fiancé?"

Colleen just stares at him, and then nods. Michael stares at the game, but he thinks about a break-up so bad that it leaves a young woman in a wheelchair with a broken hip.

As halftime nears, Colleen decides to go help Sadie. Even though they are in the visitors' stands across the field, they can see that Sadie's limp is definitely pronounced.

Colleen carries the prop box planning to set out and collect props while Sadie sits on the players' bench to give directions. As Sadie limps in the grass, she slips in the mud. To catch herself, she jams the wrong leg. Electric pain shoots up her back and down her leg. Stumbling, she makes it to the bench.

The band performs in the rain. Not their best performance, the band muddles through. As they exit the field, Colleen carries off the prop box. Sadie tries to stand, but to no avail. Each attempt brings shooting pain. Colleen returns to help, but she can't seem to get her up. Michael appears beside Sadie. Colleen and Michael help her off the field. The band director instructs them to take her home.

Once they are beside the bleachers out of the main view, they stop. The rest of her friends catch up. Sadie clings to Michael. The walk to the parking lot and then out to the van suddenly seems miles away. When Michael and Sadie take a step, he feels her cringe with pain and she digs her fingers into his arm.

Leaning down, he lifts her into his arms, carrying her to the van. He sets her in the middle row and Aidan, Michael, and Stephanie squeeze in the back. Colleen sits by Sadie who explains about her raincoat.

Once home, Sadie tries to walk, but the pain still radiates. Again Michael lifts her with ease. Sadie feels scared as he carries her up the stairs burying her face in his neck. Michael comforts her, "Trust me."

Inside, Colleen takes charge, "We have to get those wet jeans off her, and dry her up. She needs warm pajamas, a heating pad, and hot cocoa. Sadie, will you take an over-the-counter pain killer?"

To Colleen's surprise, Sadie agrees. This tells Colleen just how bad the pain must be because Sadie usually avoids taking pain killers.

"Where would you like her?" Michael asks still holding her.

"Put me on a dining room chair," Sadie directs. As he moves to the dining room, Colleen repeats, "We have to get those wet jeans off her."

Before setting her down, he whispers in her ear, "Would you like me to help you with that?"

Sadie playfully hits him in the chest.

Colleen and Stephanie stay to care for her. The rest call it a night. Stephanie is annoyed that everyone stood back while the new guy took care of her. She doesn't like that a minister is joining their group and she doesn't want Sadie to end up with him. The attraction between the two is undeniable.

Sunday morning, Sadie still has a limp, but she feels better. At the end of the service, Sadie slowly descends the stairs to the fellowship hall. Michael comes down beside her offering help. Sadie refuses to be carried or lean on him in front of everyone. He wants to know how she climbed down all the stairs at her apartment to which she responds, very slowly.

"Rev. Donnelly," Gina approaches, "My mother, Ruth Johnson is in the nursing home. The doctor told me that he only gives her a couple weeks. She's dying." Gina turns to Sadie, "Thank you for all of your visits."

When Gina leaves, Sadie informs Michael that Ruth came to church every Sunday Sadie's first year. She really liked Ruth. Since Ruth had a stroke, she has been in the nursing home and Sadie visits once a month.

Later that afternoon, Michael goes to the nursing home to call on Ruth, but she is not in her room. A nurse directs him to the multipurpose room. As he approaches the room, he hears a piano and someone singing Gospel. From the door, he sees Sadie seated at the piano singing for five of the residents. He loves the sound of her voice.

"Reverend," a woman in a wheel chair sitting in the hall calls, "I can't hear from here very well. Will you take me in?"

"I'd be happy to," Michael releases the brakes and pushes her in with the others.

As Sadie finishes the song, she sees Michael, "Ruth, Rev. Donnelly is here to see you. I better stop now."

The residents groan, so Michael quickly interjects, "What are you trying to do, get me lynched? You go ahead. I'm in no hurry."

Pulling a chair over, he sits by Ruth's wheelchair and the ladies call out old time Gospel songs. Sadie has two large Gospel books in which look them up. She plays and sings.

As Michael listens, he thinks about carrying Sadie in the rain, the way she wrapped her arms around him burying her face in his neck. He thinks about the kiss in the stairwell the last day of Bible School. He thinks about how playful she had been helping him shop and set up his house in July. He remembers their little paint fight. Sadie sings five more songs.

After the mini concert ends, Michael and Sadie sit in a corner for a private conversation with Ruth who assures Michael that she is ready to be called home. She gives him her wishes for the funeral including specific songs that she wants Sadie to sing, *In the Garden* and *Just a Closer Walk with Thee*. He writes all her requests down, reads scripture, and prays with her.

As they are about to leave, Ruth reaches for Sadie, "Wait, I have something to tell you, Dear. You are a wonderful teacher and your work with the children at church is special, but Dear, God gave you all your talents and love to raise a family. I know you want a baby."

"Thanks Ruth. I love you, but I have to go," Sadie kisses her cheek.

Michael thinks she's running again. Grabbing the back of her shirt, he pulls her back down on the couch, "What's your hurry? Ruth is trying to talk to you."

Ruth continues, "When your time to leave this earth comes, the only thing you think about is the people you loved. I know that man of yours hurt you; he hurt you badly, but sweetheart, not every man will hurt you. You have to unlock your heart."

Chapter VII

After an away game, they meet at the bar. Stephanie didn't make the game, but plans to join them. Ambrose Comets lost, but it was a close game. The cool, damp evening leaves Sadie with a slight limp. Michael joins her at the table.

Leaning in close he asks, "Sadie, how did you break your hip?"

"It was just an accident, I guess," she blows off the question.

"What kind of accident?" he presses.

"Oh, it's a long story. I don't want to go into all that now."

"You never want to go into it," he accuses.

"Speaking of my hip, you know what helps? Exercise, I think I'm going to dance," she leaves with Michael shaking his head.

Michael goes back to sit with Aidan and Steve, as the girls dance with Sadie. Michael leans over to Aidan, "Do you know how Sadie broke her hip?"

A strange expression crosses a face, "Yeah, I do. I was there when it happened. Steve and I were both there when it happened."

"When what happened?" Michael pushes.

"I wish I could tell you. I'm sorry man, but it really is up to Sadie," Aidan sighs.

"Why won't she tell me?"

"I don't know. I think that it hurts her to think about it and I also think it embarrasses her. But, I'm just guessing. I don't think anyone in Ambrose knows what happened to her except for us. It's not just you, she doesn't tell anyone. I don't think anyone that she works with at the school knows. I'll encourage Colleen to try to convince her to say something soon."

"Thanks."

Stephanie enters with a tall, handsome, blond man with big dimples and an athletic build.

"Oh shit, Stephanie," Aidan elbows Steve, "Look who Stephanie brought."

"Is something wrong with him?" Michael asks.

"No, he's an okay guy," Aidan sighs, "but you don't like him."

Michael looks back at the man as he walks onto the dance floor and dances behind Sadie who turns recognizing him. Kissing her full on the mouth, he lifts her off the floor.

"Okay," Michael asks, "so who is that exactly?"

Steve replies, "That's Jack. Sadie dated him last spring."

"I thought Sadie doesn't date," Michael states.

"Well, she goes out sometimes. It was just a hand full of dates. I don't think she's seen him since May. Stephanie set them up trying to push Sadie back into dating. He works somewhere in the same building where Steph works. It didn't last long. Five dates, maybe?" Aidan explains.

Jack and the girls return to the table with Sadie appearing uncomfortable. Steve and Aidan greet him and introduce Michael.

Jack turns to Sadie, "How about I take you out tomorrow?"

"I don't think so," Sadie declines.

"I know it's been awhile since I've called you. Don't be sore. I have a surprise," he reaches in his pocket pulling out two tickets, "I have dinner theater tickets for "*42ⁿᵈ Street.*" I know you love Broadway shows."

Sadie looks interested.

"Gee Stephanie," Brenda observes, "Didn't your boss give you tickets for the same show?"

Michael shakes his head and looks down the table at Stephanie who snubs him as she answers, "I couldn't use them and I know how Sadie loves the theater, especially musicals." She does not like that a minister has been joining their group. After last week, Stephanie thinks the two are becoming too close and she wants him to go away.

Sadie stares at Jack, but doesn't answer. Jack kisses her on the cheek, "You think about it. We've had some fun together. I'm going to the men's room, excuse me."

Sadie glances at Michael who is staring at her. She turns walking to the jukebox with Michael following her over.

"I thought you don't date?" he accuses.

"Well, I've gone out here and there," she mumbles.

"You told me you haven't dated in three years," he reminds her.

She faces him, "I have gone out, but I haven't been interested in a relationship. You don't want **a** date; you want **to** date. Trust me; Jack only wants to have fun and nothing serious."

"Isn't that kind of slutty?" he accuses.

Angry, Sadie points out, "Well, since I've made it clear that we're not dating; I don't think it is any of your freaking business and if we are supposed to be friends, what kind of friend says that to me?"

She storms away. As Jack returns, Sadie grabs him and plants a big kiss on him, "I'd love to go out with you tomorrow."

"How long was I in there?" Jack asks looking around.

"See you guys later. I'm going home," Sadie tells her friends.

"Wait up, I'll walk you home," Jack offers.

Steve wanders over to Michael, "I don't know what you said, but smooth move."

"Oh shut up."

Colleen and Brenda confront Stephanie. Colleen accuses, "You did that on purpose."

"Did what? Sadie told us she doesn't want to date Michael. She said if she ends up with him she'll lose her job and move away from us. Besides, whatever the hell he said to her over there is not my fault," Stephanie defends herself. "I don't understand why you guys want to hang out with a minister anyway. I like to have fun. No one asked me if I wanted to spend Friday nights with some preacher."

Colleen defends him, "Michael never acts like he's judging us. He hasn't gotten in the way of any of my fun. I think it is odd how much time Aidan and Steve are spending with him for not being church goers. Did you know that they have been working out several mornings together and Steve offered to fix the church sink for him? Michael hasn't said anything to Steve or Aidan about not going to church."

"Well, I don't like him," Stephanie huffs.

When Jack and Sadie reach her apartment, Jack asks to come up. Sadie shows him into the living room.

"I've missed you Babe," Jack croons reaching for her. He tries to kiss her, but she pulls away.

"Slow down. I haven't seen you since May."

He touches her hair, "You seem to be having mood swings. What's going on with you?"

"You know what?" she moves away from him, "This is a mistake. I think I'm done with casual dating and I don't see us in a serious relationship."

"Is it the new guy at the bar?" he observes.

"Not exactly, maybe a little," she admits.

"Here, take these tickets. *42nd Street* isn't really something I want to see," he gives her a kiss on the cheek and leaves.

Sunday morning, Sadie leads the opening exercises for the Sunday school. All the teachers came this morning, so Sadie has free time until church. As she heads down the hall to the library, Michael approaches her asking to speak to her in his office.

"Go away," she snaps.

"Sadie,"

"I don't want to talk to you," she insists.

Michael looks around, then grabs her arm, "Wait, this isn't personal. I have a church matter to discuss with you." She looks skeptical, "Oh, just give me a minute."

They go into his office with Sadie giving him a cold shoulder. Michael half sits on his desk, "I didn't want you to hear this during the service. I received a call this morning. I'm sorry Sadie, but Ruth died in her sleep last night."

Sadie sits on the couch with her eyes tearing up. "Let me know as soon as possible when the funeral is so I can request a personal day from work."

"I will. You can stay in here as long as you need," he begins to leave.

"Thank you for letting me know. I'm sorry I was like that to you."

With his hand on the doorknob, he adds, "On a personal note, you were right. A friend shouldn't have spoken to you that way."

As the service begins, Michael is surprised to see Aidan enter the sanctuary with Colleen. Colleen had been attending more regularly, but this is the first time Aidan had joined her since his first Sunday.

After church, Michael goes to his office before he leaves. Aidan enters closing the door behind him. "Reverend, I want to tell you something."

"If it is about Sadie's date, I don't want to know. I'm not her boyfriend or anything," Michael interrupts.

"Are you done? Do you feel better now?" he teases.

Michael drops into his chair, "Okay, what is it?"

"Sadie took Colleen to the show last night. Apparently, she changed her mind and sent Jack packing. I could tell that was what she was going to do before you opened your big mouth." Michael rolls his eyes as Aidan continues, "Secondly, Sadie's birthday is Wednesday. We are having a small party for her at the bar at six o'clock. You should come. It's just our Friday night group. She and Colleen are going to visit her parents over the weekend."

Michael doesn't answer him, but inquires, "Did you enjoy the service?"

"Yeah, to tell you the truth, I couldn't picture you as a minister even though I've seen you once before. You seem like just a regular guy. So, I came out of curiosity," Aidan admits.

Michael laughs, "So, how did I do?"

"It seemed odd to see you in your robe at first, but you're definitely a minister," Aidan gives his approval.

Wednesday, Sadie meets her friends at the bar. Stephanie asks about the extra chair to which Aidan comments that she knows exactly who they are expecting. Sadie doubts he'll come after last weekend, but she is wrong. Michael joins them sitting across from her.

Steve orders seven gyro platters. Since that will take a while, they give Sadie her presents. She finishes her first drink and orders a second. Sadie opens the gift from Colleen and Aidan to find a soft pink v-neck sweater. Steve and Brenda give her a bottle of her favorite perfume.

Next she opens Stephanie's gift. Sadie pulls out a glittery gold triangle top which would leave her back bare and a very mini, mini skirt.

"What is this?" she jokes, "a handkerchief and a belt?"

"Oh Sadie, it's a dress. You are in your twenties and you dress like you're always going to church or school," Stephanie complains.

Michael shifts in his chair annoyed.

"That's because I'm always going to church and school," Sadie laughs.

"At least try it on. With all your exercise, you have a killer body. Don't be a prude," Stephanie pushes.

Michael reaches in his inside jacket pocket pulling out a narrow wrapped box which he slides across the table. Sadie glances at him and opens the present pulling out a beautiful pearl necklace to her friends' surprise. Colleen takes the necklace and puts it on Sadie.

The waitress brings their food and Sadie orders another drink. They enjoy the evening. After eating, the girls dance. When slow song begins, Michael takes Sadie's hand leading her to the dance floor.

"Why did you buy me such a nice present?"

"Why did you buy me that painting?" he counters.

As the evening progresses, Aidan leans over to Steve and Michael,

"Is it me or are the girls getting drunk?"

Steve shakes his head, "Getting? They are drunk. I don't remember the last time they drank like this."

The girls stumble back to the table in fits of out of control laughter.

"I want my presents," Sadie announces crawling in front of Michael, practically on his lap reaching for her gifts.

Sadie opens her perfume spraying her neck. She leans over putting her neck in Michael's face, "Doesn't that smell pretty?"

He agrees. Then Sadie sprays Michael three times before he can get the bottle away from her. He brushes at himself, but Aidan laughs pointing out that won't actually help.

Sadie opens the box with the sexy dress, "Steph is right. I do have a killer body. I think I'll try this on."

Standing, Michael snatches the box away from her holding it behind his back, "I don't think this goes with drunk."

Sadie tries to reach behind him. "Give me that." Leaning on him, she declares, "You know, you smell pretty."

Rolling his eyes, he sets her on a chair. Then he gathers her presents into a bag, "Maybe I should take you home. You have school in the morning."

Waving a camera, Colleen calls, "Pictures first."

The four girls gather giving Steve the camera. Pretending to be models, they strike several poses.

Aidan laughs, "We can use these for blackmail once the girls sober up."

This comment gives Sadie an idea. The girls huddle. Colleen laughs loudly stomping her foot. Brenda lines up three chairs. The girls begin to wander around with their hands behind their backs whistling innocently pretending to be casual and making the guys suspicious. They surround Michael and before he realizes what is coming, the girls pounce. They drag him to the middle chair. He tries to get back up, but they pull him down. Sadie jumps on his lap. Brenda and Colleen sit on each side of him with Stephanie behind him. They begin to pose around him, so Steve takes several pictures.

"Now these are blackmail pictures; a minister surrounded by beautiful women," Stephanie purrs.

When they are done, the girls move away. Sadie almost falls off his lap, but he catches her. Steve snaps another photo. It looks like Michael is dipping her and they are smiling at each other.

Steve decides they need a nice group shot so he calls one of his waitresses over. Steph, Steve, and Brenda sit while Aidan, Colleen, Michael, and Sadie stand behind them. Facing him, Sadie wraps her arms around Michael's waist. Then Steve decides that they need a nice picture of just Sadie and Michael. Michael stands behind Sadie lowering his chin down almost to her shoulder and wrapping his arms around her waist.

The guys discuss who will drive Stephanie home, but Stephanie insists she is not drunk like the others pulling out her keys and heading for the door. Michael catches her around the waist with one arm and takes the keys with his free hand.

She leans against him, "Hey, you smell pretty."

Rolling his eyes, Michael gives her to Aidan. Then taking Sadie's hand and picking up the bag of presents, they head across the street.

Sadie pulls out her keys, but can't manage to get it in the hole. Michael takes them unlocking the door. Worried that she is unsteady, Michael walks up the stairs behind her touching the small of her back.

Sadie turns, "Are you touching my butt?"

"No!" Michael denies firmly.

They climb a few more steps and she turns again, "You're looking at it though."

"I am not," he insists.

They climb a few more steps and she turns around yet again. Reaching out to touch his cheek, she tells him, "You are amazingly handsome."

Michael responds, "You are drunk."

"I'm not that drunk," Sadie climbs the rest of the way up. Michael unlocks the door as Sadie coos, "It's so sweet the way you made sure I didn't fall down the stairs. You wouldn't let me fall down the stairs would you?"

"No, I won't let you fall down the stairs," he leads her into the apartment.

She leans on the wall, "Kiss me."

"I don't think so," he replies.

"Why not?" she demands.

"I'm not taking advantage of you while you are drunk," he explains.

"Taking advantage? I didn't ask for sex. I just want a kiss. You kiss me whenever you feel like it. Come here," she pulls him close by his jacket, "You have to lean over. I can't reach you."

He gives in kissing her. Sadie looks up into his eyes, "I really like you."

He sighs, "Why can't you talk like this when you are sober?"

"Because I think too much. You see, my heart and my head are having a fight."

"Well, I am rooting for your heart," he kisses her again.

"Michael... I really have to pee," Michael laughs stepping aside. Sadie hurries into the bathroom.

He looks down the hall. The first bedroom is set up as a study. The bedroom across the hall is pretty, but doesn't look lived in. The door beside it is filled with boxes and junk. The door at the end of the hall leads to a large balcony. The door across from the storage is another bedroom. There are clothes on the floor and books, papers, and jewelry are all over the dresser. This is her room. Her bedspread is yellow with blue roses. A rag doll lies on the pillows. Michael goes to her nightstand to look at her alarm clock. It is set for seven which sounds about right for school, so he turns it on. As he leaves, he notices an old fashioned oval sepia photo with Sadie and her three girlfriends dressed as saloon girls. She looks cute.

He returns to the front door by the bathroom. Sadie comes out wearing a short, light blue, satin nighty trimmed in lace. Shocked, he becomes both uncomfortable and attracted.

"I turned your alarm on for you. Go straight to sleep. It's only ten-thirty. You should be fine for school tomorrow," he kisses her on the forehead.

She wraps her arms around his neck, "I'll be fine. I'm not that drunk," she promises pulling him into another long kiss looking very sexy in her satin nighty. Michael runs his hands up and down her back for a moment, before making a hasty retreat.

That Friday, the Ambrose Comets play their last game of the season on a very cold night. When they arrive at the bar, the girls order hot cocoa with butterscotch schnapps for everyone. Sadie and Colleen plan to spend Saturday and Sunday with Sadie's parents.

Sadie feels awkward about her birthday, because she had been all over Michael. She made it clear that they weren't dating, but now she made the lines fuzzy. She still does not want to live the life he offers, but she feels excited and warm all over when he is near. She sits quietly at the table, which her friends find strange.

Later, Sadie sits at the bar with Brenda when a slow song begins and Brenda goes to Steve. Michael leans his elbows back on the bar, "Do you want to dance?"

"No."

Michael rolls his head and takes her shoulders turning her around to face him, "Dance with me."

Taking both of her hands, he pulls her onto the dance floor. Holding her close, he lays his cheek on top of her head. Then, he leans down nuzzling her cheek and neck causing chills to run up and down her spine. He steals several quick kisses. Her heart pounding, she does not resist him. Soon, they are kissing long and deeply.

After the dance, she returns to the bar where her girlfriends join her. Stephanie shakes her head, "Honey, if you two are just friends, what the hell would dating look like?"

Sadie covers her face with her hands as Colleen adds, "Maybe it is time that you admit that you are dating."

Sadie sighs, "Or it's time to put a stop to this."

The girls return to the table. She sits by Michael and asks Steve for her bill claiming she's tired and wants to go home. Steve passes out the bills. Sadie looks at hers, and then lays it on the table. As she turns to get money out of her purse Michael sneaks her bill and goes up to pay for both. Sadie searches for her bill until Aidan tells her Michael took it. Grabbing her coat and purse, she leaves in a huff.

As she unlocks her door, Michael catches up to her, "Sadie, are you okay?"

"Do you realize we just ate, danced, made out in public, and you just paid my bill?"

"Yes."

"We're dating," she snaps.

"I was hoping you wouldn't notice," he teases reaching out to gently caress her hair.

"Well I did and it's a mistake. I have to go."

"Sadie," he begins, but she runs inside pulling the door shut behind her.

Chapter VIII

The next Saturday afternoon, Sadie runs the Sunday School Halloween party. At the planning meeting two months ago, Michael and she had butted heads about the party, because he believes it is the devil's holiday. Sadie strongly disagreed. She believes it is the night before All Saints Day and a harmless fun American tradition. They argued back and forth while the others just sat back and watched. Finally, Michael called for a vote. Not one of the women on the Education Committee agreed with Michael.

Michael suggested that they call it a Fall Harvest party, but Sadie scoffed that it is a cop out. A rose by any other name smells just as sweet. He surrendered and the ladies planned the Halloween party.

Michael walks down to the fellowship hall to check in on the party. Sadie looks beautiful dressed as Snow White surrounded by excited children. As she passes him to go into the kitchen, he whispers to her, "You make a beautiful princess."

She responds, "Oh shut up."

He cocks his head and squints at her. As Sadie sets out treats on the table, she watches Kelly Mitchell run to Michael.

"Rev. Donnelly, do you want to see my dress twirl?" Kelly, dressed as Cinderella, asks.

"Of course," Michael smiles as the little girl spins.

Spencer, dressed as Spiderman, and Mason, dressed as a Power Ranger, joins Kelly to vie for Rev. Donnelly's attention. Michael smiles as they jump around showing off for him.

Dorothy Martin calls the children to a table to make a craft. After the children run off, Sadie approaches Michael whispering, "You were right. This is all so evil. Those kids will be chanting to Satan by midnight."

Michael glares at her as she walks over to help with the craft. Aidan, who plans to help Michael put the tables away when the party ends, arrives and motions to head upstairs.

Aidan remarks, "Sadie looks pretty in that get up."

"Don't be fooled. She may look like Snow White, but she really came as the Wicked Bitch of the West."

"Ooo, problems?"

They go up to his office to talk. Aidan asks, "Are you planning on going to Brenda's big Halloween bash? They are hoping for some big profits which are badly needed that night."

"Sure, I guess I'll go," Michael agrees.

Aidan leans forward, "You know, Brenda's pushing hard for us to wear…"

"No," Michael interrupts. "I don't wear costumes."

"Come on. It means a lot to Brenda," Aidan persuades.

"No way,"

"Steve found something for all three of us to wear," Aidan informs him.

"Give me a break," Michael rolls his eyes.

"It's just a jacket."

"What kind of jacket?"

"Hell's Angels," Aidan smiles. "Come on. Just wear a t-shirt, jeans, and a jacket."

"Maybe," Michael begins to cave.

Aidan slides Michael a pack of pictures which are his copies of the pictures from Sadie's party. He kind of likes the one where she almost fell off his lap. He also likes the one of just the two of them and wishes she would just let go and date him. He wants her to admit that she loves him. He believes what she said that night about her heart and head fighting, but she has a wall built up around herself that he cannot seem to break through.

Monday night, Brenda has high hopes for her party. Michael arrives early wearing jeans and a t-shirt and joins the others in the backroom. Sadie is running late having had a long hard day with twenty-six wound up first graders and is not there yet. Brenda, dressed as Marilyn Monroe, thanks Michael for coming even if he doesn't care for the holiday.

Colleen, dressed as a French maid, and Stephanie, dressed as a Playboy Bunny, ignores Michael's protests and fuss over him. Colleen hangs chains on his jean loops. Brenda wets his arm with a sponge. He asks what she is doing, but she ignores him as she slaps a piece of paper on his arm and rubs it. Pulling it back, it leaves a large fake tattoo of a skull and cross bones. Michael rolls his eyes. Brenda comforts him that it's cold out and to just wear long sleeves until it wears off in a couple of days. Stephanie struggles to tie a dew rag on his head. He draws the line at a clip-on earring.

Aidan and Steve wear make-up to look as if they had been in a fight. Michael puts his foot down to the make-up, but compromises finally allowing Stephanie to tie the dew rag on his head. He pulls on the jacket and they take several pictures.

Colleen tells Michael that Sadie will be dressed as a saloon girl. Michael remarks that he saw a picture of her wearing a dress like that.

"Really?" Stephanie saunters up. "Isn't that picture hanging in her bedroom?"

Embarrassed, he heads out to the bar with Steve and Aidan and sits at the bar. To Brenda's excitement, the bar begins to fill with people, many wearing costumes. Colleen and Aidan stand behind the bar talking to Michael. Suddenly, Colleen and Aidan's eyes widen and their jaws drop. Michael looks over his shoulder. Sadie, wearing the tiny, glittery gold outfit from Stephanie with knee high boots, ratted hair, and heavy make-up, looks like a hooker. Anger flashes through Michael.

Michael grumbles, "I thought she was going to be dressed as a saloon girl."

Aidan observes, "Well, right profession, wrong century."

Colleen comes out from behind the bar. Michael comments to her that Sadie spends too much time with Stephanie.

"That's not about Stephanie," Colleen starts to walk away, but Michael grabs the back of her dress and pulls her back.

"Tell me," Michael orders.

"We've been teasing her about dating you. I mean, the last time we were here you were trying to suck out her tonsils."

"Why is the thought of being with someone so terrifying to her?"

Colleen sits on the stool next to him and explains, "After Sadie experienced a traumatic break-up with her fiancé, she went through a bit of hell. She pulled herself up by moving here, getting her dream job, and finding her way back to God at your church. She rented her first apartment on her own, plus she exercised her way back to health. We were so proud of her. In her eyes, ending up with you takes all she has worked for away. She would lose her job and home and being close to us. The problem is she is obviously crazy about you. It looks to me like she is freaking out a little bit tonight."

"Please tell me, what happened between Sadie and her fiancé?" he pleads.

"That's for Sadie to tell you," Colleen shrugs.

Michael just shakes his head frustrated.

"Uh, Michael, there's a man hitting on Sadie and Steph," Colleen tells him.

"A Playboy Bunny and a hooker are dancing. They are going to be hit on all night," he grumbles.

"Yeah, but he isn't taking no for an answer."

"That's their problem," he snaps.

"Fine, I'll get Aidan," Colleen leaves. Michael looks over at the dance floor. A man pulls Sadie toward him. She pulls away. As she turns to walk away, he smacks her on the butt. She turns back toward him and he tries to dance with her.

Rolling his head, Michael gets up. He steps up to them, "Excuse me," he takes Sadie's arm, "I need to speak to her."

"Hey, I'm dancing with her," he slurs.

"Well, she's with me," Michael states.

The man argues. Balling up his fist, he attempts to punch Michael who ducks and pushes the man over. The man stands up and charges Michael. Before he gets to Michael, Aidan pushes him over. When the man gets up again he faces Michael, Aidan, and Steve. The man stops.

Steve orders, "I own this bar. I need you to leave or my wife will call the police."

The man and his two friends leave. People, who are standing around, clap for the Hells Angels.

Sadie walks away, but Michael follows her barking in her ear, "How did you think men at a bar would treat you dressed like that?"

"It's none of your business," she snaps.

"I just got in a bar fight for you," he points out.

"I didn't ask for your help."

"Come here. I want to talk to you," he takes her hand and leads her to the office.

Before they reach the office, she jerks her hand away, "Just leave me alone."

Frustrated, Michael grabs her from behind around the waist. Lifting her, he carries her into the office.

"What is wrong with you?" he demands.

"Nothing, what's your problem?" she shoots back.

"Is this because of last week when you said we're acting like we're dating?" he demands.

"We are not dating," Sadie declares.

"On your birthday, you admitted that you like me," he reminds her.

"I can't get involved with you. You are temporary."

"Can't you relax? Don't worry about years from now," he suggests.

"No. Last week I turned twenty-six and I have lived in nine different towns. Trust me, you're temporary. Before you know it, you'll be gone and I have twenty-seven more years here before I can retire," she rants. "Unless, when the Bishop calls to move you, you leave your job to stay with me."

"Don't be ridiculous."

"My giving up my job is possible, but you giving up your job for me is ridiculous," she crosses her arms.

"I can't do this anymore. I don't even want to be friends," he barks.

"But Michael," Sadie begins.

"No. You want me in one spot. If I move away, you pull me back and if I try to get closer, you push me away. I'll work with you at church, but that is it."

Michael storms out of the office. Sadie gives herself a minute before she leaves. Back in the bar, Brenda orders her, no more drama. This night is important to Steve and her. Sadie smiles insisting she is fine. The bar attendance exceeds their hopes.

Sadie quietly tells Aidan, Colleen, and Stephanie that she ended dating Michael and he ended being friends. Stephanie, who is thrilled about this, offers to buy her a drink.

Aidan catches Michael leaving and pulls him back to the office where Michael recounts his conversation with Sadie.

Aidan reminds Michael, "Steve warned you that she is a whack job. Everyone acted like he was just joking, but he wasn't. Listen to me, because of Sadie and Colleen I lost one of my best friends. I lived with the guy for four years and he isn't even invited to my wedding let alone in it and that really bugs me.

"I don't want to lose another friend. The girls act like I only hung out with you to get Sadie to date you. That's not true. I invited you to sit with us the first time to be nice. After that, I liked hanging out. I am tired of the girls being most important. Sometimes I feel like I come in second to Sadie with Colleen. Now that you aren't friends with Sadie, I don't think we should have to stop being friends."

"I'm glad to hear it. For at least a while, I can't be part of the Friday group, but we can keep working out in the mornings and have lunch sometimes like we have been."

Sadie spends the rest of the party with Stephanie and Aidan stays with Michael. Poor Colleen runs back and forth. Steve and Brenda feel frustrated that Sadie pulled their group apart again. However, their party ends a success.

That night, Michael cannot sleep. Two women now have dumped him because he is a minister. He fought hard to become a minister causing a rift between him and his family and friends. After working as minister for four months now plus his student pastorate, his family and friends still have not attended one service. He also sacrificed financial leisure.

He still feels confident in his calling. His mind drifts back to his senior year of college. Michael went to Rev. Foreman's office to ask him about a letter of recommendation for Harvard. Rob said he would be happy to write it, but he asked about the other career he had been considering. Michael denied there was another choice and left.

Two hours later, as Rev. Foreman was leaving, he discovered Michael sitting in the sanctuary. Michael looked up at him and quietly asked, "Do you think I would make a good minister?"

Rob sat in the pew in front of him, "I think you would be a great minister. Do you feel a calling?"

"I think so. I keep saying I'm going to be a lawyer, but I can't picture myself as a lawyer. I can picture myself as a minister. I feel comfortable here in the church like I belong here. I try not thinking about being a minister, but I think about it almost every day now."

Rev. Foreman takes him back to his office and gives him a packet of information about a seminary that he had prepared just waiting for Michael to ask.

Five months later, Michael was home during spring break. One day as Michael came in from playing tennis his dad grabbed him and threw him down on the couch. James had never been physical with his children, so the attack took Michael by surprise.

His dad has a fraternity brother on the Harvard Law School review board. The friend told James that Michael blew his Harvard interview. They still accepted him because of his video, references, essays, and transcript, but they would keep a close eye on him. Apparently, he demonstrated a lack of interest. When asked why he wanted to be a lawyer, he responded because that was what his parents want him to do.

James called his friend to find out if Michael had even applied because he found an acceptance letter in the mail to a seminary. Michael stood just to have his father knock him back down as he ranted and raved accusing Michael of being too lazy to work hard enough to get through Harvard or to be a lawyer. James couldn't believe he'd choose to be a minister who works one morning a week at a dead end, do nothing job.

Sophia stood behind James crying. She said that ministers had nothing. Thirty years of work and he would have nothing to show for it. James lamented that he should never have allowed Michael to take all of those religion courses.

Michael responded, "I am not now nor have I ever been interested in being a lawyer. I tried for four years. I don't belong in Harvard."

His parents paced around the room. James roared, "Fine, if you don't think you can handle Harvard then don't go! You will have your business degree in a couple of months. Go get a real job!"

Michael stood, "I am going to go to seminary and see if that is what I am supposed to do."

"I'm not paying for it," his father threw the acceptance letter down on the table.

"I have plenty money in my trust fund and since I'm over twenty-one, the money is mine," Michael countered.

Graham and Colby took the news hard reminding him about Worthington, Donnelly and Stark. All Michael could say was "Sorry." They yelled and made fun of him for hours feeling betrayed by him. Michael felt frustrated that his friends refused to look at any of it from his point of view. Colby worried about going to Harvard without Michael to help him. Michael assured him that he would have a study group to help him.

Barbara probably took it the worst. She actually smacked him across the face. Michael had confided in her that he didn't want to go to Harvard and she promised to stand by him. However, he had not revealed that he was considering a seminary. She had assumed he was going to use his business degree or wanted to try being a tennis pro. She had cried pitifully.

Back at college, she went and spent an afternoon with Bonnie Foreman asking questions. Bonnie told the brutal truth about what it would be like to be a minister's wife. She said that the church people would watch her every move and judge her. She explained that they would be hard on her if they thought that she had more than them and that if she didn't attend church and all the extra activities, they would hold it against her and the minister. Bonnie said the only reason she was willing to do it was because she wanted to be with Rob enough and her strong faith in God provided her with the patience and understanding that she needs.

Barbara had loved Michael for as long as she could remember, but she didn't want to live like that and she didn't want to raise her children with nothing in a parsonage being constantly watched and judged.

While Barbara had been talking with Bonnie, Michael was lying on his back on the couch in Rob Foreman's office tossing a baseball straight up and catching it. Rob sat at his desk listening as Michael shared his parents', friends', and fiancé's reaction to his news that he would be attending seminary.

"You know, it's not easy being a minister's wife. If you marry the wrong woman, she will be miserable, which will make you miserable, and it would hurt your ministry. I had a friend whose wife refused to go to church at all and the parish became angry and resentful. They requested that the conference move him."

"How do I know who the right woman is?"

"She will need three things: her own strong faith in God, a willingness to make the necessary sacrifices for your work, and of course, she has to be able to excite you sexually."

Michael leaned up on his elbow and looks at his friend shocked by his last remark, "I can't believe you just said that."

"Why? I'm not a priest and sex is important in a marriage. Just you wait until you have spent years counseling married couples with troubled marriages. Trust me; sex is important if you are going to be married. Bonnie still excites me after all these years."

Michael lied back down laughing. He knew in his heart that if he married Barbara, she would be miserable and she would most definitely make him miserable.

Later that afternoon, they walked back to campus together. Tearfully, Barbara told him that if he goes to seminary, she would not marry him. To her horror, Michael simply told her that her understood why she needed to break up with him. Devastated, she had thought that he would fight harder for her than that, but he just walked away.

Michael looks at the clock, midnight. His mind drifted back to his second year in seminary. The first day of classes, he saw a pretty little blonde woman with big blue eyes and a sweet gentle smile. She, too, was studying to be a minister. She understood the life he was choosing and had chose it for herself already.

After class, he introduced himself to her. She was painfully shy and blushed easily. It took him a few minutes to convince her to go for coffee with him. She had been difficult to talk to at first. Her name was Monica Popavich. They began to date.

After a month, she had fallen in love with Michael. They studied together and discussed theology. Michael, however, had been unsure of his feelings for her. One evening, she told him that she liked studying theology, but she didn't really want to be a minister. She would rather teach religion in a college or she would be happy marrying a minister and assisting him. She could run Bible Studies, help with hospital calls, and raise children.

Michael wondered that night if part of her plan in attending seminary was to meet and marry a minister. He thought, why not. It would be good to have such a partner. She seemed perfect for a minister's wife, except for one thing. She did not excite him.

Despite being pretty, with a cute bob style blond hair, he found her to be too pious and frankly, boring. She never seemed to understand jokes. When he had a beer one day, she looked at him disapprovingly. She was shy and quiet. She never said much unless they were discussing theology.

Monica didn't allow him to kiss her for over two weeks, and when he did, she always ended them before he was ready. She liked leaning up against him with his arm around her, but if he tried to really kiss and hold her, she would shyly pull away.

It was clear that she believed in absolutely no sex until after marriage. As a man studying to be a minister, he knew that he should be okay with that, but he wondered if she would be boring in bed after they were married. Rev. Foreman said that his wife should excite him. Monica just didn't excite him.

However, he tried to make it work with her for almost six months. It was awkward breaking up with her. She clearly wanted to be his minister's wife and have his babies. It was hard and painful to explain that he just didn't think that they were right for one another. Monica had cried pitifully. He felt terrible, but he just didn't want to marry her.

Michael checks the clock again. The night had passed already. He must have drifted in and out of sleep. He pulls himself out of bed and dresses. Sitting on the edge of the bed he thinks about the three things Rev. Foreman said that a woman needs to be a minister's wife.

Barbara had been fun to be with and they had shared a wonderful sex life. Barbara definitely excited him, but she did not have a strong enough faith in God and she was not willing to make the sacrifices needed. Monica had been more than willing to make more sacrifices than needed and she had an extremely strong faith, but she did not excite him and they had no sex life.

Sadie possesses a strong faith and understanding of church life. She is extremely fun to be with and definitely excites him. They share a powerful chemistry whether they are kissing or running a Bible School opening together. While Sadie always runs away after a kiss, she usually allowed him to kiss her first. But, Sadie clearly, does not want to make the sacrifices or trust him enough to share her secret with him.

He wonders that if he could break through her wall and find out her secret, maybe she would be more willing to work things out with him. If only she was willing to return to the parsonage life she already knows, she would be perfect for him. However, he is losing hope that Sadie will work out either.

Completely frustrated, he presses the palms of his hands to his forehead falling back onto the bed. He thinks maybe he should give up and remain a bachelor, who focuses on his work, but he has only been a minister for four months and he is already lonely. He wants a wife and children.

Chapter IX

By the time Michael drags himself down to the kitchen, Aidan and Steve are at the door. It is too cold out to jog, so they go to the community rec. center to lift weights and swim laps. Michael works out with vengeance.

That night, after a meeting, Michael lies on the couch staring at the ceiling. On a whim, he calls Barbara, "Hey Barbie. It's me. It's been so long since we talked."

They talk for over an hour about her job as a graphic artist for an advertising agency and about Michael's work in the church. They talk about old times. She tells him about Graham and Colby.

After they hang up, Michael lies in bed thinking about Barbara. It had been obvious to him that she had a crush on him since she was a little girl. When he was a junior and she was a freshman in high school, their tennis coach paired them up to play doubles for the next two years. He never knew for sure, but he suspects that Barbara had begged the coach to pair them up.

At the end of the two years, they won a large tournament. After the winning shot, he picked her up swinging her around. He lifted her and perched her on his shoulder. Photographers loved that pose. That photo still hangs in the pro-shop at the country club.

Shortly after that, Michael left for college. May, at the end of his freshman year, Barbara asked him to come home and take her to the junior high school prom, but he declined explaining that that was the weekend before finals. Two weeks before prom, she called her brother, Colby, to tell him she had a date to the prom. The Wednesday before prom, she called Colby crying. Her prom date made up with his girlfriend and will take the girlfriend instead of her.

Colby relayed what she told him to Graham and Michael. Colby and Graham stared at Michael until he took the phone and offered to come home to take her to the prom. He then called his mother to have her to buy the corsage, pull out his tux, and make dinner reservations. Colby and Graham rode home with him studying together for finals all the way.

Michael always thought Barbara was one of the cutest little girls he'd seen. She had long silky light brown hair and big round brown eyes. As she smiled she squeezed her shoulders up toward her ears. That night, she walked down the stairs looking older in a strapless shimmering purple dress with a full knee length skirt. She looked beautiful. At dinner, they talked easily as old friends.

He thought everything was going fine at the dance, but after they were there for half an hour, she told him she regretted coming with him and ran out of the hall.

Michael found her outside in the courtyard, "What's wrong? Why are you upset?"

"This is my prom. I wanted a date, but you treat me like you're my big brother. It feels like you're just humoring me. Well, let me tell you something Michael Donnelly, I am not now nor have I ever been your little sister! I'm only two years younger than you and I'm old enough to date."

Michael pulled her close, kissing her gently, their first kiss. She wrapped her arms around his neck and they kissed some more. They enjoyed the rest of the evening.

Two weeks later, Michael and his friends came home for the summer. Michael took Barbara on a couple of dates. One day, at the tennis courts, Michael leaned on the fence flirting with Melinda, a tall blond, who he dated on and off. Just as he was about to ask her out, something hit him in the back with a sharp pain.

He turned to see Barbara storming off after throwing a tennis ball at his back. He couldn't catch her before she drove off in her car. Michael jumped into his car and followed her to her house. Colby informed him that she ran up to her room. Michael knocked on her door. Assuming it was her brother, it startled her to see Michael enter her room. She sat at her computer chatting on-line with a friend. Michael sat on the edge of her bed while she logged off.

"So, why did you hit me with that ball?" He questioned.

"I'm sorry. I shouldn't have, but don't ask me out again."

"Why?"

"I like you more than you like me. I don't want to just be one of your girls. I want all of you or none of you so just go away."

Michael sat thinking for a moment, "I won't promise anything I might not keep, but if you want to try dating exclusively for a while to see what happens, I will."

Barbara jumped on him knocking him back on the bed. He flipped her on her back, leaned over, and kissed her. Colby came in to check on his sister. Finding Michael lying on the bed kissing her, Colby became angry.

"What the hell are you doing with my sister?!" he yelled.

Michael jumped up, "What? I thought you wanted me to date her."

Colby lunged at Michael who rolled across the bed and ran out the door. Colby chased Michael down the stairs and around the dining room table with Barbara running after them.

"Colby, stop it!" Michael demanded.

"I'm going to kill you!" Colby threatened and continued the chase.

As they ran through the kitchen, Colby's mother, Victoria Stark, stopped them, "Now what are you boys fighting about?"

They both froze for a moment and then said in unison, "Nothing."

They quietly walked out of the kitchen and out of the house to the backyard, where they took off running again. Finally down by the pool the chase ended. Michael walking backwards with his hands raised tried to calm his friend down while Colby slowly advanced still angry.

Just as Colby seemed about to tackle Michael, Barbara jumped on Colby's back. Colby lost his balance and fell in the pool with Barbara still on top of him. Michael jumped in with them. By the time the three crawled back out, they were all laughing.

On their next date, Barbara begged Michael not to be angry with her as she confessed, "Do you remember the date I had for the prom that dumped me? Yeah, well, he never existed. I made him up. I actually turned down four guys."

"Why?"

"Duh, I wanted you to take me. I thought if I was hurt, you'd rescue me."

"What if I didn't?" he asked.

"I knew you would and you did. Are you mad?"

"I guess not," he said laughing.

That summer, Barbara attempted to talk him into having sex, but he was in college and she still had a year of high school. It just seemed wrong to him plus Colby would kill him.

The following summer, on June eighth, Barbara graduated. On June ninth, she took Michael to her family's guest house. Declaring that they had dated for a year and that she had graduated which meant she was no longer in high school, they both experienced their first time together.

After they broke up, Michael found himself missing her at times, especially when he would go home for a holiday or for the summer. During Christmas his last year of seminary, after he had broken up with Monica, Colby and Graham came to see him. They seemed to have finally forgiven him for not attending Harvard with them. They admitted that they missed his friendship. Colby invited Michael to join them to go skiing for News Year's Eve. Michael happily accepted the invitation having missed his friends as well.

The day his friends came to pick him up, he was surprised to find Barbara in the backseat. She was going skiing with them. Graham and Colby were in the front seat, so Michael had to sit in the back with Barbara.

After Michael relaxed, they had great fun like old times. They laughed and joked. Once they registered at the lodge, they went skiing. Barbara was as good as any of them and they had a great time skiing down the toughest runs.

That night the lodge hosted a big New Year's Eve bash. They drank, laughed, and danced. He even slow danced with Barbara. At midnight, Michael grabbed Barbara and gave her the biggest kiss he had given her in years to her sheer bliss.

After the party, Michael walked her to her room where she invited him in. He hesitated, but followed her inside. Barbara told him that she missed him and that she hoped that he was happy. They stood there staring into each others eyes for a moment.

"Well, I should go," Michael stutters, "I had fun with you today. It has been great seeing you again like this." Barbara didn't answer, but just continued to stare at him. He continued to stutter, "Okay then... You sleep tight... Goodnight."

Before he could turn to leave, Barbara jumped up on him wrapping her legs around his waist and her arms around his neck. Catching her, Michael automatically, began kissing her passionately. With her in his arms again, he stumbled across the room and climbed onto the bed where he spent the remainder of the night.

Alone in his parsonage, Michael crawls out of bed to go downstairs for a drink. He always cared about Barbara. He even loved her, but there had been something missing. He never thought about her night and day. When she wasn't around he didn't really miss her, but instead took it for granted that he would see her later. Barbara was right. She loved him more than he loved her. Now it seems that he loves Sadie more than she loves him. He is unsure. Sometimes he thinks Sadie does love him, but she won't let her guard down, at least not for long.

The next morning, Barbara drives up to Michael's parsonage. All the men she had dated since Mike, not one lasted more than a few months. She never got over him. Hearing his voice last night gave her a driving urge to see him.

She stares at the back of his house. She thinks it looks like lower middle class and can't picture him living in there. More importantly, she can't picture herself living in there. Taking a deep breath, she knocks on the door and waits. He is not home.

As she walks back to her car, she stares at the church. Nervous, Barbara tries the door to the breezeway. It opens. She looks around and can hear a woman talking. Climbing the stairs she looks in the first open door. A frumpy woman sits at a desk talking on a phone. She holds up her finger for Barbara to wait. The woman hangs up.

"Can I help you Dear?"

"I'm looking for Michael Donnelly," she tells her quietly.

The secretary looks to her left through another open door calling, "Rev. Donnelly, there is a young woman here to see you."

Her heart skips a beat as she hears his low voice, "Send her in."

"The next door over Dear," Sue directs.

It feels odd to hear him referred to as Rev. Donnelly. She backs out of the office and walks to the next door. Since he plans to go to the hospital after office hours, he is wearing his cleric shirt with his white tab collar. Barbara finds him working at a computer.

Michael glances up, shocked to see Barbara walk into his office. He stands, "Barbie, what are you doing here?"

"Talking to you last night made me want to see you," she explains staring at his collar.

He calls through the door, "Sue, I'm going over to the parsonage if you need me," he looks back at Barbara nodding at the open door, "Cheap intercom."

He walks to her.

The secretary interrupts stepping through the door, "Excuse me Reverend. I can't run the newsletter until I have your article."

"Right, sorry. I'm almost done. Barbie, have a seat for a few minutes." The secretary leaves and Michael returns to his computer. He stares forcing his thoughts back to his article.

Barbara scans his small, shabby office. Two chairs set in front of his desk and an old couch leans against the wall by the door. She sits uncomfortably in a chair. His office consists of two tall filing cabinets, book shelves, an old desk and a small computer table. A picture of Jesus knocking on a door hangs on a wall. She wonders why He had to knock on Mikey's door. On a bookshelf the statue of Jesus signaling a touchdown that his brother Sean gave him sets. She notices the name plate on his desk that Carol had given him with the crosses and the name, Rev. Michael Donnelly. She wishes he would hurry because she wants out of this room.

Within five minutes, Michael finishes calling, to Sue. Sue offers to transfer the article to her computer for him so he and his guest can leave. He asks Barbie if she wants to see the sanctuary. She answers "Sure," half-heartedly. He seems proud of it, but Barbara thinks it is small and plain compared to their church.

He takes her over to the parsonage where she looks around unimpressed with the old house which is bare with nothing decorative on the walls or on a table. She asks about the church table in the dining room, but he just laughs.

In the living room, she notices the painting above the couch, "That's a strange painting. It's not pretty. What is it supposed to be?"

Michael cocks an eyebrow, "The hammer is casting a shadow that looks like a cross over the toddler."

He waits for her to understand, but she just stares at him, so he continues, "its Joseph's carpenter workshop with Jesus as a toddler living under the shadow of a cross."

"Huh, weird," she shrugs.

Michael looks at Barbara standing in his living room. She seems out of place. She stares back at him. He looks odd wearing the white tab collar of a preacher. They knew each other their whole lives. They slept together for years, yet here they stand feeling awkward together.

Barbara moves close wrapping her arms around him missing their closeness, wanting to want him. Michael leans down kissing her. It is no longer the same. Barbara asks if he wants to show her his bedroom. Michael looks toward the stairs, but instead offers her something to drink. They talk for a while. Disappointed with her visit, she kisses her Mikey goodbye.

Michael realizes he does not miss Barbie; he misses Sadie. Sadie fits in this house, she fits in his church, she fits in his arms, and she fits in his life. If only he could think of a way to make it work.

Thursday night, Michael attends a Pastor/Parish committee meeting run by Mac who begins with the fact that he has a list of serious concerns about their new preacher. Michael suddenly feels as if he is on trial. The first concern, Rev. Donnelly spends too much time at a bar. Michael answers that he hasn't been drunk since before seminary and only goes to the bar because his friend owns it.

Mac continues, "A friend of mine saw you in a bar fight on Halloween."

"Well, not exactly." Michael cringes. "A man wouldn't leave a woman alone. I stepped in, but I never threw a punch. I just ducked and pushed him away."

Mac accuses, "The same friend also saw you on the other occasion on the dance floor kissing a woman."

Michael sighs, "I know you are used to married ministers, but they were married because at some point they dated."

Mac persists, "Maybe you should be more discreet than making out in public."

"Maybe, are we done here?"

"What about Sadie Stevens?" Mac ambushes.

"What about Sadie Stevens?" Michael rolls his eyes.

"It is obvious the way you look at each other that something is there. Do you think that it is smart to date a parishioner?"

Anger flashes through him, "First of all, Sadie and I are not dating, but what if we did? Do you find it hard to believe that a minister would be attracted to a woman with a strong faith who is active in church, a woman who understands ministry? It seems to me that would be better than picking someone up at a bar."

"We know that you are a bachelor, but as a pastor of a church, we think you should be more discreet." Mac repeats with conviction.

Michael thinks the meeting won't ever end.

This has definitely not been a good week for him and doesn't improve Sunday morning when Michael passes through the fellowship hall to find Dorothy Martin leading the Sunday school's opening exercises. Sadie does not come to church this week.

Wednesday evening, Michael lies on his couch watching T.V. when he hears the doorbell. He opens the door to discover a sobbing Colleen. "I think I'm calling off our wedding. I thought you should know."

She begins to leave, but Michael chases her down the steps. Taking her hand he pulls her into the house leading her into the living room, but she can't tell him the problem because of her crying. He holds her until she calms down.

"Two weeks before our wedding, one of Aidan's groomsmen can't make it to the wedding because of an important work assignment. So, Aidan decides to replace him with Troy Meyers."

She stops as if that is enough. Michael cocks his eyebrow, "There has to be more to this story."

"Oh, I'm sorry," Colleen wrings her hands, "Troy Meyers is Sadie's ex-fiancé. Three years ago, when they broke up, Brenda and I actually broke up with Steve and Aidan for staying friends with him.

"My wedding is hard enough with my five parents and step parents. Now, Sadie, my best friend in the whole world will be nervous and uncomfortable. She says she'll be fine, but I don't believe her. Aidan says that it has been over three years and Sadie should be over it by now."

"Maybe Aidan's right," Michael suggests.

"Michael, I can't handle this big wedding. I can't. Can't you just take us over to the church right now and quietly marry us?" she pleads.

"I could, but I don't think it's a good idea. Over the next fifty years, you will face a lot of problems together. You might as well start with getting through your wedding. You have such good arrangements made. You'll regret missing your wedding. Stay here. There's not much in my kitchen, but help yourself. I'm going to talk to Sadie."

As he walks down the street, he thinks about Aidan's words on Halloween. He resented that he had lost a best friend and because of Sadie, he wasn't even invited to the wedding. Michael had wondered at the time if he was talking about Sadie's fiancé, but didn't want to ask about her at that moment.

Michael pushes the buzzer.

"Who is it?"

"It's Michael."

"Now's not a good time for me."

"I need to talk to you. Buzz me up."

"Not now."

"Your best friend is at my house crying and thinking about canceling her wedding."

He hears the door release and climbs the stairs.

Sadie, with a tear streaked face, meets him at the door. Standing in her dining room, he tells her about his conversation with Colleen.

Michael suggests, "Whatever happened over three years ago, maybe you should let it go. You're letting it eat up your life."

She responds, "You have no idea what you are talking about."

Frustrated, he demands, "That's because no one will tell me, but you are going to tell me right now."

He takes Sadie by the hand and leads her to the couch. She stands back up to pace around. As she looks out the window, she begins her story:

"I met Troy my junior year of high school. I had a crush on him. He was a senior and a football player. When he asked me to the Christmas Dance, I was thrilled. We dated the rest of the year.

"We decided to break up when he left for college rather than attempt a long distance relationship. He was dating someone else when I began my freshman year at his college. He asked me if I wanted to get back together. I said yes and he broke up with her.

"Aidan was his roommate. Colleen liked him right away. Aidan's best friend, Steve was dating Brenda. That is how our group began. Stephanie joined us after college.

"September of our senior year, Troy, Aidan, and Steve proposed at the same time down in the gorge. We were going to get married three months apart. Troy and I set our date first in August, followed by Brenda and Steve in November and Colleen and Aidan in February.

"Then in January of our senior year, it happened. I found out I was pregnant. I thought, oh well. It's not that much of a scandal. We dated for five years and were engaged, but Troy freaked-out. He insisted that I have an abortion. I said no, but he made an appointment for Saturday. I cried to Colleen and Friday night we left for my parents' house.

"We arrived home after eleven o'clock at night. I told my parents everything. Dad said it didn't work well for a person of faith to marry someone who doesn't practice his faith. They said to postpone my student teaching and come home. They planned to take care of me and my baby until I finished my degree and got a teaching job.

"Colleen and I stayed until Sunday evening. When we arrived back on campus, I went to the house that Troy rented with Aidan, Steve, and two other guys. Everyone was home, so Troy and I went up to his room. He was furious that I left town without telling him. He said that he made another appointment for me to have an abortion on Wednesday.

"I told him I would not have an abortion and I would not marry him. I threw the ring at him. He said in a few years, after he became rich, I would come after him for child support. He didn't want to be on the hook for the next eighteen years.

"I said goodbye, but he followed me out into the hall. The guys downstairs could see us, but ignored us. I pushed him away. We were screaming and cussing. I smacked him across the face.

"When I reached the stairs, he yelled, 'Hey Sadie.' I turned to face him. He looked me in the eye and pushed me. I fell down the stairs.

"I woke up in the hospital with a broken hip, some broken ribs, broken leg, twisted wrist, bruises everywhere and a concussion so bad that they drilled a hole in my head to relieve the pressure. Oh yeah, and I had a miscarriage. He got the baby after all.

"Troy told the police that he didn't mean to knock me down the stairs, that we were both fighting and it was an accident. Aidan and Steve backed his story up. They said they saw me push and smack him. The police ruled it an accident. He never faced charges. He actually wanted me to forgive him and still get married."

As Sadie finished, Michael comes up behind her. He touches her shoulder and she leans on his chest. He wraps his arms around her thinking about the comments on her birthday about him not letting her fall down the stairs and how tightly she held on when he carried her up the stairs.

"Why didn't you want to tell me this for so long?" he whispers.

"I don't like talking about it. I don't like thinking about it. I didn't want to tell you that I was knocked up."

"It happens. You were in a serious relationship. I'm just glad you never considered the abortion."

"Psalm 139 says 'I knew you in the womb' so I named the baby just for me. Since I didn't know if it was a boy or girl, I chose a name that worked for either, Jamie."

Michael kisses the top of her head. They sit on the couch to discuss the situation. He discusses that forgiving Troy would do her more good than him. Facing him could be good for her. She needs to face her demons so that she can move on. Sadie agrees to go to the parsonage to meet with Aidan, Colleen, and Troy.

Sadie goes to the bathroom to wash her face and redo her make-up. Michael goes into the study to use his cell phone to call Aidan on his cell phone.

"Aidan, its Michael, what the hell are you doing? Why are you messing with Colleen two weeks before the wedding?"

"It would be nice to feel like I matter to Colleen more than her friends or that my friends matter at all," he explains.

Michael wonders if he and Sadie's argument on Halloween coupled with losing one of his groomsmen had been the catalyst for all of this, "Are you sure this is the stand you want to make now?"

"Troy is my friend. He has been tortured by that day too. Sadie acts like it was attempted murder. It was a stupid accident during a fight that she was active in. Did she ever bother to tell you what happened? I know that I'm not allowed to say anything."

Michael feels defensive of Sadie, but doesn't want to argue with Aidan right now, "She told me. I can understand not wanting everyone to talk about that."

Michael arranges for Aidan and Troy to meet the girls at the parsonage to work things out. Aidan is with Troy and they agree to come. Michael calls Colleen to let her know that they are all coming back. Sadie had changed her clothes and fixed her hair and face not wanting to look like a wreck when she sees Troy for the first time in two years.

While Michael, Sadie, and Colleen wait at the parsonage, Sadie assures Colleen that she is calm, but when the doorbell rings they both jump. Michael lets them in. Troy has dark hair and eyes and is tall like Michael, but while Michael has a slim build, Troy has more of a football player build.

Troy sees Sadie as he walks through the dining room, "Wow, you are more beautiful than ever."

Sadie's heart pounds, "Hi."

They stand around awkwardly sharing chit chat. Michael stands back out of the way. After some quick catch up talk, Sadie dives in, "Troy, I never said that I forgive you, so I forgive you."

Troy hangs his head for a minute thinking, and then his eyes meet Sadie's, "I don't want your forgiveness."

The others exchange glances. Sadie stiffens, "What do you want?"

Troy moves closer to her, "I want you to believe me. I was angry that you were leaving and I pushed you away from me like fine, go. I did not realize you were that close to the stairs. I meant to push you away, not down the stairs."

Sadie thinks for a moment, "Okay, I believe you."

Troy shakes his head, "But I don't believe you."

Sadie insists, "No, I mean it. I believe you. Troy, you never strayed from this story. Aidan and Steve, who I love, believe you. The police cleared you. I'm the only person who thought it was on purpose and I woke up in the worst pain of my life stuck in a wheelchair with a miscarriage. Maybe I've been wrong, so I choose to believe you."

Troy sweeps her into his arms for a big hug. Michael stiffens but stays quietly where he is. Colleen hugs Michael calling him a miracle worker. He did in two hours what they couldn't do in over three years.

Aidan and Colleen leave to talk things out between themselves. Troy and Sadie sit on the couch to talk while Michael leans on the dining room archway, to give them some privacy yet keeping an eye on them.

Troy, excited, wants to go somewhere for a drink to talk and have a fresh start.

Sadie shakes her head, "I'm sorry, I don't want a fresh start. I want closure."

Troy keeps pushing, but Sadie explains, "Troy, I didn't break up with you because of the stairs. I broke up with you because you insisted on an abortion. I said no and you made an appointment for me anyway. The first time we faced a real crisis, and our values had a train wreck. Your main concern was money and climbing the business ladder and mine were Christian and family values. When I date again, I want a man of faith."

Troy won't give up. He is sorry for his reaction to the baby insisting that his attitudes have changed. He points out that they were together for five good years with only one bad week.

"But it was one hell of a week. I'm not going out with you tonight. I'm willing to see you and be friendly especially at the wedding, but I'm not looking to reconcile."

"Sadie," Troy reaches for her hand.

Michael steps in, "Troy, Sadie has made her feelings clear. I think it is time for you to go. Come on, I'll walk you out."

Troy glares at Michael, "Excuse me Reverend, I don't see how this is any of your business."

Anger builds in Michael, but he remains calm, "Well, Colleen came to me for help, I talked Sadie into coming here, I invited you, and this is my house. I am asking you to leave now."

Annoyed, he kisses Sadie on the cheek and leaves. Michael sits on the couch watching Sadie pace.

"Did you really believe him?" Michael asks.

"I don't know. It's possible. Whether I believe him or not doesn't change anything and I love Colleen and Aidan. I would do anything for them. I was okay until he refused to leave. Thank you for making him leave."

"Why don't you come and sit down?"

Sadie sits by him. He holds his arm out and Sadie curls up against him laying her head on his chest. He places his arm around her.

"What are we going to do about us?" she asks.

"What do you mean?"

"Last week, I acted like an idiot at the Halloween party and said I won't date you. You said you don't want to be my friend anymore and here we are a week later cuddled up on your couch."

Michael laughs, "How about until after the wedding, we go back to where we were in September and October. We were pretty happy then. After that, we can worry about what's next."

Sadie agrees and he kisses her on top of her head. Michael is relieved to finally know what happened and what had caused Sadie to stop trusting men. So much makes sense now. He remembers Martin saying that if he had not been a minister, he might have beaten the crap out of Troy. Michael believes that this evening will be good for Sadie. She needed to face her past before she can move forward.

Sadie tips her face up toward Michael, "Thank you for being here for me and for Colleen tonight. You are a very good pastor and you are a good friend."

Michael looks tenderly down at her. Leaning down, he gently kisses her lips. She then cuddles into his side with his arm around her and he holds her. They remain on the couch for a long while before Michael walks her home.

Chapter X

Aidan and his groomsmen meet in the parking lot of Duffy's to drive into the city for Aidan's bachelor party. Aidan, Steve, and Aidan's cousin Tom are in the lot when Troy arrives. Troy has missed being part of the close knit group missing Aidan and Steve almost as much as Sadie.

After Sadie's tumble down the stairs, Aidan and Steve had stuck with him and all three girls broke up with them. A few months later, Steve made up with Brenda and Troy saw less and less of him. It hurt Troy when Steve married Brenda. Not only was he not in the wedding party, he was not invited to the wedding for Sadie's sake.

A little over a year later, Aidan reunited with Colleen. Now the five of them are close again and because of Sadie he is left out. He hopes to win Sadie back and rejoin his old group. He believes he has a chance now that he has held Sadie in his arms again. He wishes they had gone out for drinks that night, if only that minister hadn't gotten in the way.

Troy is surprised when Michael walks up thinking to himself, "Who takes the minister to the bachelor party?"

Aidan tells them he wants to hang around even though they are all here because the girls are coming to the lot and he wants to see them before they leave.

"We all fit in Steve's van, so we only need one designated driver,"

Aidan leans his elbow on Michael's shoulder, "Now who wants to be the designated driver?"

Laughing, Michael agrees to do it. Aidan has never seen Michael drink more than one beer even though he had been at the bar with them once or twice a week for the past two and a half months.

Aidan hands him the keys, "I believe we all feel safe in the Reverend's hands."

Troy scoffs, "Is that why you take a minister to a bachelor party?" They laugh as if he is joking.

Michael feels strange being with the man who not only hurt Sadie, but who she had loved and slept with for so many years.

The girls arrive dressed to party at the clubs and strike several poses for the guys. Colleen wears a white baseball cap with a small veil attached to the back with the word "BRIDE" in silver letters across the front.

Troy thinks Sadie looks even more beautiful than he remembers with her thick, wavy brunette hair flowing down her back. Her dress hovers above the knees and the sleeveless, low cut bodice reveals a hint of cleavage. The white dress, trimmed with black flowers, flatters her trim, fit body.

Colleen and Brenda walk to Steve and Aidan and to Troy's surprise, Sadie walks to Michael. The girls feel happy and flirty. Sadie flirts with the minister. Troy tries not to be too obvious that he is watching them. Michael quietly complains to her that her dress is too low cut and he suggests that she be the designated driver.

She laughs, "Are you worried about not being there to protect me from the letches? Don't worry; I've hung out at clubs for years before you showed up. I have even taken down a pack of rapists." Michael smiles, Sadie continues, "Thanks to Stephanie, we don't need a designated driver."

Sadie points at a black limo pulling into the lot.

Aidan shakes his head, "The girls always do things with style." He places his arm around Colleen's shoulder, "Do you think we'll bump into you tonight?"

"Maybe," Colleen grins devilishly, "Are you planning on stopping by the male strip club?"

"You better be joking about that," Aidan warns, but Colleen only waves goodbye pulling out of his arms.

Stephanie calls, "Shall we, ladies?"

As they head for the van, Troy quietly asks Steve about Michael and Sadie. Steve informs him, they are just friends and they work together at church. Troy had waited a long time outside the parsonage for Sadie to leave the other night. The minister walked her home more than an hour later.

As the night progresses, Troy still feels like an outsider. Aidan and Steve act nice enough, but it doesn't feel like old times. Michael and Troy obviously feel uneasy with each other, but remain polite. Troy notices how close Aidan and Steve seem to be with this young preacher. Troy wonders if after all these years they are replacing him in the group and hopes he isn't too late to regain his place. By the end of the evening, Troy begins to brew hatred toward Michael.

The next Friday, Michael feels a little nervous about running his first wedding rehearsal. He talks on the phone with Sadie's dad for over an hour going over everything.

He looks in his *Book of Worship* as he enters the sanctuary.

Everyone had already arrived. Hearing people arguing, he looks up. Colleen's mother, father, step-mother, and two step-fathers are fighting. Aidan looks at the ceiling and Colleen cries. Everyone else stands around watching.

Michael steps in. Using a strong voice, he tells the parents to sit down and stop talking. With as much authority as he can muster, he explains that this rehearsal will not go like this. They can ask questions and make suggestions, but he will make the decisions period. He points out that Colleen is the bride and should look happy, not like this. The parents try to argue, but Michael wins.

Michael takes Colleen aside to find out what the problem is. She cries as she tells him. He stares at her as if he's listening, but doesn't understand a word.

He turns to Aidan, "You try to tell me."

All three men think they should be the one to walk Colleen down the aisle. One points out that he is the biological father, but Colleen says he left her when she was only three. Her step-dad raised her from six to sixteen, but her mom hates him now. Mom wants her current husband to do it, but Colleen had been twenty-one when they married.

Michael thinks for a moment and asks, "Did you ever live with anyone other than your mother?"

Colleen replies, "I lived with Sadie's family for five months in high school, but other than that, I lived with her."

Michael goes to her mother, Tammy, "Who raised Colleen from birth through college?"

Tammy puffs up, "I did."

Michael decides, "Good, you walk her down the aisle."

The men begin to argue, but Michael remains firm. Tammy had

never thought about the mom walking the bride down the aisle and is pleased with the solution. Colleen is impressed with Michael for solving the first problem.

Michael runs a fun rehearsal. The four year old flower girl and five year old ring bearer keep running down the aisle. Michael runs after them bringing them back. He tries walking with them, but on their own, they run. The organist isn't there, so he calls Sadie to sing 'The Trumpet Voluntary.' She points out there are no words, but he says to just sing "da, da, da." So she sings and finally the children walk.

As each bridesmaid appears in the door, he makes different comments about people being in awe of their beauty or stunned by the lovely vision. He tells them the photographer will jump out. Stop and smile. Then continue after he ducks back out. Taking Martin's advice, he instructs the girls not to do that strange walk where women step and then place their feet together. Women who do that end up walking like ducks. He suggests a simple slow, but normal walk.

When Colleen appears in the door, he tells her she will hear a gasp as her admirers take in her angelic appearance. Colleen giggles and tells him to stop that.

While he keeps his directions clear, he has everyone smiling and laughing. When the Reverend goes over the vows, he keeps making comments to Colleen like "are you sure, last chance, and think about it" with Aidan yelling 'hey!' When they reach the kiss, Michael keeps stopping them with suggestions and stepping between them until Aidan shoves him out of the way to kiss his bride.

After the rehearsal, Michael goes to his office and plops down in his desk chair. Sadie follows him in. She sits in a chair across the desk from him, "That was a great rehearsal. You are a natural at all aspects of ministry. No wonder God called you."

Michael just looks at her with a small grin.

Colleen and Aidan enter the office. Michael stands walking around to the front of his desk. Colleen runs and jumps on him. With her arms wrapped around his neck, she kisses his face several times.

"Thank you, thank you. I thought my wedding would be a nightmare and you made tonight so much fun. You stopped my parents from fighting. You are a miracle worker."

Aidan extends his hand, "I'll just go with a handshake."

Troy looks around for Sadie as people prepare to leave for the rehearsal dinner. He asks Steve where she is. Steve says he doesn't know, but guesses she is in the Reverend's office. Troy feels a flash of jealousy.

As the four emerge from Michael's office, the crowd stares at Michael.

Stephanie inquires, "Reverend, what exactly were you and Sadie doing in your office?"

Sadie laughs, "It wasn't me."

Michael asks Sadie, "What are you talking about?"

Steve answers, "Dude, half your face is covered with lipstick."

Michael turns to Aidan, "You couldn't tell me?"

"Sorry Reverend. It was too funny."

Sadie explains to the crowd, "Colleen thanked him for the good rehearsal."

Troy's jealousy burns in his gut.

The day of the wedding, Michael knocks on the lounge door to see if Colleen is ready. Sadie answers the door. She had been at the salon all morning and looks radiant with her hair all piled and woven on top of her head with ringlets hanging around her face. Her royal blue gown with spaghetti straps clings to her body. He gazes at her saying nothing for a moment. He takes a breath and asks if they are ready. Sadie invites him in. Colleen turns around wearing her wedding gown and veil.

Michael just says, "Wow." Colleen beams.

Michael joins the men, "Here we go," he elbows Aidan, "Ready?"

Aidan nervously checks, "God, it took forever to get here. Are you sure she's really here?"

Michael comforts him, "I saw her. She's here and she is beautiful. She is actually glowing."

Aidan smiles back, "Let's go."

Michael feels a little nervous, especially with Martin here to see his first wedding. The children appear in the door. Michael hopes they walk. They start down the aisle. The photographer startles the girl, but she seems all right. They walk about half way down the aisle when the little girl seems to have stage fright and stops. The boy stops and looks at her, but she won't move. Michael tries to wave her up, but she is frozen. Michael stoops down holding out his arms and she quickly walks to him passing her Mom. He walks her back to her mom in the second pew as the congregation giggles.

When Sadie's turn comes to walk down the aisle, Michael imagines her as the bride walking to him. Joy elbows Martin to point out the look on Michael's face. Sadie's eyes lock on his face which Troy notices.

The rest of the wedding goes off without a hitch. Aidan and Colleen's love shows through the whole ceremony. No one can watch them and not smile.

After the wedding and all the photographs have been taken, Michael stops at the parsonage to change from his clerical shirt to a regular shirt and tie and waits for the reception satisfied with his service and relieved that it is over. When Michael arrives at the hall, the wedding party is not yet there. He finds Martin and Joy who rave that he did a wonderful job. Martin likes how personal the sermon had been. It shows that they are friends.

They go to a table to pick up their place cards. Martin finds theirs which assigns them to table five. Other than the wedding party, Michael only knows the Stevens, so he hopes he is at table five also. When he finds his place card, it reads "head".

Martin says as a minister, he had never sat at the head table. Michael tells him they are good friends, but only since September.

Martin asks, "Did Sadie ever tell you about her break up with Troy?"

Michael nods, "Yeah."

Martin stiffens, "It is hard to see Troy in the same room with Sadie."

"I bet. Minister or not, I might have beaten the crap out of him," Michael agrees. "The other night, Troy grabbed and hugged her. I found it hard not to step in."

"He hugged her?" Martin and Joy obviously do not like knowing that he had touched their daughter. Martin continues, "I never liked that guy, but I never dreamed that he would, that he could hurt her."

Joy stares off at nothing, "I'll never forget Colleen's hysterical call that night. While waiting for the ambulance, Aidan had called Colleen. She and Brenda ran to the house which was only two or three blocks away. The girls were their seconds before the ambulance arrived. They saw her lying in a crumpled heap at the foot of the stairs bleeding and unconscious. I asked her if Sadie will be okay, and she wouldn't answer me. I yelled into the phone and she screamed back 'I don't know! I just don't know!'

"Colleen and Brenda thought she was going die. We waited all night in the hospital waiting room not knowing if she would make it. Martin and I were with her when she woke up. The first words out of her mouth were 'Is the baby okay? What happened to the baby?' When no one answered her, she knew and sobbed."

Martin steps closer to Michael, "Sadie swore that she would never date again. She said that she is content to simply be a teacher. Her mother and I have tried to tell her that she needs to allow someone to love her and to love, but she won't listen, so far."

Michael does not respond to this, but just returns her father's stare.

The wedding party arrives. The D.J. announces each couple as they enter with applause. Since Sadie is the Maid of Honor, her partner is Steve, who is the Best Man. Brenda is partnered with Tom and Stephanie is partnered with Troy. As the party gathers at the head table, Steve waves Michael over.

Michael tells Aidan, "Ministers don't usually sit at the head table."

Aidan answers, "You were the minister at church; here, you're just one of us."

Michael takes a seat at the end by Aidan's cousin Tom. Once Steve gives a toast, Sadie gives her toast, and Michael blesses the food and the couple, the dinner begins.

Later, Aidan and Colleen dance to their wedding song. The wedding party and parents join them on the next song. Michael watches while he visits with Eloise Crabtree, an older woman who is one of his parishioners. The next song played has the wedding party doing the twist. Troy works his way in front of Sadie who dances with him. Troy and Sadie then dance to another fast song, but next a slow song begins. Sadie excuses herself, but Troy follows her. Blocking her path, he attempts to persuade her to dance with him.

Sadie's brother, Luke, and father start to go to her, but Joy stops them pointing out that Michael is about to intercede. Michael steps up to them and speaks to Troy, "Aidan and Colleen look beautiful. It has been a beautiful day for them don't you think?" Troy nods as Michael turns to Sadie, "How about that dance you promised me?"

He holds out his hand which Sadie takes without hesitation. They walk onto the dance floor leaving Troy seething. Stephanie offers to dance with Troy.

Troy asks her, "What is the deal between those two?"

Stephanie smirks, "Sadie claims they are just friends, but I have seen him try to suck her tonsils out."

This fact startles Troy.

When the dance ends, Sadie begins to leave, but Michael pulls her back whispering to her, "Stay with me."

The two walk to Aidan and Colleen. As the music's pace picks up, Aidan claps Michael on the back, "Show us what you've got."

Michael agrees, "Okay." He grabs Sadie and begins to twirl her around the dance floor. Sadie can't keep up with him at first, so he gives directions: back two, three, four, forward two, three, four, and turn. She begins to catch on and is able to follow his directions to a basic samba. Steve, Brenda and Sadie's family gather to watch. The videographer spots them and begins to film their dance as Michael straightens his arms holding her away and then pulls his arms out to the side pulling her up against him as he walks around her turning her about first one way and then the other. Troy and Stephanie feel annoyed that he is showing off.

When the dance ends, Brenda asks, "Where did that come from?"

Michael shrugs, "I keep telling you, I was raised at the country club."

Colleen jumps up and down, "I want to dance with you." Laughing, Michael takes her hand and leads her out onto the dance floor. The videotographer again begins filming the impressive duo. Colleen easily keeps up with him.

Troy seizes the opportunity to talk to Sadie, "I hope you save a few dances for me."

"I don't know if I feel comfortable with that," she hedges.

Troy takes Sadie's hand, "Come on…Give me a chance for old time's sake."

Luke steps in to pull Sadie away, "Excuse me; I want to dance with my sister."

Martin and Joy watch as Michael and Sadie spend the evening together. Sadie keeps insisting to her parents they are just friends, but tonight they look like a couple. Martin and Joy can't hear what the pair is saying, but they are obviously fooling around.

Michael leans over and whispers in her ear, "Let's go back to the bar and get you a little drunk."

Sadie snaps her head up surprised, "Why?"

Michael smiles at her, "You were so much fun at your birthday party."

Sadie playfully hits him several times on the arm and back. Laughing, he pins her arms and holds her tightly from behind her so she can't hit him.

They join the rest of the wedding party. Colleen, laughing, tells them she has to go to the bathroom, but doesn't know how to do it in her gown especially with the train all bustled behind her. Brenda suggests that her bridesmaids could help her hold her gown up. The girls run to the ladies room to try to figure it out. Steve tells the guys that is true friendship. Laughing, they go to the bar to get a drink.

When the girls return, Stephanie has an idea. She talks to the D.J. who announces to clear the dance floor for the bride and her maids as they help to prepare the couple for the honeymoon. The girls run onto the dance floor.

Steve grabs Michael's arm, "You've got to see this. They started doing this in college."

Sexy music begins and the girls begin their provocative dance grinding their hips and shimmying around. Michael smiles shaking his head, Sadie is this sweet, pretty little elementary teacher who volunteers at church, yet she has this wild side.

Troy comes up beside Michael, "You should see her do this dance while actually stripping."

Michael cringes but tries to ignore him.

Troy continues, "You should see her do this dance naked."

Heat rises in Michael's face.

Troy can tell he is getting to him, "Look at her move. She moves great in bed. She can drive a man to distraction."

Michael tells himself he can't hit Troy in the middle of Aidan's wedding, so he moves away from him.

Aidan tells Michael he and Colleen are going around to the tables to say goodbyes, one more dance and they are off on the honeymoon. While Aidan and Colleen start their rounds, Michael and Sadie walk out on the terrace. Michael points out that tonight is like a date with dinner and dancing.

Sadie responds, "Thank you for staying with me to keep Troy away from me."

Michael asks, "Is that all I was doing?"

Sadie teases, "It was sort of like a pretend date."

Michael drops his head for a moment, "Well, you know how to end a pretend date? With a pretend kiss, come here."

He cups his hands around her elbows. Sadie tips her face toward him. They only kiss for a moment when Troy speaks, "Well, when you said the next time you want a man of faith, you meant it."

The look in his eyes scares Sadie as he clenches and unclenches his fists. Sadie demands, "Why do you care? We broke up over three years ago."

Troy glares at her, "You won't even talk to me or give me a chance."

Michael steps in front of Sadie, "Why don't you leave her alone?"

Troy takes a threatening step forward, "Back off Preacher."

"Look, Aidan went out on a limb with Colleen to get you in this wedding. Don't start a fight here," Michael tries to reason with him.

"Don't tell me about Aidan. I've known Aidan a whole hell of a lot longer than you."

Sadie steps out from behind Michael, "It doesn't matter if Michael is here or not. I don't want to spend time with you. I forgave you for closure and to move on."

Troy barks, "You're still a bitch."

"Gee, I can't imagine why she doesn't want to spend time with you." Michael jabs sarcastically.

Steve and Tom show up. Steve places his arm around Troy, "Hey buddy, why don't you come have a drink with me?" They pull him away.

Michael puts his arm around Sadie who is trembling.

The evening ends. The group waves as the limo whisks Aidan and Colleen away. Steve asks Sadie if she is ready to leave, but Michael offers to take Sadie to save Steve the extra drive.

Michael pulls up in front of Sadie's apartment. The hour is late, so there are spots right in front of the hardware store. Sadie feels awkward. They acted like a couple all evening in front of all their friends and her family.

"Thanks for the ride. I had a fun evening," she quickly climbs out of the car.

Michael climbs out of the car as well, "Hey Cinderella, now that the ball is over, did anything change or does everything turn back into a pumpkin?"

Sadie looks down, "I don't know anymore. I guess a pumpkin."

As she steps into her stairway, he catches the door following her in, "Sadie."

"Wait," she pulls off her shoes and sets them on the stairs, "My feet are killing me."

Michael moves closer, "You are still wearing your gown. You didn't turn back into a pumpkin just yet."

He pulls her into his arms kissing her with the passion that he usually holds back. His hands slide down her waist, over her hips and continue up her back for a tight embrace. His kisses travel to her ear, down her neck, and across her bare shoulder. Sadie grabs the back of his head lifting him up to her lips. Breathless, he lays his head on her shoulder as she buries her face in his neck.

Tears well up in her eyes, "Goodnight Michael." She pulls away running up the stairs. He sighs.

Before she reaches the door, Michael calls to her, "Hey Cinderella."

"What?!"

"You actually lost your shoes on the stairs."

Sadie laughs covering mouth with her hand. He picks up the heels by the straps and climbs the stairs as she comes back down to him.

She takes her shoes, "Thank you."

He sits on the stairs, "Please sit for a minute."

She sits next to him.

He inquires, "How long are you going to your parents' house for Thanksgiving?"

"I'm leaving Tuesday after school. I'll be home Saturday night. You?"

"I'll leave Wednesday and come back Friday. Sadie, I think about you a lot. I think about the things you told me after Bible School.

"You would never lose those friends. Our conference only appoints us to churches in East Ohio. You'd never be farther than a couple hours away. You could come back at least once a month. With cell phones and e-mail, you can be in constant contact.

"I know it is hard to get a teaching job, but you said teaching is a calling. Trust God to place you. I would help you. If I left the conference, I wouldn't have a church to pastor anymore. If you left your school, you'd still be a teacher and could find another job.

"The last one, the one about not being able to choose your own house or town, that's just true.

"I get so lonely. I've been praying for someone special. Every time I do, all I can picture is your face. What happens when you pray about it?"

Sadie shakes her head, "I don't pray about it. I won't pray about it."

137

"Why?"

She stands, "With my luck, God's trying to turn me into a freaking minister's wife."

She runs up the stairs and into her apartment. He smiles as he heads for home.

Chapter XI

The first Sunday of Advent, the church celebrates the Hanging of the Greens. Church members gather to decorate the church for Christmas followed by a tureen dinner. Then the children perform a Christmas pageant.

Sunday morning, Michael sees Sadie for the first time since the wedding, but she is busy with the pageant practice for the evening program. There are people around with no time for a private moment.

That evening, Aidan, Colleen, Steve, and Brenda all come. Michael is told that the attendance is up this year. The people have a good time decorating the church. Sadie is in a good mood, laughing, teasing, and bumping into Michael on purpose.

Michael's mother had always hired people to decorate the house. He would just come home one day and the house would be done. He never decorated on his own. Michael starts to wrap the lights on the tree that is in the front corner of the sanctuary.

Sadie points out, "Uh Michael, you are wrapping those too tightly. It looks like you're tying up the tree."

Michael disagrees. Sadie asks Eloise, an elderly parishioner who is a good soul and one of the hearts of the church, to look, "Lordy Pastor, what did that tree do wrong that you're tying it up like that?"

He laughs taking the lights back off. Sadie climbs up on the step ladder and puts the lights back on with his help.

At the tureen dinner, Michael walks around visiting with all the tables. He is last through the food line and joins Sadie and their friends. Aidan and Colleen have only been home from their honeymoon for two days and invite them over to their house Friday to look at the pictures. They put them on a CD so they can play them on their DVD player on their big screen T.V.

Sadie finishes and calls the children to come with her to dress in costumes. Colleen and Brenda go to help. Michael heads to his office.

Dorothy, an older woman who has been a member for over thirty years, barges into his office angry showing Michael two dolls. The first is a beautiful china doll dressed in white with dark skin and dark brown hair. The second is a goofy looking cowboy doll with red yarn hair, freckles, and a big smile wearing bright yellow fringed clothes with big colorful music notes on the limbs and stomach. She asks Michael which doll should be used as Jesus in the pageant.

He looks at the dolls, "Is this a trick question?"

Hand on hip, she informs him, "Sadie insists that we use the cowboy."

Sadie rushes into the office, "We don't have time for this."

He asks, "Are you planning to use this doll as Jesus?"

"Yes."

"Why?"

"Dorothy didn't bring her china doll to practice, so we used Kelly's doll, Bucky."

Michael cocks an eyebrow, "Does a doll need to practice?"

Rolling her eyes, Sadie explains, "Alice told me Kelly is excited about Bucky playing Jesus. She washed his face and practiced at home with him."

"Rev. Donnelly," Dorothy states firmly, "that doll looks ridiculous. Are you going to do whatever Sadie says just because she is pretty and you like her?"

The comment takes Michael off guard, "Sadie, just use the other doll."

"Are you kidding me? Fine," Turning on her heels, Sadie leaves the office and soon returns with Kelly Mitchell dressed as an angel standing her in front of Michael.

"Rev. Donnelly has something he wants to tell you."

Kelly looks at Bucky and the china doll on Michael's desk, and then looks at the floor. Michael glances at Sadie and then down at Kelly, "I wanted to thank you for letting us use your doll in the pageant. He's the happiest Jesus I've ever seen."

Kelly smiles and runs out of the room.

"I can't believe this," Dorothy whines.

Sadie apologizes to Michael, "Sorry, but I needed you to see the real issue." She turns to Dorothy, "The pageant is about the kids. It's not worth hurting a five year old's feelings."

Michael hands Bucky to Sadie, "Here, go swaddle this thing. Swaddle it tightly."

Sadie smiles taking Bucky as she quickly leaves. Dorothy huffs as she takes her doll and leaves. Michael just shakes his head.

Michael sits with Aidan and friends in the sanctuary. The congregation sings some of the hymns and the children sing other songs as they stomp up front in costume to create the Nativity scene.

Mary enters carrying a white bundle. The doll can't be seen. The shepherds enter surrounded by the nursery class, four toddlers dressed in white with hoods that look like sheep, crawling on all fours and yelling "baa." The congregation laughs.

The angel of the Lord enters, walks up very close to the microphone, and shouts her line. The congregation jumps and then laughs.

The three wise men enter; the three boys are drastically three different heights. The middle king has a large, bright orange water gun tucked into his belt.

Aidan leans over to Michael, "I don't remember one of the wise men packing heat."

Michael holds his hand over his mouth in an attempt to hide his laughter.

As the boy passes the pew where his father is sitting, the dad reaches out and confiscates the gun. The congregation laughs.

The sheep gather around the manger to sing "Happy Birthday" to the baby Jesus. Mary feels the need to pick up Jesus to listen. The blanket falls from its head. There is Bucky's red headed, large smiling, freckled face. The congregation laughs.

A set of brothers playing a shepherd and a sheep start hitting each other. Sadie sneaks up to separate them. The congregation laughs.

After the pageant, the children run back to change. Michael pulls Sadie into his office closing the door behind them. He teases, "That was a very interesting interpretation of the Nativity."

Sadie elbows him in the ribs.

He asks, "Was it supposed to be a comedy?"

Sadie hits his arm.

He doesn't stop, "It made me think of how the Nativity would have been performed on Vaudeville."

Sadie smacks his arm and back several times. Michael grabs her arms wrestling around. Falling on the couch, he pins her down.

"The church is full of people. Let me up before someone catches us. What if Dorothy comes in?"

Michael lets her up and opens the office door to come face to face with Dorothy.

"So Pastor, what did you think of the job Sadie did on the pageant?" Dorothy sees Sadie, "Oh Sadie, of course you're in here."

"I think people had a lot of fun," Michael states.

Dorothy persists, "Don't you think it should be more serious?"

"I think it was memorable," he smiles.

Dorothy leaves with her nose up in the air.

Sadie whispers, "Can you imagine if she had found you on top of me on the couch?"

Michael and Sadie go to the breezeway to greet people as they leave. Most comments are positive. The wise man's father stops to apologize, "I don't know how he smuggled that gun in here. I swear I frisked him before we left."

Eloise stops, "You two make a good team. Today was so much fun. You two look so good together. As a matter-of-fact, I think the two of you would make beautiful babies."

Michael and Sadie are startled.

"Eloise," Sadie corrects, "We aren't even a couple."

"Well you should be," she quips as she leaves.

Chuckling, Michael whispers to Sadie, "I told you so."

Sadie elbows him in the ribs.

He groans, "You better be careful. You're going to put me in the hospital with broken ribs."

After everyone leaves, Michael walks around turning out lights and locking doors. He notices a light on down the hall in the educational wing. Walking into the room, he finds Sadie folding costumes.

"I'm almost finished."

They walk out together. When they reach the door, Sadie notices it is snowing with big lacey flakes gently gliding to the ground. Michael leans over her to look out the window. She stretches up and softly kisses him.

"Goodnight Michael. I'll see you later this week sometime and we can talk."

"Why do you always leave after a kiss? You are driving me crazy."

"Goodnight," she walks outside.

Michael follows, "Did you think about the talk we had after the reception?"

"Yes, yes I did. Goodnight."

"Sadie!"

Sadie had so much to bring that she brought her car. She climbs in and drives off leaving him with his hands on his hips shaking his head.

Michael goes home changing into sweatpants and an undershirt. He crawls in bed looking at the clock which reads nine o'clock, so he gets back up. He paces around the house and then sits in his recliner to channel surf. Suddenly, he feels like he can't take it anymore. Shoving bare feet in tennis shoes, he puts on his coat, and walks to Sadie's.

Sadie, who is dressed in a knee length sweatshirt nightgown with a picture of a cute fox which reads 'Foxy Lady', hears her buzzer.

"Who is it?"

"It's Michael."

"What do you want?"

"To talk, buzz me up."

"I'm dressed for bed."

"I don't care, buzz me up."

"No."

Frustrated, Michael pushes the buzzer three more times. With a huff, Sadie hits the door release; then unlocks and opens the door. She walks into the dining room on the other side of the table. Michael comes in and places his coat on the back of a chair.

"You were ready for bed too?"

Michael smiles, "Well, yeah. You look cute."

Sadie places her hands on her hips, "What is so important that it couldn't wait?"

Michael walks around the table to face Sadie, "I am in love with you and you are in love with me. I want you to admit it." Sadie stares at him shocked. Michael moves closer, "I want you to admit it."

Sadie shakes her head, "Just because I think you are a good man and that you are amazingly handsome and sexy or that you are an awesome kisser and your eyes make me feel like I am going to melt, doesn't mean I'm in love with you."

"What?!"

Sadie shakes her head again and starts to walk away. Michael grabs her arms and pins her to the wall. "Stop walking away. Let's try again. I am in love with you. I need to know how you feel right now."

"Let me go."

"No. How do you feel?"

Sadie looks into his eyes, "Damn it, I'm in love with you. I have loved you since June."

Cocking his head to the side, he revels, "Finally. Now was that so hard?"

Leaning down, they kiss. He runs his hands over her body filling her with heat. His kisses travel over her cheek and ear making his way down her neck. He whispers in her ear, "I want you. I want you right now. Just say yes. Say yes."

Sadie answers breathlessly, "Yes."

Michael slides his hands down her hips and thighs. Taking hold of the bottom of her nightgown, he pulls it off in one smooth movement. Wrapping his arms around her, he leads her into the living room and pulls her down on the floor. Finally releasing all of the emotions that they had been holding back for so long, they make passionate love. When they are exhausted, Michael picks her up in his arms, carrying her to the bedroom. Sadie curls up against his body falling into a sound sleep.

The next morning, Sadie wakes up to find Michael propped up on his elbow watching her sleep. She asks, "Did what I think happened last night really happen?"

"Yes it did. Will you date me now?"

"I think we've been dating for awhile."

Michael kisses her, "You held me off for a long time. Are you sure now?"

Sadie sits up staring intensely into his eyes, "Michael, I choose you. I choose you over my job. I choose you over my friends. I choose you over choosing where I live. I choose you. I love you."

Michael lies on top of her and takes her again.

Sadie jumps out of bed to hurry so she won't be late for school. As Michael crawls out of the bed, her dresser catches his eye. On the edge of the mirror she slid three pictures from her birthday. One is the picture when she almost fell off his lap, another is the one with his chin on her shoulder, and the third one is the group shot when Sadie had wrapped her arms around his waist.

Sadie runs in to get something. Seeing what he is looking at, she remarks a little embarrassed, "Like I said, I have loved you for a while now."

As Sadie leaves for school Michael invites her to stop at his house on her way home.

Sadie has difficulty keeping her mind on her school subjects. If she closes her eyes, she can almost feel his touch. She is in a good mood and has the kids laughing and carrying on. She plays a spelling game called 'sizzle' and sight word bingo. In math, she runs board races and lets them work with and then play with the pattern blocks. During silent reading, she forces her attention on the children who take turns reading to her. School finally ends. The air is cold out as she hurries up the hill to the parsonage.

She knocks on the back door. Michael opens it as if he had been in the kitchen anxiously waiting for her. Without a word, he pulls her in, closes the door, and begins kissing her. He helps her off with her book bag and coat. Michael, still not saying word, lifts her onto the kitchen table taking her once again.

After, Sadie laughs teasing, "You are one horny minister."

Friday night, Michael and Sadie go to Aidan and Colleen's honeymoon picture party. Aidan and Colleen notice that they arrive together in the same car. Aidan's house is a split level. They go down the steps to the sunken family room where Stephanie, Steve and Brenda are waiting. Michael sits down on the love seat and Sadie sits beside him. He places his arm around her shoulders as she snuggles up. Their friends stare.

Frustrated, Colleen groans, "When are the two of you going to admit that you're a couple?"

Sadie sits up, "Last Sunday after the pageant."

Brenda and Colleen quickly sit on the coffee table in front of them, "What?!"

Sadie tells them excitedly, "Michael came up to my apartment. He told me that he is in love with me and that he knows that I am in love with him. Then he pinned me to the wall until I admitted it."

Their friends laugh and clap. Steve cheers, "Way to go. It's about damn time."

Stephanie coos in a velvety voice, "So what came next? A man pins a woman to a wall until she admits that she loves him. So what did you do next?"

"Nothing," Michael pulls Sadie back, but she smiles and wags her eyebrows causing her friends to squeal. Michael looks at Sadie, "What are you doing?"

"I didn't say a word," she giggles.

Michael squints at her, "uh-huh".

Colleen claps her hands, "We are happy for you. Oh, you should see the beautiful dress Aidan bought me on our trip. Come on girls. We'll be right back."

Colleen grabs Sadie and the girls disappear up the stairs in a blink of an eye.

Michael turns to Aidan, "Do you think they're actually looking at a dress?"

Aidan nods, "Yes. That dress is probably getting juicy details right about now."

Michael leans back rolling his eyes.

Steve plops down by him, "How about you give us juicy details?"

Michael shakes his head, "I'm not one to talk about that. You don't think she'll tell that much?"

The girls squeal from somewhere in the house. Michael holds his head in his hands realizing that they should have had a discussion about this before they came.

Aidan persists, "Just tell us this, did you spend the night?"

Michael quietly admits, "Yes."

The girls return.

Michael inquires, "What did you do?"

Sadie shrugs, "I told my friends some of the basics. Don't guys talk like this all the time?"

"I don't," he looks around, "So what's the best detail she gave you? Aidan and Steve want to know."

Sadie interrupts, "No, no. I don't want you to feel uncomfortable, besides tonight is about Colleen and Aidan's honeymoon. How about we look at those pictures?"

"First, we have a lot of food on the kitchen table. Let's make up our plates," Colleen offers.

Stephanie speaks up, "Oh honey, if I were you, I wouldn't let Michael anywhere near your kitchen table."

The other girls freeze holding their breath. Michael looks around confused by the comment. He thinks, kitchen table. It hits him. "Sadie!"

"Stephanie!" Sadie glances at Michael's shocked face, "Gotta go," she runs up the stairs and Michael chases her. The girls fill in the guys on what Michael had done on his kitchen table.

Steve comments, "He seems so reserved and mild mannered. Who knew?"

Michael chases Sadie up the stairs and into the living room. Catching her, he pins her to the wall again.

"Why did you do that?" he demands.

"What? I had to tell my friends that we finally got together," she defends.

"Sadie, some things are private, intimate. I can't feel free to be with you if you are going to tell the girls everything. Some things should just be between us."

"You're right. I'm sorry. I could have told them that we were together without giving them that many details. I was just excited and got carried away. I'm used to telling them everything. I'm sorry. I didn't mean to embarrass you."

"You know that we have to be discreet. People at the church would not understand."

"I know that better than you. My mom compares living in a parsonage to living in a goldfish bowl, but these are my friends. They're like family. They won't hurt us, but I'll try to be more careful about how much I say. You're right. Some things should be just between us."

Michael stares at her skeptically.

"I'm sorry," she repeats.

"Hey you two," Aidan calls from the kitchen, "you better not be doing anything in there. Come get a plate of food."

Michael hangs his head for a second and then gives Sadie another dirty look. She mouths the word sorry and they join their friends to fill their plates.

After everyone has their food and takes their seats around the family room, Michael addresses the group, "You know if rumors go through the church, I could be in serious trouble. People would probably get upset and they could request the conference moves me."

Steve assures him, "Don't worry. Anything said in this group, stays in the group."

Michael glares at Stephanie, "Are you sure?"

Stephanie stares back, "Don't look at me, Honey. I've been part of this group for more than two years longer than you. I know the rules. But since you brought it up, why would a minister have premarital sex? Aren't you suppose to be holy and of better moral character?"

"So you think that everybody who has premarital sex has poor moral character?" he challenges.

"No, but I thought ministers are supposed to be better," Steph fires back.

"No where in the Bible does it forbid premarital sex between two people who are in love. It is our society that mandates the marriage vows first."

"What about in the Ten Commandments?" Stephanie points out.

"The Ten Commandments only dictates that adultery is a sin. Both Sadie and I are extremely single, or should I say, were single," he answers.

"But if it's okay for you and Sadie to, uh, be together, then why do you have to worry about hiding it from people at church?" Steph continues to confront him.

"Because, many people will think about it like you do. The church people will judge a minister harshly. Besides, the love between Sadie and me is private and no one else's business," he glares at Sadie, "No one's." Sadie looks up at the ceiling and he returns his attention to Stephanie, "It will not interfere with my ministry. If anything, Sadie makes me better. She knows more than I do about so much of church life and church politics.

"Sadie and I didn't exactly jump in bed on the first date. It is almost December, and we have sort of been dating and we have been friends since June. There is nothing immoral about what we've done.

"You know Stephanie, if you want to read a Book in the Bible that would interest you, you should read *'The Song of Solomon.'* Remember, sex was God's idea."

"What about the conference and the bishop?" Aidan questions.

"There is nothing in the Discipline about it, unless it is an affair and I was cheating on somebody. As long as I am discreet, they don't care. They would only care if the church were to get in an uproar about it," he explains.

Their friends seem satisfied and they feel overjoyed to see the couple finally get together. Even Stephanie has to admit that they appear right together. They are also relieved that Sadie finally began to date once again.

Michael relaxes as they spend the rest of the evening learning about the honeymoon. The pictures of them in Cancun are breathtaking. The newlyweds had a wonderful time. As they are leaving, the girls plan to get together the next morning to go shopping.

Once home and alone, Sadie calls her parents and informs them that she has officially begun to date again. While they are not exactly surprised, they are relieved that she is dating again and they both really like Michael.

Chapter XII

Saturday morning, Michael leaves for the conference office for a day long meeting. Sadie doesn't expect him back until five o'clock. Michael does not have any Christmas decorations in his house insisting that the church and Sadie's apartment are decorated enough for him.

Sadie, Colleen, Brenda, and Stephanie go to Wal-Mart to buy a tree and decorations for his house. Sadie's friends volunteer to split the bill four ways purchasing an artificial tree, lights, garland, and ornaments. She buys a large nativity, a fiber optic wreath, silk poinsettia table centerpiece, a Santa ceramic candy dish, candles, and table cloths to cover his dining room table. They each bring a few decorations from their own homes. Sadie makes sure to bring mistletoe.

The girls go to the house of Kirk Donaldson, the Chairman of Trustees, to beg for a key. Sadie explains that they want to surprise Rev. Donnelly by decorating the parsonage for Christmas. Kirk refuses because he is not allowed to hand out the parsonage key, but his wife, Eileen overhears and tells him to give her the key. She thinks it sounds romantic. Eileen asks if they are dating now and Sadie admits that they are. Eileen states that it has been obvious that they would eventually.

The girls go to the parsonage. Sadie puts a roast in the oven. They play CD's while decorating the house. Her friends laugh at the church table and grey metal folding chairs in his dining room.

Looking at the black leather living room set, Stephanie comments, "Now this is a bachelor's pad."

Colleen agrees, "It sure is. You can tell by the blank walls and nothing decorative setting around. This place sure could use a woman's touch."

Five o'clock, Michael arrives home. Opening his door, he immediately smells the roast and hears the music, "Sadie?"

As he enters the dining room, he sees the table covered with the cloths, the centerpiece and lit candles. On the wall, the fiber optics wreathe twinkles with changing colors. He can see the Christmas tree by the fireplace with the nativity on the mantle. Walking into the living room, he finds all four girls sitting on the couches.

They call, "Surprise!"

"Why did you do all this?"

Sadie answers, "We thought a minister should have his parsonage decorated, Merry Christmas."

Michael, who is genuinely surprised, questions, "Where did you get of all this?"

"We bought it this morning," Sadie tells him.

Michael shakes his head, "This is too much."

Colleen comforts, "We split it four ways."

"Thank you, this is a wonderful surprise."

Brenda stands, "We better be going."

Michael asks if they're staying for supper, but they explain it is dinner for two and each kiss him on the cheek saying goodbye.

As Sadie serves dinner, Michael has a warm feeling. Sadie makes everything nice. He pulls her into his arms and thanks her, but she orders him to sit down to eat before the food gets cold.

Michael stares at her for a minute, "How did you get in here? I left the door locked."

Sadie smiles mischievously, "I have my ways."

He asks her what she does for Christmas. She informs him that she always goes to her parents' house for the entire Christmas vacation, but this year she plans to stay to be with him as he serves his first Christmas Eve service. This means so much to him.

She asks about his family. He tells her that he invited them for Christmas Eve, but his mother wants to go to the Christmas party at her country club. His mother is actually annoyed he won't be there with her. Sadie asks if his parents have ever seen him lead a service to which he replies no. They are not happy about him being a minister.

After supper, Michael helps Sadie with the dishes. Sadie walks over peering into the tiny laundry room off the kitchen, "Oh Sweetheart, since we are dating, do you think it would be okay if I used your machines sometimes? I am so tired of the laundromat."

"Well, let me see. Maybe we could make a deal," he barters as he comes up behind her and wraps his arms around her waist.

"What do you want?" she giggles.

"Well, if you are here doing your laundry anyway, maybe you could throw some of my clothes in as well," he suggests.

"Rev. Donnelly, do you want me to do your laundry?" she fanes being offended.

"I can provide the soap, fabric softener, and the machines and I'd even help," he offers.

"Okay, I guess so," she turns wrapping her arms up around his neck. "How would you survive if you hadn't found me? You are completely helpless in the kitchen and when it comes to housework. What do you eat when I'm not feeding you?"

Sadie walks to the refrigerator to take a look. It only has some things to drink, a little fruit, and some basics. She opens his freezer to find a stack of frozen dinners, and turns looking at him.

Pulling her away and closing the door, he admits, "Those are only for when I don't go out. I eat at the Rainbow Café quite a bit and several families from church have had me over to eat, especially Eloise. She lives alone and she teases that I need someone to cook for me."

Sadie shakes her head and leads him into the living room where she turns out the lights and they dance to Christmas music by the lights from the Christmas tree and a few candles. Michael finds the whole evening romantic and is relieved that Sadie finally let her guard down. Dating her is as good as he thought it would be.

As Sadie tries to leave, he pesters her about how she had gotten into his house. She finally admits to him that she talked Kirk Donaldson into loaning her his key and that she would give it back to him in the morning. Michael didn't even know that Kirk had a key. Sadie explains that the Chairman of the Trustees always has a key to the parsonage. Michael opens a kitchen junk drawer and digs around in it.

"Here, you can have your own key," he offers as he hands her a key.

She also informs him that Eileen asked if they were dating and she responded yes, so by the end of tomorrow, everyone at church will know. They agree that would be better than trying to keep it a secret.

The next morning at church, the gossip flies. Everyone seems to be whispering right in front of Michael. They not only know that he is dating Sadie, but that Sadie and her friends had decorated the parsonage as a surprise.

When he finishes his sermon that morning, he announces, "On a personal note, the gossip flying around this morning is true. Miss

Stevens and I have begun dating. Many of you have been making comments that you have seen this coming. Well, you were right."

Eloise calls out, "It's about time"

A ripple of laughter spreads through the church. Sadie, who is sitting up front in the choir loft, feels startled and embarrassed.

After church, Sadie ducks out skipping the coffee hour. Michael doesn't know where she is or why she left. He is anxious to find her. Many people congratulate him for dating Sadie and seem happy for them, but several seem angry or concerned. Dorothy Martin and Mac Macintyre are clearly not happy. Alice Mitchell seems bothered by it probably because Michael wouldn't date her even though she asked him out several times. Everyone keeps asking where Sadie is, but Michael doesn't know what to say or where she is.

When he finally can break away, he runs to his house first to begin looking for her where he finds her in the kitchen chopping vegetables.

"Why didn't you come down to the fellowship hall?" he asks.

She shoots daggers at him with her eyes.

"Okay, why are you angry?"

"Are you crazy? You don't discuss you're private life from the pulpit and you sure as hell don't discuss my private life from the pulpit especially when I don't know it's coming and I am sitting up front! Why would I go to the fellowship hall afterwards so people can give us their opinions on whether they are okay or not with our dating?"

"I thought it would end the whispering. I thought being up front about it would stop the rumors. You told Eileen without telling me. I thought you would be okay with it. Most people seem happy for us," Michael defends himself.

"Why don't you have them take a freaking vote? Damn it, I have always hated being discussed at church especially in committee meetings! You make a public announcement like that and you have invited people to stick their noses in. They stick them in without invitation; you don't need to make it worse!"

"I'm sorry! I thought it was a good idea," he persists.

"Well, you were wrong! If you are going to talk about me in public, I need warning. I need the chance to say whether or not I feel comfortable with it or not."

"Okay, I hear you. I'm new to this life. I don't have your years of experience. I promise to talk to you ahead of time before I make any other announcements. I'm sorry. Are you done being angry yet?"

"No, not yet," slamming down her knife, she walks out of the kitchen.

Michael leans back on the counter for a minute to catch his breath and then walks into the living room to see if she is calming down. As he enters the room, Sadie attacks him with a pillow. Taking him by surprise, she gets in four or five good whacks before he can get the pillow off her. She tries to run, but he catches her. Tossing her on the couch, he pins her down.

Out of breath he asks, "Do you feel better now? Are you done being angry yet?"

"I suppose so. Let me up."

"I don't think so."

"Come on. Let me up. I'm in the middle of making lunch."

"As I see it, we just had a fight. If you are done being angry, then we need to make up and this seems like a good position for making up," he begins to nibble on her ear.

The doorbell rings. Sadie pushes on him, "Saved by the bell."

Mac Macintyre appears serious as he enters the kitchen, "Rev. Donnelly, I am very concerned about you dating a parishioner. You are playing with fire having this type of affair."

Michael rolls his eyes, "We can't have an affair. We are both extremely single. You should be happy your minister is interested in a woman of faith who is so active in the church."

"It still seems wrong," Mac insists stubbornly. Sadie appears in the doorway. Mac remarks snidely, "Well, I shouldn't be surprised to see you here."

Sadie uses a fake voice, "Do you honestly believe that Michael dating a parishioner will hurt his ministry at this church?"

Mac puffs up as if he is winning his argument, "Yes Sadie, I do. Business frowns on office romances. In essence this is the same thing."

Sadie answers matter-of-factly, "Okay, wait here. I will fix this for you right now."

She leaves the room. Michael cocks his eyebrow wondering what she is up to now. She returns with his laptop computer setting it up on the kitchen table and begins tapping away on the keys.

She tells Mac, "I'll just be a minute. Oh, you will need a piece of paper and pen to make a list. Michael, give Mac a pad of paper and pen."

Michael shrugs obeying her request.

Mac looks skeptically at her, "What are you doing?"

Without looking up, Sadie explains, "I'm writing my letter of transfer. I can walk to the United Church of Christ three blocks from here." Michael raises his eyebrows, but says nothing. Sadie continues, "So you need to make a list. You are the Pastor/Parish Chairman, so you will need to help Michael replace me: Superintendent of Sunday

School, Bible School Director, Children's Choir Director, and oh, I'm scheduled to play the organ in March during Donna's vacation."

Mac asks annoyed, "What is your point Sadie?"

"Well, I will no longer be a parishioner and when people ask me why I left, and they will ask, I will tell them that you twisted my arm. Then people will be mad at you instead of Michael."

Michael's eyes shift to Mac who slams the pad of paper down on the table, "Never mind Sadie. Do whatever you want."

Sadie stands closing the laptop and smiling sweetly, "I'm so glad we have your blessing. It means so much to me," she saunters out of the room.

Mac turns to Michael, "You know you'll never win an argument with her."

Michael opens the door for him, "I have a feeling you're right."

Michael finds Sadie sitting on the couch who throws the pillow at him as he walks in.

"I told you, you opened the door for people to feel free to stick their nose into our private life."

Michael sits next to her, "Yes, yes you did. Although, I believe Mac would have said something either way."

"I'll go make lunch," she starts to get up but Michael pulls her back down.

"Don't bother. I believe I owe you a dinner out, but if you ask the waitress for separate checks, I will beat you with the pillow when we come home."

He pulls her up onto his lap to kiss and hug her. He is impressed with how she handled Mac. She has a wit and brassiness that he finds appealing.

Wednesday night Sadie can't stop thinking about the rift between Michael and his parents. Nervous that Michael may be angry with her, she decides to call his parents. She knows their names and the town they live in, so she dials 411.

"Hello, my name is Sadie Stevens. I met you at Michael's ordination. I wanted to talk to you or your husband."

"Well, my husband and daughter Carol are right here. I'll put you on speaker phone," Sophia tells her.

Sadie's pulse races. Her mouth dries up. She regrets the call and considers hanging up. "Well, I, uh, I'm close with your son. I thought I would, uh, call and invite you and his sister and brother again to his Christmas Eve service. I would be happy to make a nice dinner for us before church."

His mother answers in an icy voice, "That is nice, but we already have plans for Christmas Eve."

"I understand. This is none of my business, but I know that you aren't happy about Michael being a minister. I thought there are a few things you should know."

Sophia cuts Sadie off, "You're right. It's none of your business."

James is curious, "No wait. What do you think we should know?"

Nervous, Sadie takes a deep breath, "Well, uh, Michael is an amazing minister who leads wonderful worship services. His deep, warm voice is perfect for sermons, praying, and reading scriptures. He is charismatic. Our attendance on Sunday mornings is up. Two new families have already joined and two more are talking about joining since he has been here.

"Michael is full of compassion. He is very good at making calls at the hospital, nursing homes and to our shut-ins.

"Also, when Michael came, our committees were run sloppily, and our finances were a mess. I don't think we ever had a minister with a business degree before. He is reorganizing the committees and is teaching them how to run meetings correctly. He is instructing each committee to set specific goals and then create a plan for achieving them.

"Most of the people are happy, but there are several who are fighting him. Mac is the biggest pain in his side, but Michael isn't budging. He also has ideas for improvements. He is pushing to put a screen up in the sanctuary. He wants to put the entire service, hymns, readings, and graphics in a computer to be projected during services. Mac is against it, but Michael is not giving up.

"I was a bridesmaid at his first wedding ceremony. You should have seen him run the rehearsal. When he arrived the bride's five parents and step-parents were in a heated argument and the bride was crying. He stepped in and took control. He made all of them sit down and be quiet. He told them clearly how things were going to be run. The rest of the rehearsal was fun. His directions were clear, but he had everyone laughing.

"I'm sorry I keep going on. I just… I just thought you should know that as a minister, he is a natural. If you can't make it to Christmas Eve, then you really should come on a Sunday morning. You would be proud."

The line is quiet for a moment before Carol asks, "It sounds like you two are close. Did he ever get you to go out with him?"

"Yes, he pinned me to a wall until I agreed," she regrets the comment the minute she says it hitting herself in the head with the palm of her hand.

Sophia's tone is still cold, "Thank you for your phone call. Goodbye."

After the call, James cannot stop thinking about what Sadie told them. He loves Michael, but it had always bothered him that his mother had such control. He didn't like how his friends pushed him around. He hated that when the interviewer at Harvard asked him why he wanted to be a lawyer, his answer had been because his parents wanted him to be a lawyer. When his mother went to him with her mother's engagement ring suggesting that he should propose to Barbra, he proposed a week later.

Michael stood up to his parents and friends to go to seminary. Now Sadie is saying that he is in charge and not allowing people to push him around. James had never thought about a minister running meetings and worrying about finances. He has difficulty picturing his son stopping five arguing parents to take control and then spend the evening giving directions to a large group of people.

He liked Sadie when he had met her in June. Michael had always had girls swooning for him, especially Barbara. He never had to put much effort into getting a date. He liked the thought that Michael had to chase Sadie. He wondered if Sadie's comment about being pinned to a wall had been literal. James comes to a decision. They are going to Ambrose for Christmas Eve.

Thursday after school, Sadie begins supper for Michael and her. Michael arrives letting himself in with the keys she gave him. Leaning on the kitchen doorway he inquires, "Is there something you want to tell me?"

"Why? What do you know?" Sadie responds nervously.

"What should I know?" he counters.

"I called your parents yesterday?"

"Yes, imagine my surprise when my father called to tell me that he decided that they are coming for Christmas Eve and to tell Sadie thank you for offering to make dinner."

"Are you angry with me?" she grimaces.

"Not exactly, but why would you do that without talking to me?"

"I just thought it is sad that your parents haven't seen you preach and that you weren't going to be with them on Christmas Eve, so I decided to give it a try."

Sadie recounts her call for him so that he knows what had been said and even confesses the pinning to the wall comment which causes Michael to cringe. Michael isn't angry, but the whole thing feels strange that she did it behind his back. On the other hand, it feels sort of nice for someone to go to bat for him for a change.

Chapter XIII

As Christmas comes closer, Michael becomes uncomfortable that he doesn't have the money to buy the type of presents that he had been accustomed to buying and calls his family to admit the problem. They comfort him that it doesn't matter, but it still bothers him. Sadie suggests that he go to Carol for help. Sadie was raised buying different types of presents, but Carol would have a better idea of what would be acceptable.

Carol is happy to help him select items for his family, but Michael picks out Sadie's gifts on his own. He buys her the pearl earrings and bracelet that go with the necklace he bought her for her birthday, a CD of love songs, a light purple sweater, and an apple cookie jar that he knows she likes to match her dishes.

One night, as he looks over the presents he purchased and begins wrapping them, he thinks about how different it is to have to worry about a budget and not being able to just buy what he wants. His mind drifts back to his senior year of college, the week before his graduation.

Michael again sat in Rob's office discussing life as he had become accustomed. That day, Michael asked him, "What about the fact that I have so much money? Do I have to give it all away?"

"No, don't be silly. You are not becoming a priest and you don't have to take a vow of poverty. It just seems like ministers do because churches pay so little. If you don't mind my asking, about how much are we talking about?"

"Well, last year when I turned twenty-one, I received my trust fund with a million dollars," he answers honestly.

Rob sits up straight with his eyes wide and his mouth slightly opened, "Wow, I wasn't expecting you to say that." Rob stands and paces a little bit. "Now, what I said before is true. There is no reason for you to give it away, but you will have to think about the problems it could cause."

"Like what?"

"Congregations can be funny and fickle. They might not like it if you are that much better off than they are. Also, if they know you have it, they will probably expect you to fix all their problems. Instead of giving to the church and doing fund raisers, they may just expect you to fix the roof or build an addition to the building. They might push you until you lose all your money over a few years and they probably wouldn't even appreciate it. It could cause hard feelings for you and the church."

Michael leans back and thinks. Part of him wants to just be a minister and live like most ministers live, but it would be hard to give it all up. He wonders aloud, "What would I do with it. Should I donate it to charity or give it to a children's hospital or something?"

"If you do, I would try to be anonymous. People would carry on if they knew you gave that much away. You would probably end up on the national news with talk shows wanting to interview you."

Michael doesn't like the thought of that, "What should I do with it if I just want to lead a normal minister's life?"

"Where did you get the money? Did you earn it somehow?" Rob inquires.

"No, it's just family money. My dad owns his own company. He set up a trust fund for me and my sister and brother."

"If I were you, I would simply quietly give it back to them. Just explain that you have decided to live the life of a normal minister in our denomination."

Michael had feared telling his parents that he was giving up his birth right. He knew that they are not happy that he is going to seminary and now this would really make them angry and upset. He decided to wait and used his money to pay for his last year of college as well as pay for seminary. At least he could begin his ministry dept free.

Then, once seminary was over and he had completed his student pastorate, he went to his parents' house for dinner two weeks before his ordination. Carol and her boyfriend, Drew, were there as well as his brother Sean. Sean and Michael had a falling out a year earlier and his parents were upset that this ministry phase had not yet passed. The tension in the room was quite high and Michael knew that he was about to make it worse.

They ate together quietly with unimportant chit chat. Carol despises the fact that her family was falling apart. First, Michael was going away to seminary and then her brother's life blew up with her parents and Michael last year. Their family had once been close and full of love instead of this tension.

Finally, Michael decided to bite the bullet, "Um, I was wondering if you are planning to come to my ordination."

"Of course we are." Carol assured him and then looked at her parents, "Aren't we?"

Her parents nod. Sophia comments, "I am surprised that it is going to be in an auditorium in that old resort town. I would think it would be in a cathedral or at least a big church."

"Our conference meets in that town every year. It's special to many ministers and the auditorium holds a lot of people."

"Do you want me there?" Sean asked not looking up.

Michael looked at his brother for a silent moment, "Yes, I want you there. Would you please come?"

"I guess so," Sean answered unenthusiastically.

Once everyone, but Drew, who would out of town on business, promised to be there, Michael took another deep breath, "There is one more thing. Most ministers in practically every denomination are not wealthy. I want to be a normal minister. I need to live like a normal minister."

"What are you saying?" his mother leans forward.

"I'm going to turn over my trust fund back to you," he waits for their reaction.

His father slams his fist on the table causing Michael to flinch and his family to jump, "Are you serious?! You are giving up everything I worked so hard to provide for my family?! Why do you hate me? Why would you turn your back on your family?!"

Michael's temper matches his father's, "I am not turning my back on our family! I don't hate you! Our family isn't just about money is it? Can't I be part of this family even if I don't have money?! I want you to see this from my point of view. I'm just trying to do what is best for my ministry. That doesn't mean I don't love my family!"

Sophia joins in, "I don't understand why you are doing this. I don't understand any of this. Why is it you want to be a minister? Of all the careers in the world, why would you choose that one? You were never overly religious when you were growing up. You were such a normal child and athletic. Where did all of this come from?"

Michael calms down leaning forward on the table, "It's kind of hard to explain. It's a calling. I feel it. I always liked going to church and grandma always took us to that Bible School which I always enjoyed. I felt an urge to go to church when I was in college. The more I went the more I wanted to go. I spent so much time going to the minister there asking questions. When I was in that sanctuary, I just knew that was what I was supposed to do. I tried to ignore it, but the feeling was so strong. By the time I went to seminary, I never had any doubts. This is what I am supposed to do; I just know it."

"I think it was that minister," James accuses. "He talked you into this. You just said that you went to him all of the time. I knew the day you disappeared, just to find out that that minister had taken you into his home, that he was interested in you. This is all of his fault."

Michael leaned back in his chair exhaling, "No Dad, Rev. Foreman didn't brain wash me. He purposely never mentioned my becoming a minister. He waited for me to bring it up. I think he knew, but he waited for me to find my own way."

"Bullshit," his father leaned back.

Two days before Christmas Sadie goes to the grocery store to buy needed supplies for dinner, but has no idea what to make for someone used to eating at a country club. She usually made a jell-o salad, but figures it is too low class. She settles on a spiral ham, mashed potatoes, sweet potatoes, broccoli casserole, a seven layer salad, fruit cups, and spiral macaroni with crab meat, shrimp, and green peppers in Italian dressing. Just for her, she makes her family's holiday treat, pickled eggs. Plus, she has cookies she made with her friends.

Sadie unloads her groceries at the parsonage planning to do all the cooking there, so she packs up serving bowls and kitchen supplies from her apartment to use. Michael helps her unload everything from her car.

The day before Christmas Eve, Sadie cleans Michael's house with his help and starts making food that she can make ahead of time. On Christmas Eve day, Sadie spends the day preparing the rest of the food while Michael visits all the church's shut-ins to bring them Communion. His family is expected at four. He promises to be home between two-thirty or three.

3:45, his family including Sean and Drew, arrive with Michael nowhere in sight. Sadie takes their coats and invites them into the living room. She pours drinks, sets out cheese and crackers and Christmas cookies.

The phone rings. Sadie informs Michael that his family already arrived. Michael apologizes promising to be there in twenty minutes. Sadie promises to kill him later.

"That was Michael. He's sorry. He said he'll be here in about twenty minutes."

Sophia questions her, "Where did you say he is? I don't understand what a shut-in is."

"A shut-in is a person who is too sick to come to church, usually elderly people. Michael left at 10:30 this morning to visit the shut-ins who are members and take them Communion. It sounds like they got to him," Sadie explains.

"What do you mean, they got to him?" James inquires.

"For some of them, Michael is their only Christmas visitor. They're lonely. He kept staying longer than he meant to."

"Are you upset with him for being late?" Carol asks.

"No, you kind of know going in with a minister that he has other things to do on the holidays as well as spending time with the family. Holidays are busy times for pastors. The trick is to be available when he is."

James requests that Sadie tells them more about what Michael does, so Sadie shares several more stories. She tells them about him waiting with Betty for Ed to die and taking care of her afterwards. She tells them what Alice Mitchell had told her about little Kelly going to him for help and how he kept them from losing their apartment. She explains that Mac is used to being in charge of the business concerns in the church and now that Michael is taking control, Mac is fighting him on every little decision tooth and nail.

Finally, Michael comes home. His family is surprised to see him in a clerical shirt with his black suit carrying his Bible and Communion kit. For the first time, he looks like a minister to them. As he visits with them, Sadie begins serving dinner.

"Excuse me," Sadie interrupts, "Michael, will you help me take the ham out of the oven. It's heavy."

Michael immediately follows her into the kitchen to help her serve. It bothers Sophia to watch him work in the kitchen from the dining room. She wanted so much for him. The stories Sadie shared bothers her that he would work so hard for so little. Michael sees his mom glance up at the fiber optic wreathe. He knows that she thinks it is tacky but he thinks that it is pretty.

Sean laughs, "What kind of table and chairs is this?"

Michael smiles, "I didn't buy a dining room set yet, so some guys from the church put a table and chairs from the fellowship hall in here. It works. Sadie covered it up with table cloths."

As the food is passed around, Sophia keeps making little comments. She thought that purple eggs would be more for Easter. Sadie explains the pickled eggs are a personal family tradition at every holiday. Sophia puts her nose up at the broccoli casserole, but when she carries on that Sadie put marshmallows on the sweet potatoes, Michael snaps.

Michael never speaks up to his mom always having done whatever he was told. Now, listening to her making rude comments about Sadie's food angers him. Sadie fretted over the menu, did the shopping, and spent hours preparing the food.

He surprises his family, "Mom, stop being rude. Sadie didn't call a caterer. She did all the work herself. This food may be different to you, but it is delicious."

Sadie feels embarrassed, but is happy Michael spoke up for her. Carol and Sean help by chatting about people Michael knows and asking about Michael and Sadie. They agree with their brother that the food is delicious. Drew especially likes the pickled eggs because his grandma had always made them as well.

James remains quiet. His thoughts are full of Sadie's stories of Michael caring for people and working hard. Michael had helped Sadie in the kitchen as if he had always helped around a house. However, he had been the most impressed that he would speak up to his mother to defend his new girlfriend.

Michael shares stories from his long day, "This one lady, Helen, who has been a widow for over twenty years and her children live out of state, lives in this sad little house. She has become so old and so ill that she can barely take care of herself anymore. I've never seen a house so cluttered and a thick film of dust lies on everything. It smells like…well, we're eating so I'll just go with it smells bad.

"She seems to be so lonely. She can't even stand up straight, but she got up and painfully limped out of the room. She returned with a plate of homemade cookies and sets them down in front of me. Looking around that house, I did not want to put one of those things in my mouth, but I could tell that she was waiting for me to eat one. I forced myself to eat a couple, but it wasn't easy.

"I didn't want to get her all worked up on Christmas Eve, but I swear that next month I'm going back to try to talk her into a nursing home. There would be people around to talk to, to feed her, and to clean. I bet she would feel healthier if she was cared for. I wonder what she has to eat for her Christmas dinner."

His family has no idea how to respond as he seems to stare off for a minute, but Sadie knows exactly what to say, "Well, we have more here than we can eat. When I clean up, I can make a few containers for her and we can drop them off on our way to my parents' house tomorrow."

"That's a great idea. Thanks," Michael leans over giving her a kiss on her cheek.

Carol thinks to herself that a minister needs a special type of woman who understands all of this and helps with his mission. Barbara would have only been grossed out by the story, not compassionate and helpful.

Sophia misses the point to the whole exchange, "Oh, so you're going with Sadie tomorrow to her parents?"

"Yes, luckily it is easy for me. I've known her dad for over a year longer than I've known Sadie. I've always liked him. He is a wonderful minister. I couldn't have asked for a better mentor," he compliments.

Dinner had been going well until Sophia starts in on Sadie again,

"Sadie, I know from Thanksgiving with Michael that you refused to date him because you didn't want to end up with a minister. He said you didn't want to move around."

"Mother, I didn't tell you that. How do you know?" Michael demands.

"I heard you tell Carol in the library," she turns back to Sadie, "But now you are dating him. What changed?"

Sadie answers, "I decided that he's worth it." Michael smiles. Sadie continues, "Besides, Michael would not be ignored. Truthfully, we have basically been dating since June."

Michael adds, "At Erieton, we went out to eat and then for a long walk that Wednesday. She has not been able to shake me since, not that she hasn't tried."

Carol giggles, "I knew at your ordination that you were interested in her when you chased after her to talk her into coming to your party."

James asks, "Was your comment about being pinned to a wall a literal one?"

Embarrassed, Sadie looks at Michael. Michael answers for her, "Yes, I pinned her to a wall until she admitted she's in love with me."

As they visit, Michael tells about coming home from a meeting and finding the house decorated and how Sadie and her friends had bought all the decorations and put them up for him. Carol thinks that sounds very romantic.

Dinner ends on a pleasant note. Sadie, Michael, Carol, and Sean put the food away and stack the dishes. Michael and Sadie leave for church early leaving his family in the parsonage. His family discusses how close Michael and Sadie already seem to be. Everyone seems to like her except for Sophia. She thinks that the fact that Sadie bought the decorations explains the tacky wreath in the dining room. She had been hoping that in a year or two Michael would quit and come back home. Now, she worries that with Sadie helping and encouraging him like this, Michael won't come to his senses and quit as soon as she had hoped.

As Sophia waits for church to begin, she cannot understand why if Michael had to be a minister, he would choose to serve such a small, plain church. The church she raised him in is so much more beautiful and much bigger. His family finds it odd to see Michael enter wearing his black robe and white and gold stole to lead the service. He follows the choir which Sadie is in, up the aisle.

The choir only has nine people, but they sound beautiful. Carol thinks Sadie is right about Michael's voice being conducive to preaching and reading scripture. Michael seems larger than life to her. Michael's sermon impresses Sean who finds it insightful and interesting. How many boring sermons had he sat through growing up? The family feels awkward when Michael points out that his family is here to the congregation and the people stare.

Communion is usually passed out on special trays to the congregation in their seats on the first Sundays of the month, but for the holiday, Communion is served by intinction. The congregation comes forward where Michael tears a piece of bread and hands it to them and then they dip it in the wine which Eloise Crabtree, a church lay leader, is holding. Sadie, Dorothy, and Laurie from the choir and Donna, the organist, receive Communion first. They then softly sing beautiful Christmas music as the rest of the congregation is served.

It feels special to Michael to serve his family. They seem moved as well as they each smile back at him as he says, "The Body of Christ."

Aidan, Colleen, Steve, and Brenda also come through the line.

At the end of the service, the lights are turned off. Sadie sings "O Holy Night" while Michael uses a candle to take the flame from the Pascal candle and begins spreading it to the congregation's candles. Once all the candles have been lit, the congregation sings, "Silent Night". Sadie joins Michael who lights her candle. She remains in the front with him as they sing. The two look beautiful together by candlelight wearing their robes.

Carol whispers to her parents, "She is perfect for him at home and at church."

James and Sean agree, but Sophia still wishes he worked as a lawyer or business man with Barbara at his side. She still wants Michael to make up with and marry Barbara.

After church, they wait for Michael to finish greeting people. Several people hand him envelopes. When he joins his family and Sadie, he asks Sadie why people gave him envelopes. She explains that they are his Christmas bonus. Some people give financial gifts to their minister.

Michael introduces his new friends, Aidan, Colleen, Steve, and Brenda to his family before they leave.

Carol and Sean express how impressed they are. While it seems odd to see him in the role of minister, he definitely knows what he is doing.

His father shakes his hand, "Sadie was right. She said if I came to see you preach I would be proud."

Stunned, Michael is unable to respond. As they walk to the car, Michael places his arm around Sadie's shoulders and gives her a squeeze.

As they say their goodbyes and thank you, Sophia asks Michael,

"Do you have a church service on New Year's Eve?"

"No."

"Will you come to the New Year's Eve party at the country club?"

To Sophia's annoyance, Michael turns to Sadie, "What do you think, Sadie? Do you want to go?"

Sadie wants to say no because she wants to go to Duffy's with her friends, but she exclaims, "That sounds like fun."

After they leave, Sadie returns to the parsonage to finish the dishes. Michael helps. When they finish, Michael wraps his arms around her, "Thank you for all you did today. You make everything nice. Stay with me tonight."

Sadie follows him up to his room for the night.

Christmas morning, they sit on the couch enjoying the tree. Michael thinks Sadie looks cute wearing one of his t-shirts as a nightgown. He can almost picture children playing under the tree.

"We should have children. Wouldn't it be fun to watch our children opening presents under that tree?"

"I don't think it's a good idea for a minister to knock up an elementary teacher," she teases.

Michael hangs his head, and then wraps his arms around her, "I'm not talking about knocking you up. Marry me." Michael proposes spontaneously surprising himself almost as much as her.

"What?"

"Marry me."

Sadie feels as if the wind is knocked out of her, "We've only dated for a month."

"Baloney, we have been dating since June. Marry me."

"Don't ask me. It's too soon."

"You already said that you choose me. You already decided that you are willing to move with me. You had to decide that you are willing to marry me before you were willing to date me. So, marry me Sadie. Don't say no."

Sadie sits quietly thinking for a few moments, "Okay, I won't say no, how about, not yet."

Michael settles for this response. They return to bed to enjoy each other before they need to get ready to leave to go see her family.

Chapter XIV

The day of the New Year's Eve Party, Sadie panics, as she meets Brenda, Colleen, and Stephanie that morning to help prepare the bar for their party. She carries on about not belonging at a country club and wanting to stay at Duffy's for New Year's Eve.

"I'm going to look like some kind of hick. I don't have a dress nice enough. Michael has a tux. His mother already hates me. I just don't think I can go. I would much rather stay here tonight."

On an impulse, Sadie grabs the phone, "Good morning, Michael. I have some bad news. I woke up with a severe headache and I'm nauseated. I don't think I can go tonight. I'm so sorry, but I think I'm just going to stay in bed all day. You go ahead without me and have a good time."

"So you are home sick in bed?" he checks.

"Yes."

"Did you think this call through, because according to my caller ID, you're at the bar?"

"Oh…in that case, I feel much better. I'll be ready by four," she hangs up on him.

Brenda shakes her head, "What the hell is the matter with you?"

Stephanie offers to do her hair and make-up. Colleen offers her a choice of two dresses that she thinks will be appropriate. Brenda offers her a diamond necklace, earrings, and bracelet set.

Brenda spots Michael through the window, "Here he comes."

Sadie ducks behind the bar, but Michael walks in and sits on a stool knocking on the bar, "I saw you behind there."

Sadie stands up, "Hi Honey, I'm sorry."

"For what, breaking our date, lying to me, hanging up on me, or hiding from me?"

"All the above. I had a problem, but the girls solved everything, so I'll see you later."

Sadie heads for the office, but before she opens the door, Michael catches her elbow and leads her to a booth in a far corner. He slides in the seat beside her. Sadie explains that she didn't think she had anything to wear, but her friends are planning to loan her everything she needs. Michael claims that he has seen her wear a lot of beautiful dresses, but Sadie insists none are good enough for a country club.

Michael knows that there is more to this. Sadie finally admits to being scared that she will embarrass him, and that his friends won't think she is good enough for him. She tells him that she woke up with a feeling of dread.

Michael shakes his head, "How can anyone not like you?"

Sadie replies, "Ask your mother. To her, I'm the poor trash who put marshmallows in the sweet potatoes."

"Stop it," Michael rolls his eyes, "It's a party with food and dancing. You'll love it. I want you to meet Graham and Colby. I don't remember not being friends with them. I'm friends with your friends and I want you to be friends with my friends."

"Easy for you to say. Besides, my friends liked you so much that they took your side. I told them I wouldn't date you, so they invited you everywhere I went."

Michael places his arm around her, "And mine will like you."

He starts kissing her as Steve walks by and orders, "No sex in the booth."

Sadie and Michael stay at the bar for a couple hours to help Steve and Brenda prepare for their party. Then the girls hurry home to pick up what Sadie needs while she goes home to shower.

Michael arrives at her apartment to oohs and awes from their friends. They make it clear that he is hot in a tux. Sadie enters the room with the appearance of sophistication wearing a simple little black dress highlighted with Colleen's diamond jewelry. Stephanie has left Sadie's hair down, but made it smooth and silky with it brushed toward her face instead of back like usual.

"You are beautiful."

Stephanie instructs him, "No running your hands through her hair or pulling at her dress until after she meets your friends and family."

Sadie spins, "What do you think? This is Colleen's dress, Brenda's diamond jewelry, and Stephanie's fur coat, and Steph did my hair and make-up."

"Perfect," Michael appraises her, "but whose underwear?"

"What underwear?"

Grinning, Michael leans in for a hug and kiss, but Stephanie steps between them, "I said no messing her up until after she meets the friends and family."

Despite his protest, Colleen takes several pictures before they leave as if they are off to the prom. The girls actually pose them for a few really good shots. Sadie plans to choose one of the pictures to enlarge for a frame.

"Okay, okay, enough pictures. It's time to go," Michael takes Sadie's hand.

Sadie wishes Brenda well, "Good luck tonight. I hope you have even more people than you did on Halloween."

"Thanks. Hey Michael, how about you pray for a good attendance?" Brenda requests.

Michael cocks his eyebrow, "You want me to pray that a lot of people go out to a bar tonight to drink?"

"Yes?" Brenda grins ear to ear.

"Sure, why not?" Michael agrees with a chuckle.

Sadie pulls on Stephanie's coat, "Okay, here we go. Wish me luck."

Michael smacks his hand on his forehead, "No, that is not the proper response to our leaving. They should say something like have fun. You don't need luck. It's just a party. Would you relax?"

Her friends wave calling both, "Have fun. Good luck."

Sadie's heart pounds as they arrive at the party which took a little over two hours to drive. She stares up at the country club as Michael gives his keys to the valet. The large white building is both beautiful and intimidating. As they walk up to the front Michael whispers in her ear to relax. Michael checks their coats and they walk up a staircase to the grand ballroom. The crystal chandeliers sparkle and everyone looks exquisite. Sadie is glad she borrowed this dress so that she at least looks the part.

Carol, Drew, and Sean greet them with kisses and hugs. Sadie likes his younger brother and older sister. They are friendly and seem to like her. Both rave that Sadie looks gorgeous. Carol points out the friends that Michael is anxious to see.

Michael and Sadie walk across the room to two tall, handsome, dignified men. Seeing Michael walking toward them, they call, "Mikey!"

Michael hugs each one with comments about how long it has been and questions of how have you been.

Michael reaches back for Sadie, "I'd like you to meet Sadie Stevens, my girlfriend. Sadie, these are my closest friends, Colby, and Graham."

Colby does not hide his shock that Michael has a girlfriend. Graham remembers her, "Sadie, yes I met you at Mike's ordination. Carol insisted that Mike was interested in you. I guess she was right."

They sit at a round table to chat. Colby's stares make Sadie a little uncomfortable. Sophia and James stop to greet the couple and his friends. Sophia tells Sadie that she looks wonderful as if surprised and then leave the couple to stay with his friends.

Another old friend of his mother's stops at the table. Michael stands to hug her and to talk for a minute. She tells him that she heard rumors that he is a minister, but doesn't believe it. He assures her it is true and she laughs as if the fact is funny.

Before he sits back down, a woman's voice calls, "Mikey!" Barbara walks up, embracing him, "I'm so glad you came. I've been wanting to see you again."

Michael pulls out of her arms and touches Sadie's back. Sadie stands to be introduced. "Barbara, this is my girlfriend, Sadie Stevens. Sadie, this is Barbara Stark."

Both women appear equally startled. Barbara didn't know Michael has a girlfriend and Sadie didn't know that his ex-fiancé would be here. They politely shake hands and smile at one another. To Sadie's surprise, Barbara takes a seat beside Colby across the table from them.

Sadie quickly learns that Barbara is Colby's sister and has known Michael her whole life. Sadie thinks that Barbara is perfectly beautiful with perfect hair, perfect skin, perfect figure, and perfect style.

The fanciest dinner Sadie has ever seen is served. She doesn't even know what all the food that is served is and wonders what Michael thinks about the meatloaf style dinners she prepares for him. Sadie feels nervous and out of place. The old friends reminisce over dinner referring to Michael and Barbara as Mikey and Barbie. Sadie learns that 'Barbie' had a crush on 'Mikey' for most of her life. She also learns that for two years in high school, they had been tennis partners. Graham shares the story of how the crafty 'Barbie' tricked 'Mikey' into taking her to the prom, but the scheme worked and they began to date.

Sophia watches the table from across the room. She still doesn't think that Michael and Sadie are right together and fears that Sadie is keeping Michael from quitting the ministry and from coming home where he belongs. Sophia believes he belongs with Barbara. Barbara's mother, Victoria, had been Sophia's best friend since high school. She is glad that Barbara is sitting with him. Maybe Michael will compare the two and realize that he is here with the wrong woman.

Sophia remembers how Michael had always run to her when he was little. She loved cuddling him in her arms. In middle school and high school, she went to all his sporting events. After he accomplished anything, he would always look at her. They had always been so close. She wishes she could run over and hold her son now.

These past several years had been hard for her. She doesn't like feeling a distance between them. She doesn't like him doing without so much. She doesn't like that he chose to serve a small poor church, and she doesn't like that he is dating Sadie.

Over dessert, Michael's friends tell Sadie that Barbie is a graphic designer for an advertising agency. They inquire as to what Sadie does. On hearing that she teaches first grade, his friends comment that is so cute in what Sadie finds to be a belittling way. Graham informs the group that Sadie is a minister's kid to which Colby and Barbara stare at her as if she is strange. Sadie also notices that no one seems the least bit interested in Michael's ministry and that Michael doesn't even seem to try to talk about it.

The group returns to stories of Mikey and Barbie playing tennis doubles. They tell the story of the pair winning the big tournament when Mikey had swept Barbie up perching her on his shoulder with the photographers going crazy. Apparently the picture still hangs in the pro-shop if Sadie wants to see it. Sadie thinks to herself, "Why the hell would I want to see that?"

Sadie does not like the way Barbara keeps looking longingly at Michael or the appraising scans she gives Sadie. Sadie wishes that Michael had warned her that they would probably see his ex or that his ex shares a life-long history with him. He had led Sadie to believe that it had been just a three year relationship. She also doesn't like the way his friends seem to run over him and he does not defend himself or her. She doesn't know why he just sits there allowing them to talk about his old relationship in front of her. Michael seems different here than he does in Ambrose.

Just when Sadie doesn't think she can bare sitting there one more minute, Sean walks by the table saying hi. Sadie sits up straight, "Oh Sean," she turns to Michael, "Sean wants to talk to me about something. I'll be right back."

As Sadie stands, Sean confirms without batting an eye, "Yes I do.

You don't mind if I borrow your girlfriend for a moment, do you?"

Michael seems skeptical, but agrees that it is fine. Sean escorts Sadie to a small table for two by the windows just a few tables away from Michael's. He holds her chair for her and takes his place across from her.

"Now," he smiles at her, "What do I want to talk to you about?"

"I just thought you wouldn't mind giving me a break from Mikey and Barbie stories. It might embarrass Michael if I puke on the table."

Sean laughs loudly. Michael glances over at the two. Sadie thanks him for playing along and not embarrassing her. Sean is happy to do it. Then Sadie inquires if he has a date. Sean becomes serious.

"Michael never told you about me, did he?"

"He never told me what about you?" she asks.

He sighs, "I'm gay."

"Huh, no, I'm sorry. He didn't tell me," she admits.

"Figures. If you feel uncomfortable and want to go back, I understand," he assures her.

"Uncomfortable? No, I'm not uncomfortable," she assures him.

"You don't care?"

"No, it doesn't bother me. Sitting over there is uncomfortable," she says pointing at Michael's table. Sean laughs again.

"You know, Michael isn't okay with it. He thinks I'm going to hell. I guess it's in the Bible that it's a sin. We haven't been very close anymore since I came out two years ago. My parents and Michael were not nice about me coming out although I think Michael suspected."

"I'm so sorry to hear that. I'm also a little disappointed to hear that," she remarks.

"Michael feels strongly about church law."

"Well, you should ask Michael how the church law, especially the Bishop, would feel about a pastor having premarital sex with a parishioner in the parsonage." Sadie alliterates.

Sean laughs loudly again attracting Michael's entire table's attention. Michael wonders what is going on with those two.

"I can't believe you are so okay with it," Sean marvels.

"I can't explain why in Corinthians it clearly states that it is a sin. I never heard a gay man say that he decided to be gay. They always say that they discovered or realized. If some men are born gay, then it seems that God created them that way, so who am I to judge? Who is Michael to judge his own brother?

"Besides, I personally think that more than fifty percent of men are scum. I'm not all that crazy about the heterosexuals. So many men hurt women and children or think that they are superior to women. So many men insult each other by calling them girly, as if being a girl is bad.

"Don't get me wrong. I'm attracted to Michael and he is a manly man, but he is also gentle and caring. He takes care of people in his church and he listened when a little girl came to him for help. He didn't have to stay with that old woman when her husband was dying. He just saw that she was alone and chose to stay to help her. So many men blow off women and children.

"Well, you can relax with me. I'll never judge you," she promises.

Sean takes Sadie's hand and kisses it. Michael, who has been keeping an eye on them, sees Sean kiss her hand. Graham notices it too, "Your brother definitely likes Sadie."

Michael smiles, "It's hard not to like Sadie."

Barbara grimaces.

"Would you like to get a drink at the bar?" Sean offers.

"I probably should go back to Michael," she glances over at the table where Barbara is staring at Michael, "but a drink couldn't hurt."

The two walk back to the bar. On the way, Sean tells her that he has a partner named Jeremy, but Jeremy isn't welcomed at these family functions. He hopes one day he can bring him, but that day has definitely not yet arrived. The only family member who is accepting of Sean and Jeremy is his sister, Carol.

They each get a drink and stand next to a tall table meant for standing rather than sitting. Michael joins them. Sadie apologizes for being away so long promising that she was about to come back, but Sean offered her a drink which sounded good.

Michael turns to Sean, "So, what did you need to talk to Sadie about?"

Sean looks at Sadie not sure what to say. Sadie answers for him, "Actually, I lied. Sean figured that I had my reasons, so he backed me up."

Michael points out that is her second lie to him that day so she explains that she needed a break from the Mikey and Barbie stories. She also points out that he could have warned her that they would probably run into his ex-fiancé. Michael agrees and goes to get himself a drink.

Graham joins Sadie and Sean by their table, "I'm sorry if we made you uncomfortable talking so much about Mike and Barbie. We just don't have too many memories of Mike that don't include her. Even after they broke off the engagement, they still went out on dates over the summer breaks. Why, just last New Year's Eve, we all went skiing together. Mike was supposed to room with me, but the last night, he never made it back to our room."

"Graham!" Sean interrupts, "What is wrong with you?"

"She can't be jealous. That all happened before he met her," he defends himself.

Michael returns with his drink. Graham comments that looks like a good idea and leaves to get himself a drink.

Sadie moves close to Michael whispering, "I thought you said Barbara broke up with you almost four years ago."

"That's right," Michael confirms.

"According to Graham, you were still sleeping with her last year at this time." Sadie accuses.

Michael's eyes widen, "Graham just walked over here and told you that?"

"Yes. That story was part of his apology for making me feel uncomfortable here," she informs.

Shocked, Michael looks at Sean who simply nods. Michael begins to try to explain, but Sadie interrupts, "Let's just postpone this discussion for a later time. I mean, it was before you met me, and doesn't really matter now, I guess. I don't want to make a scene. Don't worry. I'm fine."

Michael is relieved and impressed that Sadie is calm and sensible. He feels disappointed that his friends are treating her so badly.

Barbara and Colby join them with their drinks, who also apologize to Sadie if they had made her uncomfortable. Barbara keeps the conversation current asking about Michael's work and telling about her job. When she asks how long they have been dating, Sadie appreciates that Michael answers since June.

The conversation goes well until Barbie asks Sean if he has been to the parsonage to which Sean replies that he has.

Barbie laughs, "What a bachelor's pad. What is with that horrible table in the dining room?"

Michael closes his eyes as Sadie stiffens, "You were in the parsonage? When were you in the parsonage?"

Barbara makes a show of thinking, "Oh, it was the first week in November. Michael called me up on a Tuesday and I drove out the next day. He didn't mention you."

"We were broke up that week," Sadie states coldly staring at Michael.

"Oh, that explains it. That explains a lot."

Michael stands there wishing the floor would open up and swallow him. Anger flashes through Sadie, but she attempts to hide her feelings. She doesn't know if she wants to throw her drink at Mikey or at Barbie.

Sean rescues her, "How about a dance?"

Sadie gratefully takes his hand and leaves Michael with his 'Barbie'. Michael thinks about asking Sadie to dance at the wedding to get her away from Troy. Now, his brother just asked her to dance to get her away from him. Barbara asks him if he wants to dance, but Michael declines leaving the table. He watches them dance to an up tempo song. When the dance ends, he takes Sadie by the hand leading her to an empty hallway.

"I didn't cheat on you," Michael defends himself; "She came after you made it clear that you didn't want to be with me."

"I'm not accusing you of cheating," she shoots back, "You didn't tell me the whole truth. You said that you dated for three years and then she dumped you almost four years ago. You left out that you knew her your whole life and that she is your best friend's sister. You left out that she had a crush on you most of her life. You left out the years of being

190

tennis partners. You never mentioned that after you broke up, you continued to date and sleep with her over the summers and holidays. You also left out that she is clearly not over you. I don't like knowing that if I break up with you, there is a beautiful, sophisticated woman waiting in the wings!"

Michael wants desperately to defend himself, but can't think of a single argument to counter what she said. All he can think of to say is "Sorry."

Sadie turns on her heels and walks back to the bar. She quickly decides that she needs her wits about her to survive this night and orders a cola. Michael follows her and they stand together, not saying a word. Colby approaches Michael to request if he could talk to him in private. Michael says this isn't a good time, but Sadie states it is fine with her. She doesn't need him.

Sadie goes back to Sean so Michael follows Colby. Sean checks if she is okay. Sadie asks where the ladies' room is, so Sean shows her the way. The restrooms are up a flight of stairs on a little balcony overlooking the party. The end of the balcony opens overlooking the lobby. Sadie looks out at the lobby in time to see Colby leave Michael with Barbara...

Michael follows Colby out to the lobby, where Barbara is waiting. Colby leaves the two alone.

Michael rolls his eyes, "This isn't a good time. What do you want?"

Barbara starts, "I didn't know you are dating. I want to know how serious you are about her."

"I want to marry her, but she says it is too soon to talk about that," he states bluntly.

Barbara is stunned. Her gaze lifts to the balcony where she notices

Sadie watching them and moves around so that Michael turns his back to Sadie as she declares, "I miss you, but I wish you well."

Barbara throws her arms around him and he returns the hug for only a moment...

Sadie sees Barbara look at her and purposefully move so Michael wouldn't notice her. As Sean joins her to see what she is watching, Barbara throws herself on Michael who returns the hug. Sadie leaves, quickly descending the stairs with Sean close behind her.

Sadie runs into Sophia who stops her to chat, "Deana, this is Michael's date this evening, Sadie." Sadie notices that she called her a date for this evening instead of girlfriend as if this she is a casual date.

Sophia compliments her dress and begins questioning her about the designer or where she purchased it. Sadie, who doesn't know the answers, finally admits that it is borrowed.

Sophia responds, "That explains it."

After some more uncomfortable small talk, Sophia coos, "I am so glad Michael found you." Sadie smiles until Sophia continues, "I think it is wonderful that he found someone who knows so much about church life. He says that you help him with his ministry. I'm also glad that he found someone to cook for him. My boy is helpless in the kitchen. Why, I bet you even do his laundry."

This comment takes Sadie by surprise. The expression on her face confirms the fact for Sophia who laughs with her friend. Sadie wants to run away. Sean is uncomfortable and worries about Sadie not sure how to help.

Sophia continues, "I worried so much about him when he lost the love of his life, but now that he lives the way he does, I'm glad he found someone to help him, sort of a helpmate."

"Mom!" Sean interrupts disgusted.

Sadie gives a small smile, "Thank you, if you'll excuse me, please."

Sadie walks away quickly with Sean again chasing her. Michael catches up to her reaching for her, "There you are. I've been looking for you."

"Don't touch me," Sadie snaps.

"What's wrong now?" Michael snaps back.

"I'm going to the ladies' room," Sadie turns to Sean, "I don't know if it will make him feel any better, but tell Jeremy they don't treat heterosexual dates much better."

"What?" Michael asks startled by her comment.

Sadie leaves without looking at him. Michael starts to go after her, but Sean grabs his arm pulling him to the side of the room where he fills Michael in on his mother's conversation and then informs him that he and Sadie saw Michael and Barbara hugging in the lobby.

Michael covers his face with his hands feeling awful. How could he have allowed this to happen to her? Somehow she knew when she woke up dreading tonight. He wishes that he had just taken her to Duffy's. After trying for five months to get her to trust him and let her guard down, he blew it in one night. He asks Sean to find Carol and meet him at the ladies' room.

Michael waits by the restroom door for Sadie to come out. Carol runs up the stairs. Sean had briefly filled her in on Sadie's evening, so she smacks Michael across the back of the head as she passes him disappearing into the restroom for a short time, but returning alone.

"Are you sure she's not in there?" Michael asks.

"How big do you think it is in there?" Carol counters. "If I were her, I'd go to the lobby to look for a place away from everyone."

The three run down the steps and toward the lobby. Graham, Colby, and Barbara watch the three running around knowing that a fight had definitely started. Sadie is obviously missing and Michael appears upset.

A host stops Michael, "Mr. Donnelly, I was just coming to find you. A young lady left this for you."

Michael takes the paper which is folded in half with Michael Donnelly written in Sadie's neat first grade teacher printing. He unfolds the note which reads, "Just so you know, I left."

"How?" he thinks. He has the valet's ticket and they are two hours from home. She wouldn't leave without Stephanie's coat and he has the coat check ticket.

"Come on," Michael heads to the coat check.

He hands the teenager Sadie's ticket at which she glances at the number becoming nervous, "A lady already took this coat."

Michael runs his hand through his hair, "How? She didn't have the ticket."

"She talked me into it. She promised me that you wouldn't report me."

"I won't, if you tell me what she said," he bargains.

"Are you her idiot boyfriend?" the girl chirps.

Michael hangs his head as Sean and Carol answer in unison, "Yes."

The check girl giggles, "She said she doesn't belong here; that she is just a school teacher in a borrowed dress."

Michael attempts to hide his frustration, "Did she say where she was going?"

"She asked how to get a taxi. I told her to go ask the valet."

"Thanks," Michael runs outside into the cold, down the walk to the valet parking. They tell him that the taxi has been called, but has not yet arrived. They told Sadie to wait in the lobby. Michael walks back to the entrance where his siblings are waiting to inform them she is still here, but he doesn't know where to look.

"There's the taxi," Sean points out.

Michael walks back outside. As he heads for the taxi, he spots Sadie who had waited outside in the bitter cold down by the gazebo. He runs to head her off. Stepping in front of her, he takes her by the shoulders.

She looks away, "Just let me go."

"No. If you want to go home, I'll take you. That taxi isn't going to drive you all the way home."

Sadie shoves him on the chest, "I know. I'm not stupid."

"Let me take you home. We need to talk."

She looks up at him. She has been crying and her mascara is a mess. Michael feels horrible. He pulls her into his arms holding her tightly and laying his cheek on her head. "Oh Sadie, I'm so sorry. Wait here."

Michael gives the cab driver some money and tells him his services aren't needed after all. Michael attempts to take Sadie's hand, but she pulls it away.

"Come on. I need to get my coat and tell Sean and Carol we're leaving," he coaxes.

Sadie doesn't want to be seen, but he convinces her to wait by the door out of the wind. When they come close to the door Sean and Carol come out to meet them.

Carol reaches for Sadie, "Are you okay?" She sees Sadie's make-up is a mess. "Oh you poor dear, come with me. I'll fix you up."

She smacks Michael across the back of the head again and pulls Sadie through the lobby to a restroom away from the party. Carol opens her purse which contains a baggy with disposable cloths that when dampened and rubbed soap up. Sadie washes her face. They both pull out make-up and Carol goes to work on her face.

While she works, Carol comforts her lovingly, "I want to tell you something. My mother and Barbara's mother have been best friends since high school. My mom is the one who wants Michael to be with Barbara.

"At Thanksgiving, I found Michael sitting on a window seat in the library staring out the window and we had a heart to heart talk. He told me that while he had loved Barbara, he had never been in love with her. He didn't think about her much when she wasn't around. He took it for granted he would see her whenever. He said he was in love for the first time with you. You are his last thought at night and his first thought in the morning. He thinks about you all the time.

"When Barbara broke up with him, she was upset that he didn't try at all to win her back or even talk about anything. He tried harder to find you these last five minutes. I know he slept with her last year, but that was once in an entire year. Graham told you they dated over the summers. They did go out a couple of times, but they didn't act like a couple over the summer.

"Sadie, my mother is wrong. You are the love of his life."

Sean and Michael wait on a couch outside the restroom for her. While they wait, Sean tells Michael in detail about his conversation with Sadie about being gay.

"You know bro, when Sadie and I sat at that table talking by ourselves, I told her I was gay. Apparently you never mentioned it." Michael rolls his eyes as Sean continues, "Sadie is completely okay with it. I was so surprised."

Michael smiles as he hears the arguments Sadie had given Sean to use against him.

"I may never win an argument with this woman," Michael puts his arm around his brother, "I blew it tonight. Thank you for being there for Sadie."

Carol and Sadie emerge from the ladies' room. Carol and Sean say their goodbyes leaving Michael and Sadie to work things out. Carol runs to find Drew.

Michael, standing behind a couch, half sits on the back of it. Cupping his hands over Sadie's elbows, he pulls her close to him.

"I'm beginning to rethink my all men are scum theory," she mumbles.

"Don't start that," Michael grumbles tiredly.

"I didn't start this," she counters.

"Sadie…"

"Tell me the truth, the whole truth," she demands. "In November, in the parsonage, did you have sex with Barbara?"

"No."

"Did you kiss her? I don't mean a peck on the cheek. Did you kiss her?"

"Well, yes, but it didn't feel right, so I stopped," he admits.

"When is the last time you had sex with her?"

Michael sighs, "Last New Year's Eve, when we went skiing." When Sadie is quiet, Michael starts, "I'm so sorry about tonight. I wish I could start the whole night over."

"I don't want to do this night again," quips Sadie.

"My friends didn't treat you this way because of who you are or because you don't have as much money as they do."

"I know. I could tell. Their problem is that I'm not Barbara," she states coldly.

"I didn't know Colby was taking me to see her. I didn't hug her and when she hugged me, I didn't let it last long."

"I know. I saw her see me watching. She moved so you would turn your back to me and then she hugged you."

"She did that on purpose?"

"Women do crazy things when we are jealous."

Changing the subject, he states, "I have never thought of you as free help or a helpmate. You don't have to ever do my laundry again."

"I know. I always offered. In my world, taking care of someone is part of loving him. I just didn't like your mother looking down her nose at me."

Michael looks Sadie in the eyes, "Truth: Barbara was never the love of my life. You are the love of my life. I want to marry you. Don't break up with me."

Sadie returns, "Truth: I was never going to break up with you. I was just trying to get the hell out of here."

A smile slowly crosses his face. Michael gently brushes her cheek with the back of his hand and slides his other hand under her hair cupping the back of her head pulling her to him and kissing her tenderly.

Barbara watches from the doorway. She had not seen Michael with another woman since they started going out. Seeing him kissing Sadie tears at her heart. She doesn't remember a time that she didn't love him and always believed that they would get back together somehow. Sophia is hoping that after a year or two, he will come to his senses and leave the ministry, but Barbara saw him in his church dressed like a minister. He is not leaving. Picturing his house, she thinks she just can't live like that. After all these years, it is finally time to let him go.

Michael checks his watch, 11:49. He talks Sadie into returning to the party to be on the dance floor at midnight. They recheck their coats with the teenager who is happy to see that they made up. As they head for the dance floor, they meet his parents.

Sophia stops them, "Oh, Carol said you might have left. I'm glad you are still here. I'd hate to think you would leave without saying goodbye."

Michael lets go of Sadie's hand stepping close to his mother, "I know what you said to Sadie. Don't you ever treat her like that again."

Sophia tries to defend herself, "I don't know what she told you, but I don't think I said anything wrong."

Michael remains firm, "Sadie didn't tell me anything. Barbara is not the love of my life and Sadie is most definitely not just some helpmate. If you treat her badly, I won't bring her to these things and I won't come without her."

Michael takes Sadie's hand and leads her to the dance floor.

James sighs, "Sophia, you said that to her?"

After a couple of dances, the countdown begins. At the stroke of midnight, balloons and confetti fall from the ceiling. Michael and Sadie enjoy another kiss and then they go to the bar for a drink.

Once they are standing by a tall table, Sadie begins slowly, "I don't want to start another argument, but…"

Michael sighs, "Now what?"

"You just told off your mother for treating me badly, when you don't even acknowledge your brother's partner, Jeremy."

Michael looks at the ceiling for a moment, "What do you want me to do?"

"Invite both of them over for dinner Saturday."

Michael is not sure how he feels about all of this, but he has to admit that Sean treats Sadie kindly and despite the way Michael has treated him, Sean still came to his ordination and to his Christmas Eve service.

As they finish their drinks, Sean walks by. Michael calls him over inviting him and Jeremy to dinner Saturday. Sean accepts enthusiastically knowing this is Sadie's doing.

Sean asks Sadie to dance. As they move to an up tempo oldie, but goodie, Michael watches from the edge of the dance floor. Graham joins him.

Michael, not trying to hide is anger growls, "I can't believe the way you treated her tonight. I can't believe I allowed it to happen. I thought there was a chance that we could still be friends even though we went our separate ways. I guess not."

"I'm sorry, Mike. I've known Barbara my whole life. It was easy to take her side tonight. I don't want to lose you as a friend." Graham apologizes.

"Barbara dumped me almost four years ago. Am I supposed to spend the rest of my life alone as some punishment for not leading the life that my parents and friends think I should?

"Look at her. Sadie is fun and energetic. She is kind and loving. She is intelligent and witty. She has a strong faith and completely understands and supports what I am doing. She helps me and takes care of me when I need it."

"We can try again another time right? I don't want to lose you as my friend. I really am sorry. Sean is having a good time with her. I should have given her a chance. We thought you two were going to have a big fight. To tell you the truth, we are surprised how quickly you made up. You must have something special."

"We do."

After the dance ends, Sadie and Sean walk to Michael. Graham apologizes to Sadie and says he would like for them to get to know each other sometime. Sadie smiles and tells him she would like that. Graham kisses her on the cheek. Michael pulls her on the dance floor with him. Sean, Carol, and Drew join them.

In the car on the way home, Michael asks, "If you knew that a cab wouldn't take you all the way home, what were you planning to do?"

Sadie explains, "I would have asked how far he would take me, and then I would have checked into a hotel for the night. I'd slept in and watched television until at least eleven in the morning so as not to wake anyone. Then I would have called my friends to see if someone would come get me or I would have rented a car."

Michael shakes his head, "I am so glad I caught you before you got in that cab."

"Why?"

"If you had left, I would have gone straight to your apartment. When you didn't show up, I'd have gone crazy. I would have called all your friends looking for you. By eleven o'clock, we would have all been crazy." He reaches for her hand apologizing yet again for the rough evening she had.

Soon, as he drives her home, the car lulls Sadie to sleep. After he pulls into his drive at three-thirty, he gently rubs her leg to wake her up. She climbs out of the car.

"It is good to be home," Sadie yawns, "Goodnight Michael."

She starts to walk home, but Michael blocks her way, "Where are you going? Stay with me tonight."

"I don't think so. I want to go home," she answers.

"Please stay," he looks into her eyes.

"No."

"Sadie, we don't have to do anything. We can just sleep. I just need you to stay with me tonight, please."

"Okay," she caves allowing him to lead her inside.

Michael pampers her as they get ready for bed being constantly attentive. Once curled up in bed, Michael can't help himself as he begins to stroke and kiss her. It takes Sadie a little bit of time to warm up to him, but she does. The couple makes love.

They sleep until after eleven o'clock. Wearing one of Michael's t-shirts for a nightgown and his tube socks which are way too big, but her feet were cold; Sadie makes them omelets, bacon, and toast for breakfast. Someone knocks on the door. Sadie quickly hides in the den as Michael answers the door wearing sweats and an undershirt. Colleen, Stephanie, and Brenda barge in.

"Good morning Michael. Sorry to drop in on you, but we are anxious to talk to Sadie," Colleen tells him.

"She's not here," he lies.

"Oh right, and you're the one making omelets," Stephanie observes.

"Fine, I'll get her," he goes to the study.

"You don't have to tell them how badly it went, do you?" he asks her.

"I don't have to," she agrees.

She enters the kitchen and they coo that she is cute in Michael's t-shirt. Sadie asks how the party at the bar turned out. Brenda reports that it was the best turn out for a party at the bar since they opened it. Sadie tells her that she wishes she had been there. Michael rolls his eyes.

"So, how did it go at the country club?" Colleen asks.

"Oh, it was awful. It couldn't have gone worse," Sadie states truthfully.

Michael looks surprised, "I thought you said you didn't have to tell them."

"Oh, I don't have to tell them, but I'm going to," Sadie remarks.

"I'm going upstairs to get dressed," Michael leaves.

"Your omelet will get cold!" she calls after him.

"I don't care!"

Sadie reports about the evening telling them all about Barbara and how his friends treated her. She repeats what his mother had said. She tells them about childishly running away and Michael coming to find her. As Michael returns to eat his breakfast, Sadie shares the good parts about how much she likes Sean and Carol and how Michael had tried so hard to make up with her as well as him speaking up to his mother. She describes being with him on the dance floor at midnight.

Stephanie shakes her head, "It's always drama with you."

Sadie and Colleen make omelets for everyone. Stephanie ate Michael's, so Sadie makes him a fresh hot one. They all squeeze into his breakfast nook. Michael sits quietly as she and her friends loudly go over details about both parties wishing he was anywhere else.

Chapter XV

Saturday morning, the women's groups are getting together at church to practice for a special program about the Women's Aid Society in the late eighteen hundreds. Sadie stops at the parsonage on her way to church. She attempts to talk Michael into wearing a circuit rider costume, an eighteen hundred's minister who rode from town to town serving several parishes.

Michael responds, "I don't think so."

Sadie points out that all the women will be wearing costumes. Michael refuses. Eloise is sewing it for him, so chances are he won't be able to dodge it for long.

The doorbell rings. Michael finds a delivery man dropping off a large floral arrangement in a crystal vase for Sadie at his address. Sadie squeals when she sees it, asking if it's from him, but it is not. Sadie finds the card and reads it to herself smiling.

Michael acts jealous, "So, who's it from?"

"None of your business," she teases.

Michael takes a step toward her, "Give me that card."

"Okay, I'll read it to you. To a Lady who is prettier than these flowers. Love…"

Sadie takes off running into the dining room. Michael chases her. Sadie attempts to keep the table between them, but he is fast. She knows it won't take long for him to catch her. She stops, stuffing the gift card down her bra.

Michael puts his hands on his hips, "Oh, like that's going to stop me."

Sadie turns to run, but he is quick. He comes up behind her wrapping one arm around her waist and slides his other hand down her shirt. Sadie laughs and screams. Just as he snatches the card, the doorbell rings. Sliding the card in his back pocket, he answers it to find Mac.

"Good morning Rev. Donnelly. Are you killing someone?"

"Not exactly, come in," he invites.

Mac calls out, "Good morning Sadie."

Sadie enters the kitchen.

"Spend the night did you?" Mac pries.

"No, I came for the same meeting your wife is going to. I just stopped here first," she explains.

Michael asks annoyed, "Can I help you with something?"

"My wife sent me to get the church keys."

Michael takes the extra set of church keys and hands them to Mac. He stands in the doorway watching Mac leave. Just as he closes the door, Sadie pushes him into it, reaches in his back pocket and retrieves the card. Regaining his balance reaches, he back and catches her wrist. He grabs the card and holds it over his head.

Leaning on the counter, he reads the card, "To a Lady who is prettier than these flowers. Thank you for tonight, Love Sean and Jeremy. Why didn't you want me to see this?"

"Oh, I wanted you to see it. I just wanted to play first."

"Come here," Michael becomes serious wrapping his arms around her waist, "Tonight is really important to Sean."

"Of course it is. You want your family to accept you as a minister. Sean wants his family to accept him for who he is."

"You make every part of my life better. You managed to get my family to come to see me preach. You have my brother coming for dinner with just me for the first time in over two years. You helped me set up house and you help me at church. My sex life is definitely better. Marry me."

"You are one horny minister."

"Marry me."

"Not yet."

Later that day, Sean and Jeremy arrive at the parsonage. Michael greets them, "Come in, but keep your coats on. We are going for a walk. Sadie decided she'd rather cook in her own kitchen and she has a real dining room."

Sean takes Jeremy in to see Michael's dining room. Michael defends himself with the fact that he has a nice living room. As they are about to leave the doorbell rings. Mac is at the door.

Michael introduces them, "Mac, this is my brother, Sean and his friend, Jeremy. We were just leaving."

Mac intrudes, "I'm sorry to interrupt your plans, but this is very important. I'm considering calling a Pastor/Parish Committee meeting after church tomorrow."

Michael rolls his eyes and sighs, "What did I do now and how quickly can you sum it up?"

Mac begins, "I have three concerns."

"Great."

"You took another large sum from the discretionary funds."

Michael defends, "I only took money from it one other time in August."

"I am the financial chairman. I need to know why you took three hundred dollars," he demands.

"Actually, you don't need to know. It is at my discretion. I only have to give you the amounts, but if it makes you feel better, a member of our church has been laid off. The family is struggling. I gave them the money they were short for their mortgage."

Mac complains, "That's a lot of money to give out at one time to one family."

Michael stiffens, "I thought not losing their house was important. Besides, before the lay off, they had always been generous in their giving to our church. Next problem,"

Mac continues, "Someone took at least two-thirds of the food collected for the food bank."

"I bagged it up and gave it to the same family," Michael admits.

"That was for the food bank. You should have sent them there."

"It was for people in need and members of our church are in need. Next problem,"

"You submitted a request that General Fund pay fifty dollars for one of the youth to go on the trip. Fund raising paid for most of the trip, but every member has to pay fifty dollars. I'm paying fifty for my daughter. Why should we pay for only one person? It's not fair."

"Only one member can't afford to go," Michael tries to reason.

"I know who was laid off. That money would go to the same family again."

Michael offers, "I will personally pay the fifty. Now go call Eloise and if she agrees that we need a meeting, then we will have a meeting.

Right now, I'm taking my brother and his friend to dinner. Goodnight Mac."

"Fine, but I need that fifty dollars by Monday to send in the reservations."

Sean opens his wallet and hands Mac a fifty. After Mac leaves, Sean insists he doesn't want the money back. As they walk to Sadie's, Michael tells them about some of his frustrations in the church. Mac heads the list. Before Michael became a minister, Sean had never realized all the different types of problems ministers face. He is impressed with his older brother and how he had just stood up to Mac.

Sean and Jeremy think it is convenient to have a girlfriend who only lives two blocks away. They are a little surprised that she lives over a hardware store. Michael uses his own key to let them in.

Sean comments, "You have your own key? This must be serious."

Michael just smiles as they head up the long staircase. They can smell Sadie's dinner before Michael even opens the door, "We're here. Sorry we're late. Mac stopped by with another list of concerns, the cheap ass."

Sean introduces Jeremy and Sadie as Michael takes their coats. Ready to serve, Sadie invites them to have a seat in the dining room. Sean watches Michael follow her into the kitchen asking her how he can help. Sadie has him pour the wine, after all that is what ministers are good at. Sadie serves rice meatballs, mashed potatoes, mushroom gravy, green bean medley, tossed salad, fruit cups and dinner rolls.

Sean looks around, "Now this is a dining room."

Michael appears mischievous, "I have a plan to get a beautiful dining room in my house. Here, I'll show you. Hey, Sadie…"

Sadie looks at him suspiciously, "What?"

"Marry me."

Sadie shakes her head, "Not yet."

Sean and Jeremy laugh. Sean asks, "How long have you been proposing?"

Michael smiles, "Since Christmas morning."

Sean chuckles, "So that's your plan, to pester her until she says yes?"

"That's how I got her to date me."

Conversation flows easily. Jeremy works at Macy's. Sadie comments that she loves looking through that store.

"Looking? Don't you ever buy anything?" Jeremy asks.

"Heaven's no. I can't afford to shop there."

"What are you into? Shoes?" he asks.

"I'm more into purses, but I've never bought one that costs more than twenty dollars," she admits.

"You are kidding me. I'll tell you what Love, the next time there is a good sale, I'll let you know plus you can use my store discount."

Sadie likes the thought of that. They have a pleasant evening. After dinner, Michael insists that Sadie play the piano for them. Michael loves listening to her play.

After she plays some ragtime, she tells them that when she was seven, she begged her parents for piano lessons, but they said they couldn't afford lessons let alone a piano. Sadie played around on the church piano every chance she had. Finally, the church organist offered to give her piano lessons cheap and her father allowed her to practice in the church while he was in his office or in a meeting. A year later, an older lady, who was moving into a nursing home, gave Sadie her piano. The piano was an old upright which sounded like she was playing in a saloon.

Sadie tells them she dreams of buying a real piano, an acoustic piano. She purchased an electric piano, because it is less expensive and they couldn't get a real piano up the stairs and make the turn at the top. Movers had trouble with the china cabinet and dresser. Sadie shows them a brochure she has for a mahogany upright piano.

Michael reminds her, "There's room at my house for a piano. See, you should marry me."

Sadie throws a small couch pillow at him.

They spend the evening visiting and playing games. Sean and Jeremy ask if Michael would feel comfortable if they stay in a hotel and went to church tomorrow. They promise to introduce Jeremy as Sean's friend. Michael assures them that he would like that.

Sean and Jeremy enjoy church and take Sadie and Michael to a nice restaurant for lunch afterwards. Michael and Sean haven't been close since Sean came out of the closet. They were on the right path now as they embraced goodbye.

That Friday, Michael and Sadie join their friends at the bar. As they eat and visit, Michael notices a young man from church playing pool. He asks Steve "Isn't he only eighteen?"

"Yeah, but he only drinks cola."

Michael keeps an eye on him. After the pool game ends, they reset the table and pull out their wallets. Michael pulls the boy, Josh, aside asking if he knows the men he and his friend are playing. Josh says no. Michael warns him about gambling like this. It is easy to be hustled. Josh does not take his advice and continues their game. Michael returns to his friends.

As a good song begins to play, Sadie grabs onto Michael's arm, "Dance with me."

"No, I don't think so," he responds.

She pouts, "But I want you to dance with me."

"I'm not a good dancer," he lies.

"Oh no, you blew it. We all saw you dance at the wedding," she reminds him as their friends laugh.

Michael looks at her as if she is crazy, "I have no idea what you are talking about. I never danced."

The girls giggle, "Liar!"

Michael turns to Aidan and Steve, "I honestly have no idea what they are talking about. Do you remember seeing me dance at the wedding?"

"No, no I don't recall you dancing…Steve?" Aidan plays along.

"Nope, I don't remember the Reverend ever dancing," Steve sticks with his friends.

Sadie punches Michael in the arm, "Oh, you guys are hopeless."

The three friends pick up their beers in unison and take a drink while the girls glare at them.

Michael sees the boys leaving looking upset. "Hey Josh, come here," Michael calls them over. "How much did he take you for?"

Josh shrugs, "a hundred dollars."

Michael shakes his head, "Steve, can you loan me a hundred dollars?"

Stephanie jumps in, "Here Reverend, I'll give you a hundred dollars. I'm curious to see what you're going to do." She pulls out the money handing it to Michael.

"I'll give it right back," he announces heading to the pool table. His friends remain at their table.

Michael lays the hundred on the table, "I'll play you for the kid's money."

"I don't want to take your money Reverend."

"Don't worry about me."

The man takes the bet encouraging Michael to break. As Michael racks the balls, his friends gather to watch the game. On the break, he sinks a ball and then controls the table. Several shots are complicated.

About five shots into the game, the man he is playing accuses, "Reverend, did you just hustle me?"

Michael glances up, "No. I never said I wasn't good."

The game ends. Michael gives a hundred back to Stephanie. He hands the other hundred to Josh, but holds onto the money as Josh tries to take it, "You owe me for this. You can come volunteer at the church for a couple weeks. I can think of some jobs you can do."

Josh whines, "Ah man, do I have to?"

Michael smirks, "This isn't your money. You lost your money. This is mine; I won it. I'll let you earn it back. Come by after school Monday."

"Yes sir," Michael lets the money go, "Thanks." Josh leaves.

Stephanie is impressed, "Tennis champ, golf pro, competitive swimmer, ballroom dancer, and now, pool shark."

Steve asks, "Where did you learn to play like that?"

"Well, my parent's house has a billiards room, plus four years of college and three years of seminary. Student unions tend to have pool tables and my fraternity house had one."

Brenda visibly stiffens at the mention that he had lived in a fraternity house. Stephanie quickly moves the conversation along, "What other talent do you possess that we have not yet discovered?"

Michael leans back to think, "I'm a pretty good skier."

The group raises their glasses yelling, "Cheers."

Sadie shakes her head, "I can't do any of those things."

Michael disagrees, "That's not true. You can dance. You picked up the samba steps I was doing quickly and I've seen you dance often."

"Ah, ha, you just remembered dancing with me at the wedding," Sadie gloats.

"Oh crap," he slaps the table while the others laugh. "Well, you dance and of course, you can swim."

Her friends exchange glances, so he asks, "What?"

Sadie seems embarrassed, "Actually, I can't swim."

"You're kidding."

"Shut up."

"You can't swim?"

"Shut up."

"I could teach you to swim," he offers.

"No thank you."

"Swimming is fun and great exercise. There would be no pressure on your hip. Trust me," he persuades, but Sadie only agrees to think about it.

"Come on, Darling dance with me," Sadie begins tugging on his arm again.

He rolls his eyes and laughs. His cell phone plays *Amazing Grace*. He checks his watch, eleven forty-five and cocks his eyebrow at Sadie.

"I changed your ring tone. Do you like it?" she giggles.

Making a face at her he answers, "Hello, Rev. Donnelly speaking."

He listens for a second and then sitting straight up, a serious expression crosses his face, "When…which hospital? I'm on my way." He replaces his cell phone on his belt.

"What is it? What happened?" Sadie sits down next to him.

"Breanna Johnson and four of her friends were in a car accident. I have to go," Michael stands.

"How many beers have you had?" Stephanie asks

Michael lifts his bottle which still has some in the bottom, "Not quite one."

Sadie opens her purse and hands him a pack of spearmint gun, "Here, chew a couple of these on your way. You don't want to smell like beer."

He takes the gum and runs out the door and down the block to his house to fetch his car.

Brenda asks Sadie, "Who is Breanna Johnson?"

"She is a fifteen year old girl in our church. Her family comes regularly and she is in the youth group. Oh, God, I hope she's okay."

Rev. Donnelly runs into the emergency's waiting room. He does not see anyone and inquires at the desk. The young girl has been raced to surgery. Michael hurries to the surgical waiting room where he finds the girl's panic stricken parents, Bob and Cathy.

Bob paces in a short little space while he fills Michael in on what they know. Breanna was spending the night at her friend's house. The friend's seventeen year old sister decided to take the group of friends to the mall to walk around for a while and then they went to see a movie. On the way home, the girls were rowdy, playing music loudly, and joking around. Suddenly, there was an animal in the road, a cat or raccoon or something. The teen, Caitlyn, swerved and lost control of the car slamming into a tree. Breanna who was sitting on the passenger's side and a girl named Jeannie who was behind her in the backseat were hurt the worst.

Michael coaxes Bob and Cathy along with Jeannie's parents to stand in a circle and hold hands. He prays for the two girls and their friends willing God to give him the words. After, they just stand and sit waiting. Michael goes for coffee for everyone. Then at their request, he goes around the hospital to gather updates on the other girls in the car.

Michael soon returns, "Caitlyn and Taylor are going to be fine. Caitlyn has a broken arm, a small concussion, and some bruises. Taylor has whiplash and bruises. Skyler is stable, but her back is hurt and they won't know how badly it will be for her until the swelling around her spine goes down."

The parents nervously nod and continue to pace and stare out windows. Around one o'clock in the morning, a nurse comes for Jeannie's parents, Mark and Patty, to take them to a family consultation room to wait for a doctor. The mother has a bad feeling.

Turning to Michael, her voice trembles as she requests, "Reverend, I know you don't know us and we are not members of your church, but would you come with us."

"Certainly," Michael does not hesitate, but stands and follows the petrified couple.

They wait anxiously. Finally a very serious doctor slowly enters, "Jeannie sustained serious internal injuries in the crash. We did everything we could to the best of our capabilities, but there was simply too much damage. I'm sorry, but she died at one fifteen."

Her parents just stare in disbelief for a moment. Then the reality of what the doctor just said hits her mother, "Oh God, oh God, no, no, she's gone. My baby girl is gone!"

She becomes hysterical screaming. The father, sobbing walks away from her and slams his fist into a wall. Not sure what to do, Michael goes to the mother and touches her shoulder. She turns toward him and collapses. Michael barely catches her quickly setting her on a couch. He kneels in front of her as she hangs onto him pressing her face into his shoulder.

She begins to yell for her husband, Mark. Mark comes and pulls her up into his arms. Michael stands and backs out of their way. "Come on Patty. Pull yourself together. Let's go see her and do whatever the hell we are supposed to do."

Michael hands Mark a tissue and he gives it to his wife. As they calm down and prepare to leave, Mark addresses Michael, "Thank you Reverend… Uh, Reverend, we don't belong to a church. If it's not too much to ask, would you do Jeannie's funeral?"

"Of course," Michael reaches into his back pocket pulling out a small silver card holder. He pulls out one of his church cards and hands it to Mark.

Mark thanks him and leaves holding up his wife. As they stumble pitifully down the hall, Michael wonders what he was thanked for. He didn't do anything. He has no idea what he is doing.

He returns to Bob and Cathy attempting not to look all shook up himself now that he has horrible task of informing them that Jeannie has died. Cathy and Bob cling to each other crying.

Michael sits in a chair thinking about Breanna. She is tall and very thin with shoulder length light brown hair. She and Mac's daughter, Cheyenne, are always together at church. The two of them were always standing around pointing and whispering. Any time he spoke to them, they would giggle and giggle. They often sat in the back of the church on their own during the service. Michael could tell that they were passing notes back and forth and sometimes, he could swear that they were painting their fingernails.

His thoughts are interrupted as Caitlyn and Taylor's mom enters the room to check on the other girls. Cathy jumps up, furious, "Why the hell was my daughter at the mall without my permission?! I never would have allowed her in a car with a group of girls and a teenage driver!"

Cathy storms toward the startled woman. Michael jumps to his feet planting himself between the two women holding his arm across her and grabbing her arm with his other hand.

"Cathy, don't do this now," Michael orders. "Calm down. Try to calm down."

Allowing him to hold her back, she continues her tirade, "She was supposed to be at your house! She is supposed to be watching DVD's at your house. Now, your daughters are fine and mine is in surgery and Jeannie is dead!"

The woman obviously hadn't heard about Jeannie and cries out as if she had been smacked. Michael again attempts to stop Cathy, "Don't. Come on Cathy. Stop it. I understand how you feel, but this won't help right now." Michael looks over his shoulder at the other woman, "I'm sorry, but this isn't a good time to talk with her. I think you should go for now."

The other woman runs away sobbing. Cathy pulls away from Michael and runs to Bob. The agonizing wait continues. Michael tries a couple of times to get an update, but is told a doctor will be with them as soon as possible.

Finally, a little after three in the morning, a nurse escorts Bob, Cathy, and Michael to the family consultation room. To Michael's horror, the same scene repeats itself as a doctor informs them of the loss of their daughter. Sweet, giggling, fifteen year old Breanna, died.

Bob requests that Michael accompanies them to see their daughter's body and to pray over her. Michael wants to say no and leave, but instead, he nods and follows them to a room. The little girl still has a large tube down her throat. She is bruised and swollen. She doesn't really even look like Breanna. Nausea washes over Michael, but he fights hard to remain in control.

Bob and Cathy cry and kiss their daughter. They say goodbye. Then they turn and look at Michael. He knows they want him to pray over her, but he has no idea what to say to bring comfort. He prays quickly in his head begging God for help as he steps up placing his hand on the cold girl's forehead.

Closing his eyes, he begins, "Dear Heavenly Father, we thank you for the blessing Breanna has been in her family's lives during her brief life. We thank You for the joy and love she brought. We will always cherish our memories of this bright child. We ask You Most Gracious Father to take Breanna into Your Heavenly home to be with You where she now belongs.

"And Dear Heavenly Father, we pray that you will give the Johnson family the strength they so desperately need to get through this tragic time in their lives. Be with them, guide them, and bring them comfort. This I pray in the name of our Risen Lord, Jesus Christ. Amen."

Opening his eyes, he sees Bob and Cathy quietly crying. Bob nods at him. He is relieved that they seem fine with his prayer. He is not even exactly sure what he just said and figures God simply answered his prayer for help.

He remains with family as they sign papers and make arrangements to have her body taken to a funeral home. They thank and hug him. Michael is finally free to go home.

Chapter XVI

Michael arrives home around four thirty. He is exhausted. His head aches and his chest contains a strange hollow feeling. He now has to figure out what to say at two young girls' funerals.

As he stumbles through his living room, he is startled by a voice, "Michael?" Sadie, who had fallen asleep on his couch, turns on a lamp.

"Sadie, what are you doing here?"

"I waited up for you. What happened?"

Michael presses his hand to his forehead, "Breanna died. Breanna and another little girl, Jeannie, they died."

Michael shutters. Sadie goes to him. He wraps his arms around her unable to stop himself from crying. Sadie soothes him and holds him for as long as he needs and then leads him to the couch.

He stutters and tries to explain how helpless he felt, "Both families thanked me, but I don't know for what. I didn't do anything. I had no idea what to say. I don't think I brought them any comfort. I didn't know what to say that would help."

"Shh, there, there, Sweetheart, there are no words. They just lost their daughter. There is no comfort. You have to just let them go through the emotions. You were there for them. That is all you can do."

After he calms down, he tells her every detail. She rubs his cheek gently with her hand, "You did so much more for them than you think.

I am so proud of you. Come, you need your rest."

Sadie walks upstairs with him. He undresses and falls into bed. Sadie lies pressed up behind him with her arm over him. Although he thinks he won't be able to fall asleep, it only takes a minute to fall sound asleep.

The next day, Michael wakes up alone. The clock on his nightstand reads eleven forty. He notices the telephone on his nightstand is unplugged and his cell phone is gone. He dresses and goes downstairs where he finds Sadie working in the kitchen.

"Good morning, do you feel any better?" she greets him.

"I'm better than the Johnson's," he mumbles. "What are you doing?"

"I'm making two lasagnas, one for us and one for the Johnson's. I'm also making brownies for them. Now, sit down and I'll make you breakfast. You must be starved."

Michael plops down at the table and grumbles at her, "Why do women run to their kitchens when someone dies?"

"Well, they are going to need to eat and they are going to have company, but they are not going to feel like or have time to cook. I am trying to help where I can."

He stares at her for a minute, "I'm sorry. I didn't mean to be grumpy with you."

"I forgive you," she kisses his forehead, "Do you want scrambled eggs and toast?"

"Sure. Did you unplug my phone and take my cell?"

"Yes, but don't worry. If you had received an important call, I would have come to get you. I just didn't want someone trying to get you to subscribe to a newspaper or something stupid to wake you."

"Thanks," he sits back and watches her bustle around the kitchen. He thinks to himself, this is why ministers need a wife. After spending all night trying to take care of others, Sadie is here taking care of him and thanks to her father, Sadie knew to wait for him; she would be needed. What would he do without her?

Later in the afternoon, Sadie tells him that she is going to drop the food off. Michael informs her that he will come along.

"Sadie, I'm not sure what to say to them," he admits.

"Well, whatever you do, don't tell them that losing their child in a car accident was God's plan for her life. And don't tell them that God won't give them anything that they can't handle, because that sounds like God did this to them on purpose. Just say that you are sorry for what has happened and to not ask why, but to lean on God for strength and guidance. And if they need anything at all, don't hesitate to call."

"That sounds good. What would I do without you?"

They arrive at the Johnson home. A haggard looking Cathy invites them in. The two younger siblings seem confused and in a fog. Michael promises that they don't want to bother them, but Sadie wanted to drop off some food and he wanted to check on them. Cathy invites them to sit in the kitchen for a minute.

"Thank you so much for staying with us all night like you did and for being so kind to Jeannie's family. I don't know how we would have made it through without you and thank you for stopping me from tearing poor Becky's head off. I'm still angry with her, but you were right last night when you said that she and Caitlyn are going to have to live with this."

The doorbell rings and Cathy excuses herself. Sadie gives Michael a warm smile and Michael takes a deep breath. They can hear that Mac and his wife, Bonnie, are at the door.

"Hello Cathy. We can't tell you how sorry we are to hear what happened. Cheyenne is beside herself. We don't want to impose, but we brought you a casserole," Bonnie lovingly comforts her friend.

"Thank you," Cathy accepts the casserole.

Mac speaks up, "Cathy, I know our minister is young and inexperienced. You should feel free to have anyone you want to do the funeral. I bet Rev. Harper would come back if you asked."

Michael and Sadie's eyes snap up to each other. A wave of anger washes over both of them.

"Mac," Cathy sounds indignant. "Rev. Donnelly is our pastor. He stayed with us all night and when we lost her, he went with us and prayed over her. He will be doing the funeral. Now if you will excuse me, I have things to attend to."

Cathy returns to the kitchen, "Did you hear anything?"

Michael simply looks at her.

"I'm so sorry," Cathy apologizes.

"Don't worry about it. He's right. You can request anyone you wish to do her funeral. Just so you know I have done two funerals since I've been here and I did three during my student pastorate."

"You don't have to sell me. After last night, I wouldn't have anyone else. Sadie, I know you teach, but I was wondering if you could be there."

"I will be there. I have a couple personal days left," Sadie promises.

"Will you sing?" Cathy requests.

"I would be honored to. If you need anything else, please don't hesitate to call," Sadie offers.

As they prepare to leave, Cathy asks, "Reverend, I don't understand how this happened. Where was God? Why did He take her?"

"Don't ask why. It will drive you crazy. It was just a terrible accident. Try not to turn away from God in anger. You need Him more than ever now. Lean on Him for strength." Michael soothes thankful for the talk he had had with Sadie before they came.

Cathy hugs him and they leave.

Once back at the parsonage, Michael asks Sadie, "Do you think as a minister I have the power to throw Mac out of my church?"

Sadie smiles at him, "No Dear, you can't do that."

"Well, it was just a thought," he walks over to her cupping her face in his hands, "I don't know what I would do without you. You make me a better minister. I think God meant for me to find you at conference. I really do."

Michael slowly, gently kisses her savoring the warmth of her lips. Together, the two of them get through the painful funerals.

The last week of January, a blizzard blows in. The schools close for two days which Sadie spends at the parsonage. Michael still goes to the office for several hours in the mornings, but he cancels all other church activities.

Michael lights the gas fireplace. They move the loveseat across the room in front of it where they spend hours listening to music, talking, reading, cuddling, making love.

Thursday, Sadie returns to her first graders and Michael goes to the hospital to catch up on calls. He returns to find Sadie cooking pepper steak. The kitchen smells wonderful.

As Michael pulls off his snowy boots, gloves, hat, and coat, Sadie tells him, "You missed an important call." He turns his full attention to her as she continues, "Beth called. You have her wedding on your calendar for June eleventh. Her fiancé has been called up to active duty. She wants to move the wedding up to not this Saturday, but next Saturday. I went to your office. There's nothing important on the calendar. She also wants to use the fellowship hall for her reception."

"Okay, I'll go call her back," he says hanging up his coat.

"I know that there is no alcohol allowed in the church, but do you think she could have wine for the toast?"

"There are strict rules about that. I don't think I can allow it."

"We're not talking about an open bar, just wine for a toast with dinner. Even Jesus made sure there was plenty of wine at the wedding in Canaan," she argues.

Michael rolls his head, "Sure he did, because a woman, his mother, pestered Him about it. I can't promise anything, but Sunday I'll call a Pastor/Parish meeting and ask their opinion."

Michael begins to head for his study, but Sadie continues, "You know, they are losing all their deposits. They have the grand ballroom at the Ambrose Hotel, a photographer, and the same D.J. and caterer that Colleen used. They could use the money now. Wouldn't it be great if another couple gave them their money back and took over those reservations?"

"That would be great, but I don't think we have a chance of finding another couple willing to do that," Michael begins sorting through the mail he brought in as he walks into the dining room.

Sadie calls after him, "You know, the second weekend of June is a perfect date. School is out for the summer and it is a week before conference."

Sadie waits. She hears nothing and wonders if he even heard her. Then he appears in the doorway giving her a strange look.

"Are you thinking that we should be the couple to take over that date?" he stares at her.

"Well, it's just, school is out. We could go on a honeymoon for a week, come home Friday, get ready Saturday and leave for conference Sunday. I would have all of July to move out of my apartment and...fix this house up."

"Are you serious?"

"Well, how serious were you the half a dozen times you proposed?" she asks staring into the electric skillet.

Michael turns her around taking both of her hands and holding them to his chest, "Sadie Stevens, I knew from the first day I met you that you are the one I've been praying for; the one who would walk this path with me. I love you. Will you marry me?"

Sadie smiles up at him, "I love you too. Yes Michael, I will marry you."

"So you will marry me now?" he checks.

"Yes Michael, now."

Chapter XVII

Friday night, the couple meets their friends at Duffy's. Stephanie complains, "I am already tired of all this snow and we still have months of it ahead. I can't wait for summer."

Michael smirks, "I can think of something fun we can do this summer."

"What do you have in mind?" Brenda asks.

Michael smiles looking at Sadie who takes a deep breath, "Well, we were thinking on June eleventh we'll get married."

A dead silence follows for a moment and then Aidan leads the whooping with the girls screaming. Steve leaves to choose a bottle of wine for the occasion. The groom and his bride invite all of them to be in the wedding party.

Stephanie lays her head on the table, "Oh great, I'm the only single one left. I'm officially the seventh wheel."

Her friends gather to comfort her and assure her that they didn't want to lose her.

Colleen wants to know, "Where's the ring?"

Sadie shrugs, "No ring yet."

The girls glare at Michael, but he throws his hands up and assures them, "There will be a ring. I'll buy her a ring. Since it's not a surprise, Sadie can go with me to help pick it out."

Satisfied, the girls begin discussing wedding plans.

Saturday, Michael and Sadie drive out to have dinner with Martin, Joy, her brother, and sisters. Once dinner starts, Joy asks if there is any special reason that Sadie had suggested a family dinner, so Sadie announces their engagement. Luke, Mary, and Lucy begin congratulating the couple, but Joy just stares.

"What is the rush? I mean, in November you wouldn't even admit you were dating; now two months later, you're engaged? I have nothing against Michael, but why so fast?"

"We feel sure about this. We don't want to wait," Sadie replies.

"Martin?" Joy hopes for reinforcement.

"It does seem fast, but when we watched them together at conference, we both thought they were going to end up married. You said so first." Martin reminds her.

Joy concedes. The conversation turns to wedding plans. Joy offers to take Sadie shopping for her wedding gown next Saturday. The couple invites Luke, Mary, and Lucy to be in the wedding party. Martin tells them, while he wants to perform the ceremony, he would like to have another minister to assist so he can be free to do the father of the bride part as well. Michael suggests Rev. Rob Foreman who they met at his ordination. Everyone agrees.

Sunday morning, a nervous Sadie dreads going to Michael's house that evening to announce their engagement. She fears facing his mother who obviously didn't like that Sadie was her son's date for New Year's. How would she feel about wife?

At church, Sadie runs the opening exercises for Sunday school, leading several songs and saying a prayer. The children then go to their classrooms. All the teachers are present leaving Sadie free.

Aidan and Colleen find Sadie and rush her to Michael's office closing the door behind them.

Colleen questions, "Isn't Fred on Pastor/Parish?" Michael nods and she continues, "His wife, Sarah, likes you. So she gave me a heads up knowing that I'd come straight to you."

Michael leans forward, "What's going on?"

"Mac is planning to ambush you today at the meeting you called about Beth's wedding. He's going to demand that you tell them if you and Sadie are sexually active."

Sighing, Michael leans back in his desk chair. Sadie begins to pace and panic. Michael tells her to calm down assuring her it will be okay and he will take care of it.

"Oh, my dad used to say that. I've been engaged for four days and my private life is already on a meeting agenda," Sadie rants.

Michael repeats firmly, "Calm down."

Sadie yells, "Don't tell me to calm down!"

Michael jumps up, "Shh…"

Sadie's voice drops to a low growl, "I want to know exactly who says what and how you handle it."

"Don't worry so much. I'll tell you what happens."

"Oh, you're just like my dad. You'll only tell me the basics and the outcome and leave out any of the details that you think might upset me," she accuses.

Michael remarks sarcastically, "Why would I think that you might overreact?"

Sadie storms out of the office with Colleen close at her heels.

Michael drops back into his chair. Aidan stays with Michael to talk things over and help him think of what to say.

Sadie and Colleen sit in the lounge for a few minutes when Sadie's eyes light up. "Come on, Colleen. Let me show you how an experienced preacher's kid handles this."

First, Sadie returns to Michael's office apologizing for carrying on and giving him a kiss. She suggests that Michael announces their engagement which could affect the attitude of the people on the committee. They'll find out soon anyway. Michael stares at her remembering when he announced that they were dating. Sadie explains this is different because she knows its coming and an engagement is something people normally announce publicly.

Sadie then leaves with Colleen, going to the youth group's room where she searches the cupboards until she finds a set of walkie-talkies. Next, she returns to the lounge where she hides one in a large, dusty, silk flower arrangement. When she turns it on to vox, it makes a static sound until she turns on the receiver. Colleen giggles in disbelief that her friend has just bugged her fiancé's meeting.

The two see Michael heading for the prep room at the back of the sanctuary to robe up. They duck back into his office leaving the other walkie-talkie in his desk drawer. Sadie then hurries to the choir room to robe up. The rest of the choir has already left for church.

The opening hymn begins and the choir processes in. Michael follows noticing that Sadie is missing. He wishes he could look for her, but he can't. He wonders if she couldn't handle the thought of the meeting and left. As the last verse is sung, Sadie enters walking down the side aisle climbing into the choir loft. Relieved to see her, Michael can't help being suspicious about where she had been. He notices

Colleen sliding into the pew with Aidan.

Michael impresses Sadie with how calm and focused he appears. No one would guess that he had other concerns on his mind. At the end of his sermon, he states that he needs to take a personal moment and invites Sadie to join him as he announces their engagement to thunderous applause.

When Michael finishes shaking hands after the service, he heads to the lounge. Sadie and Colleen break away from the well wishers running to the office. They sit on the couch pleased with how easily they can hear the committee settling in.

Michael starts the meeting with the discussion concerning Beth and Adam's wedding reception being allowed to serve wine. Mac vehemently demands that no alcohol be allowed in the church. Michael argues being supportive of the problems facing the soldiers serving our country as well as Sadie's argument that Jesus made sure there was enough wine at the wedding in Canaan.

Sensing that most people agree with him, he calls for a vote. Only Mac stands firmly against the exception they are making. Michael thanks them for their time attempting to end the meeting, but Mac interrupts, of course; he has a concern. Michael braces himself as Mac dives right in.

"Rev. Donnelly, we have reason to believe that you are engaging in premarital sex with a parishioner in our parsonage."

Most of the rest of the committee appear to be shocked by his statement. Eloise appears annoyed and embarrassed by Mac's allegation. Michael remembers Sadie's advice to the teenage girl. Stick to the truth. Don't deny anything. Don't admit anything.

"What would that reason be?" he counters.

"Just answer the charge," Mac demands.

"Has anyone seen inappropriate behavior? Have I ever been unprepared or late for a service or meeting? Are there any legitimate complaints?" Michael challenges.

"What does any of that have to do with the question at hand?" Mac pushes.

"I am the pastor of this church and I find your question disrespectful and offensive. Unless you have a specific complaint about inappropriate behavior or a problem with my work performance, I will not dignify your charge with a response of any kind."

Eloise raps the table, "Here, here..." The rest of the committee agrees with Michael.

Thrilled with the way Michael handled the situation, Sadie hugs Colleen. Then she realizes her mistake. Michael leaves the meeting before the others and she is hiding in his office. She grabs their coats hurrying out of the office and running into him in the hall.

She quickly grabs his hand, "Let's get out of here."

However, Michael wants to go to his office first. Sadie blocks his path suggesting they can come back later. He becomes suspicious. Pushing past her, he enters to find Colleen who is standing behind his desk and smiling too big. He goes to his desk to get his briefcase, while Sadie and Colleen chatter so he can't hear anything unusual.

Knowing that they are up to something he orders them to be quiet and hears something. Opening his desk drawer, he finds the walkie-talkie under some papers and hears the committee still talking as they prepare to leave.

"I don't believe you two," angry, he turns it off.

"No!" the girls yell, "You can't turn it off. The other end just went to static. It is in there making noise."

Michael's eyes widen, "Oh shit..." He quickly returns to the meeting room where Mac is holding the other walkie-talkie.

Mac inquires, "Do you know anything about this?"

"It's mine," Michael turns to see Sadie enter the room. "I'm sorry, but I did that."

As Sadie sits down, the committee returns to their seats. Michael folds his arms and leans on the wall.

"I overheard a rumor that this meeting would be about my private life and the preacher's kid in me panicked. I reverted back to a teenager whose older brother showed her how to do this so we would know what people were saying about us.

"In eighth grade, my first boyfriend walked me home from school every day. That was it. There was no hugging, no holding hands, no kissing, just walking and talking. Still, at one of these meetings people complained that I was too young to have a boyfriend, especially publicly. They acted like they had a right to vote on it or something. Luckily, my father told them that he and my mother would decide whether or not I could walk with him.

"Another time, when I was in high school, there were these two weird girls in my church. They invited me to their sleepover. When I declined the invitation, a meeting was actually called to discuss my not being a good preacher's kid in their church.

"I'm sorry and embarrassed by what I did, but I have been engaged for four days and my life is already the topic of one of these meetings. However, I am really embarrassed and can honestly promise not to do this again.

"If it is Michael's moral character you are questioning, I can tell you he has never been anything but a gentleman. The church is his priority and the reason you caught me listening is because when he saw what I was doing, he immediately turned it off which caused the static."

Eloise speaks up, "Well, I've been in this church for over fifty years and Sadie is telling the truth. This is typical preacher's kid mischief. Thank you Sadie for your honesty about the situation. I say we accept her apology and go home already."

Despite the fact that Mac is fuming, the others agree with Eloise and leave. When Michael and Sadie are alone, Sadie asks him if he is mad. His eyes answer the question. He grabs her hand and briskly walks to the parsonage. Once inside, she tries to apologize, but Michael explodes.

"Do you have any idea how hard that meeting was for me and you go and make it worse?!"

"I'm sorry."

"I based not answering Mac's charge on there being no inappropriate behavior and you hand him inappropriate behavior! We are just lucky that that fact didn't occur to him, or at least it didn't occur to him yet."

"I'm sorry."

"I told you to trust me! I told you I would tell you what happened!"

"I'm sorry."

"Who do you two think you are, Lucy and Ethel?"

"I'm sorry. I have no defense. I was wrong and I'm sorry I embarrassed you."

Michael stomps into the living room dropping down on the couch to stew. Sadie sheepishly sits beside him. The two sit in silence for a while until Michael looks down at a throw pillow. Grabbing it, he gives her four good blows. Sadie covers her head and doesn't even try to stop him. Once he tosses the pillow aside, Sadie buries her face in his chest promising to never listen in on a meeting again and that she will trust him.

Michael smiles, "Do you know what this means? My friends, Sean, and I thought that I would never win an argument with you. I just won my first argument with you."

Sadie smiles back at him as he pulls her up onto his lap to kiss and hold. Sadie is relieved that he forgave her so quickly. Michael is relieved to know that he can win an argument with her.

The Donnelly home cannot be seen from the street. As Michael drives up the long driveway, Sadie's knees knock a bit. The house is a white accented with brick mansion complimented by perfect landscaping. Michael holds her hand as they approach the front door telling her not to be nervous, but he can see the fear on her face.

Before they reach the door, Sadie observes, "You moved from here to a parsonage?" Michael smiles. She continues, "You know, chances are you will be living in parsonages smaller than yours. Yours is old, but for a parsonage, it's a good size."

Michael kisses her forehead, "As long as I live with you."

"You are insane," Sadie informs him.

"So I've been told," Michael leads her into the house.

Overwhelmed in his house, Sadie feels out of place. Sean tells her to relax as he hugs her. She finds it comforting that Sean and Carol like her and his father's attitude is warm. Drew, who is away on business, is not here. Only his mother seems icy.

Taking her hand, Michael leads her through a rather large living room with Carol and Sean walking with them. Michael shows her a beautiful, black, full size grand piano. Sadie is surprised and thinks it is beautiful. Michael suggests that she play something, but Sadie explains that she can't play from memory. Carol opens the bench which reveals some music. Sadie looks through the books, chooses a pretty song from a Best of Broadway book, and begins to play. Soon, Michael's parents join them to listen as Sadie plays.

When she finishes she asks, "Wow, this is beautiful. Who plays?"

"What do you mean?" Sean asks.

"I mean, you have this gorgeous instrument, so who plays it?"

"No one in our family plays," Sophia responds. "I tried to force Carol to take lessons, but she just hated practicing and I gave up."

Sadie seems confused, "Then why do you have it?"

The family exchanges glances. No one had ever asked before. James answers, "We hire people to play at our parties and it is a beautiful piece."

"Oh, I see," Sadie can't imagine having the top of the line piano for just once in a while.

"That must be hard to understand, when you have wanted a piano all of your life and never been able to buy your dream one," Sean understands.

"Oh, I will get my piano some day," Sadie smiles.

Sophia shakes her head, "It's a shame that ministers can't afford the nice things in life."

Michael rolls his head and then places his hands on Sadie's shoulders, "Well, when we come to visit we will find you some time that you can play this piano."

"Do you want this piano?" James generously offers. "You can have it."

Sadie's eyes widen, "Wow, thank you, but they would never get this into my apartment and if we did I would have to throw a mattress on it to sleep."

They laugh. James adds, "In that case, you are always welcome to play it when you come for a visit with Michael."

The family gathers in the dining room. As a servant begins serving, like Joy, Sophia cuts to the chase, "Michael, why did you suggest this family dinner with your friend?"

Michael's head twitches, "Well, my friend and I want to invite you on June eleventh to our wedding."

Sean and Carol yell congratulations.

Sophia's eyes about pop out of her head, "You can't be serious!"

Michael nods, "No, I'm serious. We actually want you there."

"Michael, at Thanksgiving, she refused to date you. Why would she rush you like this?"

Sean interjects, "Actually, it's Michael who's been pushing this. I can't believe pestering her to marry you for a month worked."

Sophia smacks the table, "You mean he had to beg her to marry him?"

Michael rolls his head, "I didn't beg her." He looks at Sean, "Don't help." Turning back to Sophia, he attempts to explain, "She never said no. Like you, she thought it was too fast, so she tried to put me off."

Sean laughs, "Yeah, she kept saying not yet."

"When did you first ask her to marry you?" she quizzes.

"After we got up Christmas morning, I proposed down by the tree," he replies.

"So you're already sleeping with her," Sophia spits.

"Huh," Michael cocks his head, "I didn't think that comment through."

"You are an ordained minister. What kind of woman sleeps with an ordained minister?" Sophia demands.

"Oh please," James surmises, "He went to her apartment, declared his love, and pinned her to a wall until she admitted that she loved him. What do you think came next?"

Michael covers his face with his hands for a moment, "Well, now we have a date set and we are getting married."

"June eleventh?" Sophia shakes her head, "I don't think I can even get the country club with such short notice."

"Uh, Mom, I'm not getting married in the country club. I'm a minister. I'm getting married in my church."

"What about the reception? Your church is two hours from here."

"Yeah, we sort of have a deposit for the Grand Ballroom in a hotel. It's beautiful."

"What's next, a DJ instead of a live band?" Sophia snorts.

Sadie leans over toward Michael, "Is that a bad thing?"

Michael wags his eyebrows at her. Sophia slams down her fork, throws her napkin down, and storms out of the room.

Michael takes a drink of water, "Well, that went well. Dad, where do you stand?"

"I'm fine with it. I like Sadie. Go talk to your mother."

Michael leaves to find his mother. Sadie feels terrible, but Sean and Carol engage her in friendly conversation.

Michael sits with his mother on a couch while she cries telling him that she misses being close to him. He assures her that he wants to be close to her again and holds her. He tells her that he loves his ministry and he has no doubts that he is where he belongs. He then asks her to give Sadie a chance. Assuring her that he is in love with her, he asks his mother to trust him. Sophia tells Michael that she loves him and sends him back to the dining room promising she'll be there in a minute.

Sophia enters the dining room carrying a small velvet box which she sets by Sadie's plate. "This is my mother's engagement ring. I gave it to Michael to give his…fiancé." Sophia explains.

Michael seems uncomfortable, "You can wear it if you want to, but I'll still buy you your own."

"Don't be silly. Why would she need two engagement rings?" Sophia scoffs.

Sadie opens the box. It is an old fashioned silver ring with three large diamonds. It is not Sadie's style at all, but she smiles, "Thank you. It's beautiful."

"If your engagement ends, you would need to return it," Sophia states matter-of-factly.

"Mother," Michael sighs.

"This is not your first engagement Dear," she reminds him.

Sadie glances at the ring, "Michael, is this the ring you gave Barbara?"

Michael nods slowly. Sophia insists, "That does not matter. It's Michael's ring. Oh, you will need to sign a pre-nup."

Michael runs his hand over his face, "You don't have to sign a pre-nup."

Sadie questions, "Why would I need to? I make more than he does."

This fact causes Michael to cringe.

Annoyed by the statement, Sophia lists, "There is inheritance, family heirlooms, the trust fund."

"Trust fund?" Sadie turns to Michael, "I thought you told me you got rid of that?"

"I turned it over to my parents. They kept it in tact in case I change my mind and need to pay for Harvard or something," he explains.

"Fine, if you need to protect your things and Barbara's ring, I'll sign one. I don't care," Sadie concedes.

Michael leans over snapping the ring box closed, "You don't need to sign one."

James, Sean, and Carol attempt to lighten the mood. Michael and Sadie invite Sean and Carol to be in the wedding party. They enthusiastically accept.

Sophia points out, "You understand if Colby is one of your groomsmen and his mother is my close friend, we have to invite Barbara."

"I understand. I don't have a problem with that," Sadie states honestly trusting Michael's love enough.

"I'm not sure that I'm going to ask Graham and Colby to be in the wedding," Michael admits.

"Michael! You three were inseparable growing up all the way from kindergarten through college. How could you not ask them?" Sophia demands.

"Mom, they don't like me anymore. They don't seem to have forgiven me for not going to Harvard with them. They have never once come to one of my services and they have never invited me to go to court with them. We never talk anymore." Michael defends his decision.

"Son, I think your mother is right. You boys were best friends for almost twenty years. You need to work it out with them. Have you invited them to a service? Have you offered to go to court with them?" James agrees with Sophia.

"No, but at the New Year's Eve Party, they were not nice to Sadie," he argues.

"But they apologized and said that they wanted to try again sometime. They said that they didn't want to lose you as a friend," Sadie reminds him. "Besides, your mother wasn't nice to me and she's invited."

The comment startles Michael and offends Sophia, but Carol, Sean, and even James can't help busting up laughing. James likes this girl.

Sean quips, "Wait until I get home and tell Jeremy about all of this."

"Sweetheart, you probably shouldn't bring Jeremy with all the friends, family, and colleagues, not to mention people from Michael's church."

Sadie elbows Michael who speaks up, "Jeremy is invited, period."

"Michael, I do not think that is wise," Sophia persists.

"Oh please," Sadie, who is becoming more and more frustrated, snaps at his mother, "I'm expected to be okay with inviting the person you consider the love of his life, and wear her engagement ring, but I'm not supposed to invite Sean's partner? Well, I have met Jeremy and I like him. He is definitely invited."

Michael and his family look surprised by her outburst, but she doesn't care. After a moment, Michael agrees with Sadie. Sean is thrilled that someone spoke up for him and Jeremy like this and will gladly welcome Sadie into his family.

As the evening finally ends and they prepare to leave, Sophia asks,

"It is clear that you are doing your wedding your way. Is there any part that I can have to do?"

Sadie thinks for a moment, "You can have the flowers at both the church and reception including the table centerpieces and all the bouquets and boutonnières. My mother and I are shopping for my gown next week and the following weekend, we will shop for the girls' gowns. I'll send you pictures and color schemes. You can knock yourself out."

This satisfies Sophia and James offers to stock the bar as well as cover any other expenses that Michael needs. Michael accepts thankfully suggesting that he purchases the alcohol from a close friend of his, Steve Duffy, who will also be in the wedding, and the couple heads home.

Michael squeezes her hand, "Thank you for giving mom the flowers to arrange."

"It's selfish actually," Sadie admits, "I would have kept the cost on flowers at a minimum. She'll do it up big, and from the looks of your home, she'll do it tastefully."

Michael agrees and then he adds, "I never planned on giving you that ring. I will buy you a ring."

Sadie winks at him, "Okay. You better."

Chapter XVIII

Troy cannot let go of his disappointment. After all these years, he still wants Sadie. He still wants to be part of the group. Troy misses Aidan and Steve. Troy had thought that everything would be better after the wedding. He thought they would invite him to hang out again like the old days, but they hadn't.

Troy became obsessed with the minister. He started following him. Everyone had lied to him. The preacher and Sadie are most definitely not just friends. They spend nights together, share almost every supper together, and go places together.

Michael has taken Troy's place with his friends. Michael spends almost every Friday at Duffy's with Sadie and their friends. Even while Sadie is at work, he spends mornings with Aidan and Steve. They jog, swim laps, lift weights, and play basketball. Some days, they eat lunch at the Rainbow Café. Aidan and Steve have even been attending his church.

Hatred grows in his stomach. He has to win Sadie back. What's more, he has to get Sadie away from the minister. Troy wants his place back with Aidan and Steve. He has to find a way to get rid of the minister for good.

Sunday, after church, Troy follows Sadie and his replacement to a mall. The couple walks from one jewelry store to the next. A terrible feeling comes over Troy. He has to know what they are shopping for.

Troy enters a jewelry store after they leave walking to the showcase where they spent time talking with a sales lady.

"Damn it," he thinks, "wedding ring sets. The son-of-a-bitch wormed his way in permanently."

Sadie loves her new ring. Michael insisted on a much bigger ring with several more diamonds than the simple ones she kept selecting yet it is gold and dainty. His taste is still much higher than Sadie's. The sales lady who sold them the ring said that she doesn't usually come across a man being the one insisting on the upgrade of the selections. Her friends highly approve of the purchase.

That week, Sadie spends two evenings at school holding parent/teacher conferences. Because of the conferences, there is no school Friday. All six of her bridesmaids plan to meet Sadie to shop for gowns. Later that evening, Sadie, Colleen, Brenda, and Stephanie plan to drag the guys to a chick flick.

Sadie's car made strange noises earlier that week, so she took it to a garage planning to walk to and from school despite the snow, but Michael insists on shuttling her back and forth especially at nine o'clock at night after her conferences.

Thursday night after conferences, Michael drives Sadie home. She invites him up for a while because conferences leave her wound up and wide awake. Once in the apartment, Michael has bad news. There are problems with the church finances. The Finance Committee has to redo a report and make spending cuts by Monday's meeting with the District Superintendent. The emergency finance meeting will be held on Friday night causing him to miss the movie, but he promises to meet them after the movie. He sarcastically remarks how he hates missing a romantic comedy. Sadie playfully smacks his arm several times, so he pins her arms to stop her.

With a kiss, he says goodnight and heads for the door. Sadie blocks his way. Pushing him up against the wall, he allows her to pin his arms to it. She informs him that he is not going anywhere. Kissing his neck and jaw, she undresses him. Leaving his clothes by the door, she pulls him down the hall to her room where she shoves him on the bed and jumps on top of him. Again, he allows her to pin him down to have her way with him.

In the morning, the door buzzer slowly wakes Sadie. Rolling over, she checks the clock. Suddenly, she sits up pushing on Michael, "Wake up, wake up! We slept in."

Groggy, he moans, "So?"

"Get up. Someone's here. If it's Colleen, she has a key."

Sadie springs out of bed. Grabbing a robe, she hurries out of the room to retrieve his clothes but she is too late. Colleen and Brenda stand at the end of the hall picking up his clothes.

"Did we have company last night?" Colleen teases.

"Good heavens, apparently you two barely made it into the apartment," Brenda tisks.

"Quick, take a shower. We have to meet your mother in less than an hour," Colleen pushes her toward the bathroom despite Sadie's protests, "Go ahead, I'll toss his clothes in the room for him."

Once Sadie closes the bathroom door, Brenda and Colleen stroll down the hall to the bedroom. Colleen knocks, "Good morning Michael. You better cover up. I'm delivering your clothes that you managed to lose by the door."

Colleen opens the door; she and Brenda step into the room. Michael sits in bed with the covers pulled up over his stomach, "Good morning ladies. Where is Sadie?"

"She had to get in the shower. It is almost time to meet her mother," Brenda explains.

They set his clothes on the dresser, but instead of leaving, they climb onto the bed, one sitting on each side.

"What are you doing? Get out," he demands.

Colleen coos, "So how's it going?"

Michael has flash backs to college making out with two girls. These girls aren't kissing him, but the fact that he is naked seems worse.

Brenda points out, "I know you work out with the guys, but I didn't realize just how buff you are."

"Please leave," Michael begs.

Colleen says thoughtfully, "You know, Sunday it will be hard to concentrate on the sermon with this image of you in my head."

"Please leave," he repeats.

Colleen lies down, propping her head up on her hand, "You know what I've been meaning to talk to you about?" Michael bangs his head on the headboard a few times as Colleen continues, "Aidan and I have decided to officially join your church."

"Ooo, Steve and I are talking about joining too," Brenda adds.

"That is great. Glad to hear it. Please leave now."

They refuse to leave taking guilty pleasure in his embarrassment as they chat away about a television program they watched last night.

Sadie comes back to the room, "What the hell are you doing? Get off my bed. You were just supposed to bring him his clothes."

"We did. They're right there on the dresser. He didn't get up to put them on," Colleen shrugs.

"Why couldn't you bring my clothes before you jumped in the shower?" he whines.

"That probably would have been better," Sadie agrees. "You two, out now."

As they leave, Brenda giggles, "Wow, Stephanie is going to hate that she missed this."

Sadie joins her friends in the kitchen, "What's the matter with you two? You really ticked him off."

Giggling, they apologize, "We're sorry."

"Sure you are," Sadie giggles too.

The door buzzer sounds. Sadie answers, "Who is it?"

"Steve."

Sadie presses the door release and opens the door. Returning to the kitchen, she tells Brenda, "Steve is here."

"What? He can't be. He's at home lying under his car with the break pads off," Brenda informs her.

The three turn to see Troy Meyers standing in the apartment. "I was hoping to catch you alone."

Sadie's heart pounds in her chest, "How dare you lie to get up here."

"I just want five minutes to talk. Just hear me out. We were together five years; you can give me five minutes."

Troy hears a door open. Michael comes out of a room from down the hall. Troy knows it has to be a bedroom. Michael stops half way down the hall when he notices Troy. Slowly, he continues down the hall.

Fury rises in Troy's throat, "Hello Reverend," he turns to Sadie, "You lied to me. You said you were just friends, yet here he is coming out of what I assume is a bedroom and you are wearing an engagement ring."

"Not that it is any of your business," Sadie's voice trembles a little, "but I didn't lie. Things between Michael and I were strange in early November, but we managed to work it out."

"I still want the five minutes," Troy demands.

"What five minutes?" Michael snaps.

"Troy wants to talk to me," she explains.

"In private," Troy adds.

"I'm not leaving," Michael states firmly.

"Please," Sadie pleads, "just wait in the study for a few minutes."

Michael wants to say no. They look into each other's eyes and have a short silent argument. Annoyed, Michael gives in and stomps into the study. Troy's anger increases to see that they are so close that they can communicate without speaking.

Sadie instructs the girls to wait in the dining room knowing they will be able to hear everything and leads Troy through the dining room into the living room.

"Sadie, I know you waited over three years to begin dating again because you had trouble getting over me," Troy begins.

"No, I had trouble trusting men after you. Maybe that's why it took a minister to get me dating again," Sadie corrects.

"Sure, a tall, thin minister with dark hair and eyes," describes Troy.

"What's your point?" she asks.

"That description fits me. You are trying to replace me."

Sadie laughs, "I have never once looked at Michael and thought of you."

"Listen to me, you and I belong together. We were meant for each other. I am so sorry about my reaction to the baby. I wish I could do that week over, but I can't. We shared five wonderful years together. How long have you known this preacher? Look, just listen to me," Troy insists.

"No, you listen. I don't have any feelings for you. I stopped loving you the day you wanted me to abort our baby. Well, our baby is gone, so we have no reason to see each other ever again. Your five minutes are up. Get out," she orders.

"You bitch," he backhands her across the cheek.

"Michael!" Colleen and Brenda yell. As Michael rushes in, Colleen yells, "He hit her!"

Michael runs into the living room. Troy throws a punch, but Michael dodges, blocking with his forearm. Michael grabs Troy's right arm twisting it behind his back. Michael uses his free hand to grab the back of Troy's shirt ramming him into the wall.

Once Troy stops struggling, Michael growls, "Don't you ever come near Sadie again." Keeping his hold on Troy, Michael shows him to the door.

Michael hurries back to Sadie taking her in his arms. Sadie doesn't want to tell him all that was said, but Michael insists. She promises him that she never thought of Troy when she looks at him. Michael believes her.

Running late, Sadie and her friends leave to meet the others to choose bridesmaids' dresses. Sadie's face bares a rather large bruise on her right cheekbone. Everyone is upset by the incident, especially Joy.

They attempt to put it aside to enjoy their shopping. Sadie likes pastels, but can tell her friends don't. Sadie's favorite color is green in any shade. Hunter green is too dark for a June wedding and sea foam green does not look right on the girls. Finally, they find a pretty shade of green called citron that they all agree on. The dress is sleeveless with a v-neck and is tea length with a kerchief cut.

With the dresses green, Sadie plans to tell Sophia she can go with any spring colors she likes for the flowers. Sadie prefers a nice colorful mixture, but trusts Sophia's taste.

The gowns ordered the happy group head out for a pleasant luncheon.

Troy's anger builds all day. The fact that he could not land a punch on Michael and that Michael had so easily pinned him was more than Troy could stand. Sadie had laughed at him. She told him to get out. She had no feelings toward him. The way she treated him felt like she stuck him with a red hot poker.

Since he lost his temper hitting her, he knows that Aidan and Steve will take her side. Besides, they are best buddies with the minister now. Troy decides to kill Michael. He decides to kill him in front of Sadie and their friends. Today is Friday. On Fridays the group either goes out or hangs around Steve's bar. They never invite him, but he will be joining them tonight.

Sadie and her friends stand in front of Duffy's waiting for Stephanie. Michael's finance meeting already began. Steph walks up declaring that Sadie is her date for the night hooking her elbow around Sadie's. The theater is only two blocks away. Before they leave, Sadie spots Troy. Instinctively, she moves behind Aidan. The others see him now and are angry that he hit her.

"What the hell do you want?" Aidan snaps.

"I want to talk to the preacher," he demands.

Troy plows through the crowd muttering about the minister. They notice something is off about Troy. His eyes have a wild look as they dart around. It is clear that he wants to confront Michael.

"He's not with us tonight," Steve informs him.

"Bull shit! He's always with you. He came out of Sadie's bedroom this morning. You two," he jerks his head toward Steve and Aidan, "You are always with him, jogging, swimming, lifting weights, playing basketball. You eat lunch at the Rainbow Café; hang out with him at the bar. You even go to his church! You've totally replaced me with a god damn preacher!" Troy rants.

"We didn't replace you," Aidan stammers. They all wonder how Troy knows so many details of their lives realizing that he must have been stalking them.

"Bull shit! You four are married and now Sadie and the preacher are getting married. That was supposed to be me! You wouldn't even know Colleen if it weren't for me."

Colleen speaks up, "Well, I guess you threw it all away or should I say you threw it all down the stairs."

Troy, seething with anger, takes a menacing step toward her. Aidan rushes between them staring Troy down.

Troy's attitude suddenly shifts to pleading, "Sadie, I want you back. I need you."

Sadie charges Troy pushing him in the chest with her palms, "Now listen to me. It is time you move on. People break up everyday. We broke up almost four years ago. So, move on!"

She turns walking away.

"Hey Sadie," Troy calls.

An eerie feeling fills her as she has heard those words in that tone before. Terrified, she slowly turns to face him. Troy pulls a gun from his pocket and aims it at her chest. Aidan charges him. As his shoulder plunges into Troy's ribs, the gun shot rings out.

Sadie screams as she falls back. Lying on top of Troy, Aidan yells, "Is she hit?"

Everyone is screaming. Brenda yells, "Oh my god, oh my god! He shot her!"

Aidan drives his fist into Troy's face three times, picks up the gun, and stands. Stephanie calls 911 on her cell phone. Steve removes Sadie's coat. Using his scarf, Steve applies pressure to her wound. The blood seems to be coming more from the shoulder than by the chest and coming from more than one place. He believes that the bullet must have ripped all the way through. Blood gushes onto the sidewalk. As he pushes down, Sadie cries out.

Police arrive quickly. The ambulance soon follows. Brenda gives her name to the police informing them that she needs to get Sadie's fiancé.

Chapter XIX

The Finance Committee combs the budget searching for cuts. Mac and Michael square off on the priorities. Michael lays down the law that salaries and utilities are off limits.

The money paid to the conference called apportionments, bring the most arguments. The church seldom pays all or any of this. Mac again wishes to include this in the cuts. Michael insists that they pay every penny.

"Our church is small. Unless you want to risk being put on a circuit, being appointed a part-time minister or being forced into a merger which could close these doors, we need to pay the conference to prove that we are a viable congregation," Michael debates.

"What are you willing to cut?" Mac challenges.

"Sadie requested a substantial amount toward an excellent Bible School program. We had a successful Bible School in August creating our own program. I say we cut it."

Surprised, Mac comments, "I didn't think you would touch Sadie's request."

Annoyed, Michael rolls his eyes and continues, "The choir submitted a request for new music. I think we need cut that amount at least in half. Now, here I got a little creative..."

The door bursts open. Brenda stumbles into the room out of breath.

Her pale, tear streaked face holds a look of terror. Michael jumps to his feet. Brenda cannot bring herself to say a word.

Michael moves around the table to her, "What is it? What's wrong?"

Breathing heavily, she stutters, "It's Sadie... Troy... he shot her. He just pulled out a gun and shot her."

Michael cannot believe it and has difficulty catching his breath. He swallows, "Is she... is she..."

Brenda grabs his arm, "She was alive when the ambulance took her. Colleen went with her."

Mac offers, "Go. I'll start the prayer chain."

Michael runs to his office for his coat and keys. As Brenda and Michael run to his car, Aidan's car squeals through the parking lot. They jump in the back with Stephanie. Aidan peals out. Stephanie quietly, steadily recounts what happened for Michael. Steve adds that the blood seemed to be coming from her shoulder and not her chest.

Michael asks where Troy is. Brenda tells him that the police took him to the hospital because Aidan broke his face. This fact pleases Michael.

Once they arrive at the hospital, Michael runs to the reception desk. The receptionist informs him that the doctors are working on her and sends them to a waiting room. As Michael paces around, he notices Aidan's busted knuckles. Then he looks at Steve, who is covered in blood, his chest, legs, arms, and especially his hands. A wave of nausea floods through him, causing him to feel light-headed. Steve can't bear to return Michael's gaze. Stephanie takes Michael's arm coaxing him to sit. He leans his arms on his legs hanging his head.

Once he recovers, he asks if anyone has called Sadie's parents.

Stephanie had. Michael pulls out his cell phone to call his parents and speaks with his dad asking him to call Carol and Sean.

Colleen appears running to Aidan. She has some blood on her. Colleen reports the doctors took Sadie to surgery. The group changes waiting rooms. Michael realizes that it is the same waiting room where he had spent the night with Bob and Cathy causing a sick feeling to sink into his stomach.

As they wait, a police detective interviews them one at a time. The police bag Steve's clothes for evidence and allow him to wash up. A nurse provides him scrubs to wear.

Michael learns more details as he listens to the police interrogation. Michael hears Aidan tell the detective that Troy was gunning for Sadie's fiancé, Michael Donnelly. He also learns for the first time from Brenda that Troy had pretended to be Steve to gain entrance to Sadie's apartment that morning.

Sadie's parents arrive running to Michael and embracing him. Stephanie sits with them to recount the events of the evening. Another person waiting for a family member in surgery pours coffee. Her hand shakes burning her finger which causes her to drop the coffee pot. The sudden loud noise causes everyone to jump. The girls can no longer hold back their tears. Aidan holds Colleen, Steve comforts Brenda, and Stephanie leans on a wall staring out a window alone. Michael goes to her placing his hand on her back. She turns toward him and he catches her in a tight embrace.

As the wait drags on, Sean and Jeremy arrive. Michael surprises them by introducing them to Sadie's friends and family as Sean and his partner, Jeremy instead of his friend.

Michael moves away from the group and sits alone to pray in

earnest, "Dear God, please don't take Sadie. So many people love her here. She can't be done yet. I need her here. I just found her, please don't take her yet.

"You don't have enough good people on this earth. You need her here a little longer. Think of her students, her family, her friends, the people in her church. She needs to have and raise children.

"I need her. I want her. She makes me a better minister. She makes things better with my family. She makes me a better man. Please God, don't take her. Please, don't let Troy's evil win. I love her."

Martin finds him and sits beside him. Quietly, without interrupting Michael, he silently joins him praying once again for the life of his beloved daughter.

A nurse enters the waiting room calling for the family of Sadie Stevens to follow her to a consolation room. The thought of that room sends a wave of fear and panic through Michael as he stands along with nine other people. The nurse suggests they wait where they are since there are so many and she will send the doctor down to them.

Finally, a doctor comes to speak with the family, "Sadie is out of surgery. The bullet tore up her shoulder, but she should have a full recovery. Whoever tackled the shooter probably saved her life. Had he shot her in the chest at that close range…"

Everyone looks at Aidan.

The doctor continues, "She lost a lot of blood. We gave her a transfusion. The person who held pressure on the wound also helped to save her life."

Everyone looks at Steve.

The doctor continues, "Her biggest danger now is staph infection. We have her on antibiotics. We will send her home in the morning.

Most infections are caught in the hospital. You'll want to wash her bedding in hot water and place a clean sheet on the couch. All visitors should wash their hands. Most of you may not see her tonight, but a few can go in two at a time."

The doctor notices Martin's collar, "Are you her minister?"

"I'm her dad," he answers.

The doctor seems confused, "Is your name Michael?"

"No, this is Michael. He's her fiancé," Martin answers.

"Oh, I see. So you're a minister also?" the doctor asks.

"Yes, why?" Michael asks.

"She's coming out of the anesthetic and is asking for you," the doctor tells him as he tries to suppress a smile.

Michael wonders what she is saying as he turns to her parents, "You go in first. Then I'll give you the key to her place so you can stay in her guestroom. I want to stay here with her tonight."

Joy agrees, "That's a good idea. It will give me time to wash her bedding for her."

Joy and Martin leave to see her. Michael seems concerned. Colleen asks, "Is something wrong?"

He lowers his voice, "Sadie's mother is going to wash her bedding. Think about how you found me this morning."

Colleen assures him, "Don't worry. I think Sadie straightened up before she left for the movies."

After a few minutes, Martin and Joy return to the waiting room attempting not to laugh.

"Is she alright?" Colleen asks.

"Oh, she is great," Martin chuckles, "She is still drugged up."

"Yes," Joy glares at Michael, "She is asking for you."

"Why are you looking at me like that?" he wonders if he should ask.

Joy does an impression of a drugged Sadie, "She asked, 'Where's Michael?' We said you were here, just outside. She said, 'I love him. He is one horny minister."

Michael shuts his eyes and hangs his head. The others have the first good laugh of the night. Michael grabs his coat, hands her key to her parents, and makes a hasty exit.

A nurse shows Michael the way. She tells him that many people come out of anesthetic crying or groggy, but Sadie came out rather happy. She apparently really likes her minister.

Michael runs his hand over his face, "Well, I'm not just her minister; I'm her fiancé."

The nurse giggles. He sees Sadie lying in a bed behind a partially closed curtain. "Hi Sweetheart."

"Hi, where have you been? I've been waiting for you," she sounds drugged.

"I've been here all evening," he assures her.

Sadie tells the nurse, "See? I told you he's hot." Michael shakes his head as she turns back to him, "Want to make out?"

Michael leans over her, "Now's not a good time, maybe later."

The doctor checks on her, "Hello Sadie. Do you remember who I am?"

She points at him, "Yes, you are my hot doctor."

The doctor addresses Michael, "She woke up a little horny."

Michael shakes his head. The doctor steps out with him. Michael requests to spend the night.

The doctor jokes, "There is no sex in the hospital."

Michael runs his hand over his face again, "Seriously, if she wakes up in the night, if she remembers what happened, I don't want her afraid and alone."

The doctor permits it. Once she moves to a room for the night, Michael slumps in a chair drifting in and out of sleep. Around four in the morning, Michael wakes hearing her moaning and grunting. She tosses her head from side to side as if trapped in a nightmare. He leans forward rubbing her arm gently to ease her out of her sleep.

She wakes with a startled cry pulling away from his touch, "Don't touch me! Leave me alone!"

"Shh... It's okay. It's me. It's just Michael."

"Michael?" she tries to sit up.

"I'm here. Don't get up, just lie back. Take it easy."

"I had the worst dream," she wipes her eyes, "I dreamt that Troy shot me."

He touches her face, "You're okay now. Go back to sleep."

A nurse enters the room to check the IV's. Sadie stares at her.

The nurse asks, "How are you feeling dear? Do you have any pain?"

"You're a nurse," she mumbles confused, "Am I in a hospital?"

She looks to Michael who nods. Her eyes scan the room. Her right hand reaches over and touches her left shoulder. She flinches with pain and examines her IV's. Her eyes fill with panic.

"Did he really shoot me?" Michael doesn't answer, "Michael! Did Troy shoot me?"

Michael nods. Sadie sobs. He puts the side rail down so he can comfort her. He holds her hand lying his head on top of hers.

In the morning, Joy and Martin arrive to find Michael bent in half sleeping with his head beside her on the bed. Their presence wakes him. He slowly sits up, stiff and sore.

"How is she?" Joy frets.

"She knows she was shot. She thought it was a nightmare until she figured out she was in a hospital."

The conversation wakes Sadie. Michael gives his seat to Joy. Martin suggests that Michael should go to the cafeteria for breakfast. The nurse said the doctor won't be by for a little bit. Martin offers to go with him. Michael agrees needing to walk more than eat. As they reach the elevator, he realizes he left his wallet in his coat by the room and goes back to retrieve it. As he stands by the curtain he overhears Sadie talking to her mother.

"I loved him. I was going to marry him and he shot me. I dated him for five years and never saw any of this coming; although, he always had a bit of a temper. I almost believed that the stairs really had been an accident, but now… Yesterday, he hit me. I could have ended up a battered woman. How could I not have seen this coming? Now I'm engaged again to a man I haven't even known a year. Am I crazy?"

Michael quietly backs away. His chest and head ache. Was she going to pull away from him again? Does she really think that he could hurt her?

"Are you okay?" Martin finds him.

"Yeah," he stammers, "You know, I'm really not hungry. I think I'll go outside for a breath of fresh air."

Michael heads out of the hospital pulling on his coat. The air is cold and crisp. Thursday night, she had jumped him loving him freely, openly. How could he lose it all so suddenly? It took him five months to break through the wall she had built around herself. Would she put the walls back up? He definitely did not like being referred to just as "a man".

He stands around for awhile. Taking a deep breath, he returns to her room to wait for the doctor. Joy sits next to her with Martin standing behind Joy's chair. Michael leans against the wall on the opposite side of the bed.

Finally, the doctor's rounds make it to Sadie's room. He explains the discharge instructions. An at-home nurse will come by every other day to change the dressing and examine the wound.

He prescribes antibiotics and pain medication. Sadie refuses the pain killers. The last time she took pain killers, she had difficulty getting off them. The doctor presses her to take them promising to get her back off them. He warns that the pain of ripped muscles will need the medicine.

Sadie feels relieved to arrive home. Her bad hip throbs with pain. When she was shot, she landed on the sidewalk on her bad hip leaving it bruised. She limps from the car to the stairs. She only struggles up the first two steps before Michael scoops her up carrying her rest of the way.

Michael places her on the couch already covered with a clean sheet. Her mother tells her that she washed Sadie's bedding last night. Sadie's eyes grow wide thinking about the mess she had left in her room and of the evidence laying around to what she had been doing.

"Don't worry Sadie," her mother smirks, "We already knew before we came last night."

Embarrassed, Michael looks out the window.

"You knew what?" Sadie asks.

Joy's face lights up with a good idea, "Did you know that anesthetic acts as a truth serum? As people come out of it, they babble their thoughts."

"Oh no, what did I say?" she asks.

Michael turns back toward Joy who smiles at him.

"When Daddy and I came to see you, all you could do was talk about Michael. Where is Michael? I love Michael. I'm going to marry him. Oh yeah, and my favorite, he is one horny minister."

Sadie slaps her hand over her mouth and looks at Michael who smiles at her, "I'm so sorry. Did I embarrass you?"

"I didn't mind. I was just so relieved you were awake and talking. You did tell the nurse that I'm hot. I'm glad Mac didn't stop by to see you."

Martin and Joy plan to stay two or three nights, but need to go home first. They will be gone three to four hours and suggest Michael and Sadie sleep. Michael checks the alarm clock for Sadie's pills, and then falls asleep in the recliner.

The sound of Sadie's heavy breathing and moaning wakes him. He assumes she is having a nightmare, but finds her awake.

"What's wrong?" he asks.

Breathlessly, she groans, "Nothing, I'm fine."

Michael checks the clock to discover that she is over an hour late to take her medicine, "You missed your pills."

"No. I took the antibiotics," she assures him.

Annoyed, Michael reminds her, "The doctor told you, you have to take the pain killers. He will get you back off them. I'll help you. Trust me."

Sadie doesn't answer him. She just cries. Michael fetches a glass of water and her pill. He slides one hand behind her back and takes hold of her hand with his other. He instructs her to take a deep breath and blow it out as she sits up. As he pulls her up, she cries out in pain.

After she swallows her medication, he knows it will take a while to be effective. He sits behind her placing his legs on both sides of her and pulls her back so she is lying on his chest, with his cheek on the side of her head. He tries to soothe her, speaking gently and helping her to take deep, slow breaths.

When Martin and Joy return, they find Sadie asleep in Michael's arms. People from church drop off tons of food. That evening, Sadie's friends and siblings stop to see her. Thanks to the church, Joy has no trouble with supper.

Martin asks Michael if he is ready for church in the morning. Michael simply responds, "Nope."

Chapter XX

Sunday morning, to Michael's surprise the church fills with people. Because of the prayer chain, every member knows what happened. Michael called her principal who used the snow emergency phone chain to notify the teachers of the incident. Michael scans the congregation from the back of the church seeing members who are not regulars as well as many teachers, her principal with his wife, and teen girls from her flag corps. Sadie's friends are here. His biggest surprise comes when his parents walk in with Carol, Drew, Sean and Jeremy. Ushers have to set up folding chairs in the back to accommodate the large crowd.

Five minutes before the service starts, Michael rushes back to his office to call Sadie, who stayed home with her mother and Stephanie. He tells her of the overwhelming love and support wishing she could be here, but it would be too much too soon. Sadie is moved to tears.

Michael hurries back to begin the service. He begins the announcements by informing them of Sadie's condition since that is what most people came to hear. Since they ran out of bulletins, Michael leads the parts of the service the people should read in the bulletin as "repeat after me".

Finally, the time for the sermon comes. Michael steps behind the pulpit, "Wow, I can't believe how full the church is this morning. It sort of makes me wish I had finished preparing a sermon," the congregation laughs. He continues, "Well, I'm just going to wing it. I have heard many times people say, 'Why should I go to church? I can believe in God without it. I can pray from anywhere.'

"Today is an example of why you should come to church. Sadie is a member of both this church and community. She is going through a traumatic time in her life. Look at this support and love. She is not alone. Look at all the prayer support she has.

"Thank you to those of you who brought food. It was nice that her mother didn't have to make supper or we didn't have to eat pizza. Heaven knows nobody wants me in the kitchen. Yet, we had plenty of nourishing, delicious food. I never understood why people brought food during troubled times or funerals. I never realized that when everything goes crazy, everyday tasks, like making supper or finishing a sermon is easily skipped. To be part of a group like a church who takes care of you in time of need is a blessing.

"Being part of a church isn't just a comfort in bad times. It enhances good times. Coming to church makes Christmas more special. Who didn't have fun at Sadie's crazy Christmas pageant?" The congregation laughs again. Michael goes on, "We celebrate many events in church, weddings, baptisms, and holidays. We enjoy socializing together as evident by the youth group, women's groups, men's groups, tureen dinners, church picnics.

"While it is true that you can read a Bible anywhere, do you? It is true that you can pray anywhere, but church reminds you to do it. And there are times in all our lives that are so difficult, we can't even pray. At those times we have a prayer chain here, where many do the praying for us."

Michael continues relating Gospel references off the top of his head which seem to apply to his message. He even finds a connection to today's Old Testament reading.

"So in conclusion, as it turns out, my sermon ended up being about how important church can be in your life. It enhances celebrations; it comforts and brings support in hard times, and brings the presence of God to our forethoughts in our regular everyday lives.

"I want to thank the guests who came from other churches today for sharing in this prayerful support. To those of you who I don't usually see who came today for Sadie, thank you, but next Sunday consider coming back for yourselves."

After church, Colleen and her friends tell Michael they are going home since there are four parents and many siblings heading to see Sadie. They will come another time.

Michael walks beside his parents toward the apartment hoping his mom doesn't fuss about Sadie living above a hardware store.

Martin catches up clapping Michael on the back, "You, my boy, are something else. I've been preaching for almost thirty years and I'm telling you, you are a natural born preacher. You saw your church full to the brim and you wing a sermon on reasons to attend church on a regular basis." Michael laughs. Martin goes on, "You had those people's attention and you didn't waste it. I sat there thinking, 'Go Michael go."

Luke steps up, "You know what else you did? You said how much you appreciated the food. Half those women went home to their kitchens. You and Sadie won't have to cook for a month."

"You're kidding," Michael grins.

Martin and Luke shake their heads. They are not kidding.

Sophia looks surprised when she sees them entering the hardware store, but wisely doesn't say anything. They go up to the apartment where Joy has lunch set out. Sadie sits at the table, but seems tired. Lucy and Mary give Sadie details about church. Martin summarizes the sermon. Michael lists people who came like teachers, the principal, several flag corps girls and some church members.

It bothers Michael that Sadie's smile appears forced. She does not quite look like herself. A certain light in her eyes seems to be missing. He suggests that she should go lie down. The others are concerned as well. Her sisters and brother each gently hug and kiss her goodbye. Carol, Drew, Sean and Jeremy follow their lead saying goodbyes.

Sophia asks Michael if there is somewhere private they can talk. Michael leads her to the study. She takes his hand, "I think I'm starting to understand. You are supposed to be a minister. You handled yourself professionally up there today. I'm proud of you. Sadie always saw this in you. She understands this life and you."

Michael hugs her, "Thanks Mom."

"You know, she has this apartment decorated very tastefully. For an apartment, it is big."

"Yeah, that's what she likes. It's big and close to everything."

His parents say their goodbyes. Michael checks on Sadie who simply sits staring off and then goes to help Joy clear the table and do the dishes.

Joy pats Michael's hand, "Don't worry so much. She will come back. This is just an injured shoulder. Last time, she had so many broken bones, she was in a wheel chair, and she had lost her baby. She felt betrayed by her fiancé. She pulled herself out of that. Just be patient."

He knows she is right. Of course, Sadie has to go through the emotions. She told him she would not date him and he just didn't leave. If she pushes him away now, he just won't budge.

"Michael! Michael!" Sadie sounds scared.

He runs in to see what she needs. Her eyes are filled with tears as he sits by her. Her breaths are shallow. She stares directly into his eyes, "I remember more. I keep thinking about it. What he said. He hardly said anything about me. He was ranting about you. I think he came to kill you."

He rubs her leg, "I know. Aidan told me. According to Troy, I have his fiancé and his friends. Apparently he went nuts. I don't know why."

"Where do you think he is now?"

"He's in jail. He went nuts in front of a lot of witnesses, plus Aidan took him down."

Sadie cuddles up against him, "I'm so glad you weren't there."

He leans over kissing her, "I wish I had been there."

Monday, Michael struggles with his office work staring at his computer, but can't concentrate. He wishes he could go for a jog, but it is too cold out and he doesn't have time to go to the rec. center.

Sadie's parents went home today, so he needs to go to check on her at lunch to make sure she takes her medicine. When he arrives at the apartment, she is not in the living room. He finds her in bed not looking well. Sweat sparkles on her forehead causing him to worry about a fever and infection. Sadie insists she just needs sleep.

Michael heads to the kitchen to find some lunch, but first stops to use the bathroom. While washing his hands, he notices the dressing from Sadie's shoulder in the waste basket. The visiting nurse is not scheduled to come until later that evening. Picking up the gauze, he discovers fresh blood on it. On a hunch, he lifts the hamper lid where he finds a hand towel with blood.

Rushing back into her room, he demands, "What did you do?"

"What?" she plays dumb.

"I saw the blood in the bathroom. What did you do?" he demands again.

He pulls the blankets off her and unbuttons her nightgown to expose her shoulder. As he begins to peel up the tape, she tries to stop him. His glare convinces her not to fight him. Some of her stitches have been pulled out. Her wound is open, bleeding, and seeping in spots.

"What did you do to your shoulder?" She doesn't answer. Michael's anger grows, "Tell me what happened."

"I did my kick boxing video," she mumbles.

"You've got to be kidding me," Michael utters in disbelief.

"I thought I just wouldn't use my left arm. I thought it would make me feel better. I guess I got carried away."

"Didn't it burn? Wasn't it painful?" he asks.

"I guess," she stammers.

"Why didn't you stop?"

"It felt good. It was sort of a release. I didn't finish the video. I stopped," she defends herself.

Smacking his legs as he stands, Michael collects clothes for her. She replaces her dressing. As he brings her clothes, she asks what he is doing. He replies, "We have to go back to the hospital."

"I don't want to go," she whines.

"Then you shouldn't have ripped your wound open," he snaps. He dresses her and takes her to the hospital.

In the car, on the way home from the hospital, Michael suggests, "Maybe we should make an appointment for you with a psychiatrist?"

"I'm not crazy," Sadie snaps.

"Of course not, but someone tried to kill you...again. I think it would be a good idea to get help handling it," Michael persuades.

"I'll be fine," Sadie promises.

"You just injured your shoulder trying to handle it yourself," he points out.

"I'm tired. I don't want to discuss this anymore," she mumbles.

"Okay, but we will talk about it later," he reaches over to touch her leg, but she pulls it away.

Tuesday, Michael doesn't want to leave the apartment, but he has work to do. Sadie promises not to do anything stupid. He decides to leave, but stops in frequently. Sadie just lies on the couch watching TV. Then he notices her movie selections tend to be violent. As he walks in the living room, a man on television jumps on top of another man stuffing two guns under his chin. The first man shoots the second with blood splattering all over the shooter's face.

"Why are you watching this?" he asks.

"It's a good movie," she answers.

He sits on the recliner for a minute, "No, this is not a good movie."

Later that day, he stops in again, to find her watching a rather graphic werewolf movie. The werewolf hits an old man decapitating him sending the head flying through the air. She insists everything else bores her.

Sadie hates being trapped at home. She went from being constantly busy with school, church, exercise classes and friends to lying on a couch watching TV. She can't even play the piano. As he prepares to return to work, Michael leans over to kiss her, but she turns her head so his kiss lands on her cheek.

Luckily that evening, her friends visit. She seems better as she talks and laughs, but Michael still thinks she looks different. He begins to notice her friends also seem different somehow. Michael, Aidan, and Steve break away to talk in the study. Even though Sadie is the one who had been shot, all the girls have been traumatized. They are all jumpy and depressed. Brenda doesn't sleep much and Colleen is having nightmares.

As they get ready to leave, Aidan acts strangely. He sits next to Sadie as if he wants to say something, but can't find the words.

"What's wrong Honey?" Sadie coaxes.

His eyes fill with tears, "I'm sorry, I'm so sorry."

"For what?"

"This is all my fault. You had Troy out of your life for two years. I brought him back into your life. I insisted that you should get over it. I insisted that he be in the wedding. I forced you with our wedding to face him. You forgave him for my sake. It was because of me that he found out about Michael. It was because of my witness statement that Troy was never charged with anything when he pushed you down the stairs."

"Stop," Sadie soothes, "This is not your fault. You couldn't know he would do this. I never saw this coming. And as far as the stairs go, you told the police the truth. That was all you could do. You did nothing wrong. I don't blame you. Aidan, you saved my life."

Aidan hugs and thanks her, but still repeats that he is sorry.

Once everyone leaves Sadie takes her medicine and goes to bed. Michael turns out the lights, locks up, and heads home. Exhausted, he crawls in bed falling asleep before his head hits the pillow.

The phone rings. Michael can barely lift his arm to answer. "Hello?" he mummers.

"I'm so sorry to wake you," Sadie apologizes.

Michael checks the clock, three ten. "What's wrong, Sweetheart?"

"Nothing really, I feel like I'm having a nightmare and can't wakeup," she explains.

"It's probably all that crap you watched today. Do you want me come over?" he offers.

"No. I thought if I talked to you for a minute it would help. It feels like someone broke in, but I know I'm alone. I feel stupid now. I shouldn't have waked you. I'm sorry. Goodnight."

"Sadie," he begins, but she hangs up. Michael pulls out of bed and walks to Sadie's. From outside, he sees the lights are on. Letting himself in, he calls out so not to scare her.

He discovers Sadie sitting on the floor between the living and dining room trembling with a large kitchen knife and a baseball bat. Every light in the apartment is on including the closets. She feels embarrassed to be caught like this. First, Michael disarms her and puts her back to bed and then walks around turning out all the lights. He climbs into bed with her kissing her forehead and assuring her she is safe.

Wednesday evening, their friends come to visit again. After a while, Sadie tells about being scared in the night.

"Oh, I went through that," Brenda admits, "its called night terrors. Because of your attack, you don't feel safe. At night, your fear attacks you. Yeah, it happened to me after the rape. Does Michael know about the rape?"

"Yes. My dad told him," Sadie answers.

"Huh, that's really weird," Brenda looks at Michael.

He shrugs, "I asked him why Sadie didn't trust men. Since he couldn't tell me about the stairs, he told me about you. Only he didn't tell me your name."

Sadie asks, "What did you do to stop the night terrors?"

"I took your advice. You said to say a prayer and then say the Lord's Prayer over and over until I calmed down." Brenda reminds her.

Steve turns to Michael, "Prayer huh? I'd of thought you would have come up with that one."

"You'd think," Michael agrees.

That night, Michael stays over hoping if he stays with her, she won't be scared in the night. However, around two-thirty, Sadie pulls on his arm yelling to get up. She believes the apartment caught on fire. He wraps his arms around her trying to calm her and then takes a walk through the apartment to make her feel better before crawling back in bed.

"You want to pray together?" he offers.

"No. I just want to go back to sleep," she turns away from him feeling embarrassed.

"Goodnight Sweetheart," Michael kisses her arm.

"You know, you're not stuck," she whispers softly.

"What's that suppose to mean?" he asks.

"We aren't married yet. If you're worried that I'm crazy…"

He interrupts, "Hey, hey, sweetheart, you were a bit of a whack job when I met you."

Sadie doesn't know if she should laugh or cry and rolls over on her back.

He continues, "I always say that I'm attracted to you because you share my faith, which is true, but that crazy side of you is so much fun: the side of you that ends an argument with a pillow fight or throws celery at her friend to shut her up or does a provocative dance at a wedding or bugs a committee meeting, or breaks into my house to decorate it for Christmas or jumps me when I tried to leave to have your way with me. I love you baby. Don't be so hard on yourself. You were shot less than a week ago."

"I love you too," tears run down her cheeks, "You are one horny minister."

Michael kisses her long and deeply for the first time since the shooting.

The next morning, Michael attempts to discuss seeing a psychiatrist again, but once again, Sadie refuses.

"Sweetheart, psychiatrists can help you feel better. You didn't hesitate to go to the doctor's take care of your shoulder. Why not go to a doctor to take care of your feelings?" Michael attempts to persuade her.

"I'm thirsty," Sadie walks out to the kitchen. Her evasion reminds him of how she acted in Erieton every time he brought up Troy.

The rest of the day, Sadie tries to keep busy cleaning the house and working on the computer. Michael still catches her watching a bloody movie about assassins and suggests one of her many musicals.

Colleen and Aidan arrive with a duffle bag. "Dude," Aidan announces, "you have not had one night of uninterrupted sleep in a week. So, go home. Go to bed. Colleen and I are going to stay with Sadie."

"I don't know," Michael leans back in his chair.

"It's a great idea," Sadie exclaims. "I'm sure you're tired. You've been trying to keep up at church and take care of me. I know you're behind on the newsletter. You're going to break neck tomorrow to finish aren't you?"

"Actually, yeah," Michael agrees to go.

The three friends spend the evening playing Scrabble. Then they turn in. Sadie decides that no matter what, she will not call for help. If she gets scared, she promises herself, she'll stay in bed repeating the Lord's Prayer.

Four o'clock in the morning, Sadie hears strange sounds. The sounds are coming from the balcony. The door to the balcony is at the end of the hall between her room and the bedroom she uses for storage.

Sadie tells herself over and over the sounds are in her head, but she still hears it. She starts praying, but the sound persists. It sounds like the patio furniture being moved and a woman crying 'no'. She can't take it. Climbing out of bed she walks to the hall. She picks up a bat setting by the door looking through the door's window.

"Sadie?" Aidan whispers from behind her startling her. "What are you doing?"

Colleen comes out of the guestroom.

"I'm not crazy. I hear something on the balcony," Sadie defends herself.

"Give me the bat and I'll take you back to bed," Aidan takes away the bat. Sadie stares at the floor embarrassed. Crash, something on the balcony falls over. Sadie and Colleen scream. Even Aidan jumps.

Aidan directs the girls to wait in Sadie's room and unlocks the door. The girls, terrified, beg him not to go out. Trembling a little, Aidan takes a deep breath and steps out on the balcony. Sadie turns on the outside light. Aidan gripping the bat tightly doesn't see anything. From nowhere two cats dart pass Aidan's legs. He jumps back. The cats jump up on the cement rail and leap to the apartment in the next building.

Aidan goes back in locking the door behind him. He informs the girls that it was two cats chasing each other around and that sometimes a cat's scream can sound like a woman yelling. Sadie is relieved that the noise wasn't in her head. Colleen, exhausted, heads back to bed, but Aidan sits on the edge of Sadie's bed.

"I'll stay for a little while until you fall asleep," he offers, but she has trouble falling back to sleep.

At eight o'clock, before Michael goes to the office, he stops to check on Sadie having had a good night. Going to bed at nine o'clock, he slept until seven o'clock; he slept hard for ten uninterrupted hours and feels good.

The sound of the door wakes Colleen and she meets him in the hall. Colleen tells him about the cats and then looks in the bathroom, then the kitchen. He asks what she is looking for to which she mumbles that Aidan isn't in bed. He's not in the living room. Then she stops and smiles. Colleen and Michael walk down the hall to Sadie's room. There they find Aidan and Sadie sound asleep; Sadie curled up against him.

"Well, good morning," Colleen wakes them.

The two wake to find Michael and Colleen at the foot of the bed. Then they look at each other. Realizing they are cuddled up in bed together, they jump up. Michael and Colleen shake their heads leaving the room.

From nine to twelve, Michael and his secretary, Sue, work on the monthly newsletter. At twelve, the end of office hours, Sue tells him not to worry. No one would mind if it is late this time. Everyone knows what happened last week. He tells her to go, but he plans to keep working on it.

A half hour later, Sue returns and sets a bag on his desk. Having brought him a lunch, she goes back to work. The two finish up at five-thirty. Michael thanks Sue encouraging her to put in for the overtime. The newsletter is ready for Sunday.

Michael goes to Sadie's for supper. She is dressed up with make-up wearing a sling.

"Going somewhere?" he asks.

"Yes, I'm going to Duffy's tonight," she announces. "I declare myself healed and I am not staying here one more day. If I don't get out of this apartment and do something fun, I'm going to go crazy."

Michael agrees.

As they walk up to Duffy's, Sadie slows. Flashes of last Friday shoot through her head. Placing his arm around her shoulder, Michael checks if she is okay. She insists she is and continues inside.

Sadie feels happy to be out. Michael thinks all the girls look better. Sadie's sparkle is not back yet, but she looks better. Colleen tells Steve, Brenda, and Stephanie about finding Aidan and Sadie in bed which provides plenty of material for jokes.

Sadie orders a margarita, but Michael points out that she is not completely off her pain meds. Sadie insists on one drink. They argue a bit. The girls decide to dance. Again, Michael gives Sadie a hard time. She assures him she won't tear open her wounds and besides, the wound is much more healed this time.

Once the girls begin to dance, Steve and Aidan tease him about becoming a mother hen. Michael defends himself that she had to be forced to take her medicine, she watches gory, violent movies, and she already tore her wounds open once sticking him for another long wait in a waiting room. Not only did she hurt herself, but she attempted to hide it from him. Then he had to force her to go to the hospital. Her moods swing from depressed, to rage, to annoyed, to scared. It has not been an easy week.

Michael relaxes as he watches her dance. She takes it easy on her arm, but manages to have fun and smile a genuine smile. Jack enters the bar going straight to Sadie and giving her a surprise kiss.

"Oh hell no," Michael declares, "I don't have to take this, this time."

Sadie and Jack come back to the table with the girls following.

"Hey babe, I heard someone shot you," Jack tells her.

"Yeah, an old flame burned me," she says matter-of-factly. "I'll be fine."

"You look great," he moves to put his arm around her.

Sadie holds out her left hand even though it is in a sling, "I also look engaged."

Jack drops his arm, "You? Engaged? Are you joking?"

"No, I am not joking," Sadie snaps.

"I thought all men are scum," he counters.

"He changed my mind," she nods toward Michael.

Jack looks at Michael, "Aren't you a minister?"

"Yep," Michael answers.

"Wow, from one night stands to a minister's wife. That's a leap. I'm glad you're alright."

Michael cocks his head and narrows his eyes. Jack kisses her on the cheek and says his goodbyes.

"Excuse us," Michael stands taking Sadie's hand and leading her back to the office.

"What's wrong?" she asks.

"What's wrong? Did you sleep with Jack?" he glares at her.

Sadie replies nervously, "I thought you already knew. I mean, what were you so jealous about the first time you met him?"

"You wouldn't date me, but you apparently dated him. Aidan told me you only went out five times over the course of months. How many times did you sleep with him?"

"Four times," she admits quietly.

Michael becomes angrier. She points out that all of that happened before she met him, but he does not like that she would have a one night stand at all. Troy had been a serious boyfriend, but this was slutty. Michael demands to know how many other men she had screwed. Sadie insists that Jack was the only one. Michael leaves her there and goes home. Her girlfriends join her to talk and comfort.

Michael falls into bed at eleven-thirty tossing and turning unable to fall asleep. He gives up by one o'clock and takes a walk to check on Sadie. As he approaches the apartment, he sees all the lights are on again and lets himself in yelling up the stairs that it is him. As he opens the door, he calls to her again. Sadie lies on the couch watching a movie about a killer shark. As Michael walks in the shark swallows a girl whole as her friends scream. Michael cocks an eyebrow and looks at Sadie.

"What do you want?" she snaps without looking at him.

"I worry about you."

"Why? I'm just a slut," she states coldly.

Michael rolls his head and plops down into the chair.

"Get out," Sadie orders.

"Why?"

"I don't need another jealous man who rages in my life."

Michael does not respond, but simply rocks in the recliner. She continues, "I thought I'd never fall in love again. I had been alone for years. I was lonely. I slept with him. Shoot me. You know what else? If you and Barbara broke up and then once or twice a year slept together, that is still a one night stand. You weren't in a meaningful relationship."

"Touché," Michael replies. "Are you armed?"

Sadie lifts her afghan to expose the butcher knife setting beside her. Michael takes it and places it on the table. He takes hold of her hand pulling her to a sitting position, sliding behind her with a leg on each side. He lies down pulling Sadie down on his chest and whispers sorry in her ear.

As she goes back to watching the movie, the shark starts attacking a group of screaming teenagers. Michael complains, "Sweetheart, about your movie selections."

"Darling, I don't want to fight anymore tonight, so…shut up."

Michael lays back shaking his head and kissing the top of her head.

Later that night, after they go to bed, Sadie wakes Michael as she screams in her sleep. Once he calms her, he again brings up a psychiatrist, but Sadie claims to be too tired to discuss it and falls back to sleep while Michael just stares helplessly at her.

Chapter XXI

Saturday morning, Sadie wakes up alone after ten. She finds Michael in her living room flipping through a book the doctor at the hospital gave her which has a part with a list of local psychiatrists.

"What are you doing?" Sadie demands.

Without looking up at her, he responds firmly, "I am making you an appointment."

She attempts to grab the book away, but Michael is quick and jerks his arm away before she can touch it.

Anger flashes through her, "Why is it that when I tell one of my fiances that I don't want an appointment, they just go ahead and make one for me anyway?!"

Michael's anger matches hers as he jumps to his feet roaring, "Don't you dare compare this to that! Troy was being selfish and was causing you harm; I'm doing this because I love you. I'm not hurting you! I am trying to help you."

Sadie backs down, "I'm sorry. I shouldn't have said that."

He points at the couch, "Sit down."

Sadie obeys. Calming down, Michael sits beside her and reaches for the phone. Sadie climbs up on her knees touching Michael's shoulder and trying to take the phone, "Please don't Michael."

He turns his back and ignores her as the receptionist answers,

"Hello, my name is Rev. Michael Donnelly. Dr. Memintosky was referred to us at the hospital for my fiance, Sadie Stevens... Yes, she was recently the victim of attempted murder and needs to talk to someone... How soon can he see her...? That's great, thank you."

Michael hangs up, "You have an appointment this Friday morning."

Sadie returns to bed without speaking to him. Michael leans back exhausted on the couch. After a minute, he calls Martin. Telling him all that has been going on, Michael wants Martin's opinion. Martin validates Michael's actions and thanks him for taking care of his daughter.

Sunday, the church is not full to capacity, but the attendance is significantly up. Everyone greets Sadie, who is wearing a sling, enthusiastically. Michael had worked extra hard on his sermon to be sure it holds interest.

The next day, Sadie returns to work. Michael thinks she is returning too soon and wants her to wait until she sees the psychiatrist, but Sadie needs to continue her life.

Michael takes her and drops her off because she is not allowed to drive for six weeks. She promises him to take Friday off for 'his' appointment. Her students are thrilled to see her and offer to help with all her work. They do not allow her to lift or carry anything. The children give her stacks of get well cards and pictures they made for her. Her first grade class makes her happy. She loves teaching.

Friday morning, Michael wakes up alone finding Sadie already dressed and in the kitchen making scrambled eggs and toast and cutting up oranges. He gives her a kiss on the forehead as he squeezes her shoulders. She hands him things to put on the table. He discovers the book from the hospital laying open on the table to the page with the psychiatrists and other services available.

As they begin to eat, Sadie begins to talk without looking at Michael, "I've been looking through that book. I think the Victims of Violent Crime Counseling looks like a good place to get help. I think I want to go there."

Michael pulls the book toward him to read, "That sounds like a good idea."

"Good. I'm glad you agree. They have counselors and special group therapy sessions, and even legal advice if we need it," Sadie now looks at Michael who is nodding. "Good, then I will call and cancel today's appointment."

"Whoa, I don't think so. If you want to look into this group, that's great, but I want you to see an actual doctor. At least give this guy a chance. They squeezed you in rather quickly because they consider you an emergency. I'm taking you there today." Michael puts his foot down.

Sadie hits the table, "But I don't want to go."

"Why?"

"I didn't like the man my parents took me to after the last time. He put me on medication and I don't want that again. I have nothing against people taking pills to help them, but I just don't want it for me this time."

"All doctors, whatever their specialty, hit some people the right way and some the wrong way. If you don't like him, we'll try another on the list until you click with someone, but you need to give him a chance."

"I did better getting back on my feet on my own last time. I used exercise, work, and church to feel better. I did great and I'll be just fine this time," she reminds him.

"When I met you, you were determined to never date again and had a huge cinderblock wall built around yourself," he argues.

"I'm not going!" Sadie insists.

"Yes you are," Michael stubbornly won't give in. Sadie stands and begins to walk away with most of her breakfast left on the table. He orders, "Sadie sit back down and eat your breakfast."

"Stop telling me what to do!" she yells.

Michael stands and goes to her, "I don't want to tell you what to do, but you're not taking care of yourself. You're not eating or sleeping enough. You don't take your medicine if I don't tell you to and you keep watching those horrible movies. Give this a chance today and stop walking away from me and your problems. Now, you made a good breakfast. Sit down and eat it. "

Reluctantly, Sadie slams back into her chair and begins stabbing at her food. Michael reminds himself to be patient; it has only been two weeks since the attack. Every now and then he sees flashes of the old Sadie. She just needs to deal with what has happened to her.

Michael sits in the waiting room while Sadie talks to the doctor with his laptop so he can do some work, but he cannot seem to focus on anything. He is worried about Sadie and he is not sleeping enough. He misses feeling close and having fun with her. She has pulled back into her shell which frustrates him.

Soon, Sadie comes out of the office. Michael stands to help her with her coat inquiring how things went.

"It was a big waist of time," Michael rolls his eyes as she continues. "The doctor didn't say anything useful. He just kept asking me how I feel and what I think. I just want to go home."

"The doctor has to find out what you think, how you feel, and learn something about you before he can say anything useful," Michael argues.

The door opens, and a short, balding, overweight man steps out to speak to the receptionist and stops to watch Michael assisting Sadie. He then approaches the couple. "Excuse me, may I ask who you are?"

Michael turns to him, "I'm Michael Donnelly, Sadie's fiancé."

"Did you just arrive?" he inquires.

"No, I've been out here the whole time," Michael glances at Sadie who is staring at the floor.

"That's odd. When I asked Sadie if anyone was here with her, she claimed she was alone," he too glances at Sadie. "I'm Dr. Memintosky. Would you care to step into my office?"

Michael cocks his head, "Sadie?" but she simply shrugs. Michael takes her hand and follows the Doctor into the office. They sit in front of his desk as he takes his place behind his desk.

Dr. Memintosky begins, "Sadie is going through an anger stage and she is in denial that she needs help."

Michael nods thinking to himself, "Tell me something I don't know."

"This is a very normal reaction to what she has been through. She was able to open up enough to tell me about the shooting and about being pushed down the stairs. I would like to see Sadie twice a week, but she said that she is unwilling to miss that much school."

"Do you have any evening hours or weekends?" Michael requests.

"No I don't, but I believe that the school would be willing to give her a couple mornings a week off for a couple months considering all she has been through."

"Mornings are reading groups. A sub can't run all the learning centers and keep up with the small reading groups which are the most essential part of the day. I also don't believe the school wishes to pay that much out for a sub," Sadie argues.

"Sadie gets out of school at three twenty. How late are you here?" Michael checks.

"I might be able to work out a four o'clock appointment at least once a week," the doctor offers.

"That would be great," Michael feels relieved to work it out.

"Here take these in case Sadie changes her mind," the doctor hands Michael two prescriptions. "Those are for sleeping pills and antidepressants. She refused to take them earlier. I then asked if anyone was with her. That's probably why she lied."

Michael nods again and thanks the doctor. Sadie leaves without saying a word. Despite his best efforts in the car, Sadie simply stares out the window silently.

Once home Michael tries again, "I think you should give this guy a chance. Go for a month or so."

"I would rather go to the Victims place. They don't hand out the drugs. According to the internet, they believe in coping techniques," Sadie argues.

"Fine, we can look into that too, but I still want you to give Dr. Memintosky a chance."

"I want to go to the other place right now," Sadie demands.

"Not today. I'm tired and I have work to do at church. Go ahead and make an appointment for sometime. I gave you a copy of my schedule. Now, you take it easy and I'm going to go down the street and have these filled."

Sadie snaps, "I don't want sleeping pills."

"You might feel better with a good night's sleep," he coaxes.

"Don't you mean you will feel better with a good night's sleep? You don't have to stay here at night you know. People at church might notice anyway. Starting tonight, sleep at the parsonage. It's not like you've made love to me since I was shot."

Tired and annoyed, he replies, "I have just been giving you time. I didn't think you would be up to anything like that. Besides, I'm not trying to drug you because you are bothering me. I'm trying to help you feel better."

Sadie turns and walks away from Michael again. Michael leaves to fill the prescriptions slamming the door behind him. When he returns, he walks into the living room to attempt to reason with her again, but she is not there. He checks the bedroom, but no Sadie. He looks through the apartment not finding her. He decides to walk across the street to the bar to look for her when he notices a note lying in the middle of the dining room table.

"Dear Michael, I went to the Victims of Violent Crimes Center. I'll be back later. Love, Sadie."

Michael panics running down the stairs as fast as he can go. Sadie's car is gone. She is not supposed to drive for at least another four weeks. Her shoulder doesn't have full range of motion. The city is about forty minutes away, so she is basically driving with one hand on a snowy day on a major highway. Furious, he runs home, jumps in his car and follows her to the center.

Michael arrives at the center which is located in a dilapidated old brick building in a bad section of town. Michael wonders how many people have been victims of violent crimes just trying to get into the building. He yanks the old door open barging into the waiting room where he finds Sadie sitting on an old, sagging, dingy couch filling out forms attached to a clipboard.

Storming over to her, he jerks her up by her good arm, "What were you thinking? Why do you insist on putting yourself in harms way? If you want me to stop bossing you around, then you need to get a grip and start behaving like an adult."

Furious about the way he is speaking to her, Sadie shoots back, "Go to hell."

A tall, thin Hispanic man, who is standing by the receptionist, observes the encounter and quickly intervenes pushing between the couple.

"Okay, let's calm down. Everybody take a nice deep breath," he instructs. Both Michael and Sadie back off. The gentleman turns to Sadie, "Do we need to call the police on this man?"

The question startles Michael. To his relief Sadie responds without hesitation, "No, he never hurt me. He's just my fiance."

"Okay, why don't we step into my office and see if we can't sort this out," He leads them to a tiny office where they sit in chairs in front of the desk. The man sits on his desk in front of them. "I'm Tony Rodriguez. I'm one of the councilors here at the center. Now, sir, let's start with you. What's going on?"

Michael introduces himself, "I'm Rev. Michael Donnelly, Sadie's fiancé. I'm sorry if I made a scene, but she scared me. She is not suppose to drive for four more weeks, but she just drove forty minutes taking a major highway in the snow with only one fully functioning arm. Since the shooting, she has this self destructive behavior."

He goes on to tell him about her re-injuring her shoulder, not wanting to take her meds, being belligerent, and watching horribly violent movies.

Sadie takes a turn informing him about Troy and his two attempts to murder her. Sadie explains that Michael is bossing her around and refuses to listen to her. She claims that she believes in mental health care and has no problems with people taking medication to help, but she is not ready to try that. She wants to try to feel better without it first.

Tony then asks Michael to take a seat in the waiting room so that he can talk to Sadie privately. Michael leans back on a couch with his hands over his face for a moment as he begins a forty-five minute wait. Finally, Tony invites Michael back into the office.

"Michael, I think you are doing a good job taking care of Sadie with all that has happened," Tony begins. Michael thinks that he is being patronized, but listens quietly. "I understand that you want to do all you can for Sadie to help her feel better as quickly as possible, but what she needs now is time, calm time. She needs time to heal and not feel frenzied, judged, or pushed.

"She wants time to calm herself down before she tries medication. Now, we have a volunteer psychiatrist who is here on Wednesdays who can oversee medication if we decide that is the route we want to go. Right now we are stressing with Sadie to use relaxation methods. Victims often feel uptight and scared, as if they don't remember how to relax and have fun. We work toward victims making a decision to take back their lives to be able to relax and find happiness again every morning when they get up. Your solution to the night terrors by using prayer or scripture is a very good idea. Give it time to work. She also enjoys singing in the church and knows many songs. When alone, I suggest singing to help calm her and help her relax.

"I believe that those movies she has been watching have been a form of release for the anger she has inside toward Troy trying to take her life again especially after having already overcome all of this before. While this is understandable and she may still watch some of those if she wishes, I told her that you are right. She needs to begin transitioning to comedies and feel good movies as well.

"She also asked if I think you should cancel or postpone your wedding," at this Michael straightens glancing at Sadie, "It is February and your wedding isn't until June. I suggest that this decision should wait until Sadie has time to heal. You have time. I suggest that we meet back here again at the end of March or the beginning of April, and see where we stand then. Of course, this is simply a suggestion. Sadie needs to make her own decision in this matter."

Michael and Sadie thank Tony for all of his help. Michael has to admit that this does seem to be the support and help that Sadie prefers and may respond to better. She plans to come to a group therapy session in the evening every other week and come in for counseling with Tony once a week for a while and then every other week as well. Sadie promises that her friends will help with the long drive for now.

As they leave the building, Sadie heads for her car, but Michael catches her arm. He is not about to allow her to drive herself back home insisting on driving her home. Later, Aidan drives Michael all the way back into the city to pick up her car.

In one week, their parents plan to come to work on wedding

invitations, but Sadie is plagued with doubts. Michael's jealousy scared her. He tried so hard to take care of her that he has become bossy. She didn't like that he questioned her about going back to work, about ordering a drink, or about dancing with her friends. She is still angry that he forced her to go to a psychiatrist she didn't want to see and that he filled prescriptions that she clearly didn't want to take.

She lived on her own for several years making all of her own decisions and does not like his constant interference. He pushed her to date. He pushed to get married. Marrying him would mean in a couple of years leaving Ambrose, leaving her school, leaving her friends for God knows where, literally.

Had she married Troy, she would have probably been battered. He pushed her down the stairs, he tried to force her to have an abortion, he backhanded her when he lost an argument and he was jealous of Michael enough to want to kill him.

She dated Troy for five years. She knew Michael for nine months. She decides to break up with him and change churches. She does not want to wait until April. She wants out now. The memories of breaking up with Troy scare her, so she calls Colleen and asks if she and Aidan would be in the apartment. Colleen promises to be there.

Aidan, frustrated, believes Sadie is making a mistake. Before Michael arrives, Aidan argues with Sadie that Michael loves her. He didn't act jealous when he found Aidan and Sadie in bed. He refused to leave her alone in the hospital. He pushed her to date because it had been obvious to everyone that Sadie was attracted to him.

When Michael arrives, he knows from the look on Aidan's face that something is up. Aidan and Colleen sit at the dining room table. Michael finds Sadie pacing around the living room.

He asks suspiciously, "What's going on?"

Sadie refuses to make eye contact, "I'm so sorry, but I can't marry you."

Michael takes a deep breath staring at the ceiling for a moment, "Sadie, don't do this now. You were shot only a little over two weeks ago. You have gone through a lot. Just wait like Tony said."

"No, I have decided. We are over," she still won't look directly at him.

He goes to her, taking her arm above the elbow. Before he says a word, Sadie yanks her arm away and shoves him with the palms of her hands, "Don't touch me!"

Colleen and Aidan wish they are somewhere else. Even Colleen feels Sadie is wrong and thinks Sadie is being cruel as she breaks up.

Michael steadies his voice, "Calm down."

Sadie tries to work her engagement ring off her finger. Michael steps away from her. "Don't do this Sadie."

She manages to get the ring off. Holding it out to him, he refuses to take it. She still won't look at him.

"Take it," she demands.

Michael doesn't move. Frustrated, she throws it at him. It hits him in the middle of the chest and falls to the floor. Sadie crosses the room staring out the window with her back to him. He bends down. Picking up the ring, he slips it in his front pocket.

"Look at me. I want to know why," he demands.

Sadie doesn't move, "I just don't want to."

"That's not good enough," he persists, "Look at me."

Tears well up in her eyes, "I don't love you."

Anger flashes through him. She keeps her back to him. Frustrated, he goes to her again. Turning her around, he holds her just above both of her elbows, "I don't believe you."

"Let me go," she orders.

He doesn't, "Talk to me."

Sadie pulls away, "Go away." She smacks him across the face and calls him an asshole. Sadie braces herself for his reaction.

He slowly turns his face back to her. Now, she looks at him. His eyes display anger and his lips are tight. Sadie trembles with fear. With the smack and the look on Sadie's face, it occurs to Michael what is actually happening.

Michael turns, walks to the couch and plops down, "Are you finished? Is there anything you left out or forgot?"

"What do you mean?"

"Isn't this the same things you did to Troy? You broke up with him, told him you didn't love him, threw the ring at him, pushed him, smacked him, and cussed at him. He pushed you down the stairs. He hurt you and it probably wasn't an accident. Well, you threw it all at me, and I didn't hurt you. I am not going to hurt you," he promises with conviction.

"That's not what I am doing," she denies.

"I heard you in the hospital. You told your mother that you dated Troy for five years and never saw this coming. You haven't known me a year and we're engaged. You asked her if you're crazy. Sadie, I am not Troy. I would never hurt you. I admit the other night picturing you with Jack made me jealous and I yelled, but I did not hit Jack and I didn't hurt you. I didn't even stay mad long. When you bugged my office, I was embarrassed and angry, I didn't hurt you. I couldn't even stay angry long.

"Sadie, not all men hurt women. Not all men are scum. I'm sorry if I have been telling you what to do too much. I love you. I get that I was pushing too hard and I'm trying to back off. I just was trying to take care of you because I love you. Do you get that? Do you understand and really know how much I love you? Did you really stop loving me?"

With tears on her face, she shakes her head no.

"Come here," he orders.

She slowly sits down beside him.

"Talk to me. You have so many emotions to go through and that's okay. You need time to heal and I have been pushing too hard. I'm sorry. I will slow down and calm down too. You can have all the time you need, but there are two rules. Number one, no hitting," She nods. He continues, "Number two, no breaking up with me."

He pulls the ring from his pocket placing it back on her finger.

"I'm sorry," she whispers. Michael pulls a tissue from the end table and mops up her face.

"I love you. Are you still going to marry me?" he asks.

"Yes… You must think I'm crazy. No wonder you want to drug me."

He sighs, "I won't ask you to take medicine that you don't want again. I promise. Besides, I've always thought that you're crazy," he pulls her close. Taking her in his arms, he kisses her long and deeply.

"Goodbye! We left." Aidan and Colleen call, thrilled and very impressed with Michael. They quickly leave, thinking he is a miracle worker.

Michael picks Sadie up and carries her to the bedroom where they make love for the first time since the shooting.

Chapter XXII

Between being tired from work, making up with Michael, her counseling, and group therapy sessions, the night terrors subside. When she does feel scared, she uses prayer or a song to calm down.

The group therapy is good for Sadie. Instead of Michael driving her out there and then staying in a waiting room, Brenda offers to drive her and attends the meetings with her. It hasn't been that many years since her rape and she believes that she too can benefit from the meetings. The friends face these horrific events in their lives together.

Saturday afternoon, their parents meet in Sadie's dining room and sit around the table with the address books and lists. Joy uses Michael's laptop to type in all the addresses to print out for the printers. Michael attempts to convince his mother to cut down her list from five hundred to around two hundred.

Sadie listens, but seems disinterested. Their parents worry that Sadie does not seem to be excited. Michael worries that she still has doubts. Colleen, Stephanie, and Brenda stop by to set a date for a shower while the mothers are together and also notice Sadie's lack of interest

Finally, Joy decides to confront the problem head on, "What exactly about the wedding is bothering you."

"I'm sorry. I don't mean to be a problem," she apologizes.

"Just tell us what the problem is," Joy prompts.

"You spent so much money on my gown, and I don't want to wear it. We can't return it because they already started alterations," Sadie explains.

"But honey, you look beautiful in that gown," her mother comforts.

"I did. Mom, it's strapless," Sadie reminds her quietly.

"Oh, your entire scar will show."

"I won't ask you to buy a different gown," she promises.

"When is your next fitting?" Sophia asks.

"Next week," Joy answers.

Sophia instructs Joy to bring the gown home. Sophia will bring her dress designer, Roberto, to fix the gown and she will take care of his costs. It's only March. She assures her there is time to fix the gown.

Stephanie jumps in, "What you need to do is get back to being happy. You need to feel like a bride again. I remember how happy you were the night before it happened. Easter is coming in a couple of weeks. Once Easter is over, Sadie has spring break and Michael can take a break. You two should take a pre-honeymoon, one big long date to get back in the spirit of things."

Sadie's mom rolls her eyes, but Michael agrees, "That's not a bad idea. Maybe we should get away."

"And when you get back, I am going to plan an amazing, kick ass bachelorette party for you like no one has ever seen." Stephanie adds.

Sadie perks up becoming more involved in the discussions. As the afternoon wears on, she even becomes a little playful. Martin teases about watching Michael and Sadie at Colleen's wedding. They reminisce about Sadie and the girls' provocative dance. Sadie's giggles bring relief to Michael as the old Sadie begins to emerge.

Before their parents leave, Michael's father asks if they had plans for their post-wedding honeymoon. When Michael tells him they don't, his father hands him a manila envelope containing information and tickets for a cruise, Monday to Friday. Sadie becomes excited having never been on a cruise. Michael thanks them knowing that Sadie will love it.

The next day after church, Sadie prepares city chicken and mashed potatoes at the parsonage. She no longer wears her sling all the time, just when she is sore. Michael works on something in his study.

During lunch, Michael confides in her that he sometimes feels frustrated trying to get used to not having money. He wants to take her away for spring break, but between the wedding and a beginning minister's salary, he just doesn't have the money. He had been in the study trying to figure something out, but the money simply isn't there.

Michael's idea of a vacation includes resorts, lodges, and luxury hotels. Sadie informs him that there are inexpensive vacations. They can borrow her parents' pop-up camper. Campsites are between fifteen and forty dollars a night. Park trails and public beaches are free. They can save money by eating breakfast and lunch in the camper and only eat out once a day. Her dad's rules on eating out include, never buy drinks, stick to ice water, never order appetizers and never order dessert. They can have pop and treats in the trailer.

His dead pan expression shows no interest in camping. Sadie tells him stories of both tent camping and camper camping. She has a tent, but thinks Michael would prefer a camper. She points out that he chose to live in this salary range, so he should give this a try. Michael relents, promising to be open minded.

Easter keeps Michael busy. He has Maundy Thursday and Good Friday services. Saturday, Michael again spends the day traveling taking Communion to the shut-ins. Sadie spends the day making all the food for Easter day. She makes four of her special homemade bread with crosses made out of dough on the top. Michael is quite impressed. They eat half a loaf on Saturday evening hot from the oven with butter, give one away and serve the other two the next day after church.

Saturday evening Michael and Sadie spend almost an hour arranging and rearranging the flowers in the sanctuary. The variety of potted flowers consists of hyacinths, tulips, daffodils, irises, and many lilies. The sanctuary is beautiful.

There is a wonderful feeling that Sadie always gets at Easter which is her favorite holiday. This year, the weather is perfect with a beautiful sky blue day in the mid-seventies. Sadie wears a sleeveless blue dress. Along the waist and bottom of the skirt is a thick daffodil print. She sets her hair in hot rollers giving her hair a full bouncy look.

Easter morning's schedule keeps them hopping. The morning begins with sunrise service, followed by a pancake breakfast, after which comes Sunday school and finally the main service.

Before the seven o'clock sunrise service, at six-thirty, Sadie opens the door to Michael's office where he is sitting at his desk and pokes her head in, "Good morning Darling. Close your eyes."

"What?"

"Close your eyes," she repeats.

Michael leans back in his chair and closes his eyes. Sadie enters the office holding up a garment bag with a huge flowery ribbon tied into a bow.

"Happy Easter!" She calls.

Michael opens his eyes, stands and walks around the desk, "What is this? What did you do? Easter isn't a gift giving occasion."

"Any day is a gift giving day when you want to give a gift, so shut up and open it," she teases.

Michael unties the bow and unzips the bag to find a white robe. He only owns a black robe and a minister should wear a white one for Christmas, weddings, funerals, and Easter. Michael looks at her surprised and touched. She really does understand this life that he has chosen.

"Wow, this is great. Thank you sweetheart," he pulls her close kissing her.

He drapes the robe over a chair and goes to his briefcase, "Would you believe I bought you an Easter gift too?"

He hands her a small square box wrapped in floral wrapping paper. Smiling, she unwraps her present to find a beautiful gold cross necklace with her pink tourmaline birthstone in the shape of a heart in the center of the cross.

"Oh Darling, it's beautiful," she beams at him.

He takes the necklace from her. As she lifts her hair, he places the necklace on her hooking it and then leans down kissing her neck. She turns, wrapping her arms around his neck and kisses him.

James, Sophia, Carol, and Drew attend the main service, but Sean and Jeremy come for the whole morning. The organist plays for the main service, but Sadie plays for the small group who attend the sunrise service.

Sophia is moved seeing her son up front in his white robe surrounded by all the flowers. He really looks like a minister to her and her eyes fill with tears. She is not sure she understands a calling or exactly how he received it, but she is beginning to believe he did. It is an Easter that James and Sophia will never forget.

Sean is moved because he is sitting in a pew with both his parents and Jeremy. While his parents aren't thrilled about it, they are cordial and that is enough for him today. He gives the credit for this to both Carol and Sadie.

Although there are only eleven in the choir this morning, the church swells with their powerful rendition of "Because He Lives". Sadie solos on the second verse about holding a newborn baby. Michael thinks about having a family with her and silently thanks God again that she survived the gun shot.

All the songs are beautiful and strongly sung. The church is full and everyone is singing and Donna plays the organ powerfully so that people can feel it in their chests.

After church, Sadie tells Sophia, Carol, and Sean that she purchased three of the lilies for them and that they can take them. She also bought tulips for Colleen and daffodils for Brenda. She purchased lilies and irises for herself. They take all these flowers to the parsonage making the house smell beautiful.

Once back in the parsonage, Sadie sets out all the food she prepared the day before. Since she doesn't have the time or energy to cook that day, all the food is served cold. This had always been her family tradition. She serves ham, macaroni salad, a veggie tray, homemade bread, seven layer salad, crackers and cheese, kielbasa, pickled eggs, jell-o salad, nut rolls, and candy dishes full of chocolates and jelly beans. Sophia does not insult any of the food, not even the jell-o salad although she does not take any.

Once the family leaves, Michael, like most ministers at this point, falls fast asleep for most of the evening. Sadie joins him for a nap.

Monday, the couple drives to her parents' house. Borrowing the van with the hitch and pop-up trailer, they head southeast to a campsite in a warm climate near the ocean. The pair arrives to a full campground of people on spring break. There are campers and RV's of every shape and size. Some people set out yard decorations and hang strings of plastic lanterns. Some have small tents for children setting by their campers. Michael is surprised that many have satellite dishes for their televisions.

It takes Michael four tries to back in the trailer. Sadie shows Michael how to crank the camper open and pull out the table compartment. She shows him how to set up the inside and how to attach the hook-ups. He is surprised how big the inside actually opens. Sadie laughs telling him to picture it with four kids. Michael shakes his head. Sadie points out the public restrooms and showers about a block down. Looking around, he wonders where his life is taking him.

After they open up the awning, Sadie hands him white Christmas lights to trim both the poles and awning. He cocks his eyebrow at her and she elbows him. Sighing, he hangs her lights. She then has him help her move the picnic table under the awning and sets canvas lawn chairs by the fire ring.

The next morning, Sadie sits on the small couch examining her swim suit. Michael sits next to her, "Go ahead and put it on. You are in such great shape, you will look better than most even with the scar. If anyone asks or stares, we can tell them it's a shark bite."

Sadie laughs as he bites at her neck and back. She puts on the suit, but also wears a light short sleeve blouse like a jacket. Instead of climbing into the van to head for the ocean, he leads her through the campgrounds to the swimming pool. Sadie asks what he is up to. He plans to begin teaching her to swim. Sadie turns to walk away, but Michael's arm catches her around the waist.

"Trust me," he prompts.

"Okay, but I'm not getting my face wet," she insists.

Michael rolls his head, "Lesson one, you have to get your face wet."

Later, they spend the afternoon walking around town window shopping and strolling down to the ocean. After supper, they return to the campgrounds. Michael leads her to a small clearing behind the camper and turns on a CD to teach her a couple dances for their wedding reception. Sadie thinks it's a great idea.

They spend their week going to the beach, taking hiking trails, going into town, practicing their dancing, and swimming in the pool. By the end of the week Sadie can do the dances he taught her, she can do several laps with the basic front crawl as long as she can stand when she wants, and Michael admits staying at the campgrounds is not so bad.

When they return the van and camper, Martin and Joy are pleased to see that Michael and Sadie appear to be their old selves. Sadie talks excitedly about the wedding which is now less than two months away. The couple demonstrates their dance for her parents.

Back in Ambrose, Sadie's friends, people at church, teachers, and even her students notice the sparkle in her eyes has returned. She had weathered her storm.

The first Saturday of May, Stephanie planned the kick-ass bachelorette party she promised. Carol, Mary, Lucy, Colleen, Brenda, Stephanie, and Sadie are heading out for the day. Michael, Aidan, Steve, and Luke plan to play basketball, grab a bite to eat, and spend the evening playing poker in the parsonage.

Michael complains to Sadie, "Who starts a party at ten in the morning? Where are you going?"

She shrugs, "No one told me."

He points at her duffle bag, "Why do you have luggage?"

She shrugs again, "Colleen packed it."

Colleen takes pity on him, "Stephanie, tell the poor guy where all we are going today and when we'll be back."

Stephanie, using her sexiest voice, goes over the itinerary, "Well honey, we decided the shower is for the mothers and Aunts. Today is our gift and we are doing it all. We begin the party at a spa. We have an exercise class. Then, naked in robes, we'll eat lunch. Then, we will sit around in the Jacuzzi taking turns getting facials and massages. When we're done, we'll all go take a shower and get ready to go out."

"Wow, that's hot," Steve interrupts. Michael smacks him across the back of the head.

Stephanie continues, "After that, we have reservations at a nice restaurant. Next, we have tickets to a comedy club. Sadie loves standup. To finish the evening, we'll club hop, dancing and living it up. Then, we are all spending the night at Sadie's apartment."

"That's hot," Steve repeats and is whacked again.

Luke points out, "Hold it. Lucy isn't twenty-one."

"Oh, I'll be fine," she defends herself.

Mary puts her arm around Lucy, "Don't worry. We will take good care of her. We won't let her drink."

"Here comes my part of the gift," Carol calls as a white stretch limo pulls into the parking lot.

"You girls know how to party," Aidan observes.

Michael pulls Sadie aside, "Don't get drunk."

"Oh sweetheart, I would never break a promise to you... So, just to be safe, I'm not promising that."

"I saw you drunk on your birthday and drugged up at the hospital. You become flirtatious and horny," he points out.

Sadie kisses him, "Goodbye, see you tomorrow."

Michael catches her hand, "Are you coming to church?"

"I seriously doubt it," she answers as Stephanie pulls her away and into the limo with the whooping, cheering girls.

The guys wave as the limo pulls away. Before they begin their day, they stop at the church to set up tables and chairs for the youth group's spaghetti dinner. When they reach the fellowship hall, seven teenagers and Mac are upset. Michael inquires to what is happening.

Mac explains, "The four ladies who were supposed to run this all canceled. One is sick, two were called in to work and I don't know where the other one is. We already sold tickets and spent money on the supplies."

"Do you know who I am?" Luke steps up, "I am Sadie's older brother, a preacher's kid. I can run a spaghetti dinner."

"I run Duffy's," Steve offers, "I can help do this."

"Yeah sure, I'm in," Aidan agrees.

Michael is pleased that his friends are willing to do this. He would have no idea how to make spaghetti for his family let alone for a mass crowd.

Luke takes charge, "Reverend, you and Aidan work with the kids to set up the tables. Steve and I will go in the kitchen and figure out a plan. Oh, we will take two kids to start tearing lettuce."

One of the kids turns on a CD as they work. The guys are in a good mood and spend the day working and goofing around with the kids. They are ready in plenty of time. People not only enjoy the food, but the atmosphere is fun. As the evening wares on, more people come. Word of mouth spreads bringing in a continuous crowd.

Donated desserts run low. Michael takes some money from the ticket sales and runs down the street to the bakery. He runs wet rags to the parsonage to use the dryer. He washes dishes, buses tables, and wraps silverware. By the time the dinner ends, they and the teens are exhausted. The men allow the kids to go home while they stay to do the cleanup.

The group of men crash at the parsonage after nine too tired to play poker. After a bit, Aidan and Steve head home. Michael insists that Luke stay in his room while he stays on the couch. With four bedrooms upstairs, there is still only one with furniture.

At two in the morning, Michael wakes and wonders if the girls are back. They probably would come home between two and three, so decides to take a walk just for a peek.

The windows in the apartment are dark. He wonders if they're asleep or not home, so he steps into a store front to wait a few minutes.

In the limo, the girls head home after the perfect day. While they are tipsy, no one drank too much. Sadie tells them since the shooting Michael had been overly protective and bets that he is waiting up for her now.

Colleen agrees, "I bet he is watching the apartment from somewhere on the street."

Stephanie claps her hands, "Let's play a game. We will all pitch in ten dollars. When we get back, we will have a scavenger hunt. First one who finds him wins."

Carol sticks up for her brother, "I don't think you'll find him. I bet he is home asleep."

"Okay, if we don't find him, his sister wins," Stephanie declares.

Michael sees the limo pull up. The girls climb out thanking and tipping the driver. They seem fine and happy. He plans to head home as soon as they go upstairs. Instead, Stephanie yells, "On your mark, get set, go!"

The girls fan out and start looking around. He pulls back as far as he can. Shortly, Mary appears in his doorway shouting, "I found him. I win."

Embarrassment washes over him as Mary and a few others drag him across the street to where Sadie and Carol are standing. Carol hands Mary the money and whacks her brother over the back of the head.

She complains, "I bet you wouldn't be here."

"Goodnight ladies," Michael attempts to leave, but they block his way.

"You don't get off that easy," Brenda croons, "We have to do something."

"No you don't," he disagrees, "Goodnight." They still hang on to him.

"I have it," Colleen hands him the keys, "You have to go upstairs, unlock the door for us, and kiss each of us goodnight."

"I don't think so," he tries to leave, but the girls swarm. He gives in heading upstairs with the ladies making cat calls behind him. They line up and head upstairs.

Carol is first giving her brother a kiss on the cheek. Lucy also gives him a quick peck on the cheek. Brenda puts a hand on each side of his face and kisses him quickly on the mouth. Colleen wraps her arms around his neck kissing him quickly on the mouth as well. His embarrassment increases.

Mary steps up next, "I don't know. He's going to be my brother-in-law."

"He isn't yet," Stephanie points out.

Mary shrugs, takes his face giving him a quick kiss on the cheek.

Stephanie steps up with an evil gleam in her eye. Michael backs away, but she grabs him pressing up against him. He turns his head, so she kisses his jaw and neck until Sadie quickly yells, "That's enough. Get off my minister."

Once she goes in, Michael gives Sadie a hasty kiss on a cheek and runs down the stairs. Sadie calls after him, "Hey, I'm the bride and I got the worst kiss." Sadie stomps into the apartment.

As Michael reaches the door, he pauses. Turning, he charges up the stairs. Pushing through her friends, he pulls Sadie into a small dip giving her a real kiss. He then leaves without saying a word while her friends cheer and applaud.

"What in the world have you done to my brother? He used to be shy, quiet, reserved," Carol ponders.

Sadie wakes about an hour before church and decides to go. As she gets ready, others begin to wake. Carol wants to see her brother preach. Colleen and Brenda figure Sean and Aidan will probably be there. Mary and Lucy, who seldom miss church, decide to go too. Stephanie, who has never been to Sadie's church, doesn't want to be left out. Reluctantly, she gets ready.

Michael prepares in his office for the service. Aidan, Steve, and Luke enter to ask if he'd heard from the girls. They know from his expression something happened. Aidan persuades him that he might as well tell them, because the girls will later anyway. Michael closes the door to fill them in about being caught checking up on them. The guys think the story is hysterical.

Five minutes before church, they head for the sanctuary. As they come to the breezeway, Sadie and her friends arrive.

"I didn't think you were coming," Michael greets her.

"We woke up in time. Who knew?" she explains.

Stephanie purrs, "It's my first time here, so try not to be too boring."

"I'm surprised you could walk through the doors without bursting into flames," he taunts.

Giving Sadie a quick kiss on the cheek, he heads up to the small prep room to pull on his robe. The large group takes up the second and third pews; Stephanie breaks away into Michael's prep room as he pulls up the zipper on his robe.

"Do you need something?" he asks.

"Do you really dislike me that much?"

He sighs, "I was just joking."

"There is some truth in jokes. I don't think you like me," she pouts.

He checks his watch. The service is about to begin. The choir lines up outside the door. He assures her, "Of course I like you. The group would not be the same without you."

"Oh thank you," she quickly kisses his cheek and leaves.

As the organ begins to play, he puts on his stole. The choir processes down the aisle singing the hymn. Michael follows. As he walks down the aisle people giggle. Something feels off. He reaches the front turning to face the congregation; as the second verse begins, giggles turn to laughter. Confused, he looks at Sadie who puckers her lips and points to her cheek. His eyes scan over to Stephanie who smirks with bright red lips. He closes his eyes for a second.

He ducks down behind the pulpit where he keeps a box of tissues. Taking one he rubs his cheek and sees the lipstick on the tissue. The choir behind him snickers. He looks at the choir director and points to his cheek. She shakes her head, so he rubs some more. He checks with her again. This time she nods, so he straightens back up. The congregation has difficulty singing the third verse for the laughter. After church, he plans to kill Stephanie.

When the hymn ends, Michael steps up to the pulpit for morning announcements, "Good morning," the congregation responds and he continues, "We have some guests here this morning, my sister, Carol Donnelly and Sadie's sisters, Mary and Lucy Stevens and her brother, Luke Stevens, as well as a group of our friends, some of whom you already know. They are here this weekend helping with wedding arrangements since our wedding is only a month away. Apparently I greeted them too quickly and should have checked a mirror," the congregation giggles one more time.

He goes on to other church announcements and reminders. When he finishes, he asks if there are any more announcements. Mac responds yes walking to the front of the church.

Mac begins, "Yesterday, I brought my daughter here to work on the spaghetti dinner just to find that the ladies couldn't make it. We had no idea what to do and were panicking. Rev. Donnelly and his friends, who already had plans, stopped by. When they found out what was happening, they volunteered to spend the day and they ran the dinner. We had a very successful dinner thanks to our youth group and Rev. Donnelly and his band of merry men who I see are here this morning. Thank you."

The congregation applauds. The girls are surprised to learn how the men ended up spending their day. Sadie winks at Michael assuming they didn't allow him near the food.

After church, as Michael takes off his stole and robe in the prep room, Mac joins him, "You know Reverend, it is nice having a young preacher who has the energy and willingness to do all that yesterday, but the dating and kissing is kind of odd."

"Well, I'm done dating in a month. Besides, the kiss was obviously an innocent peck on the cheek," he responds.

The group decides to walk down the street to the Rainbow Café for lunch before Sadie meets Sophia and her dress designer. As they walk, Michael and Stephanie begin to snipe at each other. The tension builds until they explode.

"What is your problem?" Steph demands.

"You embarrassed me in front of my congregation during a worship service on purpose!" he explodes.

"I didn't mean to," she denies flatly.

"Baloney! I put up with your crap at the bar, but I thought an adult would know the difference between a bar and a church. I know you don't attend church, but I thought you had some respect for it. I guess that would be too much to ask from a low class whore!"

"Michael!" Sadie reprimands.

Stephanie quickly walks back toward the church where she parked her car.

"She was wrong, but don't you think you went too far?" Sadie asks.

"Oh please, she uses language worse than that when she's not mad. I have enough troubles at church being young and dating a parishioner without her making me look like an idiot, like some kind of playboy."

No one can argue with his point, yet they feel sorry for Stephanie. They go in the café and order lunch. For a while, everyone sits quietly feeling awkward until Sadie speaks up.

"Okay, we have to take Michael's side on this one. He has always been a good sport. We did that kissing line to him last night. When Colleen and Brenda caught him naked in bed, they sat on the bed to bug him. We made him uncomfortable on purpose with the blackmail photos at the bar. He even wore a Halloween costume just for Brenda. At the honeymoon picture party, he made it clear that hurting him at church is off limits. Stephanie is the one who crossed the line."

Everyone quickly agrees. Michael feels relief that Sadie finally stuck up for him and squeezes her hand. This attitude allows him to relax, remembering how important it became to Aidan to feel like he wasn't second to Colleen's friends. He understands the feeling.

Carol leans forward, "You people got my brother to wear a Halloween costume?"

Everyone laughs as she continues, "I think you have some stories to tell me later especially the one about being caught naked in bed?"

They talk about the spaghetti dinner and the girls adventures the day before. When they finish dinner, the group waits for Sophia in Sadie's apartment.

Sophia arrives with the flamboyant Roberto who prances around the room pointing at each man ordering, "You, you, and you out. Out, out, out."

Michael heads over to kiss Sadie, but Roberto cuts him off disgusted, "Save it for the honeymoon lover boy. Out, out, out." And throws him out of the apartment.

"Now, which one of you is my bride?" Sadie shyly stands up.

"Wow, beautiful. I'm done. You are already a beautiful bride. Put your gown on and let's see what we have." He claps his hands, "Chop, chop."

Stephanie lies on her couch staring at the ceiling. For the past two years, her friends have been her family. She remembers meeting Colleen who thought Steph was funny. She and her two friends were bitter and depressed. They found Steph funny and fun to be with. Then Brenda married Steve. Steve's best friend Aidan came around. Colleen rekindles with him. Now Sadie has found Michael. They are happy and no longer need her. Now she is alone again.

Someone knocks on her door. She drags off the couch to answer it, "What do you want?"

"Can I come in?" Michael asks.

Reluctantly, she lets him in.

"They're at Sadie's doing a wedding gown thing. You should be there."

"Why? They don't need me anymore. When they were depressed men haters, I amused them. Now they are going to all be happily married. That makes me pathetic or a low class whore."

"Sorry about that. Look, you and I would not normally be friends, but we like the same people. We must have something in common. So let's call a truce. You don't embarrass me at my church and I'll try to be less judgmental," he offers.

"Thanks, but you are all couples. I don't fit in. They don't need me anymore," she repeats.

"Of course they need you. Who planned the bachelorette party that they talked about all through lunch? Who thought of the pre-honeymoon? You still bring the fun. You don't want them to turn into boring housewives do you? Especially Sadie, she's going to be a minister's wife."

Roberto looks Sadie's dress over, "Your arms are beautiful. You lift weights. The bridesmaids gowns are sleeveless, v-necks. I can remove the bodice and replace it with the same style of material with the v-neck. That will cover your shoulder, leave just a hint of cleavage, and show off your lovely arms."

They hear the door buzzer. Colleen answers it returning with Stephanie.

Sadie smiles, "I'm glad you decided to come back."

"I wasn't planning on coming back, but Michael can be persuasive. He came over and talked me into coming. He's nicer than I give him credit for being."

"There is something special about him," Sadie agrees smiling ear to ear dressed as his bride.

Sophia also smiles. Sadie is beginning to grow on her.

Chapter XXIII

The last weekend in May, the outdoor pool at the rec. center opens for the summer season. Sadie and her group of friends go. Sadie sits on the edge with her feet in the pool wearing the short sleeve blouse as a jacket to cover her shoulder. Steve climbs to the high dive, and does an impressive dive. Stephanie goes next performing a beautiful swan dive. As Aidan dives his body twists around twice before going into the water.

Michael climbs up next. He turns backwards with only the balls of his feet on the board. He bends his knees deeply and jumps high. Keeping his knees straight, he touches his toes and then goes over backwards and is perfectly straight when he enters the water. His friends cheer but Aidan carries on about him being a show off.

Aidan tells Michael that he used to be on a swim team as well and that he has seen Michael doing laps in the pool. Aidan thinks he can take him and challenges Michael to race which he accepts. Steve and Stephanie clear two lanes for them which catch others' interest, so people line up to watch. Four teens in the church youth group, including Mac's daughter, Cheyenne, and Josh, line the route cheering for their pastor.

Michael and Aidan take their starting positions and Stephanie starts them. The two plow through the water reaching the other end of the pool practically at the same time as they turn and head back. Michael pulls ahead for a small lead. The second Michael hits the wall, he pulls himself out of the water and turns to sit, so when Aidan, who is only seconds behind him, stands, Michael is already sitting out of the pool. The crowd cheers and then disperses.

Aidan splashes him, "You are such a show off. You come across quiet and reserved, but you are so competitive."

Steve laughs, "That is so true." He turns to the girls, "When we jog, we just relax and jog, but one day we went onto the high school track. Aidan starts pulling ahead little by little. Michael catches up, and slowly that turned into a race. I quit, but the two of them raced faster and faster around the track at least twice until they collapsed out of breath and laughing. Aidan is just as bad."

The friends go back to swimming and diving. Sadie sits by the deep end with just her feet in the water. She does not possess the confidence to swim in front of all these people and is uncertain about how much she even remembers. She spots Michael deep under the water swimming towards her. He comes up in front of her and gives her a kiss and then disappears back under the water. He emerges a second time, wrapping his arms around her and pulling her in.

Sadie yells at him to stop and fights him. He coaxes her to relax assuring her that he has her. Sadie is not happy, and pleads for him to at least take her down to the end where her feet touch. He doesn't listen right away simply telling her to trust him. Once in the shallow end, she refuses to take lessons or to practice in this big crowd. Colleen begs to see her do a little of the front crawl, but Sadie is adamant.

Michael encourages her to go underwater so that she loosens up, but she still refuses. Michael lifts her up and instructing her to hold her breath; he is taking her under. She begs him not to, but he falls over backwards pulling her under with him. She stands back up shoving him away. Finally, she peels off her blouse and swims a lap down the pool and back for her friends who are impressed. Colleen and Aidan have wanted to give her lessons for years, but she is stubborn. Apparently, Michael can get her to do things, like swim, go for therapy, and date him.

The following Saturday, Sadie spends all morning working on end of the year papers and report cards. Tuesday will be the last day of school followed by an in-service day. Next week at this time she will be at her wedding. She works on the fellowship hall table in the parsonage, because Sean insists someone be there between eleven and one.

Colleen, Brenda, and Steph stop by. They want to go out tonight while the guys go to the bachelor party, but Sadie is too tired. The end of the year wipes teachers out. They decide to lie around the parsonage watching movies, but Sadie is not allowed to choose. They pick romantic comedies.

Sadie's counseling and therapy sessions have been a great help. She finally agrees to take a mild medication for her nerves which she admits do take the edge off. She also occasionally takes the sleeping pills when she feels too hyper or stressed to sleep. She feels happy and prepared to marry Michael.

The guys are at Memorial Park. Steve and Aidan plan to learn tennis better, since Michael played basketball all winter with them. Aidan and Steve return to the parsonage dejected. Michael sits across from Sadie.

"How did it go?" Colleen asks.

"He beat both of us," Aidan answers.

"Of course he did," Brenda shrugs.

"No, you don't understand," Steve explains, "He beat both of us at the same time. We played doubles while he played singles."

The girls laugh.

"You'll get better. I'll teach you," Michael offers.

"Don't try to argue with him," Sadie warns, "He won't listen. He is stubborn and pushy."

Michael smiles at her.

"Are you excited about tonight?" Steph leans on Michael.

"No, not really. Graham and Colby planned it without any of the other groomsmen. I think it sounds like a boring cocktail party. We should have had you plan it," Michael teases.

"Think there'll be a stripper?" she coos.

"I doubt it. Like I said, we should have had you plan it," he repeats as the others laugh.

They hear the front doorbell. A large delivery truck arrives. The driver gives Michael a note. The movers back the truck up to the front porch placing a ramp between the truck and porch. Sadie inquires about the note. The card reads a wedding gift for you from Sean and Jeremy.

Sadie cannot believe her eyes. The movers haul in the piano from her brochure. Michael directs them to place it on a wall in the dining room.

"How did they remember the exact piano I wanted?" Sadie wonders aloud.

Colleen knows, "I saw Carol take the brochure out of your bench the night of the bachelorette party."

"That is one hell of a wedding present," Steve remarks.

Tears fill her eyes. Sadie has wanted a good quality piano since she was seven. Michael sits on the bench and pulls her onto his lap.

Wrapping his arms around her waist and setting his chin on her shoulder, she begins to play. Everyone quietly listens. Michael will enjoy the gift as well. He loves listening to her play.

Michael, Steve and Aidan drive to the party together. Michael insisted that Jeremy be invited to come with Sean. Martin and Luke are invited. There will be about thirty other men there from Michael's country club days.

Michael gave in and asked Graham to be his best man and Colby to be in the wedding because they had been friends for so long. However, it bothers him that they don't know Sadie. The only time they spent with her at the New Year's Eve party, they had been mean and cold. Sadie had been shot and neither had come to visit or help. There were only a few phone calls and a flower arrangement they sent.

The party takes place in one of the smaller rooms at the country club. Michael dressed casually to match his new friends in a polo shirt and Dockers. As they walk to the door, they run into Barbara who is dressed to play tennis.

"Hello Mikey," she beams at him. He introduces his friends to his ex whom they find to be beautiful.

"So, you are getting married next week. I'll be there," she promises.

"You don't have to come if you feel uncomfortable," Michael discourages her.

"Oh, I wouldn't miss it for the world. Although, I always assumed I would go to your wedding as the bride," she flirts.

"We better go in. They're waiting for us. Have a good game," he pulls open the door. He wonders if her bumping into them was a coincidence, but doubts it.

Graham and Colby greet them at the door. Michael makes

introductions. Awkwardness sits between Michael and his old friends. Aidan and Steve sit with Martin, Luke, Sean, and Jeremy as Michael walks around greeting old friends and acquaintances. When he can break away, he joins them. He quietly admits to them that he wishes they had just stayed at Duffy's or played cards at the parsonage.

Graham notices Michael laughing and visiting with his new friends. Graham hates that he feels like he has lost his closest friend. Now Mike lives somewhere with people and a life style that Graham knows nothing about. It bothers Graham that Michael seems to feel uncomfortable and restless where they had been raised together.

Graham, Colby, and James join Mike's group. Graham shares the story of a drunken Mike making out on the couch with two sorority sisters and being caught by Barbie. He includes how he disappeared with the police searching for him only to have been at church.

Aidan and Steve laugh and laugh. When the story ends, Steve tells the story of their wives catching the Reverend naked in bed, so they sat on the bed talking to him. Michael points out that this isn't fun for him. Martin points out that Sadie's father is sitting at the table.

Michael points at Aidan, "Yeah, well, he slept with Sadie too."

Aidan yells, "Hey, hey, don't throw me under the bus."

Aidan shares his story of waking up with his wife and the Reverend standing at the foot of the bed and Sadie curled up against him.

Shocked, Graham asks Mike, "Weren't you angry?"

Michael shrugs, "No, I had ten hours of uninterrupted sleep."

He and his friends laugh as if they have a private joke that Graham and Colby aren't in on. Martin simply shakes his head.

Graham inquires about the night terrors. Michael explains that they had only been bad for a couple of weeks after the shooting, but she made a quick comeback, even though they still occur. He recounts the night she was convinced that the apartment had caught on fire.

Steve and Aidan brag about the bachelorette party which had been given for Sadie, especially the end where the girls caught the Reverend checking up on them. Graham is annoyed that Michael comments that the girls really know how to party. Michael wants to know why this party is all about embarrassing him. Graham asks why Mike would feel the need to check up on her. Aidan explains that for awhile, after the shooting, Michael became a bit over protective.

Martin observes that Michael sits between his two worlds as two friends refer to him as Michael and Reverend and the other two friends call him Mike and Mikey. While Steve and Aidan seem relaxed, Graham and Colby appear uptight. Michael looks uncomfortable.

Michael goes to the bar for a drink wishing Stephanie really had planned the party. Graham follows him pulling Michael aside for a private word. "Mike, what the hell is going on with you?"

"What do you mean?" he asks half heartedly.

"I thought you are some kind of man of God or something. It sounds like you're off swinging with your new friends. Didn't they teach you not to swap partners in Seminary?" Graham accuses.

"It's not like that," Michael rolls his eyes annoyed.

"You've clearly been sleeping with Sadie. Is it okay for a minister to be sleeping with one of his parishioners?"

"Our love is a private matter, not open for discussion," Michael states flatly.

"I'm your best friend. Maybe you can talk to me. What about their wives in bed with you?" Graham challenges.

"They were dressed and I was covered. There was no touching

involved. They were just joking around for a few minutes," Michael defends himself.

"What about Aidan sleeping with Sadie?" he persists.

"Again, they were completely dressed. He was helping, unlike you. My fiancé was shot and you never once came. Sadie took a bullet meant for me and you didn't even act like you cared," Michael accuses.

"Meant for you?" he asks shocked.

"Yeah, Troy was gunning for me that night, but I had a meeting at the church. I wasn't there for her when it happened."

This fact startles Graham, "Look, what is your hurry? Why are you marrying her so fast? Is it out of guilt?"

"I'm in love with her. I want to marry her. We were already engaged when she was shot. You don't know what we have been through because since ordination, you haven't had much to do with me."

"I'm sorry, but I'm starting a law career. I work long hours. You're not the only one with a life," he shoots back.

"I'm sorry to have bothered you," Michael sneers.

"Mike, I have been your best friend for most of your life and I am telling you, I think you are making a mistake."

Michael grumbles as he walks away, "You have no idea what you are talking about."

He is almost back to his table, when Graham walks up behind him muttering, "For god's sake, she sounds like a mental patient."

Michael whips around punching him in the mouth. The room, stunned, falls silent. Graham rubs his jaw for a second. Then he flies at Michael punching his eye. A full blown fist fight erupts. Years of frustration pour out as punches fly. They wrestle, falling over a table.

Aidan and Steve pull Michael off Graham. Sean and Colby try to gain control of Graham. James runs to the host to talk him out of calling the police with promises to pay for any damages.

"There is no way I'm going to be your best man next week," Graham growls as Colby holds him back.

"I don't want you there," Michael shoots back while Aidan hangs on to him. "I should have made Sean my best man to begin with."

"I'm sure your fag brother is the perfect best man for you."

Breaking free from Aidan, Michael dives at Graham. Their friends pull them apart again. Martin steps between them. Steve suggests they should go back to Duffy's. Despite the long drive, James decides to go with them. Martin and Luke head to the bar as well. Michael refuses to tell anyone what caused the fight.

Michael says little on the drive back. Steve shows them to the backroom. He gives Michael a bowl of ice water for his swollen knuckles and an ice pack for his black eye and fat lip. His father sits across from him.

"Two grown men, a minister and a lawyer, in a fist fight, what happened?"

Michael makes it clear that he does not want Sadie to ever know what was said. He then tells them about the argument. Steve goes to the bar for drinks as Sadie and her friends enter. He hurries back to the others, but not before Brenda spots him. He warns the guys that the girls are here and he thinks they saw him. Michael scoots down in his chair covering his face with his hand. Steve and Aidan stand together behind Michael to obstruct the girls' view of him just as the door opens and the girls enter.

"What are you doing here?" Sadie asks.

"The party ended," Steve replies.

"The party was only two hours?" she asks.

"Not everyone parties for twenty-four hours like you girls," Steve persists.

"Where's Michael?"

"He's around," Steve assures her.

Colleen circles around the guys. Her jaw drops open and her eyes widen. Sadie walks around the other side to find Michael scrunched down. He looks up at her.

"Someone beat you up?" She notices his hand in the ice water, "You were in a fight? You have to be kidding. With whom?"

She sits beside him as Michael straightens up, "Graham and I had a little disagreement."

"About what?"

"It doesn't matter. It is safe to say our friendship ended. He and Colby are not going to be in the wedding. Two of the girls will have to partner up."

"But why?" she persists.

"Our lives are just too different now. They can't accept my life as a minister or the choices I have made."

"Did any of this have to do with me?" she wants to know.

"Not really," he answers.

"Tell me what really happened," she demands.

"No. It's between me and Graham," he states firmly.

"And you worried about me on my bachelorette party."

Michael smiles for a moment, but his lip hurts.

"What are you going to do about church tomorrow?" Sadie questions.

"I... I have no idea," Michael shakes his head.

"Sorry about your party, but we can help," Stephanie turns on some music and the girls begin to dance. Martin and James go into the bar. The girls don't strip, but they are entertaining.

After a while, Michael decides he needs to go home alone to think about what to do in the morning at church. James, Sean, and Jeremy decide to go to a hotel for the night so they can attend church in the morning to be there for him. Martin and Luke leave since Martin has his own service in the morning. This is a situation Martin had never faced.

Chapter XXIV

In the morning, Michael quietly slips into church and quickly ducks into his office. Sadie enters. Michael's face is clearly bruised and swollen as well as his knuckles. He has a black eye and his fat lip is also split. His movements are stiff and sore as his back and ribs ache. He looks at Sadie. He does not know how the congregation will react. There is no way to hide or deny this one. No matter what he says, there will be parishioners who will be angry. He asks Sadie to give him time by himself. With a kiss, she says I love you and leaves.

He has been told by several people more than once that he is a natural born minister, but this morning he feels like a failure. He spent his first year as a minister hanging out at a bar, joking around in promiscuous ways with friends, having premarital sex with a parishioner, and now starting a fist fight. What could he say today? Sorry he let them down? Reports will most likely be sent to the Bishop. He will most likely be called in to be reprimanded by the Bishop. He wonders if this is serious enough for his credentials with the conference to be taken ending his ministry.

He told Mac he had no right to question him without specific complaints of inappropriate behavior. Well, he has definitely given Mac clear-cut inappropriate behavior. Mac can pretty much ask him anything and end his career.

Michael wishes he had called in sick, except someone is bound to see him or hear what really happened. The news would travel by gossip. Besides, he did this. Now he has to deal with it. He prays for strength and guidance, but mostly, he prays for forgiveness for allowing his private life to get in the way of his ministry.

As Sadie pulls on her choir robe, tears fill her eyes. She feels as if she has destroyed his career. She knows the fight was about her. He hung out at the bar to be near her. Other than private moments with her, all inappropriate behavior had been initiated by her and her friends. The bar fight had been her fault for dressing like a hooker. She allowed her friends to tease him in inappropriate ways. She bugged a meeting causing him embarrassment. She turned on him after being shot. She hurt the man she loved, the man who loved her and did so much for her. She prayed for him and for her own forgiveness for being a selfish girlfriend.

Michael, keeping his head down, hurries to the prep room and pulls on his robe and stole. He looks in the mirror feeling like a complete idiot.

Mac enters the room shuffling papers, "Rev. Donnelly, I have a report to give this morning. How about I give it after the announcements?"

Michael turns to face him. Mac looks up, "You have to be kidding me."

"I wish I was," Michael replies, "You can give your report after announcements, but I may take awhile first."

Mac shakes his head as he leaves. The organ begins the opening hymn and Michael steps out of the prep room. The choir gasps, but begin the procession. Michael follows them down the aisle. As he reaches the pulpit less and less people sing. A mummer fills the room.

To his surprise, he spots Graham sitting in the back pew. Michael wonders about his motive in coming today. The rest of the congregation's reactions vary. Some are giggling, some seem concerned, some look angry, and many appear confused. His father, brother and Jeremy are there as well as Aidan and Steve with the girls including Stephanie. He glances over his shoulder at Sadie in the choir loft. She smiles and winks at him. The opening hymn finishes.

Michael steps up to the pulpit. He takes a deep breath leaning forward on his forearms and begins, "Well, this one is hard to explain," there is a ripple of laughter, "I think before we can focus on worship today, I need to try to explain my appearance.

"I have a friend who has been a friend since kindergarten. I even lived with him in college. When I went to seminary, he went to Harvard Law School. While visiting this weekend, we had a bit of a disagreement and instead of acting like a minister and a lawyer who have been life-long friends; we digressed to teenagers in a brawl. I have no excuses. We were just wrong, especially me. I threw the first punch. All I can do now is say that I'm sorry.

"I thought about my calling to ministry all night. I admit that I have made some bad decisions this year, but I believe that I am where I belong. I still feel my calling as strongly as ever. In the end, ministers are just humans trying their best. I'm sorry if you feel that I've let you down. It is my intention to learn from my mistakes and strive to do better, to be better.

"I always take comfort in the Bible stories. So many men in the Bible make mistakes, but God uses them anyway. I like the stories about Peter. Peter was the kind of man who jumps right in before thinking things through and he tended to be a hothead whether he was attempting to walk on water or drawing his sword to cut the ear off a soldier or even panicking to the point that he denied Jesus three times. It seems Jesus often shook his head at him, yet never gave up on him. Jesus asked Peter to feed His sheep. Now, today, all ministers are asked to feed His sheep.

"I have been officially appointed here for another year. I promise to work hard to be the best minister I can be for you."

The congregation applauds. Sadie can't hold back tears from falling. James is proud of how his son handled himself with honesty and being upfront. Sean is proud as well. Michael's heart is pounding, but he tries to appear calm. He is relieved that for at least the moment, his congregation seems to be forgiving.

Before Michael can move on, Mac stands, walking to the front. Michael sits as Mac takes the pulpit.

"Good morning. I'm Mac McIntyre, the Pastor/Parish Chairman. I was going to begin this report with how it has been a crazy year with Rev. Donnelly, but my wife said I shouldn't. But now that he showed up with a black eye and split lip, it has been a crazy year with Rev. Donnelly," Michael smiles and the congregation chuckles. Mac continues, "There are many new faces here, so let me start at the beginning. Last year, I had a meeting with our District Superintendent and Rev. Bill Harper. The Bishop wanted us to go on a circuit or merge with St. Luke's. We could no longer afford Rev. Harper's salary. Rev. Harper suggested rolling the salary back to a first year pastor's salary.

"That's how we got Rev. Donnelly. I admit I've been a little hard on him this year." The look on Michael's face causes the congregation to snicker, "But I'm a numbers man. I spent the weekend pouring over the books for this report.

"Since Rev. Donnelly arrived five new families have joined. Our attendance is up thirty-eight percent. Our offerings are up almost fifty percent. Rev. Donnelly is the first minister I have met with a business degree. Our committee meetings are run more efficiently. Although there are still serious problems, our finances have made dramatic improvements.

"Two years ago, our Bible School enrolled eleven students. This past summer Miss Stevens and Rev. Donnelly took over the Bible School planning; we had seventy-two people here each night plus the workers.

"I know that he personally kept two of our church families from losing their homes. From all accounts, I've heard he is one of the best ministers we've had for calling at hospitals, nursing homes, and with our shut-ins.

"At a recent planning meeting, Rev. Donnelly presented a list of suggestions he would like to try this year. I think we will have another very good year. He said just now that he feels a strong calling. I personally believe him which doesn't mean I won't still keep a close eye on him.

"He is getting married next week. We all hope your face heals in time. We took up a collection for a wedding present. I am shocked by the generosity not just for Rev. Donnelly, but for our Sadie who is loved as well. Kirk Donaldson and I have decided to combine it with some other funds. When you two get back from conference, you can go shopping. We are going to paint the downstairs and the upstairs hall and install new carpet in the dining room, living room, on the stairs, and the upstairs hall. We are also thinking of installing a new kitchen floor.

"We wish Rev. Donnelly and Miss Stevens a wonderful wedding day and many happy years."

The congregation applauds. Michael shakes Mac's hand. Mac walks to the choir loft and gives Sadie a hug. Michael takes over the service. When he gets to the sermon, he goes over the announcements that were skipped and then skips the sermon so that the service does not run over.

After the service, Michael takes Sadie's hand and they go to the foot of the stairs and greet everyone on their way out receiving many best wishes. Graham comes through the line first having been sitting in the back. He tells Michael he'll wait to talk with him later.

Mac runs into Graham in the breezeway, "You must be the lawyer."

Michael gives his dad the keys to the parsonage telling him to take Graham there to wait while Michael and Sadie greet and visit with their parishioners.

Michael and Sadie greet the parishioners of his church who he has come to love over the past year. Eloise Crabtree, the elderly woman who is the very heart of the church hugs each comforting Michael, "Don't be too hard on yourself Pastor. You have had a very difficult year. The stress was bound to build, even for a minister. You have a long ministry ahead of you. I'm happy to be part of the beginning with you."

Alice and Kelly Mitchell each hug Sadie and Michael. Alice smiles at them, "Congratulations on your first year. I don't know where we would have ended up if I hadn't seen that large wooden sign advertising your Bible School and decided that I should bring Kelly. You helped me so much. I am glad we joined your church. It has changed our lives."

Dorothy Martin stands in front of Michael shaking her head,

"Young ministers are different than I'm use to, but it is never dull with you two in charge."

Sadie and Michael laugh.

Bob and Cathy Johnson come through the line next. Cathy touches Michael's cheek, "I don't care what problems you have had this year. All I know is that you have been there for us during the worst time in our lives. I don't know how to thank you for all of your counseling and for staying with us that night. Breanna really liked you. It's ironic, the last time I almost got into a fist fight; you were the one who held me back."

Sue Anderson, the church secretary, shakes hands, "I'll let you in on a little secret. Of the three ministers I have worked for in this church, you are my favorite. I hope you stay here for many years."

Ruth's daughter, Gina embraces Sadie, "My mother adored you. Thank you for all you did for her. Reverend, you gave my mother a beautiful funeral. I was nervous having such a young new minister do her funeral, but I was very happy and satisfied with it. You know, after the visit when you both ended up there together, my mother told me that there was an obvious spark between you two."

Beth Bergenstein greets them next, "I can't believe the two of you gave me all my money back for my wedding and took my date. You gave me a beautiful wedding and even got permission for me to have the wine. I hope you enjoy your wedding next week as much as I enjoyed mine."

Betty Hart takes her turn, "Congratulations on your first year. You know, my children didn't want me to unplug Ed when I did. They refused to be there with me. After you prayed over him, I was so surprised that you stayed there with me for all of those hours. You will never know how grateful I am to you for getting me through that."

Jim and Tanya Pizar stop next, "Thank you for all you did to get us through this year. The time after the layoff was one of the scariest times in our marriage. You helped keep a roof over our head and food on our table. Now that I have a new job and once our bills are straightened out, I would like to help someone in need. If you ever find someone who needs special help, you can come to us."

Don, the church custodian, roughly shakes Michael's hand, "Have a great wedding, Pastor. I just love that you taught my grandson, Josh, a lesson. We can't afford him losing a hundred dollars like that, but that you not only got it back for him, I loved that you made him work at the church for it. He still helps me out now and then. I love having him coming around to help me and spend time like this."

Their friends are the last through the line. Aidan shakes hands, "Who knew that Steve and I would ever end up attending a church on a regular basis. Brenda had stopped going to church after what she went through at college and now she is back. You even managed to lure Stephanie in. You said you would try to save her, 'but from over here.'

"We were sweating for you this morning. We are really impressed with how you handled it. I'm glad we're friends and proud to stand up with you next week. Thank you for all you did for Sadie. You breathed new life in her that we haven't seen in years. We thought it had all been for nothing after she was shot, but you have helped to bring her back again. May you have a long and happy marriage."

Michael had been afraid that his congregation would be angry with him for having been in a fight; instead he is overwhelmed by the love and support that he received this morning. He hopes to remain in Ambrose for as long as he can, not only for Sadie's sake, but because he has fallen in love with his parish.

Once back at the house, Michael faces Graham who begins, "It took a lot of courage to face your church today. I am impressed. I was also impressed with the report on your first year. I should have listened when you tried to explain your calling. I'm sorry about last night. You may have thrown the first punch, but I started the fight." He looks toward Sadie, "I'm sorry."

Michael interrupts, "She doesn't know specifics."

The two friends talk for awhile. Graham wants to renew their friendship and wants to get to know Sadie. He also wants to be in the wedding, even though Sean is now the best man. Michael agrees to everything. Colby, however, has decided not to be in the wedding party because of Barbara and his own estranged feelings.

Laughing, Graham tells them he is taking courage from Michael facing his church this morning. He has to go to court tomorrow to defend a client on an assault case. The room laughs.

"You're going to be short a groomsman," Graham states.

"That's okay," Sadie informs him, "You will just have to figure out how to dance with two girls."

Michael suggests, "I bet Jeremy looks good in a tux." Sean and Jeremy look up surprised. Michael continues, "You're sort of like a brother-in-law, right? I know its last minute."

"I'll do it," Jeremy offers.

Sadie is pleased. James does not know how he feels. He has been upset with Sean, but Jeremy has been around more lately. He hates to admit it, but he sort of likes him.

"Good," Michael declares, "The only problem left is who's going to tell Mom?"

James throws up his hands, "Don't look at me."

The last day of school, her class gives her a bridal shower with the help of her colleagues and room mothers. They present her with a crystal salad bowl with six matching little bowls. They also give her a garden sign with two rabbits and flowers which reads, "Rev. and Mrs. Donnelly." Sadie loves it. She thinks she can take it with them to set out the next time they use the camper.

The rest of the week flies by, and it is time for the rehearsal. Michael and Graham's faces have healed for the most part. Despite protests, Carol insists on using cover-up make up to conceal lingering bruises on both of them.

Michael is happy to see Rev. Foreman and his wife, Bonnie, again. Rob is proud of Michael. They had lunch together that day and Michael was able to tell him about his first year in the church and about his courtship with Sadie. He even tells him about walking up the aisle once with bright red lipstick on his cheek and once with a battered face.

Michael boasts to his mentor that he has managed to find a woman who has a strong faith and knowledge about church people and politics. He has found a woman who excites him romantically and physically and who, while not at first, eventually decided that she is willing to make the necessary sacrifices to be a minister's wife. Michael thanks Rob for all of his guidance and support during his crucial years of decision making during college.

Before their wedding rehearsal begins, Michael pulls Sadie into his office. Holding her hands to his chest, he stares intensely into her eyes, "Sadie, I need to know the truth. Do you have any doubts about marrying me left? I love you, but I don't want to get married if you are not one hundred percent sure. You tried so hard not to fall in love with me. You pushed me away when you were hurt. I know the sacrifices that you will face marrying me, especially your teaching. Darling, are you absolutely sure that you want to be my wife, that you want to be a minister's wife?"

Sadie shakes her head, "After all I put you through, it is amazing to me that you are still here. You stood by me no matter what I did. I actually trust you and that is not easy for me. I have so much fun with you. I feel so safe with you. You are so handsome and sexy. I am so in love with you.

"As far as being a minister's wife, I am very proud of the kind of minister you are and I am proud to share in your ministry with you. I know the sacrifices that I will need to make, but I also know for sure that the benefits will outweigh the sacrifices. I've seen my mother cry, but I also know that she loves her life and has no regrets. She told me that over and over again last Thanksgiving.

"So, to answer your question, I choose you. I choose you over my friends, over my career, over where I live. I love you more than I knew I could love. I am one hundred percent sure that I love you and I choose you."

Michael hugs and kisses her filled with relief, love, and passion.

Martin runs the rehearsal. When he comes to the vows, he explains to them there are many unspoken vows that only they know as a couple and starts adding vows for just the rehearsal.

"Sadie, do you promise to live wherever the Bishop sends your husband? Do you promise to attend all church functions and stand by his side? Do you promise to be patient and try to please the parishioners for your husband's sake?" Sadie promises.

"Michael, do you promise not to use personal home life stories as sermon illustrations? Do you promise to automatically take your wife's side in disagreements between her and parishioners at least publicly? Do you promise not to always put church matters before your family?" Michael promises.

"Is there anything either of you wish to add just for today?" Martin asks.

Gazing down at her, Michael adds, "Promise that no matter what happens, you won't push me away again." Sadie promises.

Sadie adds, "Promise you won't take an interest in the mission field and drag me off to Africa." Michael throws back his head and laughs loudly and promises. He pulls her close kissing her, but Martin breaks it up scolding not yet.

When the time comes for the kiss, like Michael had done to Aidan, Martin keeps stopping them instructing them to keep it simple. Finally Michael grabs Sadie picking her up and swinging her around as he kisses her.

After Michael sets her down, he turns to Martin, "Too much?" Everyone laughs.

Graham watches intrigued by Michael's behavior. He acts livelier and more in love than Graham had ever seen him. He realizes that he missed something not being around for this courtship.

Michael partnered Graham with Stephanie who are both happy with the arrangement. They all have a good time at the rehearsal dinner which has been elegantly provided by Sophia who believes that she is ready to accept Sadie into their family.

The next morning as Sadie and her bridesmaids are having their hair and make up done, storm clouds roll in. Sadie insists she feels so happy; the pending storm doesn't bother her. The beautician provides the girls with plastic head covers to keep their hair from blowing around as they run to the white stretch limo Carol again provided.

Sadie takes some over-the-counter pain relievers for her hip. She does not want to limp down the aisle or have problems dancing at her reception. Her hip is not in too bad of shape. Despite the moisture in the air, it is a warm windy day.

Once at the church, the girls run up to see the sanctuary. Sophia's florist placed spring floral arrangements on the end of every pew. Flowers cover the chancel. The church is beautiful. They find their bouquets which they think are perfect.

As they head for the lounge, Stephanie sees Michael and the guys in the breezeway. Even though the girls are wearing jeans and blouses, they do not want to be seen. Carol volunteers to get rid of them.

Carol runs down the steps, "Good morning boys. Go down to the fellowship hall. Sadie is in the sanctuary and needs to get to the lounge."

"Really?" Michael heads toward the stairs to the sanctuary, but Carol catches his arm instructing Graham to take him away. Sadie hurries to the lounge to dress. Roberto did a fabulous job on her gown. She feels like a princess. She is finally Cinderella and would definitely not turn back into a pumpkin tonight.

The church fills to capacity. Just before Sadie leaves the lounge, the sky opens with torrential rain pounding on the roof and blowing against the windows. Martin, wearing a tux, walks Sadie, who is smiling ear to ear down to the aisle to her smiling groom.

As Sadie moves from her dad to Michael, lightning flashes through the windows. Rev. Foreman begins, "We are gathered here today in the presence of God." A loud clap of thunder shakes the building.

Sadie turns to Michael, "There He is now."

The pair catches a case of the giggles which quickly spreads through the wedding party. It takes a moment for everyone to settle down. After Martin gives her away, he heads to Michael's prep room where he pulls on his robe and stole and then joins Rev. Foreman.

Thunder rumbles throughout the service, but the groom and bride are not bothered. They enjoy their wedding and the congregation enjoys watching the couple. Their happiness is contagious. When her dad comes to the vows, they think of the extra ones said the night before which causes them to smile again. Their eyes lock as they clearly repeat the vows.

Although Colby decided not to be in the wedding party, he attends with his sister and mother. Watching Michael, Sean, and Graham upfront, Colby regrets not staying in the wedding party. He belongs up there with his friends. He promises himself to try to mend the fences between him and Michael after he returns from his honeymoon the way Graham has.

Barbara regrets coming. Watching becomes harder than she expected. She does not remember Michael ever looking at her this way. She always pictured weddings somber and serious, but Michael and Sadie smile and laugh and wink at each other. She is jealous of their happiness.

Martin pronounces them husband and wife. To no one's surprise their kiss lasts longer and is bigger than it is supposed to be. They turn to face the congregation.

Martin introduces them, "I'm honored to introduce for the very first time Rev. and Mrs. Michael Donnelly." The church erupts with applause. Sophia and Joy cry. The organ plays. The couple exits the sanctuary running down the stairs to look out the window. The storm has passed. The sun peeks through. All that is left is a steady light rain.

Sadie beams at her new husband, "I have always thought that you are a natural born minister. It doesn't surprise me that He came to your wedding."

Michael kisses her again.

At the reception, before dinner is served, Sean toasts the couple. He tells that he liked Sadie the day he met her and he feels guilty pleasure that Michael had to try so hard to get her to date him. He also reminisces that Carol guessed that Michael was already attracted to Sadie at his ordination even though he had only met her the day before. It seems that this is a case of love at first sight.

Colleen then gives her toast. She shares that watching the two date and fall in love was fun and romantic. "We know this couple will make it, because they have already been through for better and worse."

Next, Martin takes the microphone, "I had the privilege of being the one who introduced these two. It took them all of three seconds to begin flirting. The first thing Sadie did was make it crystal clear that she would not date Michael, and they have been dating ever since. Her mother, like Carol, guessed that they would end up together. God bless these two as they walk the difficult road as a minister's family. Don't worry, Michael, she may throw the occasional temper tantrum, but she will be good at it."

Michael lifts his glass and nods.

James takes a turn to speak, "Michael's mother and I did our best to raise a self-centered spoiled child who would live in the lap of luxury. We apparently failed miserably as Michael has chosen to live on a minister's salary to serve people. His mother and I are very proud. The first time Sadie called us to invite us to Christmas Eve, it was clear that she loved him."

Lastly, Michael takes a turn. He thanks everyone for coming and then acknowledges his new friends, "I know that they don't want me to say anything, but there would not be a wedding today if it weren't for Aidan Phillips and Steve Duffy. Both the police and doctors told us that the night Sadie was shot, these two saved her life. So we lift our glasses to our good friends with thanks."

As dinner begins, Aidan and Steve steal the microphone, "Hey Reverend, we were thinking about the first time we met you and we again triple dog dare you to kiss Sadie," Michael stands pulling Sadie to her feet. His kiss brings cheers. When Aidan sits back down, Graham asks, "Did that really happen?" Aidan smiles and nods.

The dance begins with the groom twirling his bride around the dance floor. The newlyweds spend most of the evening dancing and having a great time. Stephanie suggests their special dance.

Michael steps in, "I don't think that's a good idea. There are so many church people and family here."

Sadie places her fists on her hips, "I have been a minister's wife for only half a day and you already want me to change my stripes?"

Michael hangs his head for a second as Stephanie runs to the DJ. Within minutes, Sadie, Colleen, Brenda, and Stephanie perform their college dance routine to hoots and cat calls. Lucy and Mary join them. Carol watches for a minute and thinks what the hell; she can follow this and joins them. Graham and Colby join Michael to watch.

Graham comments, "That is one beautiful wedding party."

Colby apologizes, "I wish I would have stayed in the party for you. Like Graham, I would like to fix things between us."

"I would like that," Michael agrees.

Later, Sadie and her girls run to the restroom to freshen up. Barbara takes her chance to pull Michael away for a private moment. She concedes that she has never seen him happier and that she is happy for him. He embraces her for a moment, touches her cheek, and then walks back to his friends. Barbara knows that she has to accept that she and Michael are now completely done forever. Tears fill her eyes as she takes a deep breath.

At the end of the evening, Michael sweeps his bride off her feet and carries her out of the hall.

Sadie loves the cruise. If this is Michael's idea of a vacation, she thinks, no wonder he hadn't been all that impressed with camping at first. She had never been on an airplane, never had been on a cruise, and had never been on a tropical island. The food is fantastic, the island is beautiful, the stars are brighter, the water bluer. She had never been so pampered.

One night, they get on a smaller boat called a tram that transports them to an island for a midnight buffet. They lie on lounge chairs eating barbequed pork and dipping strawberries and bananas in chocolate with large margaritas. Later they lie together in a hammock. With no city lights, Sadie has never seen so many stars or the Milky Way look brighter. She hates to see this week end.

Chapter XXV

Michael and Sadie return to Erieton this year as husband and wife staying in Sadie's old room in her parents' cottage. Michael feels a little awkward spending the week next to her parents' room. Sadie teases him about being one horny minister.

Once they unload the car, Martin and Michael need to register. Joy and Sadie go for the walk with them. Mary and Lucy insist they want to stay at the cottage. After they register at the auditorium, the four stroll down the main street toward the pier. Everyone seems to know the Stevens. They can't go four steps without being stopped all of whom know that Sadie has married a minister. Countless ministers' wives ask her if she is crazy or what was she thinking. Then they look at Michael and tease that they can see what she was thinking. They also invite her to various ministers' wives functions during the week.

Sadie can no longer be a delegate, since ministers' wives are not permitted to fill this function, so Eloise Crabtree is their delegate. Michael teases about who will sit with him to keep him entertained during sessions.

As they reach the pier, they run into Michael's District Superintendent, Bob Kavinsky.

Bob signals to him, "Hey Michael, I received a complaint letter about you."

"Just one?" Michael asks.

"So far. Is it true you led a worship service with a black eye and split lip following your bachelor party?" he asks.

"Uh...yeah."

"Were you drunk at the bachelor party?" Bob inquires.

"No. I managed to do that sober," Michael replies.

Shaking his head, Bob dictates, "We are going to have to sit down and discuss this."

"I bet," Michael nods.

Bob leaves with Martin and Joy staring at Michael. Placing his arm around Sadie and whistling, he continues toward the pier. As he looks out over Lake Erie, he remembers sitting here last year by himself just before ordination. What a year he has had. He leans down kissing Sadie on top of the head.

After a walk by the lake, they return to the cottage. Lucy and Mary sit on the couch looking as if they were up to something. They claim they didn't feel like standing around all evening as their parents visit with everyone they see, so they just hung around the cottage.

Michael and Sadie go to their room to unpack. He lifts a large suitcase onto the bed. As it lands, jingle bells ring. He stares at the bed, and then looks over at Sadie. Dropping down on the floor, he peers under the bed discovering strings of small jingle bells zigzagging under the mattress. He stands pulling the suitcase back onto the floor.

Slowly, he saunters into the living room, where Mary and Lucy cover their faces with their hands to hide laughter. Martin and Joy ask, "What was that noise?"

"Ask your girls," Michael quips. The two jump up and take off running, but Michael quickly catches Lucy around the waist and Mary by the arm. He half carries, half drags them to the room as their parents quietly watch. Michael tosses his sisters-in-law onto the bed.

"Ha, ha, very funny. Now take them off."

The girls roll around laughing. Lucy sits up, "If you want them off, you take them off."

"No. You aren't leaving until you take them off." He turns to Sadie, "Your sisters are as strange as your friends." He leaves the room.

Sadie attacks her sisters filling the room with the sound of jingle bells and giggles. Martin and Joy look up at him as he shakes his head, "Don't ask."

"We don't need to, dear. It's obvious," Joy replies.

Conference ends and the newlyweds return home. The last week of June and first week of July parishioners parade in and out of the parsonage painting the rooms. The carpet is scheduled for installation the third week in July. Sadie plans to empty her apartment by the end of the month.

There is some discussion over the living room furniture. They both prefer theirs, but Michael really works to persuade her to keep his black leather set. He pushes her down on his couch instructing her to notice how comfortable it is while he kisses her. Laughing, she gives in and compromises that they will keep his furniture, but she is going to pack away his white with black trim kitchen dishes for her apple design dishes. He agrees, "Deal" as if he even cared about the kitchen dishes.

Michael's bedroom suit is a better quality than hers. She plans to use hers for a guest room. She gives her guest room and her living room to Mary who is moving into a new apartment.

All month, Michael and Sadie transport boxes, books, pictures, and household items with them as they go back and forth. She takes her clothes over one day with Brenda.

One day, Michael discovers Sadie sitting in the nursery staring at the forest mural she had painted, "I never dreamed when I was working on this that I would ever use it."

"Why, are you pregnant?" he asks quickly.

"No, but I'm hoping we stay here for as many years as possible," she replies.

He sits on the floor beside her impressed with her work. "Hey, I know. Let's practice." Climbing on top of her, Michael begins smothering her with kisses causing her to giggle.

Later that day, Michael meets Sadie after making calls at the nursing home. He is still wearing his clerical shirt when they arrive at the Rainbow Café where he holds the door and pulls out a chair for her. As they sit, Michael asks if she notices two older ladies giving them the evil eye.

Sadie giggles, "This happens to my parents too. I bet they're Catholic. They see your collar and they are assuming that you're a priest. Lean over and give me a big kiss."

Smiling, Michael leans over and kisses his wife. They can hear the ladies gasp and attempt not to laugh. The women stand and leave the restaurant in a huff.

The waitress, who knows the Donnelly's as regulars, comes to take their order. Sadie asks for separate checks. Michael pinches at her waist.

Once they order, Sadie points out, "Do you realize that when we were dating, I actually paid for way more dinners than you?"

"How do you figure?"

"Every time I cooked for you, I used groceries that I purchased. You my dear are a chauvinist. You insisted on paying in public, but didn't think anything of letting me cook for you."

Michael laughs realizing she is right, but had never once thought of that.

The third Wednesday in July, they need to go to court for Troy's sentencing. Luckily, he made a plea deal, so there was no trial to go through. He pled down to a lesser charge of assault with a deadly weapon. A large group attends together, their group of friends who witnessed the assault, Sadie's parents, and Graham. Sadie prepared a statement to give. She agonized over it for hours and still thinks it sounds dumb, but Michael approves of her final draft.

As she waits in the courtroom, her stomach fills with butterflies while sitting between Michael and Graham. A guard escorts Troy wearing an orange prison jumpsuit into the courtroom. He appears beaten down with lifeless eyes, an empty shell of the man she used to know. The court proceedings begin, but Sadie doesn't pay attention. She itches to leave. Michael takes her hand.

The time comes for her to read her statement. In a fog, she hears her name called. When the judge calls her Sadie Donnelly, Troy glances up at him, and then his gaze turns to Sadie who feels frozen. Graham whispers in her ear not to look at him assuring her that she is safe here.

The judge asks if she has anything to say and she nods. Michael whispers that she can do it. Michael stands up and walks her to a small podium, and then backs away.

Sadie lays down her paper with trembling hands. Taking a deep breath, she reads, "I don't understand why this happened. I know that Troy had loved me at one time. I feel the need to forgive him, so I will, but I am still very much scared of him. He has left me with physical and emotional scars. He accused me of leaving him for my husband, but the truth is I broke up with Mr. Meyers three years before I met my husband. I did not deserve this. I ask the court to give him the maximum sentence allowed."

Michael places his arm around her leading her back to her seat. Looking at Troy, she notices him still glaring at her causing her to feel jittery. Again Graham whispers not to look at him, and leans forward with his elbows on his knees to obstruct Troy's view of her.

The judge instructs Troy to stand as he sentences him to fifteen years without the possibility of parole for eight years. After Troy is led away, everyone stands. As friends and family talk, Sadie quietly slips out of the courtroom.

Michael reaches for her realizing she is gone. He and Graham hurry out of the courtroom to find her. Michael scans the hall to no avail. Graham checks with a security guard who is standing by the door if he saw an upset brunette run by. The guard points toward the door to the stairs. Hurrying to the stairwell, they can hear her running down several flights below. Michael calls to her, but she doesn't stop. He and Graham rush down the stairs. As they leave the stairwell, Graham slows Michael down, because security guards would stop men chasing a woman through the lobby. They see her leave the building and walk quickly after her.

Outside they hurry down the steps looking in every direction. Michael spies her running across a grassy area and sprints to catch her. Running ahead of her, he catches her in his arms. She tries to pull away, but he wraps his arms around her. She sobs into his chest.

As she quiets, Michael pulls out his handkerchief to clean her up,

"What happened? What's bothering you?"

"I panicked. I had to get out of there. I didn't want everyone gathering around asking me how I feel," she chokes.

"You're safe now. He's in custody. He's going away for a long time," he comforts.

"No, he's not. He can be out in eight years. Our oldest child would be seven or less and we will probably have even younger children. Did you see him looking at me? He's not going to leave us alone. This isn't over. I have a bad feeling, a very bad feeling about this," she explains.

He pulls her into a tight embrace looking over her head at Graham who only shrugs. Sadie is probably right. Graham noticed Troy's reaction when the judge referred to her as Sadie Donnelly.

That evening, Michael hates that the strange expression Sadie had the weeks following the shooting has returned. She says little during dinner and barely eats anything going to bed early. Michael joins her. In the wee hours of the morning, Sadie bolts upright in bed.

Startled, Michael asks, "What is it? What's wrong?"

Sadie responds, "Shh… Did you hear that? Someone's in the house."

"No honey," he exhales, "No one's here. It's okay."

As he holds her, he feels her entire body trembling. Disappointed that the night terrors returned, he does his best to soothe and comfort her reciting the twenty-third Psalm with her three times before she calms down enough to sleep.

Over breakfast, she apologizes for waking him, but he assures her that they will get through this together. He suggests that they work on Bible School materials to get her mind off things since they only have two weeks left to prepare.

"Michael," she begins quietly, "have you ever seen the gun club out on route fifty-eight?"

He freezes, "Yes, why?"

"I want to learn how to use a gun," she informs him.

"I don't think so," he replies.

"It wouldn't hurt to learn how to handle one," she pushes.

"When you have a night terror in bed with me, I don't want you to have a gun."

"I never hurt you with the knife or bat," she reminds him.

"No guns. Absolutely not," Michael puts his foot down.

"I won't bring one in the house. I just want to learn how to handle one," she insists.

"Darling, I feel strongly about this. I'm against guns."

Sadie doesn't finish her breakfast going back to bed. Almost half an hour later, Michael checks on her, sitting next to her and rubbing her back.

"Sweetheart, you need to calm down. We are okay. In eight years, we will figure things out. All kinds of things can change in eight years. Some prisoners find Jesus and change their lives. There are other safety measures we can take, but right now you are fine. You are safe."

"I'm fine except for the pain in my hip and the shark bite on my shoulder and the feeling that someone is coming after me."

"No one's coming after you. You survived. He tried twice and you survived. God will watch over you less you dash your foot on a stone," he quotes from the Psalms.

Michael lies back. Sadie rolls over laying her head on his chest and putting an arm and a leg over him as he rubs her back.

Sadie busies herself with work appearing to feel better. She continues her counseling with Tony. Despite a few nightmares, she does not have anymore night terrors. That Saturday, Aidan brings his pick-up truck. Steve, Sean, and Jeremy also come as well as Sadie's girlfriends. The crew completes her move to the parsonage. She feels a little sad leaving her apartment of three years, but the parsonage fixes up nicely. Between the paint, the new carpet, the new kitchen floor, and the dining room suit, it looks like a whole new house. The girls spend the day hanging pictures and arranging knick-knacks, the bareness of his house gone. They pack away his white with black trim dishes replacing them with Sadie's apple design set.

Any disagreements that come up during the day as to how to set up the house and whether to keep something of Michael's or replace it with Sadie's, are referred to Sean and Jeremy with gay jokes about interior design to which Sean and Jeremy play up their roles causing everyone to laugh.

The friends are all in the living room when Colleen lifts an empty box to move it out of her way. Aidan scolds, "I said not to lift anything!"

Colleen smiles, "It's empty. Relax."

Brenda, Stephanie, and Sadie exchange glances. Brenda cocks her head, "Colleen, are you?"

Colleen's face lights up. All the girls scream jumping up and down hugging each other while Michael and Steve look around, clueless.

Aidan announces, "Colleen is pregnant."

Steve, Michael, Sean, and Jeremy join in the celebration. She is seven weeks pregnant, due in February.

The first week in August, the Donnellys run another successful Bible School. The following week, Sadie leaves with the marching band for a week on a college campus in Pennsylvania for band camp. When she returns home, she prepares for her new school year with a new class of first graders. Life seems to be back to normal. Sadie appears to have allowed her fears and thoughts of Troy Meyers go.

Michael helps her arrange and organize her classroom. Sadie fills out name tags, laminates them and cuts them out. After sticking magnets on the backs, they hang name tags on the lockers and desks. They sort papers, decorate four bulletin boards, wash shelves and sort math manipulatives. Sadie likes having a tall husband to hang her alphabet above the chalkboard.

With September and the beginning of school comes Friday night football games followed by time at Duffy's. This almost feels like they are dating again. Colleen enjoys the evenings as well although there is no more drinking for her. The girls write out lists of baby names and discuss how to fix up the nursery. All four girls plan to paint the nursery using Sadie's overhead method.

The last Saturday of September, Michael has a meeting with the District Superintendent about an hour drive away. Before he leaves, he receives a call canceling the appointment. Now unexpectedly free, he invites Sadie to do something with him. Sadie answers that since he wasn't supposed to be here, she has lunch plans with Stephanie.

After she leaves, he hears someone at the door. Graham stops by for a visit.

"I wanted to tell you something," Graham begins. "I took this woman out a couple times and now we are starting to see each other on a more regular basis."

"Hey, that's great. Do I know her?" Michael inquires.

"Well, as a matter of fact, you introduced us at your wedding."

"Really? Who?" Michael questions.

"Stephanie Jones."

Michael is visibly surprised. Graham is on his way to Duffy's to meet Stephanie so Michael decides to walk with him, since Sadie will be there with her. Graham inquires to how Sadie has been. Michael relates to him that she is doing great. She had a couple tough days, but that passed.

At Duffy's, Michael walks up to Stephanie, "We have to be compatible. We still like all the same people."

Stephanie laughs giving him a kiss on the cheek which she then immediately wipes off.

"Thanks," Michael looks around, "Where's Sadie?"

"I don't know. I haven't seen her today," Stephanie replies as she places her arm around Graham's waist.

"Didn't you have lunch plans?" he asks.

"No," it dawns on her that Sadie must have told him they were together. "Well, I mean, we had plans, but I…"

He interrupts her, "Stop. Don't lie to me, too. Where is she?"

She shrugs, "I honestly don't know."

Thinking about the strange feeling he had over the past several weeks, he turns to Colleen, "Did you go out with her Thursday?"

"Yes, yes I did," Colleen nods.

"Really? Where did you go?" he traps her.

Colleen's eyes widen, "To the mall?"

"Wrong," Michael snaps, "But good guess. Where is she?"

"Go home and talk to her about it," Brenda suggests.

"I would, but she's not there," Michael turns to Aidan, "I know the girls stick together, but you're my friend. Do you know what the hell is going on?"

"I swear, I'd tell you if I knew," Aidan promises.

Michael returns home pacing around. Opening the front door, he brings in the mail which consists mostly of junk mail. He notices a piece of junk mail from the NRA which he doesn't remember receiving this before. Thinking for a minute, he tosses the mail on the kitchen table, grabs his keys, and leaves. Michael drives out to the gun club on route fifty-eight. As he pulls in the parking lot, he spots Sadie's car.

He informs the person at the front counter he is looking for Sadie Stevens. The man checks the roster not finding her. Michael realizes his mistake and requests the man check for Sadie Donnelly. Checking again, he tells Michael that she should be out at any minute.

He takes a seat on a wooden bench to wait. Sadie enters with another man who speaks to the one behind the counter, "Damn, you should see this little girl's target. She took out his paper heart and brain. She is deadly for a little thing."

The other man nods toward Michael, "Your ride is here."

Sadie's heart jumps when she sees Michael glaring at her. Without saying a word, he leaves. Sadie follows him out, but he drives home. She jumps in her car and follows.

At home, she finds him pacing angrily around the living room, "How long have you been going there?" he demands.

"Since the beginning of September about three weeks ago," she admits quietly.

"So, we disagreed on something and your answer is to lie to me and sneak around," he barks.

"I'm sorry."

"For what?!" he yells, "For lying or for getting caught? Did you bring a gun in the house?"

"No," she answers.

"I don't know if I can believe you. You have been lying for weeks. Where do women keep guns, in their purse or bedroom right?"

He grabs her purse dumping the contents out on the coffee table. When he finds nothing, he runs up to their room with Sadie close at his heels. They yell and shout at each other while Michael digs through her nightstand and dresser drawers. She gives up returning to the living room where she sits on the couch. Soon he returns leaning on the wall. His eyes show his anger and his lips pull tight.

"I'm so sorry," Sadie repeats.

"You promised at our wedding rehearsal that you wouldn't push me away again," he reminds her.

"I'm not pushing you away," she denies.

"What do you think happens when you lie and sneak around on someone? How can a marriage work without trust?" Michael storms out of the house.

Sadie lies on the couch sobbing.

Outside, Michael doesn't know where to go, so he takes off jogging around town. He eventually ends up at Duffy's where Steve works behind the bar. The others have gone. Michael sits at the bar ordering a beer. Steve remarks that he looks awful. Michael recounts what happened. Steve agrees about the lying.

"What do you think about the gun club?" Michael asks.

"Everyone feels different about guns," Steve hedges.

"But what do you think?" Michael prompts.

Steve reaches in a drawer below the cash register pulling out a hand gun, "I feel safer knowing it is here and Brenda can use it. The semester after her rape, she took a marksmanship class in college. Men are naturally stronger than women. Brenda said a gun made her feel powerful. It made her feel safer.

"I know living alone, Stephanie owns a small hand gun. Aidan's dad hunts and taught him. Aidan has a couple of guns and he taught Colleen how to use them."

"I didn't realize you all had guns," Michael remarks.

"We don't goof around with them or make a big show of it," Steve shrugs.

Michael finishes his beer and heads home where he discovers Sadie in the living room working out to one of her kickboxing DVDs. She turns it off when she sees him.

"I was scared you wouldn't come home tonight," she comments.

"I'll always come home. You can trust me," he states flatly.

"I promise to never lie to you again, at least not about anything important," she promises.

A smile tugs at the corner of his mouth, "What about the gun club?"

"Maybe we can talk about it later without you refusing to consider it," she suggests. "If I could go back and do this again, I would tell you that I'm an adult and you shouldn't just put your foot down with me. We should have discussed it. When I went and checked it out, I should have just come home and told you instead of being scared you would stop me. I should have just fought it out with you instead of hiding it like a little kid."

"That would have been better. I probably should have discussed it with you more. I should have listened," he agrees.

"Now that I have been going, I don't want to quit."

"Fine, you go to the gun club, but don't bring a gun into the house," he compromises.

"Agreed."

"Why do you want to go?" he asks.

"I just want to know I could handle one if I needed to. I don't want to feel helpless. I don't want to be so scared of one anymore," she explains.

"Okay," Michael crosses the room taking her in his arms. They tease because they are both very sweaty from their workouts. He suggests they go take a shower together.

After supper, Sadie slips away to her bedroom where Michael had left a big mess. She starts trying to put it all back where it goes. Soon, he joins her helping to fold the clothes that he had strewn on the floor.

October winds blow in. Michael comes home late from a long drawn-out Finance Committee meeting to discover the house covered with Halloween decorations. A jack-o-lantern tablecloth covers the kitchen table with a ceramic jack-o-lantern setting on it. There are statues, candy dishes, and pictures on the coffee table, on the mantel, on the hearth, and hanging in the windows.

"You have to be kidding me. This is a bit much," he complains.

"You know I love decorating for the holidays," she reminds him.

"You know this isn't my favorite holiday. I have to look at all of this for the next three weeks?"

Sadie wraps her arms around his neck nibbling at his jaw and neck, "Yes you do."

"Is this how you plan to get your way?" he taunts.

"Yes it is," she bites his ear. "The party will be even better this year. I promise not to be mean to you this time."

"You better not and you better not wear something indecent. I'm not wearing a costume this year," he informs her.

"Oh please. It is just one night out of the whole year," she begs.

"Last year, you dressed like a hooker, I got into a bar fight, and you broke my heart," he reminds her.

"I'm so sorry. This time it will be fun. I promise."

"No."

"This year, Brenda came up with a theme, 'Couples in History.' Steve and Colleen are dressing like Elvis and Priscilla. Aidan and Colleen will dress like a Civil War soldier and a wife in the 1860's dress with a hoop. Graham and Stephanie are going as Cleopatra and Mark Anthony."

"I'm afraid to ask, who are you thinking about?" he cringes.

"David and Bathsheba."

Michael laughs, "You are beautiful enough to dress as Bathsheba."

"My birthday is next week," she reminds him.

"I didn't forget."

"Instead of buying me a present, dress up with me for the party. The church has Biblical robes for costumes."

"I already bought you a present."

"Please..."

"Nope," he persists.

She pushes him down on the couch to persuade him further. Lying across his lap she kisses him in between begging, "Please" over and over. Finally, he begins to cave saying in between kisses, "Alright...alright... I surrender... I'll wear a costume!"

The following night, Michael has yet another meeting. As he prepares in his office with Sue's help, Sue looks out the window and asks, "Reverend, why are there police cars at your house?"

Michael moves to the window where he sees a police car and a large black car. He runs home thinking to himself, what now? An officer attempts to block him from entering, but Michael tells him that it's his house. Sadie sits on the couch by a detective. The color has drained from her face.

Detective Kern explains, "We came to warn you. During a transport for a work assignment, three prisoners escaped. Troy Meyers is one of the missing prisoners."

"You have to be kidding me," Michael runs his hand over his face.

The detective suggests vigilance and to take extra precautions, whatever that means. They would be in contact. Then Kern predicts that Troy probably wouldn't bother them, because he knows the police will watch the house.

After the police leave, Michael plops down beside Sadie. He calls to let the people at church know that something came up and he will not be attending the meeting that night. Mac huffs, but has to admit that this is the first time he can think of that Michael missed a meeting for any reason.

They sit saying nothing for a long time until Sadie whispers, "I want to bring a gun into our house now."

She waits a few moments for him to answer, "Okay."

She points out, "There is a two day waiting period."

Michael stands, "Grab your purse."

They walk down the street feeling paranoid. He takes her to Duffy's where they go into the office with Steve for a few minutes. Steve returns to the bar and removes the gun from under the register slipping it into Sadie's purse.

That night, the couple lies in bed staring at the ceiling unable to sleep. Sadie keeps thinking that Troy had wanted to kill Michael. Eventually, Michael falls asleep, but Sadie slips downstairs to watch television. After a short time, Michael comes down looking for her. They lie on the couch together and he falls back to sleep while she continues watching.

Chapter XXVI

As Sadie dresses for school, Michael sits on the bed. She suggests, "Why don't we just leave?"

"We can't just run," he replies.

"Why not? Troy has been here. He knows where we live. Hopefully the police will catch him soon, but until then we are just sitting ducks here."

"Where do you want to go? Do you want to stay with one of our friends?"

"No. If he follows us, I don't want any of our friends or family caught in the middle of this," she answers.

"Let's just go to a hotel," he suggests. "We can keep working and just spend the evenings there. They tend to have security and cameras."

"A week or two in a decent hotel will cost so much," she reasons.

"When I tell my parents about this, they will pay for a really nice one for us for as long as we want. Let's pack. We'll leave after flag corps practice."

Sadie arrives at school with Steve's gun in her purse. She stuffs the purse under the driver's seat and walks quickly into school. She goes to the principal's office where she informs Mr. Bell about Troy so that he can help watch that Troy doesn't get into the building and endanger the children. They give pictures of him out to the secretary, teachers, and custodian. Mr. Bell decides that Sadie should not do any recess duty, but stay inside during the day with the blinds pulled. He even arranges with the high school principal for her to have her flag corps practice in the front hall instead of outside. Both principals plan to escort her to and from her car.

At three o'clock, Michael arrives home. He leaves the door unlocked and runs upstairs to collect the suitcases that they packed that morning. He carries them out to the car and returns to the house to wait for Sadie. Checking the clock, he sees that he has about an hour and a half before she comes home, so he locks the door.

As he walks into the dining room, a sharp pain cracks him across the back of the head knocking him forward onto the floor. Stunned, he lies face down for a moment. Propping up on his elbows, he looks up over his shoulder into the barrel of a gun.

"Hello Rev. Donnelly," Troy, who had been waiting outside, had slid into the house while Michael had gone upstairs for the suitcases. He waited in the laundry room for his chance. Troy warns, "Don't do anything stupid. Now, get up on all fours and crawl into the living room."

Slowly, Michael obeys. Once in the living room, Troy orders him to lie flat on the floor with his hands on his head, which has a sharp pain from the blow with the butt of Troy's gun. Michael's hands touch a warm sticky liquid and he realizes that his head is bleeding. Keeping the gun pointed at Michael, Troy backs out of the room. He returns carrying a dining room chair that he sets in the middle of the room. Troy orders Michael to sit in the chair.

Michael slowly pulls himself up. Troy aims the gun at him, as Michael walks to the chair. Troy walks behind Michael warning him not to move and orders Michael to put his hands behind the chair. Michael hears Troy pulling on a piece of duct tape. Deciding that Troy is probably using both hands on the tape, he drops off the chair tackling Troy. Rolling on the floor, they exchange several punches. With the existing injury to Michael's head, Troy's blows are more effective. Troy regains control of Michael shoving the barrel of the gun so hard into Michael's temple that he causes bruising and then yanks Michael back into the chair.

Troy wraps Michael's arms together behind him using so much duct tape that Michael's hands look as if they are stuck in a beehive. Troy then wraps tape around his chest and arms to the back of the chair. Kneeling in front of him, he uses more tape to secure each of his legs to a leg of the chair.

When he finishes, Troy sits on the couch across from Michael, "Now we'll just wait for Sadie."

"She's not coming," Michael informs him. "She is expecting me to pick her up at school."

"You're lying. She has her car at school," Troy counters.

"She's planning on leaving it there. She's going to wait at school for me. When I don't show up, she will call the police," he explains.

"I still think you are lying. I guess time will tell," Troy leaves the room going into the kitchen to make himself something to eat.

Michael prays for divine intervention. He pulls and pulls at the tape, but it has no give at all. He tries to think of some way out. The pain in his head remains sharp causing him to feel dizzy and his vision blurs now and then. After what feels like a long time, Troy comes back to sit on the couch. Michael looks over at the clock on the mantel.

"It's after four," Michael tells Troy. "Her school got out at three fifteen. I told you, she's not coming."

"Nice try, Reverend, but I know that she has flag corps practice," Troy smirks.

"She didn't have practice today. She cancelled it because we planned to leave town. Go look in my car. There are suitcases in the trunk."

Troy stands. Walking over to Michael, he picks up the tape directing, "Shut up Reverend." He tears off a piece and firmly pulls it across Michael's mouth.

At four-thirty, Troy sits on the coffee table close in front of Michael, "Now we will see if you were telling the truth. Flag practice is over and I think she is on her way here. Don't look so worried. I'll let you in on a little secret. I have no intention of killing you. Oh, I plan to hurt you and make you bleed, but I won't kill you. See, from where you are sitting, you have the perfect view of the couch where I plan to rape and kill Sadie and you can live for many years remembering it."

Laughing, Troy returns to the couch leaving Michael visibly scared and feeling completely helpless. He can't move at all and he can't make much noise. A few minutes later, they can hear keys in the door. Michael's heart pounds loudly in his chest.

"So, ministers can lie," Troy observes.

"Honey, I'm home and I have a surprise for you," Sadie calls, dropping her purse on the kitchen table.

"We have a surprise for her, too," Troy whispers.

Sadie walks through the dining room from where she sees Michael taped to the chair. Terror freezes her to the spot. Michael locks eyes with her and then he looks toward Troy so she knows where he is. Sadie turns running back to the kitchen. As she grabs her purse, Troy comes up behind her. Wrapping his arms around her, he drags her kicking and screaming back into the living room.

Michael pulls on the tape so hard that the chair tips over. As he hits the floor his left shoulder dislocates. Lying on the floor, Michael is still securely taped to the chair, unable to move. Pain radiates through both his head and shoulder blurring his vision.

Troy tosses Sadie on the couch, pointing the gun at her, he orders her to shut up. He takes her purse away from her dropping it on the coffee table. Looking down at Michael on the floor, he tisks, "Now Pastor, you can't see anything from down there."

Troy pulls the chair back up sending waves of pain through Michael again. He smacks Michael's face a couple of times commenting that's better and then checks to make sure that the tape is still tight everywhere. Satisfied that Michael can't move, he turns his attention back to Sadie.

"So, you married a minister and after all the bitching you used to do about being a minister's kid and living in a parsonage. Now you went and moved back into a parsonage. Your daddy must be happy. Your daddy always hated me," Troy moves closer, "But you used to like me. Do you remember being in love with me? Do you remember all the time we shared together in college? Do you remember all the sex we had back in college? I'm sure I'm better than some god damn minister."

He pushes her down on the couch and lies on top of her. Michael feels overwhelmed with helplessness as Troy begins kissing her. Troy straddles her on his knees. As he reaches to undo his pants, Sadie knees him in the groin. Troy falls back and Sadie rolls off the couch. Her purse sets at the other end of the coffee table from her.

Troy rolls off the couch on top of her. Pinning her to the floor, he waits to recover from her blow and then stands, yanking her to her feet, "There are punishments for bad behavior."

Dragging her by her hair, he pulls her to the kitchen. When they return, Troy clenches a butcher knife and threatens Sadie, "When you misbehave, the preacher here takes the punishment."

Troy moves toward Michael with the knife. Sadie yells, "Wait! Don't cut him. I can make you happy." She walks between Troy and Michael wrapping her arms around Troy's neck and kisses him the best she can. She begins to pull Troy toward the couch away from Michael, but Troy stops.

"I'm glad you are ready to cooperate, but you already kneed me," Troy states. As Troy turns his back on her to face Michael, Sadie snatches her purse throwing herself face down on the couch on top of it. Troy slashes Michael's upper left arm twice leaving about three to four inch cuts, but Michael can only groan.

Troy turns back to Sadie setting the knife down on the coffee table. He walks over jerking her up finding her purse opened underneath her and snatches it away. Michael scans the couch and Sadie, but he does not see the gun.

"Let's see what's in your purse that you want so much, shall we," Troy dumps Sadie's purse out onto the coffee table. Michael watches closely, but still no gun. Troy pushes the contents around finding her cell phone. "Is this what you are looking for? Are you trying to call for help?"

Troy hurls the phone at the fireplace where it breaks into pieces and stands next to Michael. "I think we need another punishment." Using his middle finger, Troy draws an imaginary line across Michael's cheek from his eye to his jaw. "How about this one goes here?"

Troy picks up the knife with one hand and grabs Michael by his hair with his other hand. Michael closes his eyes tightly waiting for the cut when he hears Sadie threaten in a low growl, "Don't do it or I'll kill you."

Michael opens his eyes. Sadie, still sitting on the couch, aims Steve's gun at Troy. Troy stares back at her as she dares, "Go ahead. Give me a reason to kill you." No one moves. Sadie continues, "Before you decide whether or not I can actually hurt you, you should know that ever since you shot me, I've been going to a gun club. I can take this gun apart, clean it, and put it back together. I can load it and I can definitely unload it into you."

Troy releases Michael's hair and steps away. Sadie orders, "Throw the knife on the stairs." Troy obeys. Sadie demands, "Where's your gun?"

Troy doesn't answer, so she looks around finding it on the end table. She is between Troy and his gun. Troy steps back further while Sadie stands facing him. She needs to get past him to get the portable phone from the den, but Troy appears as if he is waiting for his chance to pounce. If he confiscates her gun, she and Michael are finished. Sadie shoots him in his right thigh. The shot startles Michael as Troy yells and falls onto the floor. Michael is relieved to see the blood coming from the leg.

"You bitch! You shot me!" Troy spits holding his leg.

"I know. What should I do now?" she glances back at Michael. "I should get the knife and cut your arm like you did to Michael. Oh, what the hell…"

Sadie shoots his upper left arm causing Troy to scream out. Sadie shakes her head, "Damn it. You're bleeding all over my new carpet."

Sadie moves Troy's gun to the top of her entertainment unit and she retrieves the knife placing it with the gun. She runs to the den returning with the portable phone standing over Troy.

"I should call the police, but then what? You keep coming back. You won't leave us alone. Maybe I should just kill you now and end this. Look what you did to Michael. You escaped from prison. You were convicted for shooting me. No jury would convict me. Hell, I doubt the prosecutor would even charge me."

Sadie raises the gun as Troy cowers with his eyes opened wide. Sadie peers over her shoulder at Michael who looks her in the eyes and shakes his head no. Sadie's gaze returns to Troy.

"You know those Christian values of mine that you made fun of? They just saved your life." Sadie dials 911. "Hello, this is Sadie Donnelly. The escaped prisoner, Troy Meyers is bleeding all over my rug. We need two ambulances and the police. Oh, and be sure to thank Detective Kern for all of his protection."

Ignoring the operator's questions and instructions, she hangs up and sets her gun with the other. She examines Michael's arm and the tape and decides to wait for the police. Sadie sits on Michael's lap, laying her head on his good shoulder and wrapping her arms around his neck. She cries while he rubs his cheek on her head.

Sitting up, she uses both hands to slowly and gently peel the tape off his mouth. Once the tape is removed, he smiles at her. She kisses him gently and then sits staring at each other.

Michael asks, "Are you okay?"

"Me? I'm fine. How are you doing?"

"I'll live," he assures her.

"I love you," Sadie hugs him tighter.

"I love you, too," Michael kisses her. "Where was the gun? I didn't see it on the couch or in your purse, and then you had it."

"I barely was able to pull it out of my purse when he started pulling me up. I didn't think I could win a struggle with him, so I shoved it down in between the cushions. When he wasn't paying attention, I pulled it back out." Sadie smirks, "And you didn't want me to go to the gun club or bring a gun into the house."

Michael shakes his head, "What is that? Is that like the world's biggest I told you so?"

She smiles not answering and kisses his sticky mouth again.

The police with Detective Kern arrive, followed shortly by the ambulances. Sadie remains on Michael's lap while the paramedics quickly take care of Troy. Kern looks over Michael and a paramedic examines his arm. Before they attempt to free him from the chair, the paramedic wraps the cuts on his arm tightly causing Michael to groan. Michael tells him that he thinks his shoulder is dislocated and that his head hurts. Anyone can tell that his shoulder is dislocated just by looking at it, but the paramedic discovers a large goose egg of a bump that is open and had bled on the back of his head.

Detective Kern asks if Sadie is injured. She states that she is fine, but does want something checked at the hospital. Sadie shows Kern where to find the guns and knife. As the paramedics work on his arm, Sadie recounts for Kern what happened.

The detective comments, "I'm surprised you didn't kill him."

Michael and Sadie exchange glances as she answers, "I wanted to, but I guess I'm not a killer."

"Do you have a permit for the gun?" he interrogates.

"No, I borrowed it because I didn't think you could protect us. Do I get points for not killing him?" She questions.

"Most likely," he answers.

Sadie finally stands. Kern takes a pocket knife and frees Michael's legs. He also removes the tape from his chest. Michael's hands are another issue. When he pulls at the tape, it hurts Michael's shoulder and he can't just cut through it, because he can't see where Michael's hands or fingers are. The paramedic tries to stabilize the arm while Kern slowly works at the tape. It takes more than fifteen painful minutes to free Michael from the chair.

They lay him on a waiting stretcher with the head propped up on a slant. They place a cold pack under his head and secure it by wrapping a bandage around it. They also wrap his arm to his body so it doesn't move around. A police officer enters asking about a gift bag he found on the kitchen floor. Sadie answers that it is a gift she brought home for Michael.

"What's it for?" Michael asks.

"Like I said when I came home, I have a surprise for you," Sadie takes the present from the officer and hands it to Michael. "This isn't exactly how I pictured this moment in my head."

Michael uses his good hand to pull the gift out of the bag and peers down at a small blue baby's bib that reads, "I Love My Daddy." He stares at it for a moment and then closes his eyes. Looking up at Sadie, he asks, "You're pregnant?"

Sadie nods leaving Michael is speechless. The paramedics and detective sit by and give the couple a minute. Michael asks, "When did you find out?"

"I'm over two weeks late, so I bought a test yesterday. I was going to take it this morning, but I forgot with all the talk about Troy. I saw it in my purse this morning before I went into school, so I took it in with me. I took the test while my children were in gym class. I bought the bib when I bought the test."

"This is probably really selfish, but I am so glad I didn't know this a few hours ago."

"I bet. I thought Troy was going to cause a second miscarriage. I think I'm okay, but I'll get checked at the hospital." Sadie leans over the stretcher and Michael hugs her tightly with his good arm kissing her as he tears up.

As they wheel Michael out to the ambulance, they hear people calling to them. Their Friday night group plus Graham are being held back by the police line. Sadie requests that the driver waits for her while she runs to her friends. Steve and Brenda had seen the police cars and ambulances race by turning into the church parking lot and have been waiting outside the house for over an hour. They called the others who had plenty of time to arrive. The group saw Troy wheeled out, but no one would tell them about Michael and Sadie's condition leaving them frenzied.

Sadie promises more details later, but quickly fills them in on the basics and Michael's injuries. She then climbs into the ambulance with Michael and their friends jump in their cars. Graham calls Michael's parents and Stephanie calls Sadie's.

In the emergency room, Michael has his head and arm stitched up. One doctor holds him down while another doctor pops his shoulder back into place. Michael yells loud enough that his friends hear him in the waiting room after which he quietly mutters a long string of cuss words. The one doctor teases the other doctor about causing a minister to swear.

Michael has a concussion and will need to stay awake for twenty-four hours. Michael then sits with Sadie holding her hand as she is given an internal sonogram. They are both surprised by the size of the instrument the doctor inserts to take a look. The doctor points to a small flutter in the middle of what looks like a white arrow explaining that it is the baby's heartbeat. The baby appears to be fine and she is six weeks pregnant. Both Sadie and Michael tear up.

By the time Michael is wheeled to the waiting room with his head and arm bandaged and his arm resting in a sling, both of their parents had arrived, plus Mary, Lucy, Carol, Sean, and Jeremy. More than half the waiting room has been waiting for them.

"We're okay," Michael assures them, and then adds with a smile, "all three of us."

It takes a moment for everyone to realize what he means. The realization that Sadie had been pregnant during the ordeal brings looks of terror instead of just jubilation. Colleen is due in February and now Sadie is due in May.

The following weeks, Michael goes through a depression unable to shake the terrible feeling of helplessness. He could not protect his own wife and unborn child. The feeling of not being able to move for so long haunts him. Sadie is patient and understanding, but also concerned.

Sadie, however, has taken her power back. She no longer fights night terrors or nightmares. The feeling that someone is coming for her is gone. She has now survived three attempts on her life and figures that God must really want her here.

Two weeks after the shooting, Rev. Rob Foreman and Bonnie come to visit. While Bonnie and Sadie talk in the kitchen, Rob takes Michael over to the church office to speak in private. Michael holds back, not saying much. It reminds Rob of their first meeting when it took Michael awhile to warm up. Rob remains patient and waits for Michael to open up. Eventually, Michael begins to talk rather reluctantly. He just hates discussing what happened despite the fact that he thinks of little else.

Rob asks, "What did you do during the time you were alone and tied up?"

"Nothing, I couldn't do anything," Michael mutters.

"I bet you did something," Rob persists.

"All I could do was pray," Michael sighs.

"I thought so," Rob nods. "Think about it. You were tied to a chair and he was free. You had no weapons and you had a concussion. He was fine and he had a gun and a knife. He planned to rape and kill Sadie, yet he didn't manage to get one piece of clothing off her. Other than a few bruises, Sadie walked away this time. You were tied up and all he managed to do to you was hit you over the head and cut your arm twice. You dislocated your own shoulder. He was shot twice. His injuries ended up being the worst of the three of you.

"Sadie said when she saw you, she froze. She said that without talking, you let her know where he was and that's why she ran for her purse with the gun. She said that when he threatened to hurt you, is when she started thinking clearly. Sadie said she almost killed him after he was already incapacitated, but despite being tied up and gagged, you stopped her.

"Michael, your prayers were more powerful than his will to seek revenge. Tied up you were stronger than the man with the gun. You were never alone and you were never really helpless. Sadie was strong with the help of both God and you."

In the privacy of his office, with his dear friend who had helped him to begin this life, Michael breaks down and cries for the first time in two weeks. Michael admits that since that night when he had prayed thanks for Sadie and the baby surviving, that he hadn't been able to pray at all. He hadn't led a church service or done any work at church.

Rev. Foreman assures him that is okay and that when he wasn't praying; he had a lot of people praying for him. However, it is time for Michael to begin to talk with God again. Taking Michael's hand, Rev. Foreman bows his head and begins to pray aloud. Soon he stops and patiently waits for a rather long uncomfortable silence. Taking a deep breath, Michael begins to pray.

This talk with Rev. Foreman is a turning point for Michael. He begins to climb back out of the depression. In a week, he returns to work and he and Sadie begin making plans for their new arrival.

Michael knows without any doubt that God called him to ministry and that God meant for Sadie to walk with him.